# TORUS

She was about to yell at him to get back when the sensation of the Skyliner's steepening dive made her forget him. Only the left-hand digits of the maddened blur of racing numbers on the altimeter were changing slowly enough to be read. Lesa instinctively grabbed the control yoke and hauled it into her stomach. The nose came up sharply causing the air-speed to drop. Her weight seemed to double, making her arms leaden and forcing her body into the seat cushions. The sea disappeared from the forward windows to be replaced by sky and the tumbling altimeter digits went into reverse. The howling noise that was punishing her eardrums slackened off. To her horror, the sea appeared above her head and she realized that the Skyliner was upside-down. She looked at Elliot for guidance and saw with a terrible sick feeling that the pilot was dead.

By the same author

*available from Mandarin Paperbacks

James Follett

# Torus

Mandarin

**A Mandarin Paperback**

TORUS

First published in Great Britain 1990
by Methuen London
This edition published 1991
Reprinted 1991
by Mandarin Paperbacks
Michelin House, 81 Fulham Road, London SW3 6RB

Mandarin is an imprint of the Octopus Publishing Group

Copyright © James Follett 1990

A CIP catalogue record for this book
is available from the British Library
ISBN 0 7493 0492 8

Printed in Great Britain
by Cox and Wyman Ltd, Reading

In fond memory of Simon Dally,
a great editor.

# PART ONE
# Harry

Happy he, who could understand
the causes of things.

*Georgics*, Virgil

# 1

## EARTH ORBIT

Matt Gosling grinned mischievously at Stella Richards, the payload master, and pushed himself into the shuttle's left-hand seat. He switched on his cordless infrared headset link and adopted a matter-of-fact but immortal phrase that he guessed would freeze about a hundred hearts in the control room.

'Houston – we have a problem.'

Stella Richards frowned at him from her position by the shuttle's aft windows. 'Hardly necessary,' she observed curtly.

Capcom Mike Connors answered Matt's call without the usual contrived bored note in his voice that he used for the benefit of the specialist news services, schools and space enthusiasts who regularly tuned in to shuttle communications on the NASA Information Channel – the space agency's own twenty-four-hour satellite television channel. 'Roger, *Colorado*. Would you care to amplify on that? Over.'

'We think you should take a close look at PacSat 19 and advise before we go any further with this recovery, Mike. She's gotten herself a windmill of a tumble.'

'Roger, *Colorado*, can you get a lens on it?'

'Roger, Mike. Paul's just started his EVA.'

Gosling flipped comm channels and spoke to Paul Balchin who was extra vehicular activity with a manned manoeuvring unit. He was a hundred metres from the shuttle and about as near as he dared approach the crazily tumbling satellite and its windmilling solar panels. 'Houston want some pics for their album, Paul.'

Paul Balchin acknowledged and operated his manned manoeuvring unit controls. Tiny jets set into the chair-like backpack spat gas and orientated him so that the earth's shining silvery-blue crescent would provide a fixed reference point at the foot of the frame. Once in position, he aimed the TV camera mounted above his left shoulder at the somersaulting satellite. A tiny TV monitor set into the arm of his manoeuvring unit showed the colour picture he was sending to earth via the shuttle's transmitters. His spacesuit radio was patched through to the earth down-link so that he could join in the exchanges between Matt Gosling and mission control.

Balchin hated going EVA. He didn't mind crawling around in a shuttle's open hold, stowing recovered defunct satellites. What he loathed was separation from his mothership. His recurring nightmare, one that he had managed to hide from NASA's shrinks, was that the thrusters on his manoeuvring unit would jam open and send him jetting away from the shuttle to end up orbiting the earth like that French astronaut whose body he had recovered the year before. The poor guy had been working on the Eurolab when his thrusters started firing on their own account. His corpse had ended up in a long elliptical orbit that took him clear half way to the moon at its apogee. The trouble was that the Hoover Space Programme was all EVA and damn all else.

'How's that, Houston?' he asked.

'Hold that a few seconds for a recording dump.'

Balchin kept the camera trained on the satellite. PacSat 19 was the size of a mini-bus. Five tonnes of tumbling 1990s hardware that had given ten years' service, beaming thirty-two channels of direct broadcasting television to the Pacific Basin from Japan to the West Coast of the United States in addition to one hundred video conferencing links. The new global high definition television standards, such as letter-box aspect ratio screens that projected scaled-down CinemaScope-like images onto living room walls, meant that the giant satellite was obsolete even before the last of its high-power transponders had finally ceased operating three years earlier. Now it was junk. Nuisance junk.

He glanced at the earth – clear weather across the Pacific with the wind systems making delicate threads of cirrus white smoke patterns parallel to the equator. There had been no shift in their position over the mighty ocean since they had 'parked' two hours ago. All that had changed was the westward creep of the terminator marking the boundary between night and day as darkness cloaked its way towards the Rockies. At this height of thirty-seven thousand kilometres, smack over the equator, anything in a west to east orbit took exactly twenty-four hours to girdle the earth, keeping pace with its spin. A satellite in such an orbit, known as the Clarke orbit or the geosynchronous orbit, appeared to remain fixed in the sky so that Joe Public could train his backyard dish onto his favourite TV satellite and forget it. And it wasn't only TV satellites that were attracted to the Clarke orbit; the explosive growth in satellite communications that had started back in the 1960s resulted in just about every country in the world dumping some sort of package in geostationary orbit: communication satellites; remote sensing satellites; orbital observatories and so on. After nearly half a century of this free-for-all, the Clarke orbit had become a vast orbital junk-yard girdling the earth like one of Saturn's rings.

Satellites at that height didn't suffer orbital decay like low-orbit earth satellites; they didn't end their days by conveniently re-entering the atmosphere and burning up: they stayed put. By the end of the century there were over twenty-five thousand derelict packages circling the earth, ranging from football-sized sputnik look-alikes to twenty tonners as big as tour buses with solar panels the size of tennis courts: a hazard for new satellites being 'walked' into their orbits.

The Hoover Programme represented an international effort to clean up the Clarke belt. The United States, as one of the worst offenders, had agreed to mop up nearly sixty degrees of belt which was why Paul Balchin was flying his fortieth shuttle mission and trying to forget an itch in his crotch while training a TV camera on a tumbling cylindrical six-tonne mass of junkware aluminium and electronics that promised to be the biggest recovery pig of all time.

'That sure is one helluva spin, *Colorado*,' the Houston capcom conceded. 'Thirty-two revolutions per minute. Any indication why it should be doing that? Over.'

'Nothing that we can see,' Gosling answered. 'According to our onboard data, the thing was stable last month when it was scheduled for Hoovering on this mission. Over.'

'Roger, *Colorado* – we confirm that. Over.'

'Any ideas on this, Paul?' Gosling asked.

'No. And I don't plan on going any closer to find out,' Balchin's voice answered in Gosling's earphone.

Stella Richards drifted over from the aft windows where she was testing the Canada manipulator arm controls and pushed her weightless body into the pilot's seat. Gosling tried not to look at her generous breasts that moved with a fascinating life of their own in the weightless conditions. Stella favoured loose T-shirts when flying missions. She was a forthright 35-year-old brunette from Boston. Pretty in a tough sort of way, and very professional. She studied the tumbling satellite for a few moments and switched on her intercom link.

'Houston. Payload master Richards. Suggest we abort the Hoover on this beast.'

Mike Connors' voice came back: 'Roger, *Colorado*. Stand by.'

'No way will they buy that,' said Gosling softly, flipping his intercom off.

Stella looked levelly at her flight commander. 'I think recovery will be too dangerous, Matt.'

'Risky maybe. But then everything's risky, Stella. Making love in a shower stall is risky. If we leave that thing, the French will Hoover it just to show us it can be done.'

'Mission control to *Colorado*.' Mike Connors' voice. 'Sorry, guys, but that's a negative on your abort suggestion. Suggest you attempt recovery with a PSM.'


## 2

Paul Balchin's third attempt with a payload stabilization module was a success. This time the guided package he had launched smacked into the PacSat satellite square amidships. There was a puff of gas as the barbs in the module's head stabbed through the skin of the satellite and hooked themselves firmly in place. The unit consisted of propellant tanks and a cluster of five miniature radio-controlled rocket thrusters pointing in different directions.

'Gotcha,' said Balchin cryptically.

'Neat,' Gosling's voice observed in his headset. 'Must be all that spear fishing you indulge in.'

Balchin made no reply. Having been in his spacesuit for three hours, he wasted no time in using a remote control to activate the module. Its computer needed a few milliseconds to measure the satellite's tumble and to calculate which of its thrusters would have to be fired to cancel that tumble and for how long. It flashed the results onto the screen in front of Matt Gosling.

'PSM estimates one hour twenty to stabilize,' Gosling relayed to Balchin. 'What do you want to do? Come in or sweat it out?'

Balchin thought about how long it would take him to decompress in the shuttle's airlock to vent excess oxygen from his blood. By the time he'd climbed out of his spacesuit it would be time to crawl back into the goddam thing again. He muttered a curse and opted to remain outside the shuttle.

'Fine, Paul,' said Gosling, grinning at Stella Richards. 'Guess you won't be smelling too good anyway by now. We're happy for you to stay out there. Okay – initiating stabilization burn now.'

Balchin steered himself to a safe distance from the satellite – just in case the PSM gizmo screwed up and spun the whole shebang even faster. But it didn't screw up. After fifteen minutes of barely visible braking fire spitting silently from one of the PSM's thrusters, mission control was able to report, 'She's looking good, *Colorado*. Spin is now down to twenty-five per minute.'

Balchin was damned if he could see any difference. The unwieldy cylinder, flashing in the sunlight as it tumbled, showed no obvious signs of becoming stabilized. But after enduring another thirty minutes of sweat trickling down his spine because the suit's cooling system couldn't cope with a long EVA, it became obvious that PacSat 19 was slowing down.

'One nine decimal five per minute,' Mike Connors' voice reported from Houston. 'Still looking good, fellers.'

Balchin thought he saw something decidedly odd about the satellite. Something was not right. He said nothing. If his eyes were playing silly buggers, no one else but him was going to know about it. Not when he was pulling $75,000 per mission. Mention a suspected vision problem and they'd have you grounded and in for checks by an army of opticians before you could say Mr Magoo.

The tiny thrusters attached to PacSat 19 continued firing their gases.

'One six decimal three,' Connors reported fifteen minutes later.

Balchin edged to within ten metres of PacSat 19.

*Jesus Christ! What the hell was it?*

But he knew the answer.

*Stars were shining out from near one end of the goddam junk heap!*

Her husband was a lawyer earning close on a million dollars a year; her marriage was happy and secure; her two children were in college and turning in good grades. All was well with her world. Financial worries did not lie heavily on her. Stella Richards had no fears about being grounded because she was seeing things. She plugged her microphone into a socket that was linked directly to the capcom through a digitally encrypted radio channel. If you needed to use the channel you went straight to it. Mission control monitored it all the time. No point in alerting viewers watching the NASA Information Channel to the fact that something was amiss by asking mission control to go to a scrambled channel.

'Houston. This is *Colorado* payload master. Copy?'

'Go ahead, *Colorado*,' said Mike Connors.

'There's something weird about that satellite. I can see stars through it near the antenna section. Suggest you take a close look at some of the frames on that last video dump we sent you.'

'Roger, *Colorado*. Stand by.'

Matt Gosling leaned forward in his seat as if moving a few centimetres nearer the window would improve his view. He caught a brief glimpse of a star cluster in Orion. The pin-pricks of light winked from one end of PacSat 19 and disappeared. Then he saw them again and swore softly.

'Shit, Stella – you're right.'

## 3
# TITUSVILLE, FLORIDA

Harry Dysan's Klipfone stood no chance of waking him but it knew what to do. After sixty seconds of fruitless shrilling, it emitted a sub-audible tone that switched on his video disc player. The play head snicked straight into the middle of the chariot race in the recent remake of *Ben Hur*. The roar of the crowd, the music, thundering hooves and the anti-social wheel hubs on the chariot of Ben Hur's opponent chewing into his spokes in ambisonic sound achieved what no mortal could: parts of Harry Dysan began waking up.

The sound effects were faint at first while his brain tried to shut them out. It had all its work cut out coping with the alcohol-saturated blood that Harry's heart was sending it. After a few seconds his brain gave up the unequal struggle and allowed the sound through at full volume.

Harry Dysan fully awoke. His groping hand killed the video disc player leaving only the phone shrilling away. He yanked the Klipfone under the cover.

'Yeah?'

'Mr Harold Dysan?'

'Just about. Who's this?'

'Mike Connors. NASA capcom. Houston.'

Harry vaguely remembered being introduced to Connors at a meeting. In his present state he had only a vague recollection of the previous night's poker game.

'I was asleep.'

'Sorry to disturb you, sir. We have a problem.'

'Why should you want to share it with me?'

'If you could use your terminal so we can verify your identity,' Connors suggested politely.

'Can't it wait?'

'That's something we thought you should decide, sir.'

Harry decided that further complaining would be useless. Besides, his sleep was dead and his curiosity was wide awake. 'Okay,

Connors. Give me ten minutes to get my brain powered up.'

He hung up and stuffed his feet into a pair of slippers that looked as if they'd been set upon by a pack of starving wolverines. He shuffled downstairs. One of Florida's heavier bugs whacked against the screen door when he turned on the kitchen lights. He closed his eyes, braced his body for the shock, and took a generous swig from a carton of undiluted lemon juice in the fridge. It hit him like a bomb. For a few seconds his body felt as if it had just finished an eight-hour stint with a pneumatic road drill. Even if he didn't feel human, at least he could now act like one. He took the carton with him into the sitting room. It was a mess: dirty glasses, empty Bud and Coke cans, brimming ashtrays. He could hear Mrs Jessamine's voice when she came in once a week to clean up the house and lecture him on Bo Jessamine's philosophy of life.

'How come a regular guy like you gets to play poker with such slobs, Mr Dysan? I mean – just look at this mess. Just look at it!'

Harry Dysan was the National Security Agency's director of NASA liaison. A fancy handle – there was no one to direct but himself. Anything odd that NASA saw they reported to him: suspected drug smuggling craft running the gauntlet of the US Coast Guard cutters; unusual construction sites around the world; illegal incursions into the staked-out mining concessions of Antarctica. Reports on any of the thousand and one uncommercial matters that weren't NASA's concern now that it was a self-financing operation ended up with Harry Dysan. When NASA dumped a buck in his lap it was his job to decide which government agency the buck should be passed to. Originally the FBI had been given the job but the top brass in the bureau had recalled that astronauts back in the Sixties had a penchant for seeing mysterious lights out of their space capsule windows. Once NASA started reporting UFO's to the FBI, everyone would. The FBI was the target of enough crackpots as it was without having the ufologists climbing on the bandwagon.

In 1995 Harry was landed with the job and had been stuck with it ever since. At first he had enjoyed it. Most of the time he could work from home at his comms terminal – working at his own pace – shuffling information from one government computer to another. Great. Trouble was that a few years back he had nearly become a victim of the Home Comms Terminal Syndrome: working at home meant that you could dress like a slob, booze, snort coke, smoke yourself into an early grave; indulge in just about any vice that you couldn't get away with when working in an office or with other people. Provided you did your job, no one was any the wiser. With Harry Dysan it had been drink. It had taken Jackie running out on him – with the kids – and a series of lectures from his boss and his doctor to persuade him that getting through four six-packs of Bud a day added up to a problem. Since then he had stuck to a resolution to drink only in company. He had hung onto his job but there was no way that he had been able to get Jackie to come back. At first he had seen the kids each week; then once a month; now hardly ever.

He shuffled across to his Cray computer terminal in the corner by the bookcase with its shelves bowed under the weight of his collection of ancient 78 rpm shellac jazz phonograph records and slipped into the jacket of a business suit that he kept hanging on the back of the swivel chair. The neatly-pressed garment had its own built-in shirt-front and a sober tie. A drag with a comb through his hair and the top half of his body could have passed a Waldorf Astoria doorman while the lower half could have had him arrested as a vagrant.

Harry dropped heavily into the swivel chair. Pressure switches under the carpet or some sort of local gravitational change near the computer – he didn't really know – always switched the damn thing on when he slumped in front of it. His reflection in the screen was uninspiring: a gaunt-looking 35-year-old with a pale indoor complexion – quite an achievement living in Florida – crowned with a mop of unkempt black hair that his mother had bequeathed him along with half a million dollars that he had used to pay off the house. On top of the monitor's moulded housing was a sign that had originally read THE BUCK DOESN'T STOP HERE until a card-playing smart-ass friend had altered BUCK to BUICK.

FINGERPRINT the screen reminded him.

Harry pressed his forefinger onto the keyboard's ident pad. A light on the built-in camera at the top of the screen winked on and a message appeared on the screen advising him that it had an encrypted video conference line on hold from NASA, Houston.

'Go,' said Harry succinctly for the benefit of the machine's voice recognition memory. It saved him having to use the keyboard.

The screen snapped into bright life. A young, serious-looking man appeared. He looked unethically alert for three o'clock in the morning. He smiled uncertainly when he saw Harry's unshaven appearance.

'Good morning, Mr Dysan. We're very sorry to bother you at –'

'Yeah, yeah. We've had all that,' said Harry waving his hand in irritation. 'So what's the problem?'

A picture of a large cylindrical satellite hanging in space suddenly elbowed Connors' face into a small box at the top of the screen. The satellite was turning very slowly about its axis.

'That's a live feed from orbital vehicle *Colorado*,' explained Connors' miniaturized head. He was looking away from the camera – probably checking his own monitor. 'That satellite you're looking at is PacSat 19 on which we've nearly completed stabilization prior to routine Hoovering.'

Harry snap-tuned his brain into NASA speak. Hoovering – the mopping up of defunct satellites. 'Okay,' he said, running his hands through his hair and fighting back a yawn. 'So why should I be fascinated?'

'Take a close look at the satellite. About a metre from the end on the left of your picture.'

Harry peered at the high-resolution image. It looked like a large but ordinary satellite minus its solar panels. Jesus – these guys loved their little mysteries. 'What am I supposed to see?' he complained. 'Graffiti written by little green men?'

'Please look very closely, sir . . . right now. See it?'

Harry saw the anomaly and was none the wiser. 'Yeah – I've got it – meteorite damage. So what?'

'No meteoroid could have caused that, sir. It's too regular. Neat. Here's a close-up.'

Harry studied the enlarged picture for some moments. What he saw prompted an inner demon to jab at his guts with a sharp pitchfork. This was something else. Connors had been right to call him and he said so.

'So what do you want to do, sir?' Connors pressed.

Harry forced himself to concentrate on Connors' problem. His problem now too, dammit. 'Have you ever seen anything like that before?'

'No,' Connors admitted. 'None of us have. So what do we do?'

'Okay. Keep the thing under wraps until I can get someone to take a close look at it.'

Connors hesitated. 'There's a problem there, sir. We're not

planning on returning the satellite to earth. We stow them in the vehicle's hold, de-orbit burn down to two hundred kilometres and re-launch them in a low orbit so that they'll eventually burn up on re-entry. Standard operating procedure.'

'Not with this one,' said Harry evenly, coming to one of his immediate decisions. 'You'll have to bring it back.'

'That's not possible, sir.'

'Why not?'

'It takes a lot of fuel to send a shuttle up to geosynchronous orbit. That's thirty-seven thousand kilometres. We can't bring back a satellite the mass of PacSat 19 without extensive mission re-profiling.'

'So re-profile the mission,' said Harry, guessing what was coming next.

Connors sounded apologetic. 'It will mean re-cost structuring the mission, sir.'

More NASA speak. Why couldn't he say 're-costing' and be done with it? Anyway Harry had guessed right: NASA costed their operations down to the last cent. 'Okay. How much?'

'Stand by, sir.' Connors' face disappeared from its box in the corner of the screen and reappeared after a few moments. 'Two hundred and sixty k, sir.'

Harry thought quickly. He had authorization to go to $600,000 for discretionary payments. The most he had ever sanctioned was $200,000 two years back for photographs of the interior of an Algerian nuclear reactor installation. The photographs had turned out to be fakes and there had been a row. That mess didn't stop him coming to another snap decision now. 'Okay, Mr Connors. You've got your authorization.'

Connors looked relieved. Harry's word was all he needed – the conversation was being recorded. 'And there'll have to be ground handling and storage charges for the satellite, sir.'

Harry bit back an expletive. Goddam compartmentalized accounting practices. All it meant was that Uncle Sam was pulling dollar bills out of one vest pocket and stuffing them in another. 'I'll fix up transport,' he said curtly. 'When's the shuttle due back and where?'

'She'll be utilizing the Canaveral landing facility at fifteen thirty today,' said Connors.

In NASA speak shuttles don't land – they utilize landing facilities. 'Okay. I'll fix something up and get right back to you,' Dysan promised. 'In the meantime I'm slapping a status level three security on this so I want you to brief everyone involved. And I *mean* everyone – particularly the ground crew who'll be handling the satellite.'

'We could divert landing to a military base,' Connors volunteered. 'Patrick AFB would be no problem.'

'Let's not do anything too out of the ordinary,' said Dysan. 'Besides, we don't want to run up too much in the way of mission re-profiling costs, do we? I'll be in touch.'

He cleared the circuit and contemplated THE BUICK DOESN'T STOP HERE sign. He had a horrible suspicion that this time he was going to have a tough time finding someone to take on this particular Buick.

He yawned and touched the information request pad on his keyboard. His fingers snazzed briefly on the Cray's keyboard as he entered PacSat 19. The screen came up with an extract from NASA's Satellite Situation Report: owned by the Pacific Satellite Communications Corporation; launch date; transponders leased to; footprint coverage of the Pacific Basin, and so on. If he delved deep enough the computer would even tell him what programmes had been up-linked to the satellite at any particular time but he wasn't interested in that. All he needed right now were the dimensions and weight of the thing.

He entered: ?DIM.

Up came: *length 4.2 metres; diameter 1.8 metres; weight minus solar panels 5.8 metric tonnes*.

A big bastard.

He reflected wryly that with that sort of damage, maybe it weighed a lot less now. He called Theo Michelmore, director of the Pompano Beach Maritime Research Station, hoping that he would find him at his home upstate in St Augustine and not on the other side of the world attending some obscure symposium. You'd think there were no such things as person to person communications and video conferencing systems the way scientists got together in far-flung capitals for their jamborees. The government scientist sounded half-asleep when he answered.

'Good morning, Theo. Harry Dysan. What time is it where ever you are?'

'The same time as it is where you are,' Michelmore growled. 'I'm at home, in bed, sound asleep, and having a bad dream about someone waking me up to ask me the time. This had better be good.'

## 4

Harry slept late that day and started work at ten o'clock. He spent fifteen minutes downloading detailed information about PacSat 19 onto his printer and another hour retrieving and digesting NASA's latest Satellite Situation Report. His security level was high enough for him to gateway to a Department of Defence computer that provided him with the recent movements and current deployments of all killer satellites regardless of the countries that controlled them. No such satellite had been moved to within striking distance of PacSat 19. Anyway, who would want to waste a satellite's precious onboard propellant to move it close enough to zap a dud TV satellite?

Maybe someone who hated soaps? The thought made him chuckle. He gave up further speculation and switched to his current task – working his way through a tangle of overseas companies – trying to trace the real owners of a LearJet that had been used for cocaine smuggling. Four hours' solid work at the keyboard grilling ten computers in as many countries and he had got nowhere; all he had established was that the executive jet had to be the most leased and re-leased aeroplane in the world. He was going round in circles – no one seemed to own the goddam thing. He gave up at six o'clock and spent the early part of the evening watching the Nude Miss World Contest on the Stag Channel.

At eight o'clock he showered and shaved and managed to make himself look unusually human by changing into a clean sweatshirt and jeans. Theo Michelmore was an old friend who didn't warrant anything smarter. For years Harry had been fooling people with the jacket and shirt routine when video conferencing, and by always turning up at meetings in a smart suit.

He had an uncomfortable feeling as he swung his five-year-old Buick out of the drive and headed south on US1 that his suit was going to see a lot of wear in the near future.

## 5

# POMPANO BEACH, FLORIDA

Harry arrived at the Pompano Maritime Research Station just after midnight. The station was financed jointly by the State Department through the FBI, the US Coast Guard through the Department of Defence, and the Environmental Protection Agency in Washington. Originally the place had been a rundown marina, now it was the best ship tracking centre on the Florida coast, and its main slipway could haul two-hundred-tonne yachts out of the water and into air-conditioned sheds for meticulous stripping down and examination by Theo Michelmore's forensic technicians. In the ten years that the place had been established the station had played a vital role in the seizure of close on five hundred tonnes of narcotics and the collection of over ten million dollars in fines from shipowners whose ships had dumped industrial waste at sea, and yacht owners who ventured into United States' waters with banned toxic anti-fouling painted on their hulls. Twenty similar stations covering the entire United States coastline guaranteed that America's beaches and fishery waters were now the least polluted in the world.

Harry was cleared through two security checks and was directed to park his car near Michelmore's helicopter. The scientist was waiting for him in the reception lobby. He was an overweight, heavy-jowled man who favoured loose-fitting suits that hung on him like iguana skins.

'So what's with this goddam satellite?' Michelmore growled, shaking hands with Harry and leading the way along a corridor towards the laboratory complex. 'Are you expecting dope to be smuggled in by shuttles now?'

'Sorry to wish it on you, Theo. But I simply had no idea what to do with it. You're the nearest secure agency that can handle a thing that size.'

The government scientist grunted. 'Sure is weird.'

'How weird?'

'See for yourself.' Michelmore unlocked a security door with his thumbprint and shoved it open by propelling his bulk into it. Harry followed him into a large, pleasantly cool air-conditioned workshop. Around the walls were heavy steel benches where marine diesel engines were in various stages of disassembly. At one end of the workshop was a huge, rail-mounted gas chromoscope shroud large enough to straddle a twenty-metre yacht. Similarly, there was a mobile X-ray machine that could traverse every square inch of a hull. The facility was a multi-million-dollar investment that could probe small craft right down to their component atoms which was why the gleaming cylindrical bulk of PacSat 19, resting on two broad straps that were hanging from an overhead gantry, looked curiously out of place.

'It only turned up an hour ago,' said Michelmore. 'And we've only just got it set up on the rotator, so I've not had a chance to take a close look at it. Just a few preliminary checks.'

Harry whistled. 'Mind if I roll my voice recorder while we're talking, Theo?'

'Be my guest.'

Harry thumbed the slide switch on the recorder that was clipped to his sweatshirt and crossed the slipway rails to take a closer look at PacSat 19. The giant instrument swayed as he leaned against it. Apart from numerous handling dents and scratches in the frail outer skin, there was no sign of the phenomenon that had led to him ordering this costly recovery.

'Don't tell me I was imagining it all,' he complained to Michelmore.

The scientist grinned and pulled a remote control box from his shirt pocket. 'Stand clear,' he warned.

Harry stepped back. Michelmore thumbed a button on the control box. There was a clank and whirr from overhead motors and the two straps began turning, forcing the suspended weight of the satellite to rotate about its axis.

'We can turn a fifteen-metre cruiser upside-down with this rig,' said Michelmore proudly.

'And shake it?'

Michelmore chuckled and thumbed the control box again. The motors stopped. The two men gazed at the damage that had come into sight.

Harry was the first to break the silence. 'It looks even worse than it did on television.' He ran his finger around the rim of the hole.

'Perfectly circular and whistle clean on this side,' said

Michelmore. 'Concentric to within half a mill. I ran an internal vernier check on it just before you showed up.'

Michelmore positioned a lamp so that Harry could peer into the thirty-centimetre diameter hole that had been punched 'whistle clean' through the satellite. He could almost get his head into it. Inside he could see the remains of circuit boards, actuators and miniature gear-boxes for orientating the instrument's antennae. So clean was the hole that in some places delicate mechanisms had been exposed like explanatory cut-away drawings in a book, while hardware and components within a hair's-breadth of the wall of the hole were unharmed. It was as if a giant drill of incredible sharpness and unheard of speed had bored through PacSat 19.

'Take a close look at the edges of the circuit boards,' Michelmore invited.

Harry peered at the nearest board that had had a semi-circular lump taken out of it like a neat shark bite. The damaged edge of the board gleamed like the glaze on a china cup. 'Looks like it's been polished up,' he commented.

'Heat vitrification,' Michelmore answered. 'Okay, let's take a look at the other side.'

The motors whirred again, turning the satellite until its far side came into view. The exit hole, if that was what it was, was totally different. Instead of clean, almost machined edges, the satellite's outer skin was a mass of twisted, blackened and half-melted aluminium skin that appeared to have been blasted outwards.

'I guess we can safely say that that's the exit hole,' Michelmore observed drily.

'Exit hole for what?' asked Harry, running his finger cautiously along the jagged edge of a panel that had fractured along its welded seam.

'Search me, Harry.'

'A meteor?'

Michelmore shrugged. 'Maybe. Maybe not. It's not my field, Harry, but I don't think a meteoroid would burn such a neat hole.'

'That's what NASA thought but I read somewhere that you can fire a candle through a plank if you fire it fast enough.'

Michelmore shook his head. 'Apart from the exit hole, we're looking at something that's bored a perfectly concentric cooking-pot-size hole plumb through two metres of compact electronics. I don't think a meteoroid could've done that. No way. You don't get perfectly round meteoroids – they're just irregular lumps of rock.'

Harry stepped back and stood surveying the satellite, hands thrust into his jacket pockets, his expression even more gaunt than usual.

'I can tell you what it may have been,' said Michelmore.

'I know what you're going to say, Theo. A killer satellite. Right?'

'It's the only explanation that makes sense.'

'It doesn't make any sense, Theo. I've checked it out. Firstly the killer satellites that use physical means to zap other satellites use high-velocity soft-nosed shells that spread on impact. Forty-millimetre calibre maximum. There's no need to use anything bigger. Whatever made that hole was no killer satellite. And anyway, who would want to kill a satellite that's already dead?'

'What about the Russians?'

Harry sighed. Theo Michelmore's aversion to the Soviets was legendary. 'I've checked all satellite dispositions, Theo. The nearest killer satellite is thirty degrees away and on a different orbital inclination.'

'What the hell's distance got to do with it?' Michelmore demanded. 'You work out velocities and timing and you could hit a target at a distance of a light year with a thirty-eight Smith and Wesson. Your trouble, Harry, is you watch too many science fiction movies. An ordinary handgun in space is a damn sight smaller and just as dangerous as those crazy laser blaster gizmos. A shell in space obeys Newton's laws – it'll move in a straight line at a constant velocity until it hits something. Savvy?'

'It was no thirty-eight that caused that,' said Harry sarcastically, jerking his head at the hole.

'True,' Michelmore conceded.

'And it also happens that the Soviets are yesterday's enemies.'

'Which puts us right back at square one. So what are you going to do now?'

Harry gave himself time to think by purchasing a can of Coke from a vending machine. He sat opposite Michelmore, elbows resting across his knees, and thumbed in the can's tab. The reagents fizzed briefly, conducting heat from the liquid. Harry waited until there was a white rime of frost on the outside of the can before taking a swig. 'I don't know,' he admitted ruefully. He took another draft of Coke and passed the can to Michelmore before walking across to the satellite and taking a long, hard look at the mysterious hole. 'I'll be straight with you, Theo. I don't know what to do about this one. Just looking at that damage gives me a crawling up and down my spine.'

'I'm going to need it out of here in ten days. Miami Coast Guard are bringing in a twenty-metre motor-sailer they want taken apart.'

'Give me a week.'

Michelmore nodded. 'Okay. You're going to have to get some experts in to take a look at this thing, Harry. Real experts. We're just a bunch of bilge probers.'

## 6

The first expert to visit PacSat 19 was Professor Cummins of the Meteoroid Data Collation Centre in Menlo Park, an agile 25-year-old who looked more like a tennis professional than a professor. He sat astride the satellite, took one look at the hole, and was adamant that there was no way it could have been caused by a meteoroid impact.

'There's no secondary damage at the impact point, no gasification burns which you'd be certain to have with a meteoroid that could make a hole that size. Except that it wasn't made by a meteoroid.'

'So what did make it?' Harry asked.

The expert shook his head and slid nimbly to the floor. 'I've no idea, Mr Dysan. Apart from the mess around the exit hole, it's as neat and clean a hole as I've ever seen. The sort of hole that could've been made by an industrial spark erosion machine – you know – the type of rig that's used in machine plants to shape billets of steel for press tools. Or maybe even a high-energy gas laser shaper. A big one. Really big.'

Harry signed for Professor Cummins' expenses and returned home. He sat at his terminal, plugged his credit-card-size voice recorder into a slot on the terminal and hit the transcribe key. The machine converted the spoken dialogue into text which it scrolled onto the screen. Sounds that the voice recognition processors could not handle were reported as system messages. Professor Cummins had a clear voice therefore there were few such messages.

Harry read through the transcript of the meeting to check in case the professor had said anything that he might have missed. There was nothing. He yawned and set about the long task of extracting from twenty government data bases all the information he could find on industrial spark erosion machines and high-energy lasers. When he had finished he had the best part of a ream of paper in his printer's output bin.

At the end of six hours' solid reading and making copious notes on an electronic memo pad, bringing his remarkable power of undivided concentration to bear, he had become something of a self-trained expert on the subject of high-tech kit for making holes. The smallest machine that was capable of punching such a large hole was Chinese and weighed five tonnes. The nearest Soviet machine weighed nearly four tonnes. Both needed to be plugged into a power station and neither could work at a distance – they needed to be on top of the job so to speak. Despite huge amounts of defence budget expenditure by the Soviets and the Americans that had started in the 1980s, the reality was that lasers and high-energy beams as weapons still belonged in the realms of science fiction. No one had found a way of containing what amounted to the energy of a small atomic bomb and then focussing it into a beam. Both sides had had spectacular failures with plasma torus coils. True, the military had blown up a missile on a launch pad during a test using a laser. The press and public had been impressed. It turned out later that it had been a stunt to win more funds: the missile's tanks had been over-pressurized to the point when a pinprick would have caused them to blow up.

Harry began worrying about what he was going to put in his report. Having spent close on a quarter of a million dollars it was even money that General Gus Whittaker of the National Security Agency would be calling him from Washington any time now screaming for his head or an explanation. Okay, how about this for a conclusion:

'Input text,' he said in a clear voice for the benefit of the Cray. 'Assuming that the Soviets have stuck to the 1977 and the 1996 international treaties on the banning of Strategic Defence Initiative weaponry, the only way that the hole could have been made in PacSat 19 is with an industrial shaping laser or a spark erosion machine. Such a machine would have to have been lifted into orbit and then open quotes – walked – close quotes alongside the satellite. Experts calculate that the energy required to bore such a hole is in the order of a million watts. This is in addition to the energy required to lift such a killer satellite into orbit. Input text end.'

Harry went over his wording that had appeared on the screen as he talked. Hell – he could tinker around with it until the goddam cows came home; it wasn't going to make that much difference. Gus Whittaker would take one look at what he had written and start looking for someone else to fill his job.

# 7

# TITUSVILLE, FLORIDA

Harry was wrong. When General Whittaker's forbidding, wrinkled face appeared on Harry's video screen the next morning, the senior officer showed concern and, for once, didn't use Harry as a whipping boy. He listened attentively to what Harry had to say and remained silent for a few moments at the end of the story while he considered his options.

'Okay, Harry. Fine. Anything else I need to know?'

'I've spent two hundred and seventy thousand dollars getting the thing to the Pompano MRS, general.'

'I'll reserve comment on that until we know what we've got ourselves here,' General Whittaker replied somewhat ominously. 'Right now, Harry, I want more information. Hard information from someone who knows something about that satellite and some solid conclusions. Get onto the owners,' the senior officer glanced down at Harry's report, 'this Pacific Satellite Corporation, and get their experts to take a look at the satellite. I don't want any more soft conclusions and flabby guesswork until we hear what they have to say.'

Harry was incensed. 'That's only an interim report to put you in the picture, sir. I didn't want to run up too much in the way of expenses –'

'Don't try loading this one onto me until you've seen your side through, Harry,' Whittaker interrupted. 'You've got a six hundred k appropriation for the current fiscal year. It's up to you to use it as you see fit. Don't push this to a higher decision level before it's ready. Let me have a full report in seven days.' With that Whittaker's face disappeared from Harry's screen.

Harry cursed himself for not anticipating Whittaker's reaction. Jesus H – all he wanted to do was discuss the case. That was the trouble with working alone. You thought alone; you worked out theories alone; you worked up phobias alone. You had no one to bounce ideas off; no friendly ears; no pretty legs swinging idly from a filing cabinet. He yearned for the world of the 1970s and 1980s

23

depicted in old movies on television. In those days people worked together in offices; they dropped in on each other and listened to one another's problems; they thrashed out ideas together over lunch; traded jokes in the men's room. That was the funny thing about old movies: they were made to earn a buck and ended up as historical/sociological documents.

He pulled information on the Pacific Satellite Corporation onto his monitor. It turned out to be a typical multi-national company with a tangled web of tax avoidance subsidiary and holding companies. He called their headquarters in London. What was an outfit with a name like that doing in London? A feminine English voice came on the line.

'I need to talk to your technical director about your PacSat 19 satellite,' Harry told her after he had identified himself. He was shunted to several senior employees before he found someone who knew what he was talking about. Alec Sommerville was a personable young man who seemed to have plenty of facts at his fingertips.

'PacSat 19? That package has been defunct for some years now. In fact I believe we've made a payment to NASA to have it Hoovered. Yes – it should have ceased to exist now. Why? Is there a problem?'

'Nothing serious. Something to do with a correct low-orbit orientation to make sure it's a hundred per cent incinerated on atmospheric re-entry.'

'All the drawings and specifications will be in the Library of Congress databases,' Sommerville pointed out.

'I'm lousy at reading drawings,' said Harry. 'We need more information than can be learned from drawings. We need to talk to the leader of the team that designed and built the thing. Someone who knows PacSat 19 inside out.'

'Fair enough, Mr Dysan. Now let me see . . . Yes – your best bet is my predecessor, Tony King.'

'British?'

'Oh, yes . . .'

Harry hit a function key combination that logged him straight into the EC Census Bureau database in Brussels without him having to pick his way past the computer's user vetting and welcome screens. A cursor appeared on his monitor, waiting for voice or keyboard input.

'. . . He's retired now. Living in Spain. That ought to be enough to find him.'

Harry had entered ?KING, TONY, ?BRITISH ?SPAIN on his keyboard before Sommerville had finished speaking.

'Fine,' said Harry as nine possible matches scrolled onto his monitor. 'What's his second name or initial?'

'Delta – David.'

Harry entered the second initial. The database filtered out eight of the matches leaving his screen filled with information on Anthony David King. 'Okay, Mr Sommerville. Looks like I've found him. Are the last three digits of his Klipfone number 934?'

'That's him, Mr Dysan.'

'Thank you, Mr Sommerville. You've been most helpful.'

Harry cleared the line and called Tony King's Klipfone number, drumming his fingers idly while waiting and reading the EC Census Bureau information on Anthony David King:

*Born 1940. Technical Director Pacific Satellite Corporation 1980– 1999. Retired 1999. Permanent address. Villa Jaconne, La Canuta, Spain.* A woman's voice answered the phone.

'Hallo?'

It threw him. Klipfones were invariably answered only by their subscriber and no one else. That was the whole point of having them – you always got through to whoever you were calling. The conversations were digitalized and encrypted – a hundred per cent secure. He could hear children splashing and yelling in the background.

'Have I called Mr Anthony King's personal number, please?'

'Yes, you have. Who's calling please? I have a United States number showing but no name.'

Harry explained who he was. The woman said that she was Mrs King, adding, 'I'm sorry, Mr Dysan, but Tony's gone camping in the Sierras with our eldest grandson. I've no idea where he is or when he'll be back. Within the next five days, I think. They don't usually go for longer than two weeks.'

'And he's left his Klipfone behind?' Harry tried to keep an incredulous note out of his voice.

'Oh, yes. He always does.'

'So how do I contact him?'

'You can't.'

'But that's crazy. Supposing he had an accident or something?'

'What my husband does is his affair,' said the woman primly.

Without going into details, Harry impressed on her the urgency of the matter. She promised that her husband would return the call immediately he got back.

Harry copied the information on Tony King onto his printer and reflected that only mad dogs and Englishmen went out in the Spanish sun without a Klipfone. For the time being Tony King would have to wait.

He waded through the Federal Personnel Resources database. A few keystrokes filtered the backgrounds and résumés of two million employees down to a string of a hundred promising names which he was able to further refine to ten by a closer examination of their career profiles (more jargon) and the work they were currently engaged on. He started making calls. The third name on the shortlist was in Florida on vacation. Harry got through to him fifty miles off Fort Lauderdale and about to gaff a marlin. Steven Krantz was deputy project research director at the Texas Particle Accelerator Centre. He was sufficiently intrigued by the little Harry had to say to offer to present himself at the Pompano Maritime Research Station the following day. He sounded young and eager. Harry thanked him, cleared the line and checked Krantz's age. Twenty-three. He groaned. Jesus Christ – another post-teen professor. At thirty-five Harry suddenly felt old.

## 8

# POMPANO BEACH, FLORIDA

Steven Krantz was gifted with a boyish, fresh face. When in his forties he would look as if he were still in his twenties. He was agile from regular workouts, keen, very likeable with a warm sense of humour and had a quick, ready wit. Women liked him which meant that older men – who drank, smoked and never went near a gym – hated him on sight. Harry didn't exactly hate Krantz on sight, but what the youthful physicist had to say about the hole in PacSat 19 did not help endear him to the older man.

'It came from outer space,' Krantz announced in a mock menacing voice from his perch. He was sitting astride the satellite like a pygmy riding an elephant. He gave Harry an approximation of a bug-eyed monster's leer.

Harry blinked. 'What did?'

'Whatever drilled this hole. No – drilled is the wrong word. Whatever vaporized this hole.' Krantz grinned down at Harry, swung his leg over the satellite, and dropped lightly to the concrete floor. He moved his lips close to Harry's voice recorder and said in his deep, mock menacing voice, 'We are not alone.'

This clowning did not go down well with Harry. 'Just what the hell are you driving at, Mr Krantz?'

'Call me Steven. Or Steve. I'm easy.' He headed for the Coke machine with Harry in tow.

'What do you mean, it came from outer space?'

Krantz fed a credit card through the machine's reader and took a Coke from the hopper. He swallowed a deep draught when the can had cooled. 'As I said – whatever made that hole wasn't of terrestrial origin. Firstly – we're still a hundred years off that sort of technology anyway. Maybe a lot less than that if Alexi Hegel hadn't stupidly given up his work on plasma physics. Secondly – the angle of the hole means that whatever made it wasn't on earth.'

'Another satellite?'

'No way.'

'How can you be so sure?'

'Because we don't have the technology. Simple as that.'

'No – I mean, how can you be so sure that whatever made the hole wasn't on earth?'

Krantz took Harry by the arm. The two men moved to the end of the giant cylindrical-shaped instrument where it had been holed. Krantz pointed. 'Those brackets on this side were for mounting the antennae transmitting and receiving dishes. Okay?'

Harry nodded. 'I know that. I've looked at the drawings.'

'That's the antenna module. As the satellite orbited the earth, motors contra-rotated the end section of the satellite so that its dishes were always aimed at the earth. The rest of the satellite had to spin slowly to prevent it from being cooked by the sun. With me so far?'

Harry found Krantz's easy-going style irritating. 'Mr Krantz. I may be an ancient thirty-five year old, but I don't happen to be senile just yet.'

'The exit hole has the same orientation as the antenna dishes – pointing at the earth. So whatever made the hole was travelling towards the earth and the satellite just happened to get in the way.'

Harry looked sharply at the younger man. 'You're sure of that? Whatever made the hole was travelling *towards* the earth?'

'Sure I'm sure. That exit hole damage and its orientation is a dead giveaway.' Krantz gave another of his infuriating grins. 'Still doesn't tell us what made the hole.'

'Could it have been a meteoroid?'

Krantz shook his head. 'Matter didn't make that hole, Mr Dysan. It was energy. Raw energy from a technology way ahead of terrestrial technology. It could have been fired at earth from a distance of a few hundred miles to a few thousand light-years. Maybe sent by a civilization that no longer exists. Maybe it's their way of sending "Hey, folks! We're here!" messages like the radio messages we broadcast to the stars back in the 1960s.'

This was new to Harry. 'We did?'

'Frank Drake's Project Ozma,' Krantz replied. 'Those messages would've reached several thousand stars by now. Maybe that hole is a reply.'

## 9

# TITUSVILLE, FLORIDA

Harry sat at his terminal and decided that he hated the thing and what it represented. The twenty-year-old movie playing on the television was a painful reminder of an era when people had actually communicated eyeball to eyeball. If this problem had happened twenty years ago, it would have been shared with twenty people by now. You couldn't thrash out problems like that any more. It was all to do with economics. What was the cost and point of a group of people groping in the dark for a solution because they didn't have all the information at their fingertips, when one man or woman working at a terminal with all the world's knowledge at his or her command could analyse the information and pass on a report on the report?

Right now Harry knew passing on his report in its present state would be putting his job on the line. Gus Whittaker would not take kindly to references to alien lifeforms and Frank Drake's Project Ozma in which the scientist had spent several months broadcasting digital pictures of a man in the hope that they would one day be received by intelligence in distant star systems. There was another name that Steve Krantz had mentioned. Harry rummaged in a drawer, found his pocket voice recorder and plugged it into the slot in the terminal. The transcript of the meeting flowed onto the monitor. He scrolled through the dialogue until he found the speech he was looking for:

KRANTZ:    It came from outer space.
DYSAN:     What did?
KRANTZ:    Whatever drilled this hole. No – drilled is the wrong word. Whatever vaporized this hole. We are not alone.
DYSAN:     Just what the hell are you driving at, Mr Krantz?
KRANTZ:    Call me Steven. Or Steve. I'm easy.
DYSAN:     What do you mean, it came from outer space?

(SYSTEM MESSAGE: UNIDENTIFIABLE EFFECTS. PROBABLY VENDING MACHINE FOLLOWED BY KRANTZ DRINKING OR SWALLOWING)

KRANTZ: As I said – whatever made that hole wasn't of terrestrial origin. Firstly – we're still a hundred years off that sort of technology anyway. Maybe a lot less than that if Alexi Hegel hadn't stupidly given up his work on plasma physics.

(SYSTEM MESSAGE: HEGEL – PHONETIC SPELLING PROVIDED. VERIFY CORRECT SPELLING WITH ORIGINATOR)

Harry considered tracing Alexi Hegel, whoever he was, and getting him to take a look at PacSat 19. Naw. Another 'it came from outer space' wise-cracking expert he could do without.

His Klipfone shrilled.

It was Tony King calling from Spain.

# 10

## POMPANO BEACH, FLORIDA

'Amazing,' said King, walking around the satellite with his hands thrust in his pockets. He was a tall, big-boned man with a weather-beaten face. Another keen outdoor type who looked in far better shape than Harry.

'Initial reactions?' Harry questioned. He felt happier with Tony King. At least this expert was older than him.

'One of amazement at seeing it again.' The Englishman paused and looked pensively at PacSat 19. 'I worked five years on this beastie. Twenty years ago when it was crated up for launching, I never dreamed that I would ever see it again.'

Harry bit back a blistering comment. He hadn't paid King's air fare from Alicante to listen to him reminiscing but he needed the Englishman's willing co-operation so he kept quiet.

King spent several minutes examining the neat, clean, perfectly circular entrance hole. He operated the control box that rotated the entire satellite and studied the mass of twisted metalwork around the exit hole.

'So what do you think?' Harry prompted.

'I don't know what to think yet, Mr Dysan. I'll need a few hours to do a strip down. I'll need wrenches, screwdrivers –'

'You'll find all the hand-tools you need in those drawers,' Harry interrupted, gesturing to the work benches along one wall.

'And I'll need an assistant. Some of the modules are heavy.'

Harry wondered if Theo Michelmore would agree to providing Tony King with an assistant and decided that it was unlikely. Besides, the less people who knew about this thing the better. He took off his jacket. 'Okay, Mr King. You've got one. Let's get started.'

# 11

The two men worked without a break for four hours. They started by removing the damaged panels around the exit hole and laying them out on the floor. At the end of the first hour they had exposed most of the complex gear-boxes that kept the satellite's antenna systems aligned.

'Why have three of everything?' Harry queried, supporting one of the gear-boxes while King unscrewed its mounting bolts.

'Triple redundancy,' said King cheerfully. 'A motor burns out at the end of its working life and another takes over. Important with multi-million-dollar satellites working by themselves with no chance of having a serviceman with a screwdriver drop in. Satellites don't just suddenly stop working – they fade away as their systems go down.'

After another hour's sweated labour they had removed all the panels from around the circumference of the damaged section and had stripped out a number of large modules so that the hole through the satellite was visible from entry point to exit.

At the end of the four hours the floor all around the two men was piled high with sub-assemblies, modules and printed circuit boards, and even the little thrusters that had to be fired from time to time during the satellite's working life to maintain its orientation. The more difficult to remove units were separated from their housings with a pair of power croppers.

'Amazing when I think of the painstaking care we took putting it together,' said King ruefully, surveying the mess. 'We worked in a clean room like surgeons. Gowns. Facemasks. Now look at it.'

Harry sat on a power supply and mopped his forehead with a drenched handkerchief. A bored 'Yeah' was his contribution to the conversation. He watched the Englishman walk across the workshop and study the satellite from a distance.

'You know something, Harry – can I call you Harry?'

'Be my guest.'

'I don't think the exit hole is an exit hole. In fact I'm damn certain it's not.'

The implications of King's casual observation alarmed Harry. 'But it's obvious that it is! Look at the mess around it!'

King nodded and returned to the satellite. He mounted a step-ladder, thrust his arm up to the elbow into the exit hole like a vet checking a cow in calf, and felt around with his fingers, his face creased with concentration. He gave an exclamation of surprise and set to work with the power croppers. The jaws opened and closed, shearing through the aluminium framework. He reached into the hole again and produced a shard of curved thick steel as big as his hand. He showed it to Harry.

'It looks like a fragment of a bomb casing,' Harry commented, turning it over in his hand.

'You're not far wrong,' King replied. 'Top quality manganese alloy. The main pressure vessel of a gas lithium fuel cell or rather, what's left of it. The internal operating pressure was in the region of two hundred bar.'

'What's that in good old-fashioned US pounds per square inch?'

'About two thousand four hundred per square inch. It was this blowing up inside the satellite that's caused the damage that we've all assumed to be an exit hole.'

'So what caused the thing to explode?'

'Whatever punched the hole through the satellite. The beam of energy, or whatever it was, hit the satellite and vaporized a hole right through it, fracturing the fuel cell in the process. It then exploded, creating the mess that we thought was the exit hole and giving the satellite that incredible tumble.'

'Shit,' Harry breathed.

King looked at his assistant in concern. 'What's up, doc?'

'Meaning that the beam was fired from earth?'

'Oh, definitely. And because it struck near the receiving antenna which was very precisely aligned on our Hong Kong up-link earth station, we can say approximately where on earth the beam was fired from.'

## 12

# THE PENTAGON, WASHINGTON

General Gus Whittaker sat in his swivel chair, his craggy face impassive as he listened to Tony King giving his evidence. Occasionally he scribbled a note onto the screen of a Hewlett Packard memo pad. The machine converted his untidy scrawl into rows of neat text and even corrected his speed-writing spelling and grammar. The text that scrolled off the screen went into a one-hundred-megabyte memory. Occasionally he shot a glance at Harry whose gaze remained fixed on the Stars and Stripes behind the general's desk. For this meeting Harry had shaved and picked the mothballs out of a smart grey suit. De-slobbing himself, he called it. He was even wearing a new pair of Italian shoes which, like their makers, knew how to pinch. The left one was giving him hell.

'And that's all the concrete evidence that I can offer, general,' King concluded. 'As for what caused the hole – I can only conjecture. I am, or rather was, a satellite communications engineer – not a particle physicist or whatever. What I *can* say with some confidence is that whatever caused the hole is the result of highly advanced technology that I would not expect to be around until well into this century.'

General Whittaker regarded King for some seconds when the younger man had finished speaking. He chose his words with care when he spoke. 'According to Mr Dysan, you can say where the beam was fired from?'

The Englishman looked concerned. 'I think I was a little over-hasty when I said that, general. It's true that the beam hit the satellite on a part that was always orientated on our up-link earth station in Hong Kong. But the satellite's been defunct for a number of years, therefore the usual orientation corrections necessary from time to time to maintain precise alignment have not been carried out. I went very carefully over my findings last night based on the likely wobble that the satellite may have developed since we stopped using it.'

'You can give me an approximate position?'

King nodded. 'Within a two-thousand-kilometre radius of Hong Kong.'

Harry surreptitiously slipped his left foot partially out of his shoe. General Whittaker chewed thoughtfully on his lower lip. He touched a keypad set into his desk. A map of the whole of the South Pacific appeared on a side wall. He centred the map on Hong Kong with the aid of a tracker ball and turned his gaze back to Tony King. 'So if we go for a two-thousand-five-hundred-kilometre radius – about one thousand five hundred nautical miles, you're a hundred per cent confident that the beam emanated from that area?'

'Yes, general. One hundred per cent confident.'

Whittaker slid a zoom control. The projected map became circular. Hong Kong remained in the centre but the area shrank to cover a radius of fifteen thousand miles. Nevertheless, the circle embraced a huge area covering a substantial portion of China to the north; reaching as far as Burma in the east; most of Indonesia to the south; and the entire Philippines together with a sizeable chunk of the South Pacific to the west.

'We're talking about an area of seven million square miles,' General Whittaker remarked drily. He went back to chewing on his lower lip. He seemed to come to a sudden decision. He sat forward, hands clasped together on his desk, and regarded King with hard grey eyes. 'Mr King. I'm sure I don't have to impress on you the seriousness of the problem we have here.'

The British engineer nodded. 'If there is such a thing as a high-energy particle beam, it could jeopardize the defence systems of NATO.'

'Fuck NATO! I'm thinking of the United States. But you've got it, Mr King. Now here's another problem. You're the only non-US citizen who has any idea of what all this is about. I understand that you live in Spain with your wife?'

'Yes, general.'

'How would you and she feel about living in the United States for a spell until this thing is sorted out?'

King looked puzzled. 'I'm not sure I understand you, general. I don't think we could afford –'

'All expenses paid,' General Whittaker interrupted. 'All the way down the line: food, accommodation, everything. In fact, I see no reason why you shouldn't come out substantially ahead cash-wise on the deal.'

The Englishman was confused. He could not see where all this was leading. 'Well. If I could call my wife –'

'One of my aides will speak to her. She'll be here tomorrow.'

'Why can't I call her?'

'Because you're not making any calls until this business is sorted out,' said General Whittaker flatly.

King looked indignant. 'You mean I'm being gagged!'

'You've got it.'

'More than gagged. Imprisoned!'

'We have a very large, very comfortable ranch. Swimming pool. Tennis courts. Gym. Pool room. Stables. We'll probably have trouble prising you out when all this is over.'

For a moment it looked as if the Englishman was about to lose his temper but he checked himself. 'Supposing I gave you my word that I would say nothing about this?'

'It won't be accepted,' said General Whittaker flatly. 'I need a few minutes with Mr Dysan, so if you wouldn't mind waiting outside . . .'

King stood and left the room without a word. Harry tried to push his left foot back into its shoe. Either his foot had swollen or the shoe had shrunk.

Despite the total ban on smoking in the Pentagon, General Whittaker unwrapped and lit a cigar. He inhaled on it while watching Harry thoughtfully. It was some seconds before he spoke. 'You've done a good job on this one, Harry.'

'Thank you, general.' Praise from Gus Whittaker!

'Even so, I'm still sorely tempted to shoot the messenger.'

That was more like it. 'I think I can understand that, sir.'

'Over the past ten years we've learned to trust the Soviets and they've learned to trust us. Our disarmament inspection teams have had unhindered access to anywhere they've taken a fancy to from satellite pics. Even at the drop of a hat. And we've done the same for them. It's been a painful lesson for all of us. And now this business.'

'It might not be the Soviets,' Harry pointed out, managing to jam his foot back in its shoe.

'That's why we can't go making accusations. Not until we've got some hard evidence. The president doesn't want to launch a major investigation until we have a better idea of what we're looking for. For the time being the less people who know about it at this stage the better. Your job is to get some hard evidence. You're to find that beam and who's behind it. Nothing else. Obviously you'll be looking for some sort of major installation. I've okay-ed the money you've spent so far and you've got authorization for another million dollars. How you get the evidence is entirely up to you.'

Harry forgot his shoes. This was heavy. Outside his experience or training. 'Thanks for the confidence, general, but –'

'I have a greater confidence in your ability to spend a million dollars of taxpayers' money than I do in your ability to find something in seven million square miles when you're not sure what it is you're looking for.'

'It's mostly ocean, general. I've only got to check out about three million square miles.'

General Whittaker grunted. 'I feel better already. Send the English guy in on your way out.'

Harry moved to the door.

'And don't come back to me until you've got something positive to report.'

Harry promised not to.

'And, Harry –'

'General?'

'Next time you're in this office, is it asking too much of you to keep your shoes on?'

Harry gave a sickly smile and opened the door. The crusty old bastard didn't even have the common decency to wish him good luck.

'And one last thing, Harry.'

'General?'

'Good luck.'

Harry was back working at his hated computer terminal and feeling that he was about to qualify for a degree in going round in circles. A first class honours degree when it came to dealing with Arnold Salter at the Environmental Protection Agency.

'And I'm telling you, Harry, that I cannot disclose the name of this particular analyst!' Salter was yelling.

'For Chrissake why not?' Harry shouted back.

Salter forced himself to calm down. 'You know as well as I do what a multi-billion-dollar business illegal dumping of noxious waste at sea and piracy has become. We've got a remote sensing analyst who knows the Far East inside-out – who's got a sixth sense when it comes to tracing rogue or hi-jacked ships – and whose evidence has been crucial in over twenty major cases. We've given the analyst a solemn promise that his or her identity will never be disclosed. We'll help on anything else, Harry, but not this one.'

'Okay, Arnie. Thanks anyway.' Harry cleared the video conference line and sat contemplating his blank screen while he considered his next move. He had spent the entire day at his terminal painstakingly tracking down the names of his country's top remote sensing analysts on the Far East. One of them had to be the one person who could interpret satellite pictures better than anyone else – someone who was so good at their job that they could identify a vehicle from its tyre tracks in a forest photographed from a satellite or a disguised ship by the shadows its derricks threw on a harbour quay. The hardware could deliver the high-resolution pictures but reading them correctly required the sort of intuitive flair that could not be programmed into a computer. He ploughed through the shortlist one by one until his Klipfone was slippery with sweat. None of them had been involved in the Environmental Protection Agency's Far East operations. None of them knew who the EPA was using. 'That's a question we'd all like to know the answer to, Mr Dysan,' one of them had admitted. 'Whoever he is, he's good.'

Maybe he could go to Gus Whittaker with the problem? Get a

White House directive to the EPA to release the name of their analyst. No – that wouldn't be such a good idea. He could hear Gus Whittaker sounding off – saying what was the point in paying Harry Dysan to ferret if he had to do the goddam ferreting for him?

Harry sighed and glanced at his watch: four o'clock. Time for the afternoon blue movie on the Stag Channel. Naw. It would have to wait. He would have to keep plugging away at this problem. He logged into the Library of Congress database for the second time that day and worked his way through the levels to trial transcripts involving joint prosecutions by the Chinese Government and the United States Government of shipowners involved in illegal dumping and cases of piracy. Maybe there was something he had missed the first time round; some seemingly inconsequential snippet of information that would lead him to the elusive analyst. He selected another recent case which involved the EPA and ploughed through the evidence presented to the United Nations' court. Ninety per cent of it was in the form of depositions: sworn statements by harbour officials, forensic experts, stevedores and so on – many of whom had had their identities concealed. He found what he was looking for: a statement by an un-named remote sensing analyst on a ship that had been tracked from Singapore. The style was familiar. There were phrases in the text that he had come across in similar depositions that day. He played a hunch by noting the EPA document reference number on his electronic memo pad:

OP11/P1OI/1/AS/LW/044567.

Harry was reasonably familiar with the document referencing systems used by most government agencies. Despite their length, they were usually fairly straightforward. In this case, the first element of the reference – OP11 – stood for Ocean Protection Department 11. P101/1 was the case number. AS were the initials of the co-ordinating officer, in this case Arnold Salter. The LW element was the most interesting. There was a faint chance that LW were the initials of the person who had originated the deposition.

Harry quickly checked back on the depositions of the other cases he had looked at earlier. The initials LW cropped up eight times in eight separate cases involving the Far East. He checked his own list of analysts. None had the initials LW. So – he was back to square one.

He sat deep in thought for some minutes. Maybe the mysterious LW was a Canadian or some other foreign national? If so, that would make his task next to impossible. Harry's tenacity was such that impossible tasks did not daunt him – they only made him angry.

Okay; start with Europe. Not because he was playing another hunch but simply because the EC databases were well-organized; working them was a pleasure. He logged into the huge Confederation of European Industries database in Paris and found the pages that identified the product codes for remote sensing and satellite survey organizations – over a thousand of them. Columns of names and addresses filled the sheets of paper that hissed out of his printer. At the same time all the names and addresses were committed to his Cray's formidable memory. He logged out of the database and went into the EC Census Bureau database in Brussels. A quick check confirmed that EC citizens were linked to the code numbers of their employers. His next moves required careful planning to get the best out of the computer. He devised a command line that would first extract all EC citizens with the initials LW. Wildcat search parameters such as L?W, ?LW, LW? and LW ensured that every combination of the initials was extracted. As he expected, such a loose definition resulted in the database reporting in excess of a million entries. It asked him:

DO YOU WANT A DUMP? Y/N

Even the huge memory of Harry's computer would be hard pushed finding room for a million names and addresses. He answered N.

The rest of his carefully-composed command line would result in the computer linking all citizens whose initials contained LW and matching them to the names of the companies he had extracted from the Confederation of European Industries database.

Harry double-checked his commands and hit the enter key. The five neatly-printed sheets of paper containing names, addresses and telephone numbers that spewed out of his printer were merged data that had not existed on any one computer until now. The listing contained about a hundred entries and was exactly what he wanted. Names such as L W Hanlan who worked for Mining Surveys of Luxembourg he ignored for the time-being. He wanted only those names with the straightforward, uncluttered initials LW. There were two: Luka Winette, employed by Surveillance Aerospacial of Paris, France; and Lesa Wessex, director of Systemation of Guildford, England.

Harry went back to the industrial database. Surveillance Aero-spacial specialized in planning highway routes for Third World countries. Systemation's skills included remote sensing services specializing in the Far East. He logged out of the database and stared at the name Lesa Wessex on his printed sheet. Now to confirm the long shot. He called Arnold Salter by video link because it was important to see his expression.

'Hi, Arnie.'

Salter looked pained when he saw Harry's face on his monitor. 'The answer's no,' he snapped before Harry had a chance to open his mouth.

'It's okay, Arnie,' said Harry easily. 'I called up your director and he gave me Lesa Wessex's name. All I want from you is some low-down on what she's like to work with.'

It wasn't necessary for Harry to see Salter's face. The outraged tone said it all. 'He had no right to do that!' Salter howled. 'That's classified information and he knows it!'

'All I want to know is what she's like to work with.'

'Screw you, Harry. You're not getting any information out of me on this one!' With that Salter cleared the line.

Harry felt pleased with himself and with good reason. The combination of tenacity, cunning use of databases, with a bit of psychology thrown in had resulted in the longest of long shots paying off. He looked up Lesa Wessex's Klipfone number.

# PART TWO
# Lesa

Good speed to thy youthful valour,
child! So shalt thou scale the stars!

*Aeneid*, Virgil

# 1

## VIETNAM July 1985

'Lesa. Wake up.'

It was Aunt Thi's voice whispering in the darkened family hut. Lesa stirred and rolled over on her palliasse to shut out the interruption that was interfering with her dream. At fourteen, fifteen in a few days, her dreams spun a strange web of excited fantasy that centred around the romantic but alien scenes in the American fashion magazines that Uncle Hinny had recently burned despite her protests. Scenes from another world: smiling couples in exotic houses, gleaming cars. Dreams, dreams, dreams.

'Lesa! Wake up!'

A hand reached under her mosquito net and shook her roughly by the shoulder. Lesa woke up.

'Lesa. You must get dressed.' There was an uncharacteristically anxious note in Thi's voice.

Lesa opened her eyes but it changed nothing. Blackness.

'But it's still dark, Thi.'

'We're going. We're all going. You must get up.'

Lesa sat up, not understanding. She pulled the mosquito net aside. 'Going? Going where?' Her hands groped for the Zippo lighter to light her oil lamp. The burst of sparks from the tungsten wheel provoked Thi into angrily knocking the lighter from her hands.

'Wait until your Uncle Hinny has the storm frames up!' Thi hissed, pulling back Lesa's homespun cover. 'You must be ready in five minutes. Wear your walking boots – the pair Hinny brought you last month. You've broken them in like I told you?' Thi managed to make everything she said sound scolding.

'Yes, Thi.'

'Good. We have a long walk. Wear black. Your black pants and a black shirt. Nothing light-coloured. I'll send Neti in and I'll be back in ten minutes. Don't strike a light.'

Perplexed, Lesa shrugged her skinny body into a pair of baggy black pants and a cotton shirt, and pulled on her lightweight boots. All around her in the hut there was movement. From behind the rattan screens she could hear Thi and Hinny and her grandparents talking in urgent, hushed whispers. There was the sound of the typhoon frames being fastened over the hut's few window openings. Little Suzi, Thi and Hinny's nine-month-old baby, started crying and was immediately hushed with soft crooning noises.

Were the soldiers coming again? But surely all that was over? And if it was Tak Noi, the new military governor, demanding new rice production levels, what was the point of hiding? He would merely post his men in the village and await their return. There was nowhere to hide but the forest, and no other village would take them in for fear of the most terrible reprisals.

Lesa knew about the soldiers. The previous year one of their Soviet-built ZIL-151 three-tonne trucks had grated into the village, belching black smoke from its badly-maintained engine. On board were about ten of Tak Noi's feared personal bodyguards armed with AK-47s. They were Kampucheans – former Khmer Rouge POWs who had opted to stay in Vietnam and transfer their allegiance to Tak Noi, the new North Vietnamese military governor of the province. They had exchanged their distinctive blood-red head-bands for black-japanned helmets but their brutality was unchanged.

Their leader looked no more than nineteen. He used a bullhorn to summon all the villagers into the compound. Lesa had clung to her mother. At thirteen she was already the taller by two centimetres. The leader had a clipboard. He had stood on the truck's cab roof and called out the name of Lesa's mother, prefixing it with an expression in English: 'good-time girl'. It was a phrase Lesa had heard before to describe her mother but she did not fully understand what it meant. She knew it was something to do with her mother having spent a lot of time in Danang during the days of Americans but that was all. No one in the village had told her the precise meaning.

The villagers gathered in a frightened, silent circle around the truck.

Hinny joined his sister and her daughter. Lesa saw that he was holding her mother's hand. Such a display of affection from Hinny was unknown.

The leader repeated his demand.

A circle of impassive white faces answered him. The hundred or so villagers merely stared back.

46

The leader shouted an order at one of his men. Not men – they were children with an ugly adulthood conferred on them by the carbines they carried with casual ease. A woman gave a scream of terror as her child was snatched from her arms. She screamed again and struggled to break the grip of two soldiers who restrained her while a third pressed the muzzle of a revolver against her baby's temple. The leader called out the name of Lesa's mother a third time and started counting.

Lesa heard her mother give a tiny whimper of terror. Hinny was now holding her arm as though he were trying to hold her back without making it obvious. She disengaged herself from her brother's grip and walked into the centre of the compound.

The eyes of the boy soldiers glittered greedily as they watched the beautiful young woman walking towards them. Not even her baggy black pants and shapeless grubby smock could disguise her grace and proud bearing. Lesa had distant memories of how lovely her mother had looked in happier days when she used to return home from her visits to Danang dressed in elegant Western clothes. But that was all so long ago. In the short life spans of the Vietnamese even the few years of childhood had a lifetime's retrospective to an adolescent.

The leader barked an order. Lesa's mother was grabbed and thrown roughly into the back of the truck. From the darkened interior came sounds of a savage beating being administered but Lesa's mother made not a sound. Lesa wanted to rush forward but she felt Hinny tighten his grip on her shoulder.

The leader jumped down from the roof of the truck and beckoned to Lesa. The terror that knotted in her stomach propelled her forward rather than held her back. She drew level with the soldier, keeping her eyes downcast, conscious that she was nearly as tall as him and that he was studying her closely. He seized her chin and jerked her head up. For the first time she saw briefly into his dispassionate eyes before he twisted her head from one side to the other like a horse dealer examining a potential purchase. He released her and shouted an order to his subordinates. They all piled into the truck. The starter growled harshly and the vehicle swung around in a tight circle, lurching drunkenly on its broken springs, and swayed back along the unmade track, its gears whining harshly in the still air. Only when the forest had swallowed the sound of the clapped-out diesel engine did the villagers break the circle and return to their daily struggle to survive.

Lesa never saw her mother again.

## 2

The sound of the rattan screen being lifted intruded on Lesa's thoughts. It was Neti. She was eighteen. Her parents and grand-parents had been killed in a Viet Cong attack on a neighbouring village when she was five. Lesa's grandparents had taken her in and looked after her ever since. Lesa loved the older girl with an intensity of passion that would have been directed towards her mother. If only Neti wasn't so teasing and provocative with boys. The older girl seemed to love letting them chase her around the stout bamboo stilts that their huts were built on because, even two kilometres from the gentle Song Yen River, the monsoons sometimes brought annual floods that could turn it into a raging torrent. While Neti played with the boys, Lesa preferred to remain above in the long family hut, reading the American magazines that were gradually rotting in the humidity – struggling with the strange writing. The magazines were precious because her mother had brought them back from Danang. After the soldiers had taken her mother away, Uncle Hinny had burned all the magazines.

On one occasion Lesa had heard Neti laughing and giggling with Diem, a much older boy who had served in the North Vietnamese Army. He was the son of the political officer who had been billeted with the village. Diem had learned English from his father who had been responsible for the interrogation of GI prisoners of war. She had peered through a crack in the floor and seen them kissing in the manner that couples kissed in the magazine photographs – which was strange. Diem had even stroked Neti's breasts – which was even stranger. Lesa had been frightened for Neti. By now she had a vague idea that it was such behaviour with the Americans that had led to her mother's disappearance.

'I've packed some things for you, Lesa,' said Neti dumping a bulging backpack on the woven straw matting. Three water canteens hanging from the pack jangled against each other. She sat beside Lesa on the bed and put an arm around the younger girl.

Lesa touched the pack. It looked like a US army kitbag. To possess anything American meant arousing the wrath of the military governor even though his soldiers had no compunction about using American supplies that had been issued to the defeated South Vietnamese army. His men had a nose for such things. Most of them were villagers themselves and knew the sort of hiding places that the villagers favoured. Sunken pots to keep out the insects had been the favourite. Their dobermans could sniff out such pots for them to unearth. Even the simplest of possessions – postcards, knives, tin openers – would earn a savage beating for those whose hut was nearest the cache.

'Where are we going, Neti?'

'I don't know,' Neti replied. 'Hinny won't say.'

'Are we all going?'

'Grandma and Grandpa are staying.'

Lesa ached for a light so that she could see the older girl's face. Neti's face could hide nothing from her.

'When are we coming back?'

It was a question that Lesa knew the answer to before Neti answered.

'I don't think we're ever coming back, Lesa.'

Lesa's thoughts were a confused whirl. She knew that many thousands of plains people had fled the country in their fishing boats. But things were supposed to be getting better now. The floor flexed beneath her feet. That was Uncle Hinny. He had finished fixing the typhoon frames in place. She knew it was him even before she heard his hollow cough from the Camel cigarettes he used to smoke. The sound earned him a sharp cuff from Thi.

'It's something to do with me,' said Lesa miserably.

'Now why should you think that?'

'The way Hinny and Thi have been arguing such a lot lately. The way they stop when they see me.'

An oil lamp was lit on the other side of the screen. It gave a brief flicker of bright light before the wick was hurriedly turned down leaving only a suffused glow that highlighted the hut's roof trusses and cast a pale light on Neti's flawless skin. Decorating the wall behind Lesa's bed were her sketches of village life. For a fourteen-year-old with no formal education, her artistic talent was remarkable. Lesa's hand stole into Neti's. The touch of the older girl was a comfort.

'That's because they don't want to burden you with their problems,' Neti murmured.

'Surely Uncle Hinny must have told you where we're going, Neti?'

'No one tells me anything. You see? I don't know what's going on either.'

Lesa's confidence in the older girl took a blow. Somehow she thought that Neti knew everything.

The screens parted. Thi entered. Two miscarriages brought about by mistreatment at the hands of North Vietnamese soldiers before having Suzi, coupled with the grindingly hard, back-breaking work in the rice paddies had made her look older than her twenty-nine years. Even her hair was pulled back into a tight, austere bun in the style of the older women. It somehow suited her permanent demeanour of bitterness towards everyone. 'Are you girls ready?' She came forward and held out her hand. 'You must rub this stuff on your faces.'

There was the sound of a tin being prised open and the strong, waxy smell of boot polish. It was a smell that Lesa remembered from when she was a baby: the pungent mixture of polish, sweat and leather from American boots flung down near her cot.

Neta took the tin and rubbed a smear onto Lesa's face. Despite the sombreness of the moment, the two girls giggled nervously as they rubbed the strong-smelling polish onto each other's faces.

'And you must wear these.'

Thi helped both girls into strange lightweight jackets with curious mottled patterns. The two girls looked at each other in bewilderment. They had seen the soldiers wearing similarly patterned garments but these had an alien newness about them; they even smelt new.

'What are they, Thi?' Neti asked, pulling the jacket's waist cords.

'American camouflage jackets. They will help keep you hidden in the forest. And you must put on your backpacks when we're down the ladder.'

'Can I take some extra things, Thi?'

'You can take what you like. But what you take – you'll have to carry.'

When no one was looking, Lesa slipped her catapult into her backpack. It was no ordinary catapult: the Farnham 50 PebbleZing had a die-cast aluminium handle with an adjustable wrist stirrup for bracing the user's forearm against the pull from its twin strands of eight-millimetre butyl elastic. It had been given to her as a child

50

by an American Marine sergeant whom she had impressed with her unerring accuracy after he had shown her how to use it. After that she had often amused herself by punching holes in tin cans at a range of fifty metres. Her successful killing of a rat led to her developing stalking skills in the woodland near the village. On one occasion she came home bearing a wild duck but no one would believe her story that she had brought it down in flight. The enthusiasm of the village boys to try out Lesa's latest possession soon waned when she demonstrated her remarkable accuracy. No boy, or man for that matter, liked to lose face to a female.

She looked around her tiny area of the hut. She considered taking her pictures down but decided that she could always re-draw them when they got to wherever they were going. She had a photographic memory for detail.

Uncle Hinny's voice spoke from the centre of the hut. 'Come on. We're going now.'

Lesa's grandparents were huddled together, sitting cross-legged on the floor in the centre of the hut's communal area. It was barer than usual because Hinny had been systematically selling his possessions over the past few weeks. The last to go had been his prized twenty-six-inch colour television. Not that there had been much point in keeping it. Ever since Lesa could remember, the programmes had been either boring diatribes against the Americans or documentaries extolling the glorious victories of the North Vietnamese army. Also gasoline for the Honda generator had become unobtainable.

The flickering light from the oil lamp highlighted the tears on the old woman's cheeks, coursing down her wrinkled face like the first rains of the monsoon finding their way onto a dried riverbed. Despite her sorrow she made no sound. Her husband stared through the gloom with sightless eyes. He had been blinded with cataracts in both eyes ever since he had trodden on one of the anti-personnel mines that the Viet Cong used to scatter in the rice paddies.

From habit Lesa put on her conical straw hat but Hinny took it from her. 'It'll show up too much in the dark,' he said. He gave Lesa a quick smile and lifted the trapdoor. He was a small, wiry man in his early thirties. He and Thi had married late. With so many villagers being killed during the war and in the atrocities that followed, there had hardly been any breaks in the periods of mourning for the village's customs to permit a wedding to take place. He stood on the rungs of the aluminium ladder, took little Suzi from Thi and disappeared into the darkness. One by one all four members of the family, five including Suzi, descended the ladder and caught the backpacks that the old woman tossed down.

With all the family standing so closely together, Lesa was uncomfortably aware of how much taller she was than anyone else. She was now at least six centimetres taller than Uncle Hinny and was still growing. It wasn't right. Although he never complained, as to do so would be to admit to a loss of face, it was obvious that he never liked her standing too close to him in public. She was also taller than Neti although she did not feel taller. Neti was always one to be looked up to.

Hinny carried two backpacks while Thi settled Suzi in a sling so that she could carry the baby on her hip. Hinny gave a low whistle and Chukki came bounding joyously out of the darkness. The little black mongrel threw himself at each member of the family in turn and, despite Hinny's training, refused to be quiet until he had received a pat from each. The boisterous creature could hardly credit that he was being taken on an adventure at night and it was all Hinny could do to keep him from running around in circles.

'We'll go single file,' Hinny whispered. 'I'll go first. Thi – you follow me. Then you, Neti, and Lesa last because she has such sharp hearing.'

The women accepted his authority and fell into place behind him as he skirted the village. The dog guarding the commandeered hut now occupied by Diem's parents gave a whine of suspicion and fell silent when its nostrils caught the familiar scents. The few pigs and water buffalo that the military governor permitted the village to keep grunted and snorted in their pens. Hinny took the well-trodden path that led to the well that the American Seabees had drilled for the village back in the days when the Americans and their Huey gunships had ruled this part of the interior.

The well was symbolic of the Americans' good but misplaced intentions born of their failure to understand the Vietnamese way of life. The well was supposed to have saved the womenfolk a two-kilometre trek to the river with their water containers. But the fastidiously clean Vietnamese women bathed and swam daily in the river at a centuries-old spot where the water flowed swiftly regardless of season and consequently there was less danger from water snakes and leeches. During the dry season the village boys regularly drove the water buffalo down river to the muddy wallows. All the well meant to the village was that the women returned from their daily bathing trips empty-handed.

The party stopped to fill their canteens at the well and moved on.

Beyond the well the path narrowed where it passed through the complex mosaic of rice paddies and cultivated smallholdings that surrounded the village. First was the heavy smell of Yan's melons, and then Tenka's long rows of pole beans trained up bamboos. Even the black, humus-rich earth, worked by countless generations, released its own rich smell after the evening's light fall of rain. The largest fields were Hinny's which he had used for growing pineapples. The Americans had loved pineapples. Hinny had been able to undercut the growers on the huge Philippines' estates by selling direct. Tak Noi regarded them as a decadent fruit and had forbidden their cultivation.

They passed the rusting hulk of a John Deere tractor. In the days of plenty, when there had been diesel fuel, the machine had been a proud symbol of the village's prosperity. Now the corroding hulk, sitting on its flattened, rotting tyres, served as a silent reminder of the economic disaster that had overtaken their beleaguered country.

A weak moon in its first quarter broke through the cloud and bathed the scene in a pale luminescence. Mosquitoes rose in swarms from the paddies but nothing stirred in the distant forest that they were moving towards. No one spoke. The only sound was the squelch of boots on the earthen path along the paddy dike and the sudden scuffle of Chukki's pads as he ran back and forth delivering affectionate licks to any hand prepared to tolerate his eager tongue.

Lesa was puzzled that Hinny should have brought Chukki. The dog often guided grandpa on his walks around the paddy dikes. Surely the old man's need for the good-natured creature was greater than theirs?

After an hour's brisk walking in the drenching humidity of the sub-tropical night they were further from the village than Lesa had ever dared venture. They came to a fork in the track. Hinny seemed to know exactly where he was going. The left fork took them in a more westerly direction towards the Annamite Mountains. Lesa shivered. As a child it had been instilled into her that west was where the enemy and therefore danger lay. Not that direction mattered anymore. These days the danger was all around.

They had been walking for three hours when Hinny stopped.

'From now on we must keep a bigger gap between us. At least twenty paces,' he told the three women. He delved into his backpack and handed out a whistle to each. 'Whoever sees any danger must give one blast on their whistle and leave the path and hide. Thi – you must go to the left. Neti to the right and Lesa to the left. We must stay separated. You will then count slowly to a hundred. If you hear or see nothing, you must re-join the trail and continue walking. Do you understand?'

The three women repeated their instructions to Hinny's satisfaction. He set off along the path with Chukki dancing in attendance. Thi waited until he was twenty paces ahead before settling Suzi at her breast in the sling and following in his footsteps. Neti gave Lesa's hand a reassuring squeeze and followed after Thi. Lesa took up the rear when Neti was twenty paces ahead.

The trail narrowed. Once or twice Lesa stumbled on the sun-baked ruts of the many bicycle tracks and water buffalo hoof marks that the rain had not washed away. She hated the separation because she was alone with her thoughts instead of chatting in a low voice to Neti. She could guess why Hinny had made them spread out: if one of them stepped on a mine, the others would not be hurt. It was as simple and as brutal as that.

She thought she heard a sound from behind. She stopped, straining her ears into the darkness. There was the sudden high-pitched shriek of a wild hamster providing a snake with its supper. She shivered – a victim of her powerful imagination. Snakes filled her with dread. They never came near the village – the noise and smells of the livestock kept them away; but out here was their territory. Common sense told her that any snakes on the path would disappear into the undergrowth long before there was any risk of them being trodden underfoot.

There was the sound again: an accidentally kicked pebble perhaps a hundred paces behind. She decided against using the whistle. Instead she quickened her pace and caught up with Neti.

'I think we're being followed, Neti.' Her whisper was low and urgent but Thi heard it and called out to Hinny. The four gathered into a group. Hinny did not query Lesa's alarm – the whole village knew about her incredibly sharp hearing. He signalled Chukki to silence. The dog obediently folded itself onto the path with its muzzle pointing back the way they had come, its ears pricked and alert like warning triangles.

Another sound. Chukki gave a throaty growl.

'Hide!' Hinny hissed.

The group separated and melted silently into the elephant grass. Lesa lay on her stomach, certain that whoever came along the track would hear her pounding heart.

A minute passed.

Another chink of a pebble. A low whine from Chukki that Hinny immediately shushed confirmed that Lesa had not been mistaken. She pulled the catapult from her backpack and felt in her pocket for the supply of ammunition that she always carried. Her fingers selected a round, flat stone that was a snug fit in the catapult's sling pouch.

The sound of a twig snapping – Lesa flattened herself to the ground and prayed that she wasn't lying on any fire ants that would indicate their objection to be being lain upon by biting her. She cupped the catapult's stirrup against her forearm, loaded the stone into the pouch, and drew back on the powerful elastics.

A slightly-built figure emerged from the gloom. A bulging backpack gave his silhouette a strange hunchback look. Lesa aimed slightly ahead of the figure, drawing the elastics to full stretch but holding her fire. There was something vaguely familiar about the stranger's walk. He passed Lesa's hiding place. A shadow leapt out on him. There was a flash of steel in the moonlight. A voice she knew cried out, 'No, Hinny! It's me! Diem!'

Lesa jumped to her feet and saw Hinny and the figure squaring up to each other. Neti rose out of the undergrowth a few metres away from Lesa. She gave a little cry and ran forward.

'Diem! What are you doing here?'

Chukki's yapping woke Suzi who started crying. It was some seconds before order was restored. The three startled women gathered around Hinny who was reluctantly releasing his grip on Diem's throat. The young man's eyes were round with terror, fixed on the long knife that Hinny was holding in his other hand.

'What are you doing?' Hinny demanded. Like the rest of the villagers, he mistrusted Diem and his father.

'Following you,' Diem replied, rubbing his bruised throat.

'I know that. Why?'

Diem's frightened eyes flickered to Neti. 'I wanted to be with Neti.'

Hinny hesitated before returning his knife to its sheath.

'How did you know we were leaving?' Thi demanded. 'Did Neti tell you?' She rounded suspiciously on the girl.

'How could I know when you never told me anything?' Neti retorted.

Diem glanced anxiously at Hinny. He licked his lips. 'The whole village knew you were planning something,' he said to Thi. 'The way Hinny was selling things and kept disappearing for several days when my father was away. I heard in Danang that it was only a matter of time before they came again, so each night I watched your house. I want to be with Neti and I want to come with you. I've brought plenty of food.'

'Did you tell your father?' Thi demanded.

'No – of course not.'

'Why should anyone come?' Lesa asked, surprising herself at her courage in breaking in on this conversation between adults.

'Go and keep watch down the path,' Thi ordered.

The custom of generations prevented Lesa arguing with her elders. She moved away from the group, leaving them talking heatedly in low tones. The wave of jealousy that Diem's arrival had aroused because she would no longer have Neti to herself if he stayed was overshadowed by the suspicion she had been nurturing that the flight was somehow connected with her mother. Diem's comments hardened that suspicion although just how she could be the sole cause of the family's flight, she could not imagine. She had done nothing to upset the authorities. Perhaps it was something her mother had done? Fear chilled Lesa's heart when she remembered the day when Tak Noi's boy soldiers had taken her mother away. Had her mother paid for something her father had done? And having punished her mother, was it now her turn?

Lesa knew nothing about her father other than that he had been killed in the war. Her questions about him among the family and villagers were not encouraged. Obviously his loss had been a source of great grief although she had always been puzzled by the lack of photographs of him. The walls of all the other huts in the village were adorned with pictures of departed loved ones, some faded with age but most, sadly, bearing the mirror-like sheen of modern photographic glazing machines and the fashionable ragged edges of the processing laboratories in Danang. But of her father there was nothing. Not even wedding photographs.

The adults finished their discussion. Hinny beckoned to Lesa.

'Diem is to join us,' he told her. 'He will take up a position between Thi and Neti. We must get moving. We've wasted enough time. We have to reach the forest by dawn.'

Lesa suddenly hated Diem and wished she had let fly with the catapult.

'Can't I walk with Neti?' Diem asked.

'No,' said Hinny shortly, and set off along the track.

After an hour's trudging the party came to a wider track that bore the deep ruts of truck tyres. They followed it for another thirty minutes. The noise of an approaching diesel engine forced them into the undergrowth until the truck was safely past.

Lesa checked the position of the stars and realized that they had swung through a wide loop and were now heading almost due east. She had only the vaguest knowledge of the geography of her country, but she knew that east was the direction the rivers flowed and east was the direction of the sea which she had never seen. She began to feel excited about the adventure.

### 3

The outskirts of the forest puzzled Lesa. It was nothing like the jungle around the village. The trunks of the trees reared up but instead of a dense crown of foliage, the branches, silhouetted against the first flush of light seeping into the eastern sky, were bare. Many had a gnarled and withered look that was not due to age. It was as if the forest spirits had vented their wrath on them. Many trees had fallen – far more than was normal even after the most savage typhoon. The larger trees had snapped and split the trunks of smaller trees so that what was left of them stood naked against the sky like drawn daggers. Beneath the trees was dense jungle that could not have grown so luxuriantly had the trees possessed foliage.

Lesa knew about trees. When a tree near the village showed signs of dying, it would be felled immediately and the whole village would join in the task of chopping it up. A dead tree was a menace. Once its fibrous roots died and lost their grip on the loose, peaty soil, the tree would be dangerously unstable. But the trees that died were old whereas these dead trees looked young. She wondered if they were victims of the tree-killing sprays that she had heard the Americans had used. There had been much heated discussion in the village about their use.

57

'Their idea had been to kill the forest so that the enemy had no cover,' she remembered Hinny saying, 'but everyone knows that when you fell a tree, more sunlight reaches the ground and makes the undergrowth grow thicker and faster. Look what happened when we cleared a new field last year. Once the trees were gone we had to work twice as hard to keep the undergrowth down until it was ready for planting.'

There had been a chorus of agreement.

'I tell you, the Americans were stupid,' Hinny had declared. 'And a stupid people cannot win wars.'

The truth of Hinny's words was borne out by the new undergrowth that was encroaching on the track. Several times Lesa tripped on vigorous young creepers that passing trucks had half-buried in the mud.

Hinny left the track and led the party into the jungle. He motioned the others to move carefully at first to avoid tell-tale damage to the undergrowth. Only when they were safely concealed did he make their going easier by slashing his way through the broad-leaved succulents with his long knife.

'We'll make camp here,' Hinny decided when they came to a small clearing. He dropped his backpack and showed the others how to assemble the ex-US army lightweight one-man ridge tents. There was one in each pack. Lesa pulled out the telescopic support poles and wondered at the planning that had gone into the flight. Even Diem had brought a tent. Everyone knew what was going on except her.

Over a meal of strips of dried pork fried on a tiny Camping Gaz cooker, Hinny parted with some information. 'We're heading for the coast,' he explained. 'We sleep during the day and travel at night. The journey will take three nights if the rains hold off.'

'What happens when we reach the coast?' Lesa asked uncomfortably aware that the others were staring at her.

Hinny carefully wiped his fingers on a handful of elephant grass. 'We make contact with a village I have had dealings with. That is all you need to know for the time being.'

Lesa knew better than to press Hinny for more information. She helped clear away the meal and bury the scraps deep so that they would not attract insects. Afterwards she relieved Thi of Suzi and spooned strained baby food into the child. One of the packs that Hinny carried was crammed with tiny Heinz tins and sachets of dried milk – more evidence of his careful planning which helped boost Lesa's confidence in the success of their mission.

Neti and Diem chased each other around until their antics started Chukki barking and earned a sharp rebuke from Thi, a scowl from Lesa, and an order from Hinny to dig a field latrine. The sun was high and warm by the time the group crawled into their individual tents.

Lesa made a hole for her hip so that she could lie on her side in some comfort. Unlike most villagers, who could sleep anywhere at any time given the chance, she always found it difficult to sleep during the day. The continuous uproar from the birds kept her awake. But here, in the rising heat of the morning, the strange, half-dead forest was still and silent apart from the occasional distant whine of a truck picking its way along the unmade road in low gear.

## 4

Lesa was woken by Suzi's crying. It was getting dark. Thi was alone with Suzi, warming an opened tin of baby food over the Gaz cooker.

'I'm a mass of bites,' Lesa complained, scratching her leg.

Thi gave a rare smile. 'That's why we brought you along, Lesa – insects seem to prefer you to us.'

Lesa laughed and suddenly clapped her hand over her mouth. She looked worriedly in the direction of the road. Chukki burst in on the camp, his tail wagging furiously. He was followed by Hinny, Diem and Neti. The two men were carrying a small wild boar – a young one. Hinny cleaned a Smith and Wesson revolver while the others helped prepare the creature and cut it into thin slices for frying on the cooker. Until then Lesa had had no idea that Hinny possessed any weapon other than his long knife.

An hour later they broke camp, carefully re-stowing the tents and utensils, and burying the evidence of their stay before resuming their long march.

The pattern of the first night was repeated: the party strung out, Lesa placing one foot in front of the other and trying to ignore the beginnings of foot blisters and the murderous stomach cramps that heralded the onset of her period.

Hinny ordered a change in their routine: they now rested for fifteen minutes every two hours. Lesa wasn't sure that it was such a good idea. It seemed that every muscle in her body locked up whenever she climbed to her feet after lying flat on her back for a few minutes.

The moon had been up two hours when a sudden cry made them freeze in their tracks. Chukki was at Hinny's side. He gave a low growl and pointed his snout straight ahead, his hackles rising like the quills of a porcupine going onto the defensive.

'Halt!'

A soldier materialized out of the shadows. The reason they had not seen the boy was because he had been sitting up-wind at the side of the road. Now he was confronting Hinny, his AK-47 slung from his shoulder and pointing with casual arrogance at the track in front of the group.

'Who are you?' the soldier demanded. His voice was filled with suspicion. It had the uneven low-high quality of a youth whose voice had only just broken.

'Hill villagers from Song Yen,' Hinny replied.

'You're a long way from home. What are you doing here?'

Lesa felt in her pocket for her catapult. Her fingers closed around the reassuring coldness of its aluminium handle.

'We heard that they have a working tractor for sale at Rochelle. We're on our way to inspect it. Our military governor said that I would have to take my family with me.'

Lesa withdrew the catapult from her pocket. She kept her movements slow and deliberate but the boy wasn't interested in her. Women rarely represented a danger. She slipped a round, slightly flattened stone into the sling. Such pebbles followed a straight and true path.

'Show me your travel permit.'

Hinny lowered his pack to the ground and unbuckled the straps while the soldier looked on with interest – there was a chance of him ending up with a profitable bribe.

Lesa held the catapult in her left hand and the sling in her right hand. She knew that there would be no time to take a proper aim. The boy soldier would be certain to see her movement. And, of course, there would be no question of getting in a second shot if she missed.

'I put all the papers at the bottom for safety,' Hinny explained, pulling out his tent.

'You have no papers!' the boy rasped. 'You're lying! You're rats leaving the ship like all the rest! Therefore you will all die like rats.' His voice was high with excitement. He stepped back and lifted the carbine. At that moment Lesa whipped up the catapult, stretched its elastics to their full extent, and fired. The stone made a soft *thrring* as it sped on its way. There was a loud crack and the boy seemed to stare glassily for some seconds before pitching forward. Hinny seized his opportunity. He snatched his knife from its sheath and drove its blade into the boy's neck as he fell. Thi gave a little cry as blood spurted from the terrible wound. Hinny kicked the rifle away from the fallen body, ready to drive his knife between the boy's shoulder blades if he stirred. But there was no need: Lesa's stone had pierced his skull – he was dead even before Hinny had stabbed him.

Hinny looked up and saw the catapult hanging from Lesa's hand. He had seen the soldier's skull cave in when the stone struck it. The girl's eyes were round with shock.

'Did I kill him?' she whispered.

'No,' said Hinny, taking the catapult from Lesa's lifeless fingers and looking curiously at it. 'I did. But you did take him off his guard. It was a good shot.' He handed the weapon back and smiled encouragingly at the frightened girl. The smile overwhelmed Lesa. Hinny had shown her a measure of respect and acceptance which made her forget for the moment the enormity of what had taken place.

Hinny and Diem carried the dead youngster shoulder-high into the sword-edged grass and emerged a few minutes later empty handed. Hinny hurled the boy's weapon into the jungle and had to whistle Chukki back to prevent him retrieving it. Thi gave Lesa a quick smile of gratitude when she insisted on carrying Suzi.

The party continued with their trek.

## 5

The terrain changed. Gradually at first, and then dramatically as the slight downward slope took them clear of the jungle and into open marshy ground, overgrown abandoned paddies, where the trail narrowed to little more than a raised strip of compacted yellow soil barely wide enough to accommodate a bullock cart. Without cover they felt vulnerable, particularly when the moon broke out from behind a low bank of cloud and spilled its pale light across the barren landscape. Hinny stopped and consulted a map.

'We're four kilometres from the river,' he told the others. 'There's a bridge. It's usually guarded during the day, and if it's guarded at night we'll have to walk upstream until we find a shallow point to wade across.'

It was the nearest that Hinny had come to admitting that he had thoroughly reconnoitred their route. They trudged wearily on. The moonlight sparkled on strange circular pools of stagnant water that seemed to be multiplying as they neared the river. There were hundreds of them of different sizes, overlapping and breaking into each other's banks. The wind rippled their surfaces and water snakes made delicate but threatening spreading vees in the moonlight. The strange pools reminded Lesa of photographs of moon craters she had seen in one of the *National Geographic* magazines that Hinny had burned. Then she realized that that was exactly what they were: craters. Bomb craters. Thousands of them that merged into a single mass of devastation around the sturdy bamboo bridge that was just coming into view. It was one of those structures that the Vietnamese were particularly adept at building using materials that were immediately to hand. Even if it were washed away in a flood, a new bridge could be built in a few days. Lesa guessed that ensuring it remained destroyed must have kept many American bombers occupied for hundreds of hours. If the appearance of the surrounding landscape was anything to go by; for every bomb that had hit the bridge, a thousand had missed.

They hid in one of the smaller craters near the bridge while Hinny scouted ahead. Lesa watched him leave – running low with Chukki close on his heels. The rushing water hid the squelching of his boots in the soft mud. Man and dog disappeared into the shadows. The moon went behind a thick cloud and total darkness returned to the wilderness. As Lesa's eyes adjusted to the dark, she became aware of a glowing point of light at each end of the bridge. They were so indistinct that it was only possible to see them by looking slightly to one side. Even then they tended to fade, sometimes disappearing altogether.

Hinny returned after ten minutes. He slithered into the crater and announced that the bridge was unguarded.

'What are the lights?' Lesa asked.

'Lights?' Hinny frowned and joined Lesa who was staring at the bridge.

'Can't you see them? A light each side of the bridge. They're very faint.'

'Your imagination, child. There's no lights.' He invited the others to take a look. None of them could see Lesa's lights. They scrambled out of the crater and moved cautiously towards the bridge.

Diem suddenly stopped. 'Lesa's right,' he told Hinny. 'I can see them now. Spots of luminous paint. There'll be snipers with their rifles trained on them. If they go out, they fire.'

Hinny could see the faint points of light now. He considered crawling across the bridge to avoid them but supposing there were other spots of the deadly paint that they might miss? The bridge was too risky. 'We'll follow the river upstream,' he decided.

## 6

The going was treacherous. The cratered heavy mud clung to their boots, dragging at their blisters and making every step an agony. Sometimes they had to wade around the dense thickets of bamboo that had sprung up in the hollows. The craters eventually thinned out and the riverbank became firmer apart from the occasional water buffalo wallows where the yellow mud reached their knees.

Two hours before dawn they came to a spot where the river widened and became a sluggish yellow soup. Cartwheel tracks showed that it was a well-used fording point. Being the tallest, Lesa carried Suzi on her back in the sling. The tepid, slow-moving water rose around her waist, tugging down her pants around her thighs. At one point it deepened and covered her breasts. She felt the caressing touches of leeches fastening hungrily onto her body. They weren't so bad in a fast-flowing river, but the presence of warm blood in still water would attract them by the hundred. Women avoided entering deep water during their period. The waistband of her pants around her thighs made it difficult to keep her balance. Her feet slipped on the large, rounded stones that lined the riverbed and she would have gone under had it not been for Diem's steadying hand. The baby didn't wake up once. The leeches were bad. What started as a barely perceptible stinging in her crotch became an insistent buzz of pain.

The water shallowed. Lesa scrambled up the opposite bank and handed Suzi back to Thi. The older woman stared at Lesa and pointed without speaking. Lesa looked down and nearly fainted from shock: her thighs and abdomen were a black mass of bloated, clinging, slug-like leeches that gleamed obscenely in the moonlight.

The loathsome creatures were voracious, opportunist feeders. Lesa had been in the water no more than ten minutes and yet they were swollen with her blood.

'Hinny!' Thi called. 'Quickly!'

Lesa suddenly felt ashamed and tried to hitch up her pants but Thi slapped her hands away. 'Stupid child!' she hissed.

Hinny saw the problem. He opened his pack and took out his cigarettes and matches which he kept in a Tupperware container. He lit one of his precious Camels and touched the glowing tip on a leech that seemed to be burrowing into Lesa's navel. It curled and dropped off. He worked systematically. She felt his breath on her body when he had to inhale at the same time as applying the cigarette to the more persistent leeches. He moved lower.

'Lie down.'

Lesa did as she was told.

'Open your legs.'

'Let me do it, Hinny,' she pleaded.

'You'll burn yourself.'

'Don't be stupid, child!' Thi scolded. 'Do as he says.'

Lesa opened her legs and fought back the tears of embarrassment that pricked her eyelids. Like other women of her culture, she was not over self-conscious of her body and did not mind others seeing her naked, but this degree of prying was intolerable. The final humiliation was Hinny telling Diem to hold a flaming Zippo steady so that he could see what he was doing.

'I'll hold it,' said Neti, hearing and correctly interpreting Lesa's little cry of misery. She took the lighter from Diem and pushed him away. Lesa felt a wave of gratitude for the older girl's understanding. There was a gentle tugging on the lips of her vagina and she felt Hinny's breath as he sucked hard on the cigarette. The heat of the glowing tip was a sudden, sharp pain, and then there was Neti's voice telling her it was all over.

Neti helped Lesa to her feet and gave her hand a reassuring squeeze before unbuttoning her shirt. Several leeches had fastened themselves to Lesa's breasts. One was sucking on her nipple like a ghastly mutant infant. One by one they fell away when Hinny touched them with the glowing Camel leaving ugly red weals on her skin. Lesa stammered her thanks and got dressed. An inspection revealed a leech on the sole of Suzi's foot and another on her ankle. Diem had one on his penis and earned everyone's contempt by making a fuss about Hinny's cigarette treatment over his one leech when Lesa had hardly made a sound.

Hinny made another trip across the river and returned holding the last of the backpacks high above his head.

The party headed for some defoliated palm groves and made camp. They were too exhausted to eat, preferring to huddle around the miserable heat given out by the camping cooker. An important consolation was that at least they had dry clothes to change into.

'We're still making good time,' said Hinny after checking his map. 'Tomorrow we cross Highway One and then we're nearly there.'

Nearly where? Lesa wanted to ask. But no one else asked the question and she knew that it would not be answered if she asked it. She crawled into her tent, too tired to even feel jealousy when she heard Neti and Diem's subdued giggling over a shared joke. Fording the river had brought one small benefit: at least she was now reasonably clean.


## 7

The next night they retraced their route along the opposite river bank and rejoined the track. Their spirits were high now that the end of their long trek was in sight, and the thickening jungle meant that hiding was no longer a problem when they heard a vehicle approaching.

The blow fell shortly after midnight when they came upon a temporary checkpoint manned by six soldiers. They had to quickly backtrack and hide in the ravaged forest because Suzi started to cry.

'They weren't there last month,' Hinny complained bitterly when they were hidden a safe distance from the checkpoint.

'Why are they going to all that trouble?' Thi asked, holding Suzi to her breast.

'It's because there are still some doing what we're doing,' Hinny answered.

'How about going through the jungle around the checkpoint?' Diem suggested.

Hinny shook his head. 'Why do you think they've set it up where the jungle is at its densest? To make it doubly difficult to avoid. And there's certain to be guards posted in the jungle. We'd make too much noise cutting our way through and it would take too long, and there might be punji traps.'

'Is there another route?' Neti asked.

Hinny studied the map. 'There is. It means at least a twenty-kilometre detour and it's almost as dangerous.'

'It can't be any more dangerous than what we've done so far,' Neti observed.

Hinny regarded her steadily. 'The detour will be extremely dangerous.'

'Do we have any choice?'

'We could return to the village,' said Thi.

Hinny glanced at Lesa and shook his head. 'Whatever the danger, we have to face it.'

Thi scowled but said nothing.

The group retraced their footsteps along the track and took a path that they had passed an hour previously. It was little more than a shepherds' track that had fallen into disuse and was badly overgrown. At times it virtually disappeared. Hinny and Diem took it in turns with the knife to hack their way through. Occasionally Hinny stopped to check their direction with a pocket compass.

The cut ends of bamboo and elephant grass slashed at Lesa's shins making her worry about cuts and the danger of infection. Chukki loved the jungle and doubled the distance he had to travel by darting after creatures that scurried away at their approach. At one point he caught and killed a wildcat kitten and caused some concern in case the creature's mother came after them hellbent on revenge. Vietnam's wildcats were not known for their good nature.

There was little point in travelling spread out in the dense undergrowth. For the first time Lesa was able to talk to Neti but the older girl was more interested in Diem's company. Smouldering with resentment, Lesa pushed ahead and took a different route from the others around a clump of bamboo. There was something odd in front of her. She went cautiously forward and parted the undergrowth.

The scream that the horror confronting her produced had Hinny at her side in an instant. The others gathered around, staring down into the pit. It was a punji – a booby trap used for centuries to catch game which the Viet Cong had adapted with deadly success for human game. It consisted of a concealed deep trench whose bottom was lined with fire-hardened pointed bamboo stakes embedded upright. The skeleton lying in the bottom of this trench was partially covered by the rotted remains of a US Marines uniform. The white bones of his fingers were still clutching his rusting rifle. He had lain there for perhaps ten years. Four thousand American servicemen had perished in such booby traps. This victim must have been separated from his platoon because it was virtually unknown for the Americans to leave a dead comrade behind.

The group moved cautiously around the trap and pressed on with Neti holding Lesa's trembling hand.

The jungle came to an abrupt end. There was no gradual thinning out. At one pace there was dense undergrowth, at the next there was a broad swathe of strangely bare moonlit soil some two hundred paces wide. It looked as if it had been recently ploughed and harrowed to a fine tilth. Ten metres from the edge of the forest was an orderly line of numbered markers at regular intervals. They all knew what a minefield was even if none of them had ever seen one before. The markers related to map grid references for the benefit of those who laid the land mines or who were responsible for their inspection and upkeep. It had a look of neat, well-ordered efficiency about it. Even Chukki sensed trouble and remained obediently at Hinny's side.

Lesa was the first to speak. 'Why is it that nothing is growing?'

'They first plough the land and then poison it with arsenic,' Hinny replied laconically. 'Nothing will grow here for years. It's a place for dying – not living.'

'Do we have to cross it?' Neti asked in a small voice.

'Yes. That's what I mean by danger.'

'Craters,' said Thi, pointing out some pock marks that disfigured the otherwise evenly harrowed soil.

Hinny nodded. 'Probably caused by wild animals,' he commented without conviction. He turned to the forest and began slashing with his knife until he had a small bundle of short lengths of bamboo. 'This is where we will cross,' he decided, pointing to a nearby number marker. 'To choose to cross near a marker with a lucky number will be too dangerous – that's where there's certain to be more than the usual number of mines. Chukki!'

The dog bounded to its feet and gave an eager yelp of anticipation as Hinny showed it one of the sticks.

'Fetch, Chukki! Fetch!'

Hinny threw the stick some twenty paces onto the sterile strip of death. The dog leapt after it, seized it in its teeth, and raced back to Hinny to drop it at his feet. His short foray across the minefield was marked by a pattern of paw prints in the soft soil.

'Good boy . . . Good dog.' Hinny made a brief fuss of the animal and turned to the others. 'We'll go across in the same order as usual except that Thi and Suzi must go to the rear behind Lesa.'

For a moment it looked as if Thi was going to object but she changed her mind.

'And you must follow in my footsteps exactly,' Hinny continued. He threw a second stick. Chukki raced forward and snatched it up but stayed put on his master's command. Hinny glanced behind him to see if the others were ready and set foot gingerly on the minefield. His weight sank easily into the cultivated soil and it frightened him.

Nothing happened.

A second step.

Still nothing.

The third, fourth and fifth steps were the same. By the time it was Lesa's turn to step into the minefield, her path was well-marked by Hinny's, Neti's and Diem's footprints. She could hear Thi's breathing behind her – short, frightened little gasps that communicated the mother's fear to Suzi who started crying until Thi put her to her breast.

When Hinny was within five paces of Chukki he called him to his side, patted him affectionately, and hurled another stick which the dog bounded after and snatched up. Chukki sank patiently to the sterile earth, tail thumping happily as he watched the cautious approach of his master. This was a great game even if it was being played in the middle of the night.

Two more sticks brought the group to the centre of the minefield. The sudden shrieking of an ape made Lesa jump. Neti reached a hand behind her and gave Lesa a reassuring squeeze – a tiny gesture but one that the frightened girl was grateful for.

Hinny selected another stick and tossed it. He resisted the temptation to throw the stick too hard. Just a few paces at a time so that the dog would return by the same route. The nagging worry was that maybe Chukki was too light to trigger a mine if he trod on one.

The group continued edging forward in single file across the hellish place that was bathed in cold moonlight like a death shroud.

Thi stumbled on the soft ground; carrying the baby and keeping her balance was difficult for her. Lesa's offer to take Suzi was refused.

'If anything happens, this way we die together,' was Thi's fatalistic reply.

They edged forward again, hearts pounding, nerves riding raw on a razor edge of agonizing tension. One foot in front of the other; feet sinking into the soft ground, dreading a sudden unyielding hardness that could mean only one thing.

Lesa nerved herself to look up from the hypnotic footprints she was stepping into and saw that they were within fifty paces of the beckoning security of the forest. At that moment it went dark: the moon had disappeared behind a thick bank of cloud.

'I can't see!' Hinny hissed. 'No one is to move! We must wait until the moon comes out again!'

Lesa twisted around to look at the moon. The cloud bank stretched from horizon to horizon. It was spilling from the west, shutting out the stars like a curse of blindness stealing across the brooding sky.

'It won't come out for a long time,' Lesa retorted. 'Can't you use a torch?'

It was unheard of for a child to question her elders like this but Hinny answered her as though he were dealing with an equal. 'I don't have a torch.'

'You didn't bring one?'

This made Hinny angry. 'I sold everything I could sell to pay for this! Besides, to show a light would be dangerous.'

'The cooker,' Diem whispered. 'Turn the air down so it burns with a yellow flame. It will give a good light.'

Hinny whispered soothing words to Chukki, carefully slipped his backpack to the ground and unfastened the straps. Chukki gave a low, impatient whine and beat his tail on the ground. A minute later the portable cooker hissed and burst alight. Hinny turned down the flame and adjusted the air vent so that it burned with a bright yellow flame. He passed the cooker to Diem who held it aloft like an Olympic torch. The shadows of the group danced on the lethal tilth like mocking demons waiting to greet new arrivals in hell.

Hinny threw a stick to land within ten paces of the edge of the minefield and safety. But Chukki gave a whining growl of delight and, without waiting for his master's command, streaked after it the moment it left Hinny's hand. The animal bounded into the air. The flying stick made a loud clomp as his eager jaws seized it in mid-air. He hit the ground, his paws throwing up soil as he skidded around to run back to Hinny.

The explosion lifted Hinny off his feet, hurling him backwards against Diem and sending them all sprawling. The flaming cooker catherine-wheeled into the air. Lesa was thrown onto her face, her ears singing at the closeness of the stunning thunderclap and her mouth filled with dirt. She covered her head with her hands as soil and bits of Chukki rained down. Suzi screamed and screamed. Lesa rolled over and thought for a terrible moment that the child had been blown out of her mother's arms. She pushed herself up and saw that Thi had fallen on her side but was still clutching Suzi protectively to her chest.

'No one is to move!' Hinny shouted above Suzi's screaming. 'You must not move!'

For some moments no one even dared to breathe. Thi was the first to stir. She sat up. Despite being badly shaken, her first thought was for Suzi. She clasped the child to her and tried to make crooning noises but the shock of the explosion made it impossible for her to control her breathing. All she could manage were shuddering half gasps, half sobs.

'Thi!' Hinny cried out. 'Are you and Suzi okay?'

'Yes – I think so,' Lesa answered for Thi.

'Neti?'

'Yes.'

'I'm okay,' said Diem, sitting up.

'And me,' said Lesa in a small voice.

Hinny climbed cautiously to his feet. He picked up the spluttering cooker and held it high. Its light fell on a fresh crater, about a metre in diameter, that was some ten paces from where he stood. He was silent for a moment as he contemplated the scene. Whatever his emotions were at the loss of Chukki, he was careful not to let them show. The sanctuary of the forest was only twenty paces distant – it might as well have been twenty kilometres. He turned and looked at Diem who was brushing dirt from his hair.

'You must all take off your pants.'

'What?' Diem looked startled.

Hinny set the cooker down and stepped out of his own pants.

The yellow light flickered on his skinny legs. 'You must all take your pants off,' he repeated.

Too frightened to be embarrassed, Lesa set an example by wriggling out of her baggy pants and passing them to Hinny. The others followed suit. Neti cautiously stood before pushing her pants down over her hips. Her legs shone smooth and supple in the flickering flame. Lesa took Suzi from Thi and steadied her while she pulled off her pants. The baby's cries were gradually diminishing.

When he had all the garments, Hinny tied the legs together to form a knotted rope. He secured one end to his backpack and swung it back and forth like a pendulum until it had gained a considerable swing before letting go. The bag plopped down a few paces to the right of the crater. He gathered up the makeshift rope and drew the backpack towards him. The heavy bag made a shallow furrow in the soil.

'Don't follow me until I say,' he ordered.

He walked carefully a few paces along the centre of the furrow, placing one foot precisely in front of the other, and repeated the trick with the pack. The unbearable suspense was too much for Lesa. She turned away and helped Thi calm Suzi. By concentrating all their attention on the child they managed to shut out the demons that filled their imagination. Only when Hinny called out did they look up. He had reached the trees.

## 8

That morning, shortly after crossing Highway One – the winding, neglected road that traversed the length of Vietnam – they made camp under a clump of stunted mangroves on the edge of a broad expanse of wetlands. Lesa cried herself to sleep. She wept because she was lonely and afraid; she wept because she was young and was treated like a child; the others might be escaping to freedom, but what freedom could there be for her – a prisoner of her youth and her sex? She wept because she longed for the security and warmth of her home and village; she wept because it was her period and she was dirty again – she hated being dirty; but most of all she wept for Chukki.

## 9

'The minefield has made us a day late,' said Hinny the following evening after they had eaten. The setting sun shone with a brilliant reddish-yellow light on the small group sitting cross-legged around a small fire that Hinny had decided could be lit because they had found some dry wood that would burn without smoke. 'But it doesn't matter – they said they would wait an extra two days for us if necessary.'

'Who will wait for us?' asked Diem.

Hinny regarded the young man thoughtfully as if making up his mind how much he should divulge. 'The people we shall be leaving with,' was his enigmatic reply.

'How much further do we have to go?' Lesa asked politely, not expecting an answer.

'Don't be impertinent, child,' Thi scolded.

Hinny gave a rare smile. 'She has a right to know,' he said. He reached out and took Lesa's hand. 'She's been a very brave girl. About twenty kilometres. Four hours if the going is easy.'

'Will there be a river, Hinny? I do so need to wash.'

Hinny waved his hand at the expanse of marsh. 'Plenty of water here.'

'But it's muddy. I'd like to wash in a river.'

Hinny's smile faded at this temerity. 'No rivers,' he said curtly. 'We have more important things to worry about.'

There was a strange sound from the west. The sun was now blood red and very low. They all shaded their eyes and tried to make out what was causing the noise. Lesa saw them first. She jumped to her feet, pointing excitedly to the long smears spreading across the sky.

'Birds!' she shouted. 'Just look at them!'

They were cranes. Thousands of them. A dark avian cloud wheeling as one in the warm golden light. The cloud swelled until it was possible to discern individual birds. Their dark-tipped wings had a span nearly equal to a man's height. Their outstretched necks were long and slender.

Hinny and his group rose to their feet and stared dumbfounded as the graceful birds settled on the wetlands. Some came within a few paces of the group and seemed unconcerned at the proximity of the watching humans. Their long bills stabbed into the shallow water seeking fish.

'Sarus!' Hinny breathed. He turned to the others and his eyes were alive with excitement. 'They've returned! This is a wonderful omen.'

The others shared his excitement and with good reason. In Vietnamese mythology the sarus cranes were a symbol of good fortune and immortality. They were souls of the innocent sent from heaven to select those destined for eternal life. They had vanished from Vietnam during the American War and now they were returning. Lesa, like Neti, had seen pictures of them only in temples and shrines. She seized hold of Neti's hand.

'Let's go nearer them, Neti!'

'You'll frighten them away,' Hinny warned as the two girls squelched cautiously hand in hand through the mud towards the nearest group of the magnificent creatures.

The cranes stopped feeding to eye the girls but showed no signs of panic. Lesa and Neti crept nearer and got within ten paces without the birds taking flight although they had stopped feeding and preening to watch the strangers intently. One of the birds spread its wings and did a strange little hop into the air. Two others did the same.

'It's their courtship dance!' Neti whispered excitedly.

Lesa spread her arms in a crude imitation of the movement. Several more of the elegant birds responded with that curious mating ritual of a loping hop into the air aided by several beats of their wings. As they dropped to the muddy water they bowed their heads and performed more hops so that they gradually gathered in a circle around the two girls.

'Dance with them Neti!' Lesa urged. 'Dance!'

The two girls moved in unison, throwing up their arms and bowing to the birds while lifting their feet in and out of the squelching mud. More cranes joined the circle until Lesa and Neti were surrounded by several dozen of the creatures who shared with the girls their strange but graceful dance of survival – the rippling, muddied surface reflected their delicate movements and the low sun threw long, distorted shadows across the wetlands.

It went on for perhaps five minutes with Hinny and the others watching in frozen silence. Suddenly the creatures tired of the dance and returned to their feeding. Lesa and Neti trudged back to the group hand in hand, their faces alive with laughter.

'Did you see us, Hinny?' Lesa cried. 'Did you see them dancing with us?'

73

'Yes,' Hinny answered. 'We saw you.' He was not sure what to think or say. He had heard folklore, stories of people dancing with the cranes, but had never seen it. Timeless legends had it that those with whom the cranes chose to dance were singled out for eternal greatness.

## 10

After a two-hour, ankle-tiring trudge across the wetlands they entered the forest where the going became even more difficult, bordering on the impossible: the weather was unstable and sudden short sharp downpours turned the soil into mud; leeches fell from the dripping leaves onto their necks. Lesa missed her conical straw hat because its broad, sloping sides deflected the creatures so that they fell to the ground. If you paused they came looping and twisting determinedly towards you.

The overgrown path that they had been following through the jungle eventually petered out, forcing Hinny and Diem to take turns with the knife. The two men battled for two hours with the bamboo thickets before their aching arms forced them to take a longer than usual rest. Lesa volunteered a spell with the knife and was pleasantly surprised by Hinny's acceptance of her offer.

After thirty minutes of sustained hacking in the will-sapping humidity of the night, Lesa felt certain that her arm was about to drop off. When they stopped for another rest, sitting on their backpacks because the place was infested with hellish fire ants, Hinny reluctantly agreed with Diem that they could not have covered much more than two kilometres in as many hours.

'They'll take another group and leave without us,' Hinny muttered dejectedly. For the first time he sounded totally dispirited. Not even the loss of Chukki had affected him like this.

'I'll take a turn,' Neti offered and took the knife from Lesa without waiting for Hinny to give his consent. She drove forward several paces into the impenetrable undergrowth without the others bothering to follow. There was no point – it was comfortable where they were sitting. They could easily catch up with Neti. Suddenly she stopped slashing at the foliage and called out. Hinny was at her side in an instant.

'Look,' she pointed at the ground. 'It's getting sandy.'

The others joined them. Hinny snatched up a handful of soil and looked closely at it in the dim, broken moonlight that filtered down through the trees. He agreed that Neti was right. He took the knife from her and started work with renewed vigour. The dense undergrowth unexpectedly began thinning out. The thickets of bamboo, giant convolvulus and spiny succulents gave way to stunted elephant grass that was only a little taller than Hinny. He could walk through it without difficulty. The rest pushed after him, hardly able to contain their excitement and praying that this was not a former cultivated clearing that had become overgrown. The grass thinned out and became even shorter. Hinny looked up at a crescent moon, unobstructed by jungle, shining down from a clear sky while underfoot the ground became dry and dusty instead of the cloying, dank-smelling rotted soil of the jungle that clung heavily to their boots.

Lesa heard the strange sound first and gave a warning cry. The others froze and fell silent. Hinny listened intently to the strange booming sound and gave a sudden smile. He beckoned the others to follow. Suddenly the grass ended and he was standing in the open. The noise was much louder now.

Lesa gasped in astonishment at the huge, open stretch of sand and what was beyond. She had seen broad expanses of water when the Song Yen River was in flood, but this was very different and on a scale that the photographs in the *National Geographic* magazines had never conveyed.

This was the sea.

## 11

Le Fong was a fishing village that had grown up around a natural sandbar that the inhabitants had built on over the centuries to form a stout harbour wall that could withstand the worst of the South China Sea's typhoons. Inside the protection of the squat stone wall fifty or so fishing boats ranging from sampans to motorized junks bobbed and nosed at their bamboo mooring jetties. Between the harbour and the village were several crude docks made by hollowing out the sand. In these docks were high-prowed fishing junks in various stages of construction, looking like plucked chickens in the moonlight. Presiding over the village like a god of the forest was a water tower supported on four massive stone columns; built by the French, it was a relic of Vietnam's colonial past and like Vietnam, it bore the scars of half a century of continuous war. The granite flanks of the main tank were pock-marked with craters. The Viet Minh had shot at it because it was French, the Viet Cong had shot at it because they thought the Americans were using it as a lookout; the Kampucheans had shot at it because it was there; the Americans had strafed with their Huey Cobra choppers when they got suspicious; and the Australians had sniped at it when they got drunk. Symbols of its survival were its talisman-like clusters of television and radio antennae. That the thing had survived was one of those miracles, like the survival of Vietnam itself.

Thi, Neti, Diem and Lesa crouched in the deepest of the sand docks awaiting Hinny's return. For Lesa there was the double excitement that their journey was at last over. For the first time since the dance with the cranes she was happy: Neti's arms were protectively around her – her head snuggled against the reassuring softness and warmth of the older girl's breasts.

They heard voices approaching but remained silent. Only when Hinny called them did they scramble out of their hiding place.

The younger of the two men with Hinny was carrying a hissing hurricane lamp that attracted swarms of mosquitoes. He raised it high, shining its harsh, stuttering light on the anxious faces. His name was Tao. He wore ragged shorts with a revolver jammed in the belt and his finely-muscled body was weathered to the colour of a walnut. He frightened Lesa but not as much as the older man, who smiled toothily at her and Neti. He turned to Hinny and said that the boat was in order and that the final payment was due. Obviously the coastal people did not mind conducting business in front of women.

Hinny said nothing but unfastened his pack and delved deep into its contents. He produced a Balkan Sobranie tobacco tin and handed it over to the older man who opened it and removed a miniature gold ingot. Reflections of gleaming yellow were caught in his eyes from the kerosene lamp's hissing brilliance.

'Ten,' said Hinny, waving at the mosquitoes. 'Just as we agreed.'

'Ten,' the older man confirmed, nodding and smiling. 'We have radio. If they are not good, Tao will bring you back.'

'They're good,' said Hinny sullenly.

'You are in Tao's hands now. The weather forecasts on the radio are good. Good luck, my friends.' With that he turned and disappeared in the direction of the village.

The group picked up their packs and obediently followed Tao onto a jetty. He boarded the largest fishing junk. It was a broad beamed, well-found motor-sailer of about twenty metres in length overall. Apart from the wheelhouse, it was flush-decked with tightly syphered afrormosia planking and neatly dowelled joints. This was a working boat: its accommodation was below – the decks were for hauling nets and gutting and cleaning fish. Like most of the larger craft, a shabby sampan with a woven straw canopy was tethered to its transom for use as a tender.

Tao hung the lamp from a hook on the wheelhouse and bade them aboard.

The smell of fish, tar and diesel oil assailed Lesa's nostrils as if the junk was a living, breathing creature. At least it swamped her own smell that she felt so self-conscious about. She looked curiously about at the unfamiliar surroundings and was gratified that Neti did not try to pull her hand away from Lesa's tight grip. The lamp picked out the junk's sheaves and rigging. The tall spruce mast described a swaying circle against the stars like a giant pen writing an invisible message for the spirits of the night. Tao led the way to a hatch in the aftdeck. Lesa ducked under the boom of a furled lateen sail and followed the others down a steep ladder into a cramped, stifling interior lit with red, low-wattage bulkhead lights. Urine and sweat added their stench to the all-pervading smell of fish and diesel oil. She became aware of two boys watching them from the bunks that lined the port and forward bulkheads. One of the boys was about two years younger than Lesa, the other she guessed was around sixteen. The older boy gave Lesa a shy smile. Tao shouted at them and they immediately scrambled up the ladder onto the deck. Lesa envied them their clean T-shirts and shorts.

'This is where you will sleep,' said Tao, waving his hand around the cabin. 'Sort yourselves out. The hands and I will sleep forward. There's a galley midships and I'll get one of the hands to show you how to use the cooker. The hand pump gives seawater and the electric pump gives freshwater – for drinking only.'

'When are we leaving?' Hinny asked.

'Now,' said Tao abruptly. He climbed onto the deck and shouted orders.

There was the sound of bare feet on the deckhead. A capstan clanked rhythmically and the sudden growl of a starter motor followed by a diesel engine chugging into life made Lesa jump. She

77

didn't know that sailing boats could have engines. The GM diesel opened up briefly and settled to a steady beat and the noise woke Suzi who immediately demanded a feed. Thi sat on a bunk and nursed the child at her breast leaving Lesa and Neti to sort out the unpacking and sleeping arrangements. A breeze bearing the scent of the ocean wafted into the cabin and the unbearable temperature dropped.

## 12

# SOUTH CHINA SEA

The builders of the junk were more concerned with seaworthiness than frivolities such as portholes, so it was not until Lesa climbed onto the deck ten minutes later that she discovered that the tiny harbour was a mile astern. The sampan tender danced in the surging wash from the propeller. She glanced at the blind windows of the wheelhouse and wondered if Tao was at the helm. The junk's turn of speed surprised her and she leaned on the rail and stared down in fascination at the wake boiling past the hull. Such was the heavenly, cooling breeze that she unbuttoned her shirt and allowed the delicious freshness to play on her bare skin.

'Hallo.'

Lesa wheeled around. It was the older of the two deck hands – the one who had smiled at her.

'Hallo,' she replied uncertainly.

'What's your name?'

'Lesa. What's yours?'

'Lin.' He sounded very polite and formal.

'Do you work for Tao?' She was suddenly embarrassed because it was such a silly question.

'Like a dog,' Lin replied. His smile was warm and friendly.

Lesa, always cautious with strangers, decided that she liked this boy.

'You smell,' he said abruptly.

Maybe she didn't like him so much. 'So do you,' she retorted. 'You smell of dead fish. Anyway – *you* would smell if you'd been through what I've been through.'

'You could have a shower,' he suggested.

'Oh, yes? With soap and hot water I suppose?'

'With soap – yes. But no hot water.'

Lesa was intrigued – above all else she wanted to be clean. 'How?'

'I'll show you.'

She followed Lin to the aft deck. The stern navigation light cast a soft white glow over the holystoned planking. The boy uncoiled a canvas hose and adjusted its nozzle. 'We use this to sluice down the decks when we've been cleaning fish,' he explained. He opened a valve half a turn and Lesa gaped in wonder at the water spraying from the nozzle.

'Where's it coming from?'

'From the sea, of course. Where do you think?' He swung the fine spray playfully towards her.

'Let me get undressed first!' She quickly pulled off her shirt and boots and yanked off her baggy pants. The sting of the warm South China Sea on her back was a truly wondrous sensation. She turned her body in the cleansing spray, giving little cries of delight as Lin played it on her face and hair. The water streamed down her body, coursing down between her bud-like breasts, washing away the filth and muck of the long trek. Lin joined in her laughter.

'What are those marks on your stomach?'

'Leeches.' Lesa grimaced at the memory.

He threw her a small block of soap which she rubbed vigorously into her skin.

'Why won't it lather?'

'It's sea-soap, but it'll get you clean.' He continued playing the water up and down her skinny body until she asked him to stop. He coiled the hose and helped rub her dry with a spotless length of sun-bleached sail cloth. The material breathed the clean, heady scent of the sea. Lesa had never felt so good in her life. She sat on a trawl winch and wrapped the sail cloth around herself like a sarong.

'Now I will wash your clothes for you,' said Lin solemnly.

In a day of surprises, this was the biggest surprise of all: a man, well – almost a man – offering to wash her clothes! Lin saw her startled expression and laughed. He bundled her garments into a nylon net which he tied to a length of cord before tossing the bundle over the side into the boiling wake.

'In ten minutes they will be spotlessly clean,' he promised. 'It's how we do all our washing.'

'What's going on here?'

Lesa turned around. It was Thi, her face a tight scowl of anger.

'I've just had a shower, Thi.'

Thi pointed to the hatch. 'Get below.'

'But I'm not tired, Thi. I've got used to sleeping during the day.'

'Don't argue with me, child! Do as I say!'

Embarrassment stung Lesa's cheeks. She blurted a hasty 'thank you' to Lin and stumbled down the ladder with the sail cloth wrapped protectively around her. She threw herself on her bunk and buried her burning face in the rough cushions.

'Behaving like her mother,' she heard Thi mutter to Hinny in the darkness.

## 13

Lesa woke and experienced a fleeting moment of disorientation before remembering where she was. The diesel had stopped its incessant pounding. She had no idea how long she had slept for but bright sunlight was filtering through the open hatch and there was a strong smell of frying pork and bamboo shoots that brought home how hungry she was. She slipped from the bunk, knotted the sail cloth around her waist and had to grab a timber upright as the junk pitched in the swell. Hinny and Diem were asleep. Thi was sitting on her bunk with Suzi at her breast. She took no notice as Lesa pushed past, following her nose to the smell.

The galley was a surprise. It was fitted out like the American kitchens in the magazines: brightly-coloured plastic working surfaces and fitted cupboards covered in the same material. There was even a freezer and a refrigerator – both bright green – the colour of good luck. Neti was cooking with a wok on a gleaming stainless-steel cooker. She smiled warmly at Lesa and gestured to the galley.

'It's nearly all made in Hong Kong. They must make a lot of money with their fishing.'

'Or with gold, like they took from Hinny.'

'Did you sleep well?'

Lesa nodded and looked longingly at the sizzling food.

Neti gave a mischievous grin. 'Thi told me what happened. As soon as I heard I went up and got Lin to give me the same treatment. Then Hinny and then Diem. I think Thi's now feeling a bit silly – especially after she had to wash in a bucket of seawater.'

The two girls giggled conspiratorially.

'Where are we going, Neti?'

The older girl frowned and shook her head. 'I asked Lin. He looked worried and wouldn't say. But then Tao was at the wheelhouse door, watching me shower.' She shovelled some food onto a plate, broke a pair of chopsticks from a partially-split board, and gave the meal to Lesa.

Lesa climbed onto the deck holding her plate. The junk was heading straight for the sun which had been up an hour and was already driving off the marginally lower temperatures of the night. The huge lateen sail was set square-rigged like a spinnaker to catch the humid South East Monsoon blowing in from the Pacific Ocean. Its stabilizing effect cancelled the motion of the swell, causing it to break in showers of wind-whipped sparkling spray that drove across the quarter deck. Water was trickling down Lesa's back by the time she sat on a coil of rope and started on her meal. She didn't mind the drenching spray – it felt good. The pork was good. She felt good. The journey had turned from misery to a heady adventure that not even Thi's moods could spoil. There was one small cloud: where were they going? What would happen to them?

There was a cry from the bow: the younger of the two boys was pointing at something for the benefit of Tao in the wheelhouse. Lesa followed his outstretched arm and saw a ship on the horizon. The sail boom creaked and lurched as the junk altered course a few degrees east, away from the ship.

A shadow fell across Lesa. She looked up. It was Lin. He sat beside her and gave her a neatly-folded bundle of clothes. Lesa held up her shirt in delight. It was cleaner than she had ever known it and amazingly dry. At this time of year the humidity made it impossible to dry anything thoroughly.

'How did you get them so dry?'

'On the engine. It stays hot for hours after it's been closed down.'

'How long have you worked for Tao?' she asked, standing up and pulling on the thin blouse. The sun was already painfully hot.

'Since I was ten.'

She stood, dropped the sail cloth to the deck and was about to step into her pants when Lin reached out and touched her little triangle of pubic hair. It was a very light touch – a gentle brushing with his fingertips.

'Why did you do that?' she wanted to know, hitching up her freshly-laundered pants.

'It's pretty.'

The gesture was treated as an insignificant break in their conversational flow. 'And how old are you now?' Lesa wanted to know.

'Sixteen. You?'

'Fourteen. Fifteen next week.'

He didn't seem to mind being pestered with questions. His parents had been killed in a raid by the Khmer Rouge. With the driving back of the Kampucheans, the village leaders had struck a deal with the North Vietnamese regular army to supply local units with cheap fish. In reality the village had survived on such deals made with whatever faction had held power in their region at any given time. Lesa's seemingly casual, almost disinterested questions were leading to what was uppermost in her mind.

'How fast are we going?'

Lin glanced over the transom at the sampan charging along in the junk's wake. 'Ten knots. Maybe eleven,' he judged. 'It's a good wind.'

'How many kilometres is that in an hour?'

Lin's laughter annoyed Lesa.

'We don't measure sea distances in kilometres,' he said. 'We use nautical miles.' He saw her frown of irritation and added quickly, 'It's about twenty kilometres an hour.'

Lesa calculated how far the boat would travel in a day. The answer shocked her. She saw from the sun that they had altered course a few degrees to the north east. Although her knowledge of the geography of her own country was sketchy, she had a good idea of what the world looked like from the maps in the *National Geographic*; her remarkable memory was such that she had retained a clear picture of them in her mind. To the north east lay China. China? Was it possible that they could be heading for China? Would Uncle Hinny plan something so senseless?

'And have all your trips in this boat been fishing trips?' she asked.

'Nearly always.'

'But not this time?'

Lin smiled and ran his fingers through his mop of black, unruly hair. 'We'll fish on the way back.'

'On the way back from where?'

'On the way back from where we're going.'

'And where's that?'

The boy looked uncomfortable. He glanced up. Lesa saw that the other deck hand was eyeing them through the open door of the wheelhouse.

'Do you have a watch?' Lin pointed to his digital wristwatch.

83

'No – of course not.'

'Do you know how to read this sort of watch?'

'Yes.'

He unfastened the watch and gave it to Lesa. 'You can have this. Don't worry. They're cheap. We can buy plenty more off the Hong Kong fishing boats.'

Lesa was too taken aback by the generosity of the gift to voice any protests when Lin fastened the strap around her wrist. 'There's a supplies locker just forward of the galley,' he said, lowering his voice even though there was no chance of anyone hearing them. 'You go through the galley and you'll see it on the left. Be there at two o'clock tonight when your people are asleep. I've got to do some work now.'

He stood and smiled down at Lesa. 'Two o'clock,' he repeated.

## 14

That night Lesa lay on her bunk under a cover, feigning sleep. Every now and again she would press the little button on the watch that she had discovered lit up the display for a few seconds. She was immensely proud of her new possession but the digits changed with agonizing slowness. 01:45 . . . 01:46 . . . It would take an age before they said 02:00. The customary patience of her race was put to the test.

Her heartbeat quicked at 01:50. She carefully pulled back the covers and listened intently. Hinny and Thi were snoring lightly. There was the faster rhythm of Suzi's breathing. Lesa's bunk adjoined Neti's but she could hear nothing from the older girl's berth. The only light in the cabin was from a few stray shafts of moonlight that flickered briefly through the open hatch when the boat lifted to the swell.

Praying that Neti and Diem were asleep, Lesa was about to sit up when she saw a movement from the direction of Diem's bunk. She froze but kept watch through half-closed eyes. It *was* Diem. He was moving towards her . . . No – he was edging towards Neti's bunk. She made her breathing sound regular as if she were asleep.

Diem was nearer now, his shirt shining white and ghostly in the gloom. It was definitely him – creeping wraith-like across the cabin. Now he was at the foot of her bunk; he whispered something; someone whispered back. It had to be Neti. There was the sound of a movement, a body shifting on a straw mattress, and Diem disappeared from view.

Lesa didn't need to hear Neti's soft, muffled cries into a cushion a few minutes later to know what was going on. To a girl brought up in a Vietnamese family hut with only rattan screens for privacy, such sounds were normal. But this time Lesa found them strangely disturbing. She pulled the cover over her head to shut them out. Her emotions were more than a tormented turmoil of jealousy at the closeness of the relationship Neti was prepared to share with Diem, and anger because of the risk that the couple might see her if she left her bunk. Not for the first time did Lesa wonder what it was like to have a man make love to her. Even after Neti's little cries died away, there was no indication that Diem was about to return to his own berth. Lesa closed her eyes and waited . . . and dozed.

When she opened them again it was daylight.

## 15

The wind strengthened during the morning and the junk smashed its way through the swell at a steady twelve knots under a full spread of canvas that had the mast shrouds groaning under the strain. Tao and his two-boy crew had reset the main sail as a square rig to extract all the energy they could from the driving South East Monsoon.

Another force was contributing to the junk's progress: the warm Kuro Shio current that swept north east along the Asian coast towards Japan where it merged with the main Pacific Kuro Shio.

It was the combination of these two powerful forces that had encouraged many thousands of Lesa's countrymen to flee Vietnam in their sampans – hopelessly inadequate craft for a long sea voyage – to escape misery and deprivation, and the terror of Pol Pot's Kampuchean Khmer Rouge raiding parties. And it was those same forces, coupled with the unpredictable storms, typhoons and voracious sharks of the South China Sea, that had led to them perishing in their thousands. The true figures would never be known. Of the quarter of a million that set out, only twenty-five thousand reached safety: a ratio of ten to one. Lemmings could do better but lemmings weren't driven to the levels of insanity that torture, rape and mass executions often achieved. As for the Khmer Rouge, their level of insanity was reached by having quarter of a million tonnes of napalm bombs dropped on them. The napalm hadn't been all that effective at first; it burned fiercely enough at a temperature that could melt lead but it didn't stick to flesh properly – if a victim was quick enough, he or she could scrape it off; until the ordnance scientists came up with the idea of adding polystyrene to the napalm so that it couldn't be scraped off. They bought unwanted dogs from city pounds, shaved them bald, and fired incandescent globs of their latest creation at them. A dime-sized spot of the new improved napalm would burn down to the bone and keep going. The scientists were satisfied but the generals reported that the enemy were setting up water tanks near their villages for victims to jump into. To keep the generals happy the scientists came up with the notion of adding phosphorus to the already lethal mix. Phosphorus burns on contact with water at a temperature that could melt steel.

The tragedy was that the scientists – basically decent people with homes and families, who went to church on Sundays – had seen the development of their terrible weapon within the narrow perspective of a series of modifications and improvements to a device that had its origins in the medieval cauldrons of blazing oil poured on armies laying siege to a castle. Even the basic ingredients were much the same. Only when it was too late did they realize the awesome power and horror of their creation; a weapon that could turn a nation of Buddhists – a gentle, artistic people with a long history of living at peace with neighbouring countries – into demented psychopathic killers.

## 16

After the evening meal with all the family, Lesa leaned on the aft deck bulwark, watching a magnificent sunset and marvelling at the unceasing energy of the wind that could drive a boat at such a speed. The little sampan racing along in the junk's foam-white wake sometimes threw its bow high out of the water when it hit a swell. Diem and Neti were at the opposite rail, their arms around each other's waist and talking in low tones. Curiously, this time their closeness did not arouse so much jealousy in Lesa. She listened to their small talk with a disinterested ear. Hinny and Thi sat cross-legged on the deck playing cards. Tao had kept Lin busy all day, so it was only now that he was able to join Lesa at the rail.

'Tonight,' he whispered. 'Two o'clock.'

## 17

Lesa's watch was showing 01:55 when she pushed back her covers. Everyone, including Diem and Neti, appeared to be asleep therefore a repeat performance of their previous morning's early matinee seemed unlikely.

She slipped from her bunk, pulled on a fresh cotton shirt that reached her knees, and crept through the galley into a narrow companionway. Lin was waiting for her, wearing a pair of his usual spotless shorts and nothing else. He opened a door and snapped on a dim red light that illuminated a paint locker whose racks were filled with pots of varnish and sail-making materials. He put his finger to his lips and bade Lesa enter. He shut the door, spread some canvas on the floor and sat down, making room for Lesa. She sat beside him, back pressed against bulkhead, chin resting on her knees. She got straight down to business.

'So where are we going?' she whispered.

'I mustn't say.'

Lesa got angry. 'You said you would!'

Lin touched her lips but she knocked his hand angrily aside. 'I didn't say I wouldn't tell,' said Lin. 'I said that I mustn't.'

'All right then. So where?'

'Hong Kong.'

Lesa turned and stared at the boy. 'Hong Kong! But it's a terrible place! They put refugees in cages!'

'Who told you that?'

'It's on the radio.'

'They're lying. They lie about everything. It's a wonderful place. There's plenty of food. Jobs. Houses. Freedom.'

'You've been there?'

'No. But we've met plenty of fishing boats from there.' Lin smiled and touched the watch he had given her. 'That's how I got that. We sometimes sell them bait and do some trading.' He kept his hand on her wrist for a moment before sliding his fingers up her arm.

'Have you done this before? Taken refugees to Hong Kong?'

Lin hesitated before replying. 'Yes.'

'Then how is it you've never been to Hong Kong?'

He slipped his arm around her shoulders. She could feel his warmth through the thin material of her shirt. Her first reaction was to pull away but then she realized that she liked the feeling of closeness and made no objection, not even when his fingertips brushed lightly against her breast.

'Well?' she asked, hoping that the slight tremble in her voice wasn't too obvious.

He kissed her on the back of the neck. The strange sensation made Lesa give a little shiver, more of puzzlement than pleasure. She didn't mind. Just so long as he went on holding her close to him. Closeness was what she needed above all else – the simple feeling of being close to and feeling the touch of another person. There was nothing sexual about it that she was aware of. Lesa had paid a high price in not having a father to play with her during her childhood to bring about an awareness of her sexuality in an atmosphere of innocence. The touch of Lin's hand, gently cupping her breast, his thumb rasping insistently across her nipple, and the closeness of him – the smell of his sweat – made up for her short lifetime of emotional deprivation. Part of that making up was allowing his hand to guide her hand under the waistband of his shorts. Part of that making up was gripping him tightly, not sure what to do while he drew up her shirt and brushed his hand over her hips so delicately that his fingertips barely touched her skin. Part of that making up was surrendering all inhibitions when his teeth took exquisite hold of her earlobe for a few seconds and not objecting when his hand traced little circles around her navel. He moistened his fingertips with his saliva before touching her. When he did, the movements of his fingers were at first very careful and gentle until the involuntary motion of her hips pushing against his hand signalled her desire for still more closeness.

## 18

Lesa slept late and was woken by the sound of Hinny and Thi arguing bitterly with Tao. She spent a few moments guiltily trying to analyse her feelings about the previous night with Lin and gave up. She had expected that such a momentous event would change her in some way and was surprised that she felt so normal. She swung her feet to the deck and stood. The motion of the boat had changed dramatically – it was rolling abominably. She pulled on her clothes and went on deck. The junk was lying stopped, its main sail furled loosely around the boom. Neti was standing apart from Hinny and Thi who were squaring up to Tao.

'What's happening, Neti?'

The older girl gave a bleak smile. 'This is as far as Tao is going to take us. We have to go the rest of the way in the sampan by ourselves.'

'I paid you to take us all the way!' Hinny was shouting.

Tao shook his head. Hinny's anger seemed to amuse him. He leaned against a mast shroud with his hand resting casually on the butt of his revolver. 'We said we'd get you out of the country. That's what we've done. You're being given that sampan loaded up with supplies and water; you'll have a chart and a compass and some distress flares; Hong Kong is a hundred and fifty miles to the north east; the wind is with you and so is the current; the weather forecast is fair for the rest of the week. You'll be there in three days.'

'We know nothing of the sea,' Thi wailed, clutching Suzi to her breast. 'We're not fishing people.'

Tao shrugged. 'The weather will hold. You'll have no trouble. But this is as far as we go.'

'Why won't you take us all the way?' Hinny demanded.

'This boat isn't registered. We could be arrested if we entered Hong Kong territorial waters.'

Not understanding international law, Hinny could think of nothing to say.

Lesa went in search of Lin and found him in the wheelhouse, holding the helm steady.

'You've known all along,' she accused.

The boy looked embarrassed. 'I'm sorry, Lesa. I couldn't tell you. He'd kill me.'

'I'll kill you if you don't stop him!'

Lin was alarmed. This wasn't the Lesa he had known last night. This coldly angry girl had a determined stance, hands on hips, looking more than capable of carrying out her threat. He did not realize that she felt betrayed.

'I can't stop him,' he said lamely, staring through the window to avoid her gaze.

'You've done this before?'

He nodded miserably. 'About ten runs. All of them were inland villagers . . . Small families like yours . . . People with money.'

'What happened to them?'

His silence answered her question. He continued to clutch the helm. She noticed the whiteness of his knuckles from his grip on the spokes.

'You don't know, do you?'

He shook his head. 'But they were all probably okay.'

'Probably!' She spat the word out.

'Tao always made sure they had good boats and plenty of supplies. He's a fair man.'

'Fair!' Lesa snarled. 'Fair? You call turning a family with a baby loose in a boat on the high seas *fair?*'

Lin met her stare. He saw the disgust in her eyes and felt deeply ashamed. 'I'll go with you,' he said brokenly. 'I'm a good sailor. You'll all be okay with me.'

Lesa was about to reject the offer out of hand but Suzi chose that moment to start screaming. Thi was trying to get the baby to accept her breast but the child was twisting her head away and bawling. Hinny and Neti were now sitting dejectedly on the deck, shoulders bowed – the universal posture that symbolized oriental fatalism. Tao and the other boy were loading brightly-coloured plastic jerry cans filled with fresh water into the sampan. Lesa relaxed her threatening stance and regarded Lin with the pensive expression of an adult rather than a fourteen-year-old. 'Will Tao let you go?'

The boy shrugged.

'What about your parents?'

'Dead. I'll speak with him. I don't suppose he'll care. Two can sail this boat and it'll save him having to pay me.' His words reflected the bitterness and despair of a whole generation of young Vietnamese, growing up without the love and guidance of their parents.

## 19

Lin watched the receding fishing junk for a few moments. He turned his attention away and saw that the others in the crowded sampan were staring at him intently. That he was now in command of his elders and that they were awaiting his orders embarrassed him.

'What do we do first?' Hinny demanded.

Lin swallowed nervously. 'We must check for leaks.'

The lowest duckboards were pulled up. Water surged back and forth in the bilges as the tiny craft rose and fell on the swell.

'It's spray water from when the boat was being towed,' Lin

explained. 'It's nothing to worry about. It's a good boat. We checked it carefully before Tao bought it.'

They took it in turns to bail with a wok. At the end of thirty minutes the bilges were reasonably dry and no serious leaks were apparent.

Tao's fishing junk had vanished. Lin set about trimming the sampan by distributing the water containers and supplies evenly about the centre line. Correct trim was essential. The tiny craft was designed for river and estuary fishing and moving supplies about in harbours. Its low freeboard meant that movements had to be carefully co-ordinated. A cot was arranged for Suzi between the water containers, and the best sleeping positions for everyone were worked out. Three eight-hour watches were agreed: Hinny and Thi kept the morning to midday watch; Diem and Neti the day watch; and Lin and Lesa the night watch. When everything was sorted out, Lin raised a badly-shredded, sun-bleached woven straw sail and secured the mast shrouds. The rolling that was threatening to make everyone seasick decreased and the appearance of a wake, although feeble because Lin played safe and kept the sail short, showed that the sampan was at last making some sort of progress. Spirits rose. Even Thi managed a wan smile as she sat under the straw canopy nursing Suzi.

Lin spent an hour showing his crew how to work the tiller and read the hand-bearing compass that Tao had provided. Diem proved an adept pupil as a result of compass and map-reading skills acquired during his service in the North Vietnamese army, but Lesa was the fastest learner. She even grasped the principles of drift and tidal set from Lin's dog-eared book on navigation.

'We don't know exactly where we are,' Lin explained to the others after a midday meal that consisted of tinned fruit. 'But we are on the right course.' He pointed to a distant smudge on the horizon. 'Chances are that that's a merchantman on the Singapore to Hong Kong run.'

'So why not fire a flare and attract its attention?' Lesa asked.

'They'd never see a flare at this distance in daylight, and even if they did, they'd ignore us. They don't want trouble with the Hong Kong authorities by bringing in refugees. There'll be a lot more ships as we near Hong Kong; their course will help keep us on course but that's all. Our only chance is to get into Hong Kong waters so that the navy or a harbour boat picks us up.'

## 20

The first night on the sampan passed uneventfully. Lin and Lesa stood their watch together but said very little. They kept a constant lookout for ships that could unwittingly run them down. Lin explained that their low wooden craft was a poor radar reflector. He said that on one occasion even Tao's junk had nearly been cut in two by a tanker. Lesa said nothing but leaned against him, wondering how she would react if he touched her while the others were sleeping. She trailed her hand in the water but Lin snatched it clear and pointed to the dorsal fin of a curious tiger shark that was shadowing the sampan. It sheered off when Lin slapped his palm on the surface of the water. Lesa took hold of his hand, kissed it, and pressed it against her breast.

The wind dropped the following morning which encouraged Lin to lengthen sail during the rest of the day to maintain what he calculated was about three knots.

## 21

Lesa woke Lin an hour before it was time to stand their watch. He knew immediately from the motion of the tiny craft that something was wrong. There were no moon or stars. The wind had veered and was now freshening from the south.

He shortened sail and sat in the stern holding the tiller while watching the sky.

Lesa sat beside him and put her hand on his knee. She smiled at him and saw his worried expression. He was shouldering his responsibilities like a man. He had made love to her in the way men made love. It was hard for her to believe that he was only two years older than her.

'What's the matter?' she asked.

He smiled and touched her face. 'Weather's getting up.'

'Will it get worse?'

'Yes.'

Lesa valued the honesty of his reply. Adults would have told her to mind her own business or that she was not to worry. She pressed her cheek against his forearm. Lin returned the embrace by putting his arm around her shoulders, making her feel warm and secure.

There was no warning. The gust seemed to come from nowhere.

It struck the tiny craft, wrenching the tiller from Lin's fingers. Two mast shrouds snapped and the flimsy sail was snatched into the darkness. The mast crashing down across the straw canopy, dislodging pots and pans, woke everyone up and set Suzi off. Lin grabbed the tiller and threw it hard over in the hope that the sampan had enough way on her to go after the sail but the ferocious wind caught the prow and nearly caused the craft to broach to. Sea poured over the port gunwale.

'Get over!' Lesa yelled, grabbing Neti's waistband and yanking her weight to starboard. Suddenly everything was surging back and forth in the water that the boat had shipped.

Hinny and Diem grabbed a wok each and started bailing frantically, at first hurling the water into the wind so that it blew back in their faces.

'Never mind her!' Lesa screamed at Thi who was trying to pacify Suzi. 'Get bailing!'

'Don't you give me orders, young lady!' Thi screamed back.

'Bail!' Lin shouted, heaving on the tiller to keep the boat aimed into the eye of the mounting gale. 'That's all that matters! Bail!' But the wind and spray snatched his words into the dark turmoil that was boiling all about the stricken sampan.

Lesa bailed and kept bailing until her arms were no longer a part of her but just automated appendages, following a scoop and hurl cycle that was beyond her will or control. How long the gale blew for she had no way of telling – just keep bailing and try to ignore the world of the flimsy little boat that was being torn apart by the howling, demented elements.

She didn't really know when the gale abated and finally died away altogether. All she was aware of was occasionally drifting off into an unreal sleep only to be woken by Lin jabbing her in the ribs and yelling at her to keep bailing. She would move her arms for a while and then slide into a sleep again, her body lolling on the thwart like a rag doll on a seesaw.


22

Daylight came quickly as it does in the tropics.

Suzi's interminable crying woke Lesa. She gazed up into a clear blue sky. The sea's long swell was back to normal. The straw canopy was gone. She tried to move and was puzzled by a sudden coldness around her thighs. She was lying back against a water container with her legs underwater. She sat up. The boat was half-swamped. Under the influence of the long swell, tins, clothes, everything that could float, was charging back and forth like a disciplined miniature platoon on a parade ground.

Lesa tried to push herself up but there was no strength in her arms. Thi was cradling her baby and staring at Lesa with an expression of hate that frightened the younger girl. Lin was slumped asleep over the tiller. Hinny and Diem were lying in the bow. Neti was propped against a thwart, blouse torn open, her head forward, long hair matted in black strands on her breasts like a surrealist painting.

'Well,' said Lesa feebly when Suzi had calmed down. 'At least we're still all together.'

'No thanks to you.' There was real venom in Thi's voice.

'I did my best, Thi. We all did.'

Hinny stirred and sat up.

'If it wasn't for you, we wouldn't be in this mess!' Thi spat. 'I should never have listened to Hinny.'

'Stop that, Thi.' It was Hinny, now fully awake. 'We've got to get this boat cleared up.'

Thi rounded on her husband. The sudden motion jerked her nipple from Suzi's mouth and the infant started to grizzle. 'We would've been all right if we'd stayed in the village. What does it matter what happens to her? Isn't the safety of your own daughter more important to you?' She angrily jammed her nipple back in Suzi's mouth.

Neti and Diem woke up.

'I don't understand,' said Lesa quietly. 'What am I supposed to have done?' She was embarrassed to see that Lin was now awake.

'It's what your whore of a mother did!' Thi snarled.

'Thi – please,' Hinny begged.

'No I won't keep silent!' Thi snapped. 'I've kept silent long enough about your sister and look at the mess it's got us into!' She kicked angrily at a can of baby food that drifted against her ankle.

'You've no right to talk about my mother like that,' said Lesa calmly, fighting hard to keep her temper in check.

'I've every right!'

'It's time she was told,' said Neti quietly. 'She's old enough now.'

94

'Old enough to be a whore like her mother!'

'My mother was not a whore!' Lesa found the strength to jump to her feet. The boat rocked dangerously.

'Lesa!' said Hinny sharply. 'Sit down and listen to me.'

Lesa was defiant. 'I won't have her calling my mother a whore!'

Thi tossed her head in contempt. 'Will you listen to the child! Talking to me like she was a grown up!'

Hinny was patient. '*Please*, Lesa. Sit down. Sit down and listen to what I have to say.'

Lesa had to sit anyway before she lost face by overbalancing. She glared at Thi but remained silent.

'I don't know how to begin this,' said Hinny unhappily.

'Just tell her,' Thi snapped. 'If she thinks she's grown-up enough to understand.'

'You've heard people say that your mother was a good-time girl?'

Lesa nodded.

'Do you know what it means?'

'She liked having a good time. She used to go to Danang a lot.'

'She was more than that,' said Hinny gravely. 'May God forgive me for having to say this, but she was what we used to call a "boom boom" girl. She used to sell herself for money to the GIs in Danang during the American War. Your father was a GI.'

Lesa felt her blood pounding in her ears at the shame of these revelations in front of Diem and Lin. 'That's a lie!' she cried, knowing that Hinny never lied to her. Suddenly the scene when her mother was dragged off by the North Vietnamese was replayed in her mind with horrific clarity. She cradled her head in her arms, more to shut out the memory of those terrible events than Hinny's words.

Lin started bailing water as if the conversation was of no consequence.

'It didn't matter to me at the time,' Hinny continued, staring down at the water slopping about in the boat. 'She was my sister and I loved her. Just as I love you – her only child. For a while it seemed that it didn't matter to anyone else either. And then Tak Noi was made military governor and everything changed. It wasn't just your mother who was rounded up, but every former good-time girl. He hated them all. And then he started on their children – those with GI fathers. Just around Danang at first.' Hinny nodded to Diem. 'Diem tipped me off. He was working in Tak Noi's headquarters when his men brought in two half-black half-Vietnamese girls about your age. Tak Noi shot them himself. And then a boy in the next village was taken away – he was tall with European looks like you – so I knew that it was only a matter of time before they came for you. That's when I started selling up everything and making plans. I planned everything as carefully as I could. I wanted everything to go just right . . . And now . . . and now . . .' Hinny was unable to finish the sentence. He bowed his head. 'The rest you know,' he concluded.

Lesa moved beside Hinny and put her arms around him. Hinny never encouraged physical contact but her courage was rewarded by him returning the embrace.

'You put the daughter of a whore before your own daughter!' Thi screamed.

Lesa's control snapped. She grabbed the nearest thing to hand, a length of broken mast, and swung it aloft with the intention of threatening Thi with it. The older woman fell backwards in surprise. She dumped Suzi on a duckboard and snatched up a knife. The baby's piercing screams merged with the deafening blast of powerful two-tone marine air horns. The group turned around and gaped in astonishment at the towering white hull of a luxury twenty-metre motor-cruiser that had come upon them unawares.


## 23

There were three men and a girl on the cruiser: Europeans. Bronzed, relaxed and laughing. The older man was short and balding – probably in his late fifties. His companion was about thirty with long black hair that blew across his face. They were wearing shorts except the girl – a redhead – who was wearing a skimpy G-string and nothing else. The man at the helm on the flying bridge was thick-set and bull-chested with heavy, Slavonic features. His skilled hands worked the Morse controls – balancing forward and reverse thrusts of the propellers so that the long white hull drew sideways to the sampan.

The half-naked redhead caught the painter that Diem tossed her. A small motorboat hoisted on davits across the transom obscured the cruiser's name and port of registration. The bow names had an awning draped over them.

The girl stepped onto a swimmers' boarding ladder near the transom and tied the painter to a rung before signalling for Suzi to be passed to her first.

'We shouldn't board,' said Lin suddenly. 'I don't like the look of them.'

'Pirates?' Diem queried.

'Maybe.'

'Nonsense,' said Hinny. 'Anyone can see that these people aren't pirates.'

'They've hidden their name and there's no flag. We shouldn't board.'

Lin's reservations were ignored. Suzi was handed up to the redhead who passed her to the balding man. One by one they all scrambled up the boarding ladder and onto the magnificent cruiser's aftdeck and stood staring uncertainly about them at their strange surroundings. The redhead took Suzi back and held the baby against her breasts. Lesa saw the spinning radar antenna on the roof of the elegant bridgehouse and wondered what it was. Idling diesels burbled their exhausts softly into the water. A brightly-coloured awning supported on shining stainless-steel uprights provided welcome shade from the burning sun. Scatterd around the deck were luxurious beach loungers and sunbathing cushions. Clamped to a rail was a clay pigeon spring gun with a half-empty magazine of clays and two rifles were lying on a mattress. Spent cartridge cases rolled back and forth on the polishcd teak deck planking. It was a world that was totally beyond the experience or comprehension of the bedraggled party of refugees.

The leader of the four Westerners came down the companionway from the bridge and inspected his new guests: he was the most powerfully-built man that Lesa had ever seen. His heavy build gave the impression that he was short but he was a head taller than his companions. His hair and eyebrows were a fine golden colour that she found frightening and yet fascinating, and his hard, unfriendly eyes were the colour of the sky. The balding man's face was gleaming with sweat, his eyes alight with anticipation. The long-haired man was lean with fine, aristocratic features. He picked up a rifle and draped it casually over his arm.

Thi took a step towards the redhead who was holding Suzi and asked for her baby back. The girl looked puzzled and said something in a language that did not sound like English to Lesa. Thi held out her arms appealingly to make her intention clear but the girl merely smiled and held Suzi closer to her bare breasts.

'Try speaking to them in English!' Neti whispered urgently to Diem.

Diem opened his mouth to say something but the bull-chested man's angry snarl at Thi made him shut up. Diem had sensed that with these people, whoever they were, it would be best to say nothing unless spoken to.

'This is bad,' Lin whispered to Lesa.

'Surely they can't mean us any harm? What could we have that they need? These people have everything.'

The leader spoke harshly to the redhead. She answered angrily and disappeared into the saloon taking Suzi with her. Thi gave a little cry and started after her but the leader lashed out with a vicious blow to her stomach. She doubled up in agony and sank to the deck. Hinny gave a scream of rage and launched himself at the leader. He took the full force of the big European's fist in his face. The huge man grabbed him before he could fall and hurled him at the rail. Hinny struggled to his feet. The leader nodded to the long-haired man who was holding the rifle. Two shots crashed out and the force of the rounds slamming into Hinny lifted his slight body over the rail and sent him tumbling into the sea. The fat man snatched up the second rifle and rushed to the rail. He took careful aim down at the water and fired three times. Then he glanced across at the big man and gave a broad grin.

Thi gave a long, piercing wail of the most terrible anguish and tried to rush to the rail but the big man snatched hold of her hair by its gathered bun. Blind rage and panic seized the distraught woman. She lashed out with her feet and fists but the leader merely held her at arm's length and ripped her shirt open. He saw the dribble of milk from her nipple and gave an exclamation of disgust before scooping her up and holding her aloft in both hands – his biceps and calf muscles bunching like living snakes beneath his skin as he braced himself against the demented woman's ferocious struggles. He did a little dance, twirling Thi around. The girl reappeared without Suzi and joined in the burst of applause as the big man's two minions showed their appreciation of their leader's performance. For an encore he bent his knees like an athlete preparing to put the shot and took a short run at the rail. A loud grunt and a heave; Thi screamed as her body arched through the air, her arms waving and legs pedalling frantically. Both rifles roared out but the men missed. Thi hit the water and disappeared. The men quicky snapped fresh magazines into their rifles and took aim. Thi broke the surface and started swimming. The rifles spoke again. Thi's head jerked and her limbs stopped moving. The redhead rushed excitedly to the rail and insisted on taking the rifle from the long-haired man. He helped her hold it steady with his arms around her while she pulled the trigger twice. The two rounds snicked streaks of silver into the water near Thi. The man gave the redhead some advice; he seemed to be telling her to relax. Her third round split Thi's skull open, spilling her brains into the sea. The girl gave a little cry of delight, returned the rifle to her grinning instructor and excitedly clapped her hands together.

It was over so quickly. Neti and Lesa clung to each other, too shocked to cry or speak. Diem had closed his eyes and seemed to have made his peace with whatever inner turmoil he was experiencing. Lin called out to the leader and walked slowly but certainly towards him. The leader grinned at the prospect of more sport and stood with his hands on his hips as Lin approached. The boy barely stood level with the leader's chest but his aim was accurate: the glob of saliva hit the big man square in the face. The broad grin didn't so much as flicker – it remained fixed in place. Nor did the leader attempt to wipe away the mess that was trickling down his tanned features. Instead he called out something to the other two who eagerly seized Lin and doubled him over the rail. Once his wrists and ankles were firmly lashed, the girl produced a knife and cut away his shorts. She giggled and felt around the front of Lin. She jiggled his scrotum playfully, squeezed hard, and seemed annoyed that the boy never made a sound. The leader dropped his own shorts and beckoned to the girl to masturbate him which she did willingly, occasionally helping things along with her mouth.

Lesa's attempts to shut out these terrible events by inverting reality and so consigning them to a detached world that she was not a part of was thwarted by her being dragged across the deck and forced to her knees a few inches from Lin's exposed buttocks. A hand yanked her head around. A tiny consolation in the whirling maelstrom of her consciousness was that they could not make her open her eyes. But her ears heard everything: the girl's laughter; the big man's grunts and heavy breathing; and Lin's whimpers of pain. She didn't see the big man finish his black deed, or the unsuccessful attempt by the bald man who tried to copy his leader's example. She heard the good-natured jeering of the others but didn't see a rifle barrel being used where the bald man had failed. The thunderclap only inches from her head deafened her; the acrid sting of cordite fumes prevented her from exploiting this temporary loss of a sense to make her delusion of separation from reality even easier. Her eyes watered despite being tightly shut, forcing her to blink. She saw Lin's lifeless body being cut away from the rail and tipped into the sea. She also saw the wetness of the redhead's excitement trickling down the inside of her thighs. Lesa's soul cried out to her God for one of the men to use the rifle on herself and end her torment.

Mercifully they suddenly abandoned her. Lesa thought the horror was over until she heard Neti's scream of terror and pain. For Neti Lesa had to open her eyes. It was an act of loyalty as if seeing the older girl's unspeakable humiliation was to share it and so bear some of the torture and pain.

The two men were pinning Neti to a sunbed mattress while the bull-chested man raped her. The redhead was down on her knees like a demented referee at a wrestling match. She was beating time on the deck with her fist and giving little wild shrieks of encouragement.

Lesa saw Diem standing to one side. He was watching the proceedings with what she thought was detached disinterest until she realized that he had a hand inside his shorts and was moving it rhythmically. Quite suddenly Lesa was gripped by reality. The unreal world born out of the horror was banished in an instant: she saw everything with a terrible, unfiltered clarity that told her exactly what she had to do: she had to remember everything about these animals: their leader, the redhead, and their boat. Especially their boat. Such a boat would be rare. Every little detail had to be committed to her photographic memory. Its shape, the layout of this deck, the configuration of the bridge. Even the fittings. Nothing escaped her. Somehow, she knew not how, the day would come when she would exact the most dreadful and bloody revenge for this hideous atrocity. But first she had to survive.

## 24

The three men finished with Neti and stood in a circle, laughing and joking with the girl, ignoring Neti's sobs of pain and terror.

They turned their attention to Lesa and systematically stripped her naked. Instead of cowering or trying to cover herself, she stood erect, staring unflinchingly into each face in turn. The big man toyed with her breasts. He threw back his head and laughingly compared them to the redhead's fuller, more mature breasts. Lesa saw the girl's eyes close-up for the first time. Even under the sun awning, the pupils were small – tiny points of closed blackness affording no insight into the creature's bleak soul.

Lesa was pushed down on the mattress beside Neti who had rolled herself into a ball and was still sobbing piteously. She felt her legs being forced apart but offered no resistance. She expected pain. Instead there was a curious sensation that puzzled her until she realized that it was due to the redhead's nuzzling attentions.

The leader gave an impatient grunt and thrust the woman aside. This time there was pain. His face was inches from Lesa. She could smell the drink on his breath. She wanted to close her eyes but she forced them to remain open so that she could print the face on her memory with the permanence and sharpness of a correctly-focussed and developed photographic print. He gave a final grunt and then the rest of the men took their turn. The long-haired man had some difficulty getting started but the redhead helped him out with her ever-willing mouth. The fat man wheezed and grunted and sweat dripped off his face onto Lesa. He gave up the attempt and used the alternative offered by crushing Lesa's petite breasts together – an innovation that earned him laughter and applause from the others. When he wiped himself on a hank of her hair and stood, Lesa had stored away a picture gallery of them all. She tried to stand, determined to show these creatures that her spirit couldn't be crushed, but there was one more torment for her. Diem moved over her – his face flushed with excitement.

This time she did not need to keep her eyes open. Suddenly there was movement. Diem jumped to his feet and a man yelled. Lesa opened her eyes in time to see Neti leap over the rail. All of them, including Diem, dashed to the side. The long-haired man snatched up a rifle and started firing. The leader cursed, snatched the rifle away, and pumped several rounds into the water.

Lesa scrambled to her feet and staggered to the opposite rail. The redhead saw her and yelled. Lesa launched herself into the sea, managing to convert her hurried fall into a semblance of a dive that took her deep beneath the surface. She felt and heard a round whack into the water. Two more smacked the water in front of her when she surfaced. One of the rounds, its energy spent, actually brushed against her leg as it sank. She gulped down a hurried gasp of air and jack-knife dived to go as deep as possible just as a fourth round tore through her left shoulder.

Despite the sudden blaze of blinding agony she thought quickly but clearly. Swimming away from the big motor-cruiser meant certain death. Paradoxically, safety, such as it was, lay with the boat. She opened her eyes underwater and saw the black, elongated shape of the hull against the sparkling light and the smaller shape of the sampan that was still hitched to the transom. Kicking extra hard with her feet to make up for not being able to use her left arm, she made a superhuman effort born of near-panic and surfaced right under the overhang of the cruiser's transom. The deep burble of the idling exhausts cloaked her gasps. Immediately above her was the protective screen of the motorboat tender hanging from its davits, and beside her was the half-swamped sampan. She held onto the swimmers' boarding ladder with her good arm in the heaving swell and brought her breathing under control.

There was some more sporadic shooting and then the leader's voice shouting at his men. The sound of someone clambering down the boarding ladder forced Lesa to press her body against the transom. A woman's foot appeared on the lower stainless-steel rungs. Lesa's first thought was that the redhead had seen her, but the woman reached down, untied the sampan's painter and climbed back into the yacht. There was a series of heavy mechanical clunks and the idling exhausts increased their tempo. A sudden powerful surge of water against Lesa's legs made her lose her grip on the boarding ladder. She was swept against the sampan that was dancing free of the cruiser. She lashed out with her good arm and managed to hook her fingers over the sampan's gunwale. The motor-cruiser's diesels opened up to a bellowing roar and water around the transom boiled white. The torque from the screws settled the stern lower in the water and the big motor-cruiser began moving away, lifting its bow as it picked up speed. It dipped below the swell and reappeared, listing to port as it turned.

Lesa twisted her body in the water to keep the screen afforded by the sampan between herself and the boat. By hanging on near the bow and peering under the raked prow she could keep the cruiser under observation. It was now about a hundred metres away.

The roar of the engines died away to a fast idle. The leader was on the bridge at the helm; the two men appeared at the stern rail with rifles which they raised to their shoulders. Oblivious of the racking pain in her shoulder, Lesa sucked air and dived just as the first rounds splintered into the sampan and whacked into the water. She opened her eyes and saw the white streaks that the rounds made through the water before their energy was spent. Lungs bursting, she swam a few metres from the sampan and surfaced. They were still firing: a round whined over her head with a frightening *kerzip* sound. She realized that they hadn't seen her but were shooting at the sampan with the obvious intention of trying to sink it. The firing stopped and Lesa swam a little way clear of the sampan just as the yacht's engines opened up – they were leaving. She dragged herself through the water back to the sampan and grabbed hold of it to try and haul herself aboard. She wanted to get as high as possible for a better view of the cruiser, so that she could commit everything about it to memory.

Instead of fading, the roar of the engines got louder. The swell lifted her and she saw that the boat was going hard about, bringing its gracefully flared bow to bear on the sampan with the obvious intention of ramming it. By now the excruciating pain in her left shoulder was dulling her ability to think clearly and react accordingly. Before she had a chance to decide on her next move, the cruiser was within twenty metres and bearing straight down on her. Terror and panic seized Lesa. It was too late to escape; the cruiser's thundering engines were lifting it onto the plane, its rapidly swelling knife-edge bow arching rigid sheets of white water like a charging mad dog with a bone in its teeth.

It was the bow wave that saved Lesa. The great surge of water first sucked her under, then hurled her aside like a rag doll before she had a chance to take a deep breath. She surfaced, floundering and choking in the foamed wake of the cruiser. That she survived was a miracle; that the sampan survived was an even greater miracle. Despite already being half-filled with water, its lightweight, all-timber construction and good design enabled it to stay upright and remain afloat. The cruiser made a half turn as if to return, but the man at the helm appeared to change his mind. The speeding boat straightened its course and moved away at an angle to the half-submerged craft.

Lesa called on her dwindling reserves of strength and started swimming towards the sampan. The fin of a mako shark broke the surface between her and the sampan, cutting a sinister vee in the swell. The creature had scented the blood from Lesa's wound and decided to investigate. Like all sharks, it had poor eyesight and therefore always exercised great caution before directly approaching a potential meal. Until now the sound of the cruiser's engines had encouraged it to keep its distance.

Despair knotted in Lesa's stomach when she saw the fin. Her grim determination to survive faltered and then reasserted itself. The shark circled at a distance of about ten metres, sizing up the situation. Lesa trod water, turning her body as best she could so that she remained facing the menacing fin. Through the clear water she could see the dark, streamlined shape of the fin's owner. Suddenly the shark veered towards her.

Lesa had no way of knowing that her next act was one that many divers, swimmers and shipwreck survivors had found to be effective in dealing with over-inquisitive or hungry sharks. She did it out of desperation and because she could think of nothing else: she put her head underwater and screamed.

The startled creature voided a cloud of excrement and turned sharply away. Through the resulting murk Lesa caught a glimpse of a cold, reptilian eye. The backwash from the shark's tail spun her around and then it was gone. She splashed her way frantically to the doubtful sanctuary of the sampan and hauled herself over the stern with her good arm. Terrified that she would suddenly feel jaws closing around her torso, she jerked her legs inboard and lay in the bilge water sobbing in pain. The fading roar of the cruiser's engines reminded her that there was no time to think of resting her tortured body for even a few seconds. She climbed to her feet, steadying herself on a thwart before straightening carefully to maintain her delicate balance.

The motor-yacht was about half a kilometre away. She stared at it – memorising every detail – and continued staring for some moments at the spot where it had disappeared into the haze. Her emotions were no longer the complex feelings of a frightened fourteen-year-old girl. Rather they were something that had coalesced into a single powerful emotion that burned inside her with the awesome sharpness and deadly brilliance of an oxyacetylene flame.

Lesa had learned to hate.

## 25

The pain in her shoulder reached into her death-sleep of exhaustion and twisted her fully awake. She opened her eyes and stared at the grey, scudding clouds. She had no idea how long she slept for. Amazingly, the watch Lin had given her was still working. It was 15:20; she had slept through most of the day. The clouds were a mixed blessing: she was cold but she did not have sunburn to add to her problems. She sat up in the slopping bilge water. Her shoulder was a lance of agony, every joint in her body ached, she realized just how cold she was – miserably cold – desperately thirsty, and hungry.

It was time to take stock. First her shoulder. Thankfully the bleeding had stopped. She could feel a small hole through the centre of her shoulder blade but the bullet's exit had left a mess of torn and inflamed, congealing tissue. Perhaps the prolonged contact with seawater would minimize the risk of infection getting into the wound – she hoped so. Or did she? Suddenly she hated her body. It had become something unspeakably vile because those animals had lusted after it and used it to gratify their perversions. Anything that such creatures wanted had to be disgusting and obscene. Covering up her body suddenly became an obsession.

All that was left in the boat was Neti's backpack whose straps had snagged on the stump of the broken mast. She tried using both hands to open the buckles but the pain was too intense. It took her trembling fingers ten minutes to work the sodden straps loose. The tears came in floods when she saw dear Neti's things: her black pants; several shirts and, among the few sad luxuries, a bar of soap carefully wrapped in a polythene bag, a brush and a comb. There was also a full water canteen. She resisted the temptation to take a long draught; she took just three small sips and tightened the stopper as hard as she could by gripping the canteen between her knees.

She struggled painfully into the clothes when the wind had dried them. Apart from the welcome warmth, she felt better now that her body was out of sight, and the touch of the garments that had belonged to Neti was a comfort.

The next problem was the water in the boat. The tiny craft was certain to be swamped if the weather worsened. At first she tried bailing with two hands but that proved an agonizing impossibility.

She thought about the problem, checked the few of Neti's possessions, and discovered that she could bail with one hand using the polythene bag. After some practice she settled down to a steady rhythm. The first two hours' work seemed to make no difference to the amount of water surging back and forth; maybe a plank had sprung and she was wasting her precious reserves of energy. For the next hour she steadfastly kept her eyes shut while she bailed. When she opened them again, it was dark but the water level had definitely gone down. She dozed for an hour, resting her head on Neti's kitbag, and then resumed bailing.

It was nearly midnight by Lin's watch when the bilges were as dry as they were ever likely to be. Her good right arm now ached as much as her wounded arm. The sampan was riding higher in the water and therefore offering a greater windage. The stronger gusts sent it scudding briefly along in short bursts as it rose onto the crests of the longer, lazy swells.

Just five more bagfuls of water, she decided. Scoop, lift and tip . . . scoop, lift and tip . . . scoop, lift and –

There was a soft tearing sound when the bag ripped open. To her dismay, Lesa saw that she had snagged it on a nail.

The disaster triggered the delayed shock that she had been fighting back all day. The frightened little girl in her seized control for the last time in her life.

She burst into tears.

## 26

She heard singing. Dance music. People laughing and shouting. She lifted her head and stared uncomprehendingly at the blaze of lights.

It was a shallow draught cruise liner that reminded Lesa of pictures of Mississippi river boats. On the lower state deck she could see women in beautiful evening dresses dancing with partners in white tropical suits. There was a long buffet laden with food at one end of the dance floor and a small band at the other where a man in a tuxedo was singing into a microphone. The entire apparition was less than a hundred metres away and was passing her like a bejewelled dowager duchess.

Lesa screamed. The wind blew her scream back in her face. She clambered to her feet as quickly as she dared in the unstable craft and frantically waved one of Neti's shirts with her good arm.

The revellers took no notice.

Lesa stood on a thwart. The ship continued slipping by like something out of a gaudy, surrealist dream.

She renewed her screaming.

The dancers continued dancing; the singer continued singing; and the band continued playing. The music faded. The sluggish wake of the flat-bottomed cruise ship reached the sampan and rocked it mockingly. Lesa stopped screaming. She stared after the receding lights and sank dejectedly to her knees. The night mist gradually absorbed the ship like a wraith returning to its secret lair but the sound of the music continued to reach Lesa long after the ship had disappeared. And then there was silence apart from the wind and the sporadic hiss of spray breaking across the sampan's prow.

Lesa's cold, pain, hunger and misery became attributes of a savage, ravening creature that was awaiting the right moment to destroy her.

## 27

The next day was bad.

The wind from the south west freshened. The energy she expended in the effort of lowering her pants and sitting over the gunwale to relieve herself left her lying in the bottom of the sampan trembling and exhausted. In the afternoon she discovered that she no longer had the strength to unscrew the water canteen stopper. She struggled feebly with it for an hour before giving up, cursing herself for her lack of foresight in always tightening it so firmly.

## 28

The day after that was worse.

The water canteen and its contents became the centre of Lesa's universe. The pain, cold and hunger were secondary to the half-litre container and its maddening contents that she could hear slopping about when she shook it. If she could no longer open it with her fingers, she needed a tool – something that would grip the flattened sides of the stopper. But there was nothing in the boat that would serve.

She bathed her wounded shoulder in seawater. It showed no sign of getting worse, or better for that matter.

The water canteen lay in the bilge where she had hurled it in anger and frustration. She looked around the battered craft and had an idea. She grabbed the canteen and crawled slowly and painfully to the mast's broken stump. The simple move took her several pain-racked minutes. She rested and tried to jam the stopper into the stump's split and splintered end. On the tenth or twentieth attempt – she didn't bother to count – she succeeded in wedging the stopper into a split. She held the canteen in position while she rested. Using her knees and her good hand, she gripped the container and turned it. The thrill of exhilaration she experienced when she felt the stopper give renewed her strength. This time the stopper turned sufficiently for her to unscrew it by hand. But the brief return of strength proved a false visitor; when she held the canteen and lifted it to her lips, her fingers failed her at the crucial moment. The canteen slipped. She snatched at it and succeeded in knocking it into the sea. She gave a cry and hauled herself to the side. Refraction made the canteen appear to be just below the surface – bubbles streaming from the open neck – but it was deeper. The neck brushed against her plunging fingers and was gone.

## 29

Lesa spent most of the next day sleeping and dreaming fitfully of the ship that had passed her in the night with its food, music, bright lights and celebrating passengers. Her dreams merged into hallucinations of sun-filled childhood days with her mother when she used to return from Danang laden with gifts.

She was too weak to take any interest in her surroundings. It was just sea and more sea and grey skies whereas her dreams were filled with a happiness that belonged to another lifetime. Had she taken an interest in the real world, even in her present state, she could not have failed to notice the increasing numbers of ships. One even passed within a mile of her. When the clouds broke they revealed occasional contrails from jetliners lacing the sky like white veins.

It rained that night just before dawn. The sting of the icy drops roused her sufficiently for her to make a brave effort to spread out Neti's shirts to soak up as much of the precious water as possible. Having nothing to store it in, her enfeebled fingers fumbled clumsily in their task of squeezing it down her throat. The squall lasted ten minutes. She managed to swallow a cupful – maybe two. She didn't care. All she wanted to do was banish the horror of this reality by lying curled up in the bottom of the boat and drifting back to sleep. She knew she was dying but death was no longer a terrible enemy to be kept at bay at all costs. Death could be allowed to draw near because it came bearing many gifts: water; warmth; her home . . . separation from her despised body . . . and Neti . . . dear, lovely Neti . . .

She felt the first gift of warmth when the brightening sun against her eyelids told her that it was daylight. There was no point in opening her eyes; just savour the gentle touch of warmth on her skin. In a tiny way it negated a little of the one-ness of the thirst, the hunger, pain and the aching misery of her loneliness.

But the gift of warmth was shortlived. It was replaced by a freezing wind – an icy hurricane that blew straight down on her from heaven. There was a throbbing *wap–wap–wap* like the wings of a giant insect beating the air as it moved its grotesque shadow over her. The punishing beat was mixed with a high-pitched whine that hurt her ears. There was still no point in opening her eyes – the thunderous reverberation and the arctic gale were just two more components in the long catalogue of misery and deprivation that death would eventually banish when it got its chance.

## 30

## HONG KONG

The sounds were commonplace in Western society but totally alien to Lesa's ears: the clip-clop of high heels on a tiled floor. They came and they went like ghosts drifting in and out of her twilight, dreamless sleep. Sometimes she heard voices: men's voices, women's voices. Some speaking in what she thought sounded like English. Sometimes in the sing-song tones of what could be Cantonese. She was warm and the terrible pain had gone.

She opened her eyes and focussed them on an overhead electric lamp on a cantilever arm. She was lying in a bed between sheets. Sheets! The brilliant white bedcovers of the glossy magazines and she was actually lying between them.

Someone was moving about at the end of her bed.

'Hallo,' she said.

The staff nurse gave an exclamation of surprise and scuttled out of the side ward. She returned a few minutes later with another nurse in tow. Small and slim with a friendly smile.

'Hallo, Lesa,' said the new nurse in Vietnamese. 'How are you feeling?'

'How do you know my name?'

'You told me. Not all of it, so they've called you Lesa Wessex. My name's Choi.'

'Wessex?' Lesa slurred the unfamiliar pronunciation.

The nurse smiled brightly. 'You were found by an RAF helicopter – a Wessex.'

'Oh,' said Lesa, and went back to sleep.

## 31

She opened her eyes and saw four shapes around her bed. The one standing against the light was powerfully built – bull-chested. He spoke to her and touched her hand. She had heard the voice before: the four Europeans who had raped her and massacred her family. The black terror returned. She screamed and screamed; running footsteps; Choi's reassuring voice; the nurse's delicate little hand stroking her forehead; the hated shapes melting away.

'They were the crew of the helicopter that rescued you,' Choi explained when Lesa had calmed down. 'They came to see how you were.'

## 32

The doctor who was attending Lesa prescribed a milder painkiller with the result that she was able to sit up the next day and take an interest in her surroundings. She learned from Choi that she was in the Kowloon General Hospital and that the bandaged bullet wound in her left shoulder was healing satisfactorily.

'You were lucky,' said Choi. 'The bullet just grazed your collar bone and made a clean hole in your shoulder blade, and there was no sign of any infection.'

'I washed it in seawater.'

Choi smiled. 'Well – it didn't do any harm. It's healing nicely.'

'They killed Neti,' said Lesa suddenly. 'And Hinny. And Thi. And Lin. And Suzi.'

'You mustn't try to talk about it. The police will be here tomorrow. Come on. The doctor said you were to get up.'

'Where's my watch?' Lesa asked suddenly.

'It's in your drawer and it's still working,' Choi smiled and pointed at the toilet. 'Do you know what that is?'

Lesa glanced at the porcelain lavatory and nodded. 'I've seen them on television.'

Choi pulled back Lesa's bedcovers. 'Come on I'll show you how to use it.'

## 33

David Janson of the Royal Hong Kong Police Force was a small, dapper man in his late thirties. He was working a three-year attachment contract from the British Broadcasting Corporation as a civilian employee stationed at Kowloon Central Police Station. Most of his childhood had been spent in Saigon where his parents had been Methodist missionaries. On his return to London, Janson's fluency in Vietnamese had won him a job with BBC External Services as a translator. In 1969 he married Carrie, a BBC studio manager, and was given an attachment to Radio Television Hong Kong who agreed to his transfer to the police when the Vietnamese boat people began flooding into the dependency.

After three renewals of the contract, Carrie rebelled, declaring that enough was enough. She had never settled in Hong Kong; she wanted to return to London, buy a house and start a family before it was too late. A leading Hong Kong gynaecologist had told her that she could not have children but she clung to the forlorn belief that the failure of her ovaries to function properly was because they weren't in England where they rightfully belonged. To save his marriage, Janson had reluctantly bowed to Carrie's pressure by agreeing to return to London. Now there were less than seven months of his contract to serve. He didn't really mind. His primary duties were the interrogation, or debriefing as he preferred to call it, of Vietnamese refugees. Thankfully those duties were nearly finished now that the numbers of boat people braving the hazards of the South China Sea had died away to a trickle. This latest girl he had been called on to debrief was the first arrival in several days.

Lesa watched him suspiciously as he set up his Uher tape recorder on her bedside table. A European who spoke fluent Vietnamese was outside her experience.

'Now then, Lesa,' said David, positioning his microphone. 'You know what this is?'

Lesa nodded, not taking her eyes off the stranger for an instant although his easy smile and gentle voice when he introduced himself had done much to allay her initial fear.

'I want you to tell me your full story in your own words,' said David easily, pulling up a bedside chair and smiling warmly at the girl. 'I'll only interrupt if something isn't clear. Do you understand?'

'Yes,' said Lesa. She looked questioningly at David. 'They killed all my family and they raped me. Will you catch them?'

David glanced down at the hospital notes on his clipboard. In addition to the shoulder wound, the poor kid had suffered multiple vaginal lesions. If Carrie had had a kid soon after their marriage as they had planned, this girl would have been about the same age. He was careful not to let his feelings show. 'We'll do our best, Lesa. Start at the beginning. Tell me about the time when you left your village.'

Lesa talked nervously at first and then with mounting confidence when she saw that this friendly little Englishman was taking her seriously. She wasn't used to having adults pay such close attention to anything she had to say. It was when she related what happened when they boarded the motor-cruiser that her voice faltered, but she kept talking.

The blood drained from David's face as he listened. Having questioned several hundred refugees he thought he had experienced the whole spectrum of the incredible brutality that man could inflict on his fellow man, but the story this girl was telling him compressed the sufferings of all those boat people down to the beginning of the scale.

For Lesa, telling the story was not as bad as she had expected. Mere words from her could add nothing to the agony of her memories. Besides, this man with his tape recorder was the first step along the path of vengeance. She finished talking just as the recorder exhausted its tape.

David switched the machine off and looked thoughtfully at Lesa. He had no doubt that the kid was telling the truth: there was her wound, the medical evidence of a savage sexual assault, and the two spent slugs that had been dug out of her sampan. Nevertheless he had to backtrack and ask her to go over a few of the more complex details. But the kid's story never varied. Even when he asked her about the watch that Lin had given her, she was able to produce it from her drawer.

'I can draw them if you don't believe me,' said Lesa emphatically. 'Do you have something I can draw with?'

David handed her his notebook and a propelling pencil. He watched in amazement as Lesa quickly sketched the head and shoulders of a man aged about thirty-five. With a few skilled strokes she had captured on the tiny piece of paper a mop of blond hair and a hard, sardonic expression. Not even the shop doorway charcoal artists along Nathan Road possessed such a remarkable talent. He stopped her.

'That's amazing, Lesa.'

'That's the leader. If I had larger sheets of paper I could draw all of them,' said Lesa simply. 'And their boat. Everything.'

David stood. 'There's an office supplies shop near the hospital, Lesa. I'll be back in fifteen minutes.'

True to his word, the Englishman returned after a quarter of an hour and gave Lesa a sketching tablet and a box of artists' pencils together with a sharpener. She ran her fingers over the paper in wonder. Never had she known such fine quality. And the pencils . . .

'Could you draw them on that for me, Lesa?'

She looked up at David and smiled for the first time. She really was an incredibly lovely kid.

'It will take me a little time.'

'Do you think you could do a drawing of me from memory as well?'

Lesa looked hard into David's kindly face for a few moments and nodded.

He chucked her under the chin and immediately regretted the gesture because she flinched away from his touch.

'Okay, Lesa. I'll be back at the same time tomorrow.'

## 34

David Janson spread photocopies of Lesa's sketches out on Detective Inspector Jack Barber's desk. The senior police officer studied the drawings of the three men and the redhead first with professional interest and then with revulsion. There was one drawing that particularly sickened him with its portrayal of obscene debauchery. 'She's good,' he commented, keeping his voice steady and professional-sounding.

'She's more than that, sir,' David replied. 'She's brilliant.'

'Okay – brilliant. But where does it get us?'

'We've got these. A drawing of the motor-cruiser. We reduce them. Print five thousand sets and –'

'And nothing,' said Barber emphatically.

David was prepared for this and had a case ready. 'We've got four good likenesses, sir, and several drawings of the cruiser. Three men and a woman with a boat like that should be easy to find.'

'We don't know that they are good likenesses,' Barber pointed out. 'The girl may be a brilliant artist but that doesn't mean she's got a good mem –' Barber broke off as David placed an excellent likeness of himself in front of him. It was more than an excellent likeness of Janson – it was a perfect likeness. He looked up at David. 'So you sat for her? So what?'

'No, sir. She drew that from memory after only meeting me once.'

'Shit,' Barber muttered. He looked sharply at his subordinate.

'The kid's a genius, sir.' David pointed to the drawing that had sickened Barber and himself when he had first seen it. It showed the bull-chested man leaning against the rail of the cruiser. He was holding a rifle while watching two other men raping a girl. A full-breasted naked woman was standing nearby, masturbating – her mouth open and an expression of ecstasy on her face as though she were seeing a vision. The atmosphere of ghastly casualness the vivid sketch conveyed was made even more horrific by the realization that it had been drawn by a fifteen-year-old girl.

'Christ,' Barber muttered. 'You can even tell what the rifle is – an M16.' He tore his eyes away from the sketch. Familiarity with the terrible scene did nothing to diminish its effect. He hated himself for what he had to say. He had read the English language transcript of David's interview with the girl twice. The first time in frank disbelief; the second with a deep sense of revulsion when he realized that the story was too horrifying to be anything but the truth. 'It changes nothing, Janson. We're talking about an offence . . .'

'Sir! We are *not* talking about an *offence* – we're talking about a fucking massacre!'

'. . . against foreign nationals in international waters on a ship that's probably foreign-registered. The whole thing's beyond our jurisdiction. We don't have the manpower or resources to chase after our own cases, never mind ones that are outside our jurisdiction.'

'I think you've got enough to track down the boat, find out its country of registration, and pass on our evidence.'

'Oh sure. I can just see the Panamanian authorities acting on our evidence. I'm sorry, David – I can understand exactly how you feel.' He glanced down at the sketches and looked away again. 'If it was up to me, I'd track the bastards down and string 'em up personally.'

David knew the futility of further argument. 'So what will happen to her?'

'You know the answer to that. Standard procedures will apply. She's too young to be offered the "move on" – having her boat repaired and provisioned, and towed out to where she was found. As soon as she's fully recovered, she'll be sent to a closed centre.'

## 35

That evening, while Carrie was watching television, David went into the hall of their apartment and phoned a probation officer at her home. Carol Turner owed him several favours. After a few opening pleasantries he got to the point.

'Carol – is it possible to carry out an IQ test on someone who can't even read or write?'

'I think so. Why?'

'We've got a Vietnamese refugee in custody. A fifteen-year-old girl. She's an artistic genius. As a personal favour, could you find a tame educational psychologist to assess her?'

'Just because a kid's good at drawing doesn't mean that he or she has a high IQ. Okay – I'll do my best. I've got a pencil ready.'

David told her everything he knew about Lesa. Carol Turner promised to call him back as soon as she had something.

She kept her promise four evenings later.

'I thought you said she couldn't speak English?' she accused.

'She can't.'

'Maybe she couldn't a week ago but she can now.'

'Carol – what the hell are you talking about?'

'According to Professor Achinson, she's got a vocabulary of about four hundred words. There's a Vietnamese nurse who's been teaching her English in her spare time. The good professor reckons she had a vocabulary of about three hundred and fifty words when he started his session with her, and about another fifty words when he'd finished. She's that fast.'

David was pleased that his hunch was right. 'So she *is* bright?'

'The professor doesn't like the Intelligence Quotient Scale. He says it's crude and imprecise but he's used it with Lesa Wessex because the likes of me and thee understand it.'

'Wessex? That's not her real name.'

'She's insisting that it is now. She's proud of it.'

'So what did he find out?'

'An IQ of one hundred to about one hundred and ten is the norm. A hundred and twenty is clever. A hundred and forty is exceptionally clever. At a hundred and seventy Lesa Wessex is nearly off the scale.'

David thanked her and replaced the receiver. He looked up in surprise at Carrie who was leaning against the lounge doorway. Like him she was in her late thirties. A tall, determined woman whose youthful good looks were being eroded by the hard lines that were appearing around her eyes. She examined her dark hair in the hall mirror as if that was the reason for her being there.

'That was about your Vietnamese girl?'

'She's not *my* girl. And yes – it was.' He resented having to sound defensive. 'That was Carol Turner. She reckons the kid's exceptionally gifted.'

Carrie examined an imaginary spot in the mirror. 'She must be to have broken through your usual detached professionalism. You've never involved Carol in all the others you've handled.'

'This girl is different.'

'Pretty?'

The question irritated him but he answered it truthfully. 'Oh yes. More than just pretty.'

Carrie turned to face her husband and wagged an admonishing finger at him. 'Don't get involved, David. Just don't get involved.'

## 36

Lesa sat in the back of the government car sandwiched between two women officials from the Hong Kong Correctional Services Department, clutching her sketching pad and drawings, and Neti's backpack which contained all her worldly possessions. Lin's watch had stopped but she still wore it. The kind David Janson, whom she had learned to trust during her three weeks in hospital, had offered to get it repaired for her but she had refused to allow it out of her sight. The watch was more than a link with the past; it was now her talisman – the shrine of the good joss wished on her by the ghosts of her departed loved ones. She would wear it until the day she died.

The smart shops and restaurants of central Kowloon, simmering in the afternoon humidity, degenerated into endless grey, washing-festooned apartment blocks as they sped north along the steaming, rain-splattered Nathan Road. After fifteen minutes the car stopped in a rundown area outside a pair of high corrugated iron gates set into an even higher granite wall topped with strands of barbed wire. All around were the high-rise blocks of the most over-crowded urban area on earth. The buildings were less than twenty years old and already they looked ready for demolition.

A tall, smiling Sikh opened the gates. The car crossed the sidewalk and entered a small compound that was enclosed by a gleaming new chain-link fence. On the other side of the fence were hundreds of Lesa's fellow countrymen and women and children. All were wearing an amazing variety of ill-fitting Western clothes. Some of the young men were clad in absurd-looking oversized business suits, complete with waistcoats, with pants rolled up at the ankles to compensate for the greater height of their original owners. Word of the new arrival spread in an instant. A crowd gathered quickly along the fence. They stared vacantly at Lesa as she got out of her car while one of the policewomen held the door open for her.

Sham Shui Po Closed Centre in north Kowloon was a former British army barracks that was now home for five thousand Vietnamese boat people refugees. The grim granite walls enclosing a two-hectare site had been used by the Japanese for their firing squads during the occupation. Lesa caught a glimpse of high, warehouse-like concrete sheds before she was ushered into a small hut where the smiling Sikh entered her name in his register. He raised an eyebrow at the second name 'Wessex' but accepted it after an explanation from one of the officials. There were no other formalities.

A brisk, no-nonsense Franciscan nun clutching a clipboard introduced herself to Lesa as Sister Veronica. She seized Lesa's hand and escorted her out of the hut. The nun spoke poor Vietnamese but Lesa had no trouble understanding her. A guard unlocked a side gate and admitted them into the main compound. The gate clanged shut behind them and the huge crowd of refugees made a path as Sister Veronica guided Lesa across the flagstoned compound towards the nearest of the concrete sheds. Lesa noticed that there were few old people among the crowd; the inmates were mostly men and women in their twenties. Also there were many children. Lacking the reticence of their elders, they fell in behind Lesa only to scatter giggling when Sister Veronica turned suddenly and shooed them away. The good sister maintained an incessant flow of conversation that was interrupted briefly by the howl of a Boeing 747 passing only a few hundred feet directly overhead, flaps fully extended, landing lights blazing and losing height. Lesa gaped in wonder at the huge apparition before it was lost to sight beyond the tenement high-rise blocks. She noticed many of the refugees had looked longingly up at the jet – a symbol of freedom – even though the aircraft must have been a familiar sight.

'We're right under the inbound approach to Kai Tak airport,' Sister Veronica explained. 'It's only two kilometres away. And that's my office over there.' She pointed to a yellow caravan standing near the perimeter wall. 'If you need anything, you will find me or one of my colleagues always on duty. We're from the Hong Kong Christian Aid to Refugees. But you must understand that unlike the resettlement camps, we don't run this place. We only help out when we can.'

They came to the shed's open sliding doors. 'This is the unmarried women's shed,' the nun explained as they entered the building's stifling, darkened interior.

The smell of sweat, disinfectant and urine was overpowering. They were competing with each other in gladiatorial combat, with the urine winning by a nose. The appalling stench made Lesa's eyes water.

'You'll get used to it,' said Sister Veronica sternly seeing Lesa's grimace. 'You'll have to.'

'I don't think I ever will,' Lesa replied, looking apprehensively around at the strange surroundings. As her eyes became accustomed to the gloom she could see what appeared to be rows of open-sided packing crates stacked three high and stretching either side of an aisle into the shadows. Makeshift curtains fashioned from old clothes were hanging across the front of each crate.

'Cargo pallets,' said Sister Veronica, consulting her clipboard and striding so fast along the aisle that Lesa had to break into a trot to keep up with her. 'We should be able to fix you up with an empty one.' She stopped and squinted around. 'It says here that you're not to use your left arm for another month, so we'll have to put you on the ground floor. Can't have you climbing ladders. Here we are – A47.'

The nun yanked the curtains aside of the numbered pallet and waved her hand at the interior. 'This is your new home. I want you to sort yourself out and come and see me about your malarial tablets after lunch. As you've come from hospital you don't need a medical or the de-lousing treatment. You shouldn't have any trouble finding someone to show you the routine here – mealtimes and so on. It'll all seem very strange at first but you'll soon settle down. There's a stewards' rota to stop petty pilfering. Any questions?'

There was one question that was uppermost in Lesa's mind: one that no one at the hospital had answered – not even David Janson.

'How long will I be here for?'

The question seemed to take Sister Veronica by surprise. For the first time Lesa saw a fleeting look of sympathy in the nun's eyes, but it was quickly gone – banished like an unwelcome intruder. 'Who knows?' she answered. 'A year. Two years. Ten years. It's all up to the politicians now. Anything else?'

Lesa was too shocked to think of anything to say. She shook her head dumbly in answer to the question whereupon Sister Veronica muttered a curt goodbye and strode purposefully back to the compound gate.

Lesa stared around and became aware that she was the centre of attention for many pairs of eyes watching her from the dark recesses of nearby pallets. She swung her backpack into her pallet and crawled in after it. Her new home was two metres long and a little narrower. A solid horsehair mattress of indeterminate age marked 'War Office Property' occupied half the floor area. The words 'War' and 'Office' she now recognized, but 'Property' was new so she decided to add it to her daily list of words to learn. Then she realized that she was unlikely to see Choi again.

She unpacked her few clothes and stowed them neatly in a corner. The drawings that David Janson had photocopied were placed carefully under the mattress. Her prized possession, apart from the sketching pad and pencils, was a toilet bag and requisites that the nurses at the hospital had clubbed together to buy her. There was even a packet of tampons whose purpose she was unsure of until she discovered a postage-stamp-sized diagram inside the packet.

The smell and heat in the vast shed was too much. She went out into the bright sunlight. Two male volunteer workers were chatting to each other in English at a trestle table while ladling out hot stew to a long, shuffling queue of refugees. Each was clutching an enamel bowl.

Lesa went to the head of the queue, rehearsing a phrase to herself under her breath. She wanted her grammar to be perfect, but, more important, she wanted her accent to sound like the women announcers on RTHK that she had listened to on her headphones in the hospital. 'Please. Can you tell me where I can get a bowl?' she asked one of the volunteers in slow, carefully pronounced English.

Both volunteers stopped dishing out stew and gaped in amazement at the striking young girl who had addressed them. The first one pointed to the yellow caravan. 'Over there,' he said.

Lesa thanked him and moved off towards the caravan.
'Blimey,' breathed the first volunteer. 'She sounds English.'
'Looks a bit English too,' remarked his helper.

## 37

Right from the beginning Lesa hated everything about Sham Shui Po Closed Centre. For one thing there was no privacy; she had to take her daily shower at a scheduled time along an outside wall together with fifty other women and there seemed to be nothing to stop the camp's youths entering the women's toilet area and ogling them. One misshapen boy of about nineteen took to following her around, exposing two rows of rotten teeth whenever he smiled at her. No – he didn't smile, he leered, usually making his intentions clear by scratching his crotch at the same time.

Then there was the loneliness. Making friends proved virtually impossible, not that Lesa was an outgoing type who made friends easily anyway. The men made it obvious from their comments and gestures that, as far as they were concerned, friendship with Lesa meant one thing only. And the women regarded her height and developing beauty – that they could never hope to equal – as a threat.

Although Lesa valued having a pallet to herself, she was, as far as she could judge, the only detainee who did not have a member of her family with her. At least there was freedom from fear and hunger – the few guards were unarmed and the food was regular and plentiful, if boring, exept when there were deliveries of fruit. There was also a generous supply of cast-off but good quality clothing provided by various charities. But what really worried her were the numbers of women and some girls of her own age with babies. Immorality was the norm in the camp. The clandestine comings and goings at night in the accommodation shed and the noises around her suggested that traditional standards had completely broken down.

Her fear was born out when she had been in the camp a week. She was woken up in the middle of the night by something touching her. Before she could scream, a hand clamped over her mouth and a knee held her pressed painfully to the mattress. She struggled valiantly but her left arm was still weak. Only when prying fingers yanked down her pyjamas and thrust painfully between her legs did she manage to sink her teeth into the hand over her mouth and scream out.

Flashlights were switched on. Feet came running. She screamed again. The curtain was whipped aside and she saw that her assailant was the youth with the rotten teeth. He jumped up, pushed past the women crowding around Lesa's pallet and ran into the darkness. None of the women attempted to go after him. They melted away leaving one of them to self-consciously comfort Lesa until she stopped sobbing. Such was her terror that it was a week before she could sleep properly at night and even then the slightest unusual sound snapped her wide awake, her heart pounding and nerves screaming.

## 38

David Janson came to see her when she had been in the camp ten days. Sister Veronica left them alone in her caravan. Lesa was pleased to see David, not primarily because she was glad to see a familiar face, but much more important, because she wanted to know how the search for the gang that had murdered her family was proceeding. David looked embarrassed when she put the question to him in Vietnamese.

'Lesa . . .' He broke off, groping for the right words, uncomfortably aware of the uncompromising, beautiful eyes fixed dispassionately on him. 'I should have told you this before . . . but there is no search.'

'You mean you've found them!'

'No . . . I don't mean that.'

The sudden light that had blazed in Lesa's eyes died. 'I don't understand.'

'Lesa – you must understand that what happened to you and your family happened on the high seas – beyond the jurisdiction of national laws unless we can find out where the cruiser was registered.'

'Beyond the laws of humanity and decency?' Suddenly there was a terrible hate in her eyes and voice.

David felt disorientated – a child talking to him in the language of an adult. He shook his head. 'No, Lesa. If it was up to me, I would hunt them down and have them brought to justice. But it's not up to me.'

'You're a policeman!'

'I'm just a police interpreter. Please believe me, Lesa, I've done my best to persuade the authorities to investigate your case –'

'No,' Lesa spat, jumping to her feet, her eyes blazing. 'I don't believe you! You're like all the rest of the *gwailo*!' *Gwailo* meant foreign devils and was the worst insult she could think of. 'I never want to see you again!' Without waiting to see the effect of her outburst, she fled from the caravan and dashed blindly across the compound to the accommodation shed. She threw herself face down on her pallet and beat her fists on the mattress in fury and frustration. She had been betrayed yet again. She had stupidly thought that these outwardly decent people would be so horrified by what had happened to her and her family that they would stop at nothing to hunt the gang down. How could she have been so stupid as to have trusted them? How could she have been so childishly naive?

She calmed down and began to think clearly with that logical, calculating brain of hers. 'I'll find them, Neti,' she whispered with passionate intensity into the darkness. 'I'll find them all and I'll kill them one by one. I swear on the souls of our ancestors, Neti. I swear it before God and Buddha – before I meet my grave, I will have killed them all . . .'

## 39

Respite from Lesa's tedium came when Sister Theresa, a kindly nun who held regular English classes for the children in a dark shed, readily agreed to Lesa sitting in on her lessons. For Lesa, listening to Sister Theresa reading Rudyard Kipling stories to the children was a revelation. She begged the nun to allow her to borrow some books. Sister Theresa smilingly handed over some of Enid Blyton's *Famous Five* children's novels and told her to write down all the words she came across that she didn't understand.

The first fifty pages of the first book were hard going. But her rapidly increasing understanding of the English language turned the struggle into a brightening light that grew steadily brighter with each page turned. By the time she was three quarters of the way through the book, she was reading it for the sheer enjoyment of submerging herself in an adventure in a wholly alien world in which middle-class children, whose parents had servants and butlers, could make camps at night in the woods without fear or danger, and go tracking down smugglers. England, Lesa decided, must be a wondrous place.

After that she was reading, or rather devouring, two to three books a day, reading every newspaper and magazine she could lay her hands on, and making life difficult for Sister Theresa who was hard-pressed to keep her prodigy supplied with new material and explain all the words on the neatly-written lists that Lesa bombarded her with.

'A wondrous gift that child has,' she confided in Sister Veronica. 'Truly a gift of God.'

'Our souls are more important gifts,' Sister Veronica snapped, which put Sister Theresa firmly in her place.

Lesa became bored with Enid Blyton after a week. The stories were wonderful but bland; they added little to her knowledge of England or its language.

Sister Theresa had no idea what a bombshell she was handing Lesa when she gave the girl her yellowing copy of *Tess of the d'Urbervilles*. If Enid Blyton had been the spark, Thomas Hardy was the flame. It was a huge intellectual leap for Lesa but once she had absorbed Hardy's style, his story of a simple country girl driven to murder as a result of her treatment at the hands of men touched a chord that led to her reading and re-reading the book and gaining new insights into Tess and her suffering with each reading. She identified so readily with Hardy's heroine that even his obscure symbolism in the sacrifice of Tess at Stonehenge made vivid sense to Lesa. What particularly struck her was the name of Hardy's makebelieve county in western England.

Wessex.

It was an omen. It was as if the ghost of this strange man, Thomas Hardy – a man as far removed from her culture as it was possible to imagine – had reached out from the grave to speak to her with compassion and understanding, and to steer her down a path of irrevocable destiny from which there could be no turning back.

## 40

From then on Lesa's literary thirst was unquenchable. Sister Theresa was driven to raiding her convent's library for Dickens, Galsworthy, Jane Austen, the Brontë sisters and even Scott Fitzgerald – it was a very liberal library. Even that was not enough for Lesa. She took to pestering volunteer workers who supplied her with paperbacks by authors such as Harold Robbins, who rarely figured in the catalogues of convent libraries.

'Goodness me,' said Theresa one afternoon when she was struggling through one of Lesa's lists of words. 'We really must buy the child a dictionary. Where did she get *this* word from, I wonder?'

Sister Veronica looked up from her desk. 'What word?'

'Fellatio. I'm sure she never got that from Jane Austen. Should I tell her what it means?'

Sister Veronica looked puzzled. 'What exactly does it mean?'

## 41

It was August. The blistering heat and smell of humanity lay in Sham Shui Po's enclosed compound like a decomposing animal, stirred occasionally by the howl of jets passing over the camp, adding the stink of kerosene to the will-sapping hell. The high walls trapped the sun and deflected what little wind there was. Even the normally boisterous play of the children was muted by the suffocating oppressiveness.

Lesa propped herself in her customary position in the shade of the women's accommodation shed's northern wall reading Ray Bradbury's *The October Country*. She was going through a fantasy and science fiction phase. This was a new book, riddled with challenging metaphors, but she found it difficult to concentrate because her thoughts were on escape. She had even considered a breakout but rejected the idea on analysis. She could scale the wall one night, she was sure of that, but she was less confident in her ability to survive in the urban jungle of Hong Kong. From what she had read it was infinitely more dangerous than the jungles of Vietnam. The Hong Kong police hunted down escapees from the closed centres with grim determination. Not out of malice towards the refugees in their care, but simply because the Hong Kong Government did not want word getting back to Vietnam and Kampuchea that life was easy in the dependency lest another flood of refugees take to the South China Sea in their boats.

Lesa realized that even if she managed to remain free, without papers or any means of identification she would be certain to end up working as a prostitute for a Triad boss. Despite the heat, the thought of a man touching her chilled Lesa's blood. Leaving legally was a remote possibility: the Canadians, British and Americans were giving priority to families who could provide mutual support in strange countries. A lone teenage girl with no dependants, who would have to be dumped in a home, was a problem no one wanted.

Lesa was reading one of Ray Bradbury's strange stories – about a dwarf in a hall of mirrors – when an idea occurred to her. Maybe she *could* escape. It meant using people but that did not worry her. She had long ago decided that if her mission of vengeance meant using people – trampling on them if necessary – then so be it.

She closed her book and crossed to the yellow caravan. Sister Theresa was bashing away at an ancient Remington typewriter. She looked up and smiled.

'Hallo, Lesa. I'm sorry but I've not had time to do your latest list.'

'That's all right, sister. Actually I've come to ask a favour. A big favour.'

Sister Theresa blinked. Whenever the child addressed her, there was always that little shock at Lesa's English which improved so dramatically from day to day. It was as if each day was producing a different Lesa. Now she was speaking idiomatic English like an adult. Amazing. 'What sort of favour, Lesa?'

'Would you send a message to David Janson at Kowloon Central Police Station please. Tell him I'm very sorry for what I said and that I'd like to see him.' The nun noted down the message and promised to send it.

Lesa returned to her favourite spot and went back to Ray Bradbury. She was disturbed by an altercation. Disputes among the refugees were normal, especially during the afternoons when the heat was at its most oppressive and tempers flared readily. But they were rarely serious and were usually settled quickly. This one was settled even more quickly than usual. An old woman was clutching a jug of ice cubes that she had scrounged. She was shouting at two youths who were standing in her way and making it clear that they wanted to share in her good fortune. Lesa had seen the old woman before, always intent on some mission, always minding her own business. Another loner. The first youth grabbed the old woman's shirt but she pushed him away in a display of agility that was remarkable in one so old. The second youth snatched at the jug. What happened next was a blur of movement that left both youths writhing in agony on the flagstones, clutching their genitals and screaming. Lesa had blinked and so missed whatever it was that the old woman had done. She clutched her jug to her chest and had vanished through the crowd by the time two guards appeared to find out what all the fuss was about.

## 42

Lesa tracked the old woman down that evening. She was at the far end of the accommodation shed, sitting on an orange box with her back to Lesa and smoking a pipe.

'What do you want with me, child?' she said without turning around. Her sharp hearing and the youthfulness of her voice astonished Lesa.

'I saw what happened to those two boys this afternoon.'

The old woman spat a glob of tobacco juice onto the bare concrete floor and turned to face Lesa. Her face was wrinkled, her skin the colour of old parchment, but her eyes were bright and alive with humour. 'I doubt it.'

'Oh, but I did.'

'Then tell me what I did.'

Lesa was at a loss. 'Well – I didn't actually see –'

'Ha!' The old woman gave a crooked grin of triumph. 'I'm still fast. I was the fastest, of course.'

'Fastest at what?'

The smile vanished into the mass of wrinkles. 'Never you mind.'

Lesa knelt in front of the old woman and took one of the gnarled hands in her own. 'Will you teach me your art?'

The bright eyes regarded her steadily. 'Are you a virgin?'

'Does it matter?'

'That's for me to judge. Well?'

Lesa met the old woman's eyes without flinching. 'No.'

'Tell me about your men.' She spoke in a matter of fact tone with no hint of condemnation that would be normal from an old woman.

Lesa looked down at Lin's watch as though she hoped to see his face there. 'The first was a boy about my own age. Only once.'

'Did you love him?'

'Yes. The second time was when I was raped by several men.'

'Pirates?'

'Yes.'

The old woman re-lit her pipe with a Bic lighter. Lesa saw the flame reflected in her staring eyes. She wanted to tear her gaze away but the old woman's eyes held her as if she were exercising a strange power over her. 'And now you hate your body?'

Lesa hesitated and nodded.

The old woman spat again. 'I cannot help you, child. For you to learn the art of Wing Chun and become a woman ninja, you must learn to love your body for it is both the weapon and shrine of the ninja.'

'If it is necessary then I will learn to love my body,' said Lesa without conviction.

The old woman regarded her for some seconds. She nodded slowly. 'You must start today. You must fast for four days to cleanse your system. Drink only water. After that you must refuse all meat for ever more unless it is necessary to defeat a warrior by sharing his table. Come and see me at this time tomorrow.'

## 43

The next day Lesa visited the old woman at the appointed time. She was sitting on her orange box unpicking stitches in an old coat using her fingernails which were long and pointed. Her sleeves were pulled back revealing a blood-red tatoo of a crescent moon on her left forearm. She motioned Lesa to sit on the floor.

'They tell me your name is Lesa?'

'Yes.'

'And that you're alone?'

'Yes. What is your name?'

'You can call me Ko,' the old woman replied. 'You've started fasting?'

'Yes,' said Lesa with some feeling because she hadn't eaten for twenty-four hours. 'I'm ravenous.'

Ko laughed. It wasn't the cackle of an old woman. Her teeth were sound, without the ugly betel juice staining that was customary in older people. 'Remember – when you've finished your fast, no more meat – fish yes. But not meat. Even if you do not become a ninja, you will be healthier in mind and body.'

'Tell me about the ninja.'

The old woman frowned. 'Even the word is forbidden in some communities.'

Lesa listened attentively as Ko outlined the history of the strange martial art. Its origins were a book, *The Art of War*, written fifteen hundred years previously by a Chinese general named Sun Tzu in which he advocated a system of guerilla warfare – of killing by stealth. For direct combat he developed a system of silent but lethal fighting that was based on the utmost economy of movement. His teachings travelled to Japan where they gave birth to the deadly ninja Clans of Death: these were remote mountain villages in the Koko area of Japan's main island in which every boy and girl from the age of five was schooled in Sun Tzu's deadly techniques. From the age of ten the girls received additional training in the art of seduction. Their modified version of Sun Tzu's combat had been developed by a priestess, Yim Wing Chun, one thousand years after Sun Tzu's death. But it was no less deadly. At night the ninja clansmen and clanswomen swathed themselves in black and melted like ghosts into the jungle to strike terror into their mortal enemies – the samurai who found that their skills with the sword counted for naught when it came to fighting these elusive wraiths of the forest. Cornered ninja used a terrible kick to the forearm that could break a samurai's sword arm like a twig; a samurai warrior with a broken sword arm quickly became a dead samurai warrior at the hands and feet of his ninja opponent.

Word of Sun Tzu's teaching spread slowly throughout the orient. Ambassadors were sent to the Koko villages to persuade their elders to send ninja teachers to other lands. Few villages were suitable; few villages were prepared to turn themselves into secret societies and live under the harsh training regimen that Sun Tzu's deadly disciplines demanded. Ko was from a village that had embraced Sun Tzu although his influence had declined with the coming of the twentieth century. She was the sole survivor of a napalm attack. The ancient skills of the ninja were no match for what Ko called 'the fire of heaven'. She believed that she was the last living ninja from Vietnam.

'The other martial arts are concerned only with combat,' said Ko contemptuously, her fingers busy unpicking stitches. 'The ninja learn not only to kill, but everything that is necessary to destroy an enemy: espionage, woodcraft, tracking, assassination, seduction, poisoning of crops and water supplies and the laying of booby traps.'

'Did the Viet Cong copy them?' Lesa asked, remembering the skeleton of the American soldier in the punji trap.

'The Viet Cong were clumsy animals compared with the ninja!' Ko snapped with sudden vehemence. 'You cannot copy the skills of the ninja. To use them you have to become one. I will show you something.'

The old woman jumped to her feet with that astonishing agility she had demonstrated the previous day and leaned a length of pallet timber against the wall. Protruding through the board about a metre from the floor was the gleaming point of a nail. She hung two plums from the nail. 'That,' she said, pointing to the fruit-decked board, 'is the enemy. A man. Do you understand?'

Lesa looked at the hanging plums and smiled. She nodded.

'Now watch carefully.'

Ko stood in front of the board and something remarkable happened. It seemed to Lesa that Ko was suddenly transformed into a young woman. Head bowed, eyes downcast, hands clasped together in front of her – the subservient stance of a demure young girl standing submissively before her lord and master, obediently awaiting his command. She stood like that for some seconds. Perfectly still and serene. Then without warning, her foot lashed out. The movement was a blur that the eye could not follow. Something wet splattered on Lesa's bare arm. The plank wobbled and once again Ko was standing shoulders bowed like a bride on her wedding night. She looked up and grinned toothily at Lesa who was staring wide-eyed at the plank. The plums had ceased to exist. In their place was a splodge of flattened skin and fruit; juices trickling down the plank dripped onto the floor, staining the concrete. It was a piece of flying plum that had hit Lesa on the arm.

'That is the way of a ninja Clanswoman of Death,' said Ko simply. 'No silly grimaces. No yells. No taking up stances. Those are the fighting ways of men. A ninja woman strikes without warning and strikes only once.' She held up her bare foot for Lesa's examination. There was no sign of any damage from the nail.

'What a woman has between her legs is her most powerful weapon,' Ko continued. 'What a man has between his legs is his greatest enemy.'

'Is that the kick you used against those boys yesterday?' Lesa asked.

Ko grinned. 'Yes. But it wasn't very hard. I wanted only to deter them.' She nodded to the plank. 'If that were a man, he would now be sure he was close to death and would be praying for it to complete its business.'

The old woman went on to explain the science behind the terrible kick: unlike the kicks in other martial arts in which the protagonists pivoted their bodies about the hip to deliver impetus to the outside of the foot, the deadly ninja kick was delivered straight up, swinging vertically from the hip with the leg kept stiff. The groin kick was particularly deadly.

'The blow is delivered with the ball of the foot,' Ko explained. 'It is not as hard as a turning kick but it reaches into a man's groin. I will give you exercises to help your toes turn up out of the way when the kick is delivered. The follow-through is to drive the thumb and forefinger of your left hand into the enemy's eyes as he doubles up. For that you will need to grow your nails longer than they are now. That's enough for today. Come to me tomorrow and we will begin serious training. You are starting late in life. There is much time to be made up.'

'Lesa!' It was Sister Veronica's voice.

Lesa turned. The nun was silhouetted against the light at the far end of the shed. 'There you are, child. You've got visitors.'

## 44

'How do you do, Mrs Janson,' said Lesa politely, shaking hands with Carrie.

'Fine, thank you, Lesa. You speak good English.'

'She's learning very fast,' said Sister Veronica primly. 'Some people have been giving her most unsuitable books. I've been trying to put a stop to it but she's still getting hold of them. This morning I had to confiscate a book by Arthur Miller. *Tropic of Cancer*. Quite disgraceful.'

'Henry Miller,' Lesa corrected.

David Janson caught his wife's eye and worked hard to keep a straight face.

'I'll leave you to it,' said Sister Veronica. She closed the caravan door behind her and set off across the compound to chastise a couple for behaving in an unseemly manner by kissing.

David smiled warmly. 'How are you keeping, Lesa?'

'Fine, thank you,' Lesa replied, uncomfortably aware that Carrie Janson was staring fixedly at her.

'And the shoulder?'

'Getting better every day.'

'Like your English,' said David.

Lesa touched her left shoulder. 'I hardly feel anything now. I'm sorry about the things I said last time.'

'Don't worry,' said David easily. 'I can understand how you feel. Let's consider it forgotten. I brought Carrie along because she's heard so much about you. I hope you don't mind?'

'No – of course not. It's very good to meet you, Mrs Janson.' Lesa smiled shyly at Carrie.

There was a hesitation before Carrie smiled back. 'We've brought you some *National Geographic* magazines,' she said, indicating a plastic carrier bag on the desk. 'David said how much you liked them.'

'That's very kind of you, Mrs Janson.'

'Oh please call me Carrie.'

'Carrie.' Lesa gave her a winning smile. She had sensed the older woman's initial wariness and hoped that she was winning her over.

'If there's anything else you need . . .' David offered.

'I need help,' Lesa replied. 'I want to go to school. I want to learn.'

David and Carrie exchanged glances.

'I don't think that will be possible,' said David cautiously, not wishing to provoke another outburst like the last one.

But Lesa seemed to have matured. She nodded gravely and said, 'I understand that. There was an article in the *South China Post*. Families are being given priority by those countries that have agreed to take boat people.' She looked at them in turn. Gaining their sympathy was crucial to her plan. 'I could be a prisoner in here for months. Maybe years. My only hope of getting out is if you can find a couple to adopt me.'

## 45

'No, David,' said Carrie firmly over their evening meal.

'Why not?'

'Because I don't think it's a good idea. It would be enough of an emotional struggle with a girl from our own culture.'

'She's absorbing Western culture like blotting paper,' David pointed out, pouring himself another glass of wine. 'She's even latched onto the name she was given by the helicopter crew that picked her up. And as for an emotional struggle, how the hell can adjusting to such a sweet, clever kid be an emotional struggle?'

'And what about *her* struggle?'

'She *wants* to be adopted. She's obviously given it a lot of thought. And even if it is a struggle for her, which I don't think it will be for a moment, it would be nothing compared to what she's already been through.'

'And how do you think she'd fit into English society?' Carrie countered, realizing that it was a feeble objection. She forced herself to face the fact that she was hunting for excuses to avoid having to bring up what was really on her mind.

'She's adaptable, for Christ's sake! Three months ago she was living the life of a peasant in the jungle. She had never even used a lavatory. Now she's reading Thomas Hardy according to Sister Theresa.'

'I'm sorry, David, but I can't help thinking it would be a terrible mistake.'

'Why, Carrie? Look – if the kid was like all the others, I would agree with you. But she's not. She's got a phenomenal IQ. Look at the way she's learned near-fluent English in only a few weeks. Think of the benefit she would get out of going to school. Think of the good having her around would do us. We're not getting any younger, Carrie. I know you well enough to know what you're thinking. Deep down you know that we can't have children but you're refusing to accept it, and we're too old to adopt a baby now.'

Carrie opened her mouth to say something and changed her mind. She shook her head. 'I don't know, David. It's just that it's not . . . not . . .'

'Not professional?'

'Yes.'

'Who the hell wants to be professional? I want to be human for once. And I don't want to have to spend the rest of my life wondering what's happened to that kid and hating myself because I chose to pass by on the other side of the highway.'

Carrie said nothing. Exactly the same thought had crossed her mind. There was something strangely compulsive about the child's enigmatic smile that lodged in the mind. It was there all the time like a persistent image of suffering from a Dali painting.

David chuckled. 'There's a guy at the station who told me that you re-live your life through your kids' eyes, but only when they get older. He reckons to hell with all the parental bonding crap. Kids should be taken away from their parents at birth and only handed back when they're about fourteen.'

Carrie smiled at the incongruity of the idea. As she did so, she had a mental picture of herself and Lesa in Oxford Street: they were shopping together and Lesa was happily accepting Carrie's choice of clothes. Every suggestion of Carrie's was greeted with that sweet, wonderful smile. It was an irresistible image of overwhelming power.

David saw the smile. It gave him hope. 'Well?'

Carrie met his eyes and nodded her head. 'All right, David.'

## 46

There was an hour of daylight left when Lesa decided to skim through the *National Geographic* magazines that David and Carrie had left her. To her surprise the magazines now bored her. The old magic was gone. Now that she could read, photographs were no longer her sole means of absorbing information. She read an article about the famine in Ethiopia and discovered that the two thousand words of well-written, hard-hitting text had greater impact than the photographs of fly-infested, pot-bellied, emaciated children that accompanied the piece.

She was about to throw the magazine back on the pile when some satellite photographs of the earth caught her eye. One of the pictures that grabbed her attention was, according to the caption, of a yacht marina on the Côte d'Azur. The neat lines of boats tied up to the mooring jetties stood out with astonishing clarity. It was even possible to make out people sunbathing on cabin roofs. On one ocean-going yacht a group of six people were seated in the cockpit playing cards. Lesa stared at the picture for some minutes, utterly transfixed. The photograph looked as if it had been taken from a height of four hundred metres, not four hundred kilometres as the caption claimed. She ripped out the article and dumped the magazines in the schoolroom.

That night, in the privacy of her cargo pallet, she switched on her pocket torch and studied the photograph in detail. She compared it with her sketches of the motor-yacht and a nebulous plan began taking shape in her fertile imagination. She switched off the torch. A mosquito buzzed around the pallet in the darkness.

'One step at a time, Neti,' she whispered. 'One step at a time, but I'll get there. I swear, Neti.'

The mosquito buzzed near her face. Her ear and hand co-ordination was such that she was able to snatch at the insect in the darkness and crush it.

## 47

'What *is* that child doing now?'

Sister Theresa looked up from her typewriter. She was writing a thank-you letter to Oxfam for their most recent consignment of bedding. She followed Sister Veronica's gaze across the compound where about three hundred excited children of all ages had formed a winding crocodile under the eye of a play leader. 'It's a dragon, sister.'

The older nun tutted impatiently. 'No – not them. The Wessex girl over by the shed. Kicking the wall – what a ridiculous exercise.'

Sister Theresa watched Lesa for a few moments. The girl was wearing high-cut boxer shorts that exaggerated her long, graceful legs. She was practising barefoot high kicks against the wall. Her headband glistened and her sweat-soaked, sleeveless T-shirt clung to her like a second skin. She had an audience of teenage youths who were watching her with obvious appreciation.

'She's being deliberately provocative,' said Sister Veronica sternly. 'You'll have to speak to her about wearing a brassiere or some such device.'

'Yes, sister,' said Sister Theresa, resolving to do no such thing. 'She's been doing that for several days now. An hour every morning and evening.'

'Just kicking?'

'There've been other exercises but mostly high kicks.'

'You'd think she'd hurt herself.'

'There's an old woman who's been giving her instruction.'

Sister Veronica gave a disapproving grunt. 'It's those books you've been giving her. Probably filling her head with a lot of nonsense about being a ballet dancer.'

'Whatever Marcel Proust is filling her head with at the moment,' said Sister Theresa equably, 'it's unlikely to be ballet.'

The older nun snorted. 'Next you'll be telling me she's reading Virginia Woolf.'

'That was last week, sister.'

'You're doing well,' said Ko, examining the sole of Lesa's foot. The old woman had come out into the compound to see how her protégée was coming along. 'Which brick is your target?'

Lesa pointed to a brick that she had scratched a cross on.

'We'll go to a higher course tomorrow,' Ko decided. 'But you're already kicking high enough and hard enough and accurately enough to break a man's jaw. You learn fast. What I could have done with you if I had had you from when you were five . . . Would you like an extra session with me in the mornings?'

Lesa looked pleased. 'Yes please, Ko.'

'Good. By the end of the week you'll be able to break his neck. And then we'll start on toughening up your hands.'


## 48

'No real problems,' said Carol Turner, sauntering into David Janson's office at Kowloon Central Police Station and dumping some papers on his desk. 'The government aren't too happy about adoption of refugees. You can't blame them. So long as they keep them in the camps and treat them reasonably well no one can level any real criticisms at them. But adoptions by Hong Kong residents could lead to scandals. We all know what happened to the poor kids that reached the Philippines.'

David understood. There were stories circulating about President Marcos' cronies in the Philippines sexually abusing Vietnamese boys and girls as young as ten, and the number of teenage Vietnamese boys and girls having to work as prostitutes for Manila vice bosses was well known.

'We'll have to get two social worker reports on you and Carrie for the courts,' the probation officer continued. 'That way we won't have any problems.'

'Thanks, Carol,' said David gratefully, looking through the forms. 'When do you want these by?'

'Tomorrow. Get Carrie to fill them in in her handwriting and to write the covering letter to the courts. It looks better coming from a woman.' She shot David a quizzical look. 'What are Carrie's views on all this?'

'She's agreed.'

'David – she's got to do more than just agree if you're going to convince a judge that you'd make suitable adoptive parents. And what about the child? What does *she* think?'

'We'll find out this afternoon.'

### 49

'Well, Lesa?' said Sister Theresa encouragingly. 'Haven't you got anything to say?'

Lesa could scarcely credit her senses. She stared at Carrie and David in turn. 'I don't understand,' she stammered, genuinely taken back by this unexpected turn of events.

'It's simple enough, Lesa,' said David. 'If you're agreeable, we'd like to adopt you.'

A football struck the side of the caravan. The sudden thump made everyone jump.

'You would become my legal parents?'

'Would you like that, Lesa?' asked Carrie. She took a step nearer Lesa and realized for the first time that the girl was the same height as her.

'But David said you were going back to England soon.'

Carrie gave her husband a worried glance. The child's obvious doubts reinforced her own misgivings. 'That's right. You would come with us. You would live with us in England and go to school. If you worked hard, you could catch up and sit your O levels next year. Do you know what O levels are?'

'Oh, yes,' said Lesa absently. She thought fast: the idea of leaving this part of the world had never occurred to her. To go to England would take her thousands of kilometres from the animals that had massacred her family. On the other hand, she might as well be thousands of kilometres from them if she remained shut up in this place. The escape route offered by David and Carrie was the only one open to her. She had no choice but to accept it. She looked at her prospective adoptive parents in turn. She knew hardly anything about them. What would it be like living with them? How would they treat her? David she was confident about. But Carrie? She saw the worried look in Carrie's eyes and realized that the older woman was just as concerned as she was. She realized that Carrie would have to be won over.

Quite suddenly the emotions of a confused little girl took over –

Lesa threw herself into Carrie's arms and clung to her. The unexpected gesture took Carrie by surprise, but that was nothing compared to the turmoil of her emotions as she held Lesa's slight form to herself. She was not a demonstrative woman – it was not in her nature to return such an embrace – but, to her own astonishment as much as David's, she did so. Lesa's warmth through her thin summer dress effectively melted the last of her reservations about the enormity of the task they were taking on.

## 50

'Three weeks?' queried Ko, turning her scrawny body under the shower.

Lesa worked soap vigorously into her hair with her fingertips. 'That's how long it takes to get the formalities sorted out.'

The two women were at the shower wall with fifty other women. Naked children shrieked around them, splashing each other by jumping in puddles. The usual group of youths had gathered near the entrance to the toilet compound. No matter how often they were chased off, they always returned. The parade of naked female flesh was a non-stop show from dawn to dusk.

The old woman pulled the overhead cord that turned off her faucet. She looked doubtfully at Lesa. 'Even with a fast learner like you, it is not possible to squeeze a lifetime's training into such a short time. But in a month you have learned much. In three weeks you will have learned much more.'

She suddenly lashed out at Lesa with her foot. Had the lightning kick connected it would have left a painful bruise on Lesa's abdomen and possibly have caused internal injury. But Lesa twisted her body to one side and brought the edge of her palm down on Ko's shin as it reached the kick's full height. Her other hand performed a whiplash arc that ended with the edge of her outstretched palm just resting on the side of the old woman's neck. Had the blow followed through it would have undoubtedly broken her neck.

Ko's wrinkled face creased even more into a grimace as she recovered her balance. 'It shows how old and slow I'm getting,' she grumbled. 'To have let you get in not one but two counter-strokes. You've learned well the first lesson of the ninja, my child. Eternal vigilance. But there is much more you have to learn. We have a busy three weeks ahead of us.'

## 51

Ko's tough training regime over the next three weeks left Lesa with no time for reading. The one-hour exercise sessions were interspersed with lectures on subjects as wide-ranging as disguise and survival – much of it was irrelevant to modern day living and Lesa would say so. But the fighting techniques she learned were timeless. With two weeks left, she was breaking pallet boards with two blows. With one week left she was using her strength and weight more skilfully and breaking them with a single blow. The perfection of her kicks was not so much in their power, but in their deadly accuracy. Ko was satisfied only when Lesa could pulverize fruit in the manner of her first demonstration without her pupil harming her foot on the nail.

It was nearly dusk when Lesa visited the old woman for the last time. Tomorrow, if all went well, she would leave Sham Shui Po and never return.

Ko's wrinkled face was sad when Lesa appeared. She had enjoyed teaching this exceptionally gifted young girl more than she was prepared to admit, even to herself. 'There is much you have learned in such a short time, child. More than I would have thought possible. But there is much you have not learned. You have not learned the art of using your body to seduce a man – you have not learned how to use your body and his body to bend a man to your will.'

Lesa shrugged. She was not sorry that this aspect of her training would not now go ahead. Ko's talk of using male volunteers had nauseated her. 'Perhaps such things will come naturally to me, Ko,' she said dismissively.

The old woman regarded her protégée steadily with those bright eyes that seemed to bore straight into Lesa's soul. 'Perhaps. You are clever enough to exploit all opportunities. But do you have the will to use your body as a sexual weapon – the most powerful weapon you have? You must not be afraid to use it, child. I say this because I know that deep down your body still fills you with revulsion despite all I have taught you.'

This talk irritated Lesa. She wanted the business over and done with. 'If I have to use my body, Ko, I will use it.'

'But there must one day be a man to whom you will give your body as a woman. It is inevitable.'

'I doubt it. Can we get on?'

'It is important, child,' Ko insisted. She rested a gnarled hand on each shoulder and fixed Lesa with an unwavering stare. 'The duties of a ninja are not only a loyalty to those that hire your skills. You must also have children to whom you can pass on your art. Fate is the only enemy you cannot defeat therefore you must know when to accept an alliance with it.'

Lesa made no reply. Ko was first to break the silence that followed. She nodded and said softly, 'I believe you are now ready to take the ninja oath of my village but there is one more thing I have to do. We must sit.'

The two women sat cross-legged on the concrete facing each other. They aroused the curiosity of other women who gathered around until Ko snarled at them. They melted away without argument. They were afraid of the strange old woman.

'Roll up your left sleeve.'

Lesa did as she was told and watched curiously as Ko removed a spatula-like strip of wood from her shirt pocket. A pin had been pushed through the end so that its point protruded a few millimetres. The old woman took hold of Lesa's arm in a powerful grip and flicked the spatula experimentally. The sharp pin caused little jabbing lances of pain as its point pierced Lesa's skin. Next, Ko opened a small jar and smeared a reddish-coloured ointment onto the spatula.

'Keep your arm still, child!'

The spatula buzzed against her arm. The tiny pin pricks felt like a concentrated attack by a swarm of mosquitoes. Ko worked steadily, the tip of her tongue gripped between her teeth in concentration. Lesa looked down at the red mass of ointment on her arm and could see no pattern until Ko spat on her arm and wiped the mess away to reveal a blood-red crescent moon identical to the tattoo on her own forearm. The old woman gave a grunt of satisfaction and wiped her arm clean.

'There you are, woman.' It was the first time Ko had called Lesa thus instead of 'child'. 'We will now make the oath and you will be a ninja Clanswoman of Death.'

## 52

His Honour Judge Joseph ('Jailing Joe') Jacoby liked adoptions; they made a welcome change from the depressing procession of fraud, robbery and murder trials that were his usual daily lot. He sat in his high-backed chair in his chambers reading slowly through the social workers' reports, indifferent to impatient stares and the occasional fidgeting of his visitors. The ceiling fan stirred the humidity without making it any more bearable. The fumes of central Victoria's grinding and revving traffic two floors below pervaded the very fabric of the room. The scales of Hong Kong's British justice were not burdened with the cost of upkeep of air-conditioning.

Mary Kendrew, the social worker who had compiled the reports, fiddled nervously with her handbag. Jailing Joe liked it to be known that he was not a social services rubber stamp. It was not unknown for him to adjourn an adoption hearing for more reports.

She was relieved when he finally looked up and smiled at Lesa. He decided that the exquisitely lovely young girl staring at him across the table was the most beautiful creature he had ever seen. Her dark eyes were quite round; decidedly not oriental, he thought. Her height, when she had first walked into his chambers, had surprised him: about five foot eight inches – he had never taken to the metric system. She was now staring back at him, not averting her gaze for even a second. 'Well, Lesa. You *have* been in the wars.'

'Yes, judge.'

It was no surprise that someone had primed her on the correct mode of address of a judge in chambers. The real surprise was her voice – the girl's correct pronunciation sounded more the product of Malvern College than a refugee camp.

'And you're happy to have Mr and Mrs Janson become your adoptive parents?'

Lesa nodded and smiled. 'Yes, judge. Very happy.'

'Mmm.' He turned to David and Carrie. 'I'm sure Mrs Kendrew has explained the responsibilities you will be shouldering if I grant this order?'

'Yes, judge,' David answered.

'You understand that Lesa will legally become your daughter as though she were your natural child. If you subsequently have children of your own, Lesa will be considered your eldest child.'

'We understand, judge.'

'You're returning to England, Mr Janson?'

'Yes, judge. We've brought our return forward to September so that Lesa will have a full academic year at school.'

'How do you feel about that, Lesa? Have you learned anything about England?'

'I've read a lot of Charles Dickens,' Lesa replied. 'And Enid Blyton.'

The judge looked taken aback. 'I hardly feel that those authors will have equipped you with a knowledge of modern day England, Lesa.'

'And modern authors: Leslie Thomas. *Stand Up Virgin Soldiers*.'

Judge Jacoby decided not to pry any further into Lesa's reading accomplishments. 'Any problems with the Foreign Office?' he asked Mary Kendrew. The new immigration act had stood the 1971 Immigration Act on its head. It was now possible to hold a British passport but with no right of abode in the United Kingdom for the holder.

'All taken care of, judge,' the social worker replied. 'Page twelve.'

It annoyed her that the miserable old bugger didn't take her word for it. He turned to the relevant page and read carefully before looking up at the gathering and saying, 'Very well. I see no reason why I shouldn't grant the adoption order.'

'There is one thing,' said Lesa suddenly.

All eyes turned on her.

Unabashed, she continued, 'Will it be possible for me to keep my second name?'

'Second name?' Judge Jacoby echoed, looking nonplussed.

'Wessex,' said Lesa.

'Lesa's very proud of the name given to her by the RAF crew who fished her out of the sea,' Mary Kendrew explained. 'They were flying a Westland Wessex helicopter at the time.'

The judge's face broke into a grin. 'Of course you can keep your name, Lesa. Any objections, Mr Janson? Mrs Janson? No? Very well – I will make it a condition of the order.'

## 53

The silence in the bedroom kept Lesa awake. From her hut in Vietnam to the hospital and then the camp, there had always been noise at night. The camp had been the worst, as could be expected with around two thousand hawking, spitting women and hundreds of babies sharing one open building. Then there was the feel of linen sheets and the silk pyjamas that Carrie had bought her on the way back from the courts. But the real heaven was feeling clean – really clean. The cleanliness that could only come from a long soak in a tub and a leisurely drying-off without being conscious of about twenty pairs of greedy male eyes watching her. Her experimental sniff at some talcum powder shaken into her hand had led to a bout of sneezing that had resulted in Carrie knocking on the door in alarm.

Lesa sat on the edge of the bed, listening to the silence. She crossed to the window and looked down at the gentle curve of Tolo harbour with its embracing silver thread of the Kowloon–Canton railway gleaming in the moonlight. The lights on the moored pleasure boats and sampans glittered and waivered in the hot night like candles in a draught.

David and Carrie rented a pleasant tenth-floor apartment in a block on the steep hillside below the Chinese University on the east coast of the Kowloon peninsula. For Lesa, the two-bedroom flat had been a revelation. For the first hour after her arrival she couldn't sit still, preferring to wander from room to room touching things while plying her new parents with endless questions. The most enjoyable part had been sitting at Carrie's dresser while Carrie helped her experiment with make-up. To David's amusement, they had spent nearly an hour together in front of the mirror, laughing conspiratorially together like a pair of schoolgirls. When they had finished, David could not recollect when he had last seen Carrie looking so flushed with happiness.

As Lesa stared down at the harbour and the luxury craft jostling each other at their moorings like bridesmaids trying to squeeze into a photographer's viewfinder, she realized that she was looking for the big white cruiser with the broad after deck upon which her family had been murdered.

The hunt had started.

## 54

The four weeks before the return to England were among the happiest of Lesa's life.

Her first adventure with Carrie while David was working was a Star Ferry trip to Hong Kong Island and then an exhilarating bus to Stanley Market where she was dazzled by the huge selection of clothes on the market stalls crammed into the narrow waterside streets. Far from being overwhelmed by the choice, she surprised

Carrie with her intuitive flair when it came to selecting clothes and shoes that suited her. She even picked out a pretty print dress for Carrie, brushing aside Carrie's protests that it was far too young, but which she bought anyway. Their last purchases were matching one-piece swimsuits. 'So that people will think we're sisters,' said Lesa, smiling happily as she held a decidedly skimpy costume against Carrie.

They were so weighed down with carrier bags at the end of their shopping spree that they had to return to Kowloon by taxi.

'I bought her a new watch,' Carrie confided in David that night. 'A nice Gucci copy but she put it in her pocket. She insists on wearing that cheap digital thing that I'm sure doesn't work.'

The next day the two women took off for a nearby beach armed with aluminium chairs and a freezer box so that Lesa could learn the curious European customs of changing under a towel and discovering that sand could get everywhere, covering one's skin with sticky gunk; lying in the sun getting burned; being stung by jellyfish, and eating gritty sandwiches. Carrie noticed the crescent moon tattoo on Lesa's forearm and accepted her explanation that it was something that the village kids used to do to each other. Highlight of the day was when they were chatted up by a determined party of American sailors from a 6th Fleet aircraft carrier. An ensign from Nebraska took a keen interest in Carrie and gave her ego a powerful boost by saying in answer to her query about his possible preference for older women that he had had no idea that she was an older woman.

They dozed during the hottest part of the afternoon. At one point Carrie became aware of a shadow falling across her. She opened her eyes. Lesa was on her feet, gazing fixedly out to sea – her lithe body rigid with tension and her fingers touching the fading scars on her shoulder.

'What's the matter, Lesa?'

'Listen!'

Carrie listened. All she could hear was some children playing in the sand and the sea breaking lazily on the beach.

'Listen to what?'

Then Carrie heard the muted beat of powerful marine diesels. A motor-yacht emerged out of the haze, heading for Tolo harbour. Lesa watched it for some moments. It was a schooner. She relaxed, flashed Carrie a smile and dropped back into her chair.

On their return from these adventures, David would listen to their animated accounts with an amused smile on his face. It was as if Carrie and Lesa had entered into an agreement to trade years: Carrie was getting younger – even the hard lines around her eyes were disappearing and she was taking a renewed interest in sex – while Lesa was advancing in years to her twenties and turning into an extraordinarily lovely young woman in the process.

'I owe you two so much,' said Lesa one evening when the three of them were enjoying a drink on the balcony of their apartment. They were relaxing after a tiring day spent packing.

David caught Carrie's eye and shook his head. 'No, Lesa. You must never think that. It's us who owe you everything.' He raised his glass. 'Here's to England.'

## 55

# SURREY, ENGLAND

Lesa made a better job of adjusting to living in England than her adoptive parents, largely because she had so much to learn and loved going to school. Merrow Grange was not the greatest centre of learning in southern England but it had a dedicated staff who took a real pleasure in responding to a gifted, eager learner like Lesa who was prepared to work hard and enjoy it, and who had such a seemingly insatiable thirst for knowledge.

David and Carrie's main problem was that neither of them liked the house in Guildford's expensive Flower Walk that David had inherited from his mother, but they were loath to sell it because the six-bedroom monster, with its acre of garden, was increasing in value at the rate of £750 per month. Even though Carrie had never really taken to Hong Kong, she was continuously irked by England's high prices and the poor quality of service in the shops. She could never understand why the owners of Guildford's multi-million-pound retail industry were happy to have their businesses run by semi-illiterate untrained children with names like Sharon and Debbie, who appeared to have received special training in manning checkouts with sulky expressions. It was all in sharp contrast to Hong Kong's hard-working, eager-to-please traders.

David's return to the BBC was not a happy one: the whole ethos of radio broadcasting had changed during his long absence. The notion of informing by entertaining had been elbowed aside to make way for worthy programmes with a decided left-wing slant. Also the Foreign Office cut in their grant-in-aid to maintain the BBC's external services had had a demoralizing effect on him and his colleagues. He stood it for a month and took advantage of his many contacts to land a well-paid job as public relations manager in the London office of a Far Eastern merchant bank.

David and Carrie's compensation was Lesa. She brought them immeasurable joy and happiness and they took tremendous pride in her considerable scholastic and athletic achievements. She turned out to be extremely popular if her wide circle of school friends, all girls, was anything to go by. The three of them celebrated Lesa's six O levels with a ruinously expensive weekend in Paris; here they discovered that Lesa's French teacher was probably right when he told them at an open night that their daughter was more accomplished in the French language than he was. On their return they made excited plans for the time when she would go to university.

Lesa shattered those dreams on a Saturday morning over breakfast. It was the last Saturday before the end of the summer break. Carrie was planning a shopping expedition for the three of them that afternoon to kit out their daughter in clothes and sportswear for the new academic year. Lesa waited until they were clearing away breakfast before she finally steeled herself to drop her bombshell.

'There's no point in going shopping this afternoon, Carrie.'

Carrie looked surprised. 'But we must, Lesa. You need new –'

'I don't need anything, Carrie.'

David looked up from loading the dishwasher. He saw the quiet resolution in Lesa's eyes. 'What's the matter, darling?'

Lesa avoided her parents' look of concern. 'I've got a job.'

Carrie smiled. 'A Saturday job? Well I think that's a marvellous idea but you might have told us.'

'I don't think she means that,' said David quietly. 'Do you, Lesa?'

Lesa shook her head. She felt sick at what she was doing but the compulsion was beyond her control. 'I've got a full-time job with Sky Surveys. Starting on Monday.'

The ensuing row had been as painful as it was protracted. Three hours of tears and recriminations from Carrie ended with Lesa storming out of the house and not returning until midnight.

David was waiting up for her. He made her a cup of coffee and set it before her on the kitchen table.

'Do you want anything to eat?'

She smiled, grateful for his calm. 'No – I'm fine thanks. I had a Wimpy and chips in town. How's Carrie?'

'Sleeping by now, I hope.'

'I've made up my mind, David. I'm going ahead with this job. I'm grateful for everything that you and Carrie have done for me. More than I can ever say. Carrie was wrong when she said that I was ungrateful –'

'She was upset,' David cut in. 'You've got to see it from her point of view.'

'I do. But you should also see things from *my* point of view. You've taught me to be independent so don't be surprised if I want to exercise that. I've got to lead my own life.'

He looked down at Lesa. It was hard to believe that the grave eyes regarding him were not those of an adult but of a sixteen-year-old until one remembered what she had been through. 'Yes,' he said heavily, uncertain as to what else he could say.

'I intend to study for my A levels at evening school. If I say I'll do something, you know me well enough by now to know that I'll do it. But I want this job. It means more to me than anything else right now.'

David poured himself a coffee and sat opposite Lesa. 'So tell me about it,' he invited.

She gave him a sheepish smile. 'It's nothing much. Not to start with. Sky Surveys are based at Fairoaks airport. I can get the train to Woking and use the Mann Avionics employees' bus from Woking Station. It's all worked out.'

He had seen that look of defiance in Lesa's eyes before and realized that he and Carrie would have no option but to climb down. He nodded. 'I see, Lesa. And what does this Sky Surveys do?'

'Aerial survey work for oil companies and mining companies. That sort of thing. They need a trainee cover librarian.'

David looked blank. 'What on earth are covers?'

'Stereo pairs, David. Aerial photographs. Thousands of them.'

### 56

On the train that took her to Woking for her first day at work Lesa experienced a terror that was even greater than the terror she had known on her first day at school. She was so accomplished at hiding her feelings that none of her new colleagues guessed her innermost emotions as they explained what was expected of her.

By the third day her fear had largely gone to be replaced by a worry that perhaps the job had been a mistake. Her rail fares, even a weekly season ticket for the short distance between Guildford and Woking, would take a substantial bite out of her meagre pay, and there was no one to give her proper training. From her first day at work, she was responsible for the storage, cataloguing and retrieval of nearly a quarter of a million aerial survey negatives and she had no help. She had to learn by her mistakes – by losing face in other words – and she hated it.

Sky Survey's customers ranged from local authorities bent on tracking down illegally-built garages and house extensions, to archaeology departments of universities looking for evidence of neolithic settlements, to mining companies on the look out for evidence of ore-bearing rocks. Their largest and most lucrative business, and one that involved the least amount of work as far as Lesa could see, was a government care, custody and maintenance contract for one hundred thousand covers originated by the Ministry of Overseas Development. The two founders of the company had left two years previously after a takeover, taking their enterprise and initiative with them, with the result that Sky Surveys jogged along, living off its library and the photo analysis skills of a shrinking team of researchers. It had added little to its library during the past year and was doing next to nothing to win new customers.

Despite her early misgivings, Lesa began to enjoy her work. She organized the library, brought the catalogue up-to-date and introduced an efficient system for booking out covers. After six months she had earned herself a substantial rise and was helping out in the photo analysis department when they were short-staffed by using the big stereo viewer for minor jobs such as checking the location of kelp beds for coastal authorities who were trying to stop their beaches being inundated with seaweed after every storm. Much of the photo analysis work was routine but she was learning. And learning fast.

Despite gaining a reputation for aloofness, she was a popular girl – well-liked by the all-male team of picture analysts who were more than willing to pass on their skills to her. Their obvious interest served to fan her feelings of guilt about herself and she found it difficult to respond to them in an equally friendly manner. She envied the style of a secretary who fended off male advances with a mixture of banter and good-natured mockery that called the sexual skills of the males into question. Lesa tried to imitate her style and found that sex and sexuality were a bitter, slow-dissolving pill that she knew she could never come to terms with. The only one whom she sensed did not sexually speculate about her, or if he did he was much too shy and polite to show it, was Darryl Grade – a bespectacled, hollow-cheeked young man of twenty-two whose arms and legs didn't seem to fit his body properly. He had an unhealthy, acneyed complexion best described as 'junk food yellow', and a dominating passion for computers that seemed to over-ride all other considerations and interests including girls. His clothes were the regulation dress of his age group: grubby jeans and T-shirt, both of which were marginally cleaner than usual on Mondays. No less an authority than an office rumour, which like all office rumours was concerned primarily with character assassination, maintained that these were the only items in his wardrobe and that he spent Sundays in a state of nakedness while he waited for them to dry. The same rumours maintained that Darryl was gay.

Sensing that Darryl's knowledge might be useful to her, and because he was the only male in Sky Surveys who didn't mentally undress her whenever she talked to him, Lesa used to deliberately seek out his company, much to the annoyance of the office lotharios. When the weather was fine they would sit on the rural airfield's grass perimeter at lunchtimes, watching Alan Mann's helicopters and executive aircraft coming and going while eating their sandwiches and putting the world to rights. It was during such a lunchtime that Lesa turned the conversation around to the subject of their employers.

'Why doesn't Jack Kelly buy in Landsat pictures?' she asked, referring to Sky Survey's general manager. 'Did you see those covers that RTZ did for the Chilean Government? All imaged from Landsat pictures.'

Darryl watched a Mann Avionics Bell helicopter performing stunts for a film crew. 'Cost,' he answered.

'You'd save on aircraft charter costs,' Lesa pointed out.

'And fear.'

She folded her arms around her shins and rested her chin on her knees. 'Fear of what?'

An executive jet landed. Darryl waited until it had shut down its engines before answering. 'Kelly doesn't understand the technology of satellite remote sensing therefore he's scared of it because it undermines his skills, therefore he latches onto its disadvantages and highlights them in his reports to head office. They're a bunch of accountants who don't understand any technology anyway except spreadsheets. As long as Sky Surveys goes on making some sort of profit, Kelly gets away with muddling along with his aeroplanes, and his Eyemo and Hulcher cameras that ought to be in the Science Museum. Sky Surveys are a microcosm of this country. We'll advance a technology far enough for it to do a job and then forget it because the people that understand science and technology are not allowed to become managers or politicians. That's why we've got a crap telephone system.' He pointed to a neat line of Cessnas and Pipers. 'That's why not one of those aircraft is British. The latest disaster is us turning our back on space because we don't understand it. That's why we have to go cap in hand to the French when we want to launch a satellite.'

Lesa seized the chance to bring the conversation around to what interested her. 'So what are the disadvantages of satellite photographs compared with conventional aerial photographs? Resolution?'

'That's the big problem. They may look good but there's nothing like the information on them that can be captured on a conventional five by five neg, and no one's come up with a sensible method of collecting rolls of film from satellites. But there are ways round that problem and the technology's in its infancy.'

Lesa was intrigued. 'What ways?'

Darryl looked uncertain. 'If you come to my house sometime, I'll show you my set-up.'

Two passing aircraft mechanics sat on the grass a few metres distant and watched Lesa, grinning. She realized that she was sitting in an immodest position but Darryl had not dropped his gaze once.

'When?' she asked, changing her posture and pulling the hem of her skirt over her knees.

For a moment he looked as if he regretted making the invitation. 'Well,' he said uncertainly. 'I'm not doing anything this evening.'

## 57

The back room of Darryl's semi-detached house in Woking was unbelievable. Lesa's eyes widened in astonishment.

'This is my shack,' Darryl explained. 'Sorry about the mess. Mind your step – there's cables everywhere.'

Mess was an understatement. One entire wall was taken up with floor to ceiling Dexion steel shelving that was bowing under the weight of oscilloscopes, spectrum analysers, signal generators and frequency counters. On one side of the French windows leading to the back garden was a workbench which was completely hidden under a mountain of the gutted remains of IBM computers, cannibalized power supplies, coils of wire, circuit board tools and soldering irons. The opposite wall was fitted with racks of television and computer monitors, satellite receivers together with a mass of amateur radio equipment that included UHF transceivers and antenna rotator control boxes. Lesa's eye followed a mass of co-axial cables and low-loss feeders that disappeared through a hole in the wall in the general direction of the back garden. The cables were strapped together into a bundle as thick as a man's leg.

'And that's my "clean" bench,' said Darryl pointing to a row of micro-computers. There were two BBC machines, a Commodore Amiga and several Taiwanese IBM PC clones. Dominating the electronic nightmare was the giant eye of a huge monitor computer with a screen nearly half a metre square. There was even a Xerox 4045 professional laser printer, and the number of IBM keyboards scattered everywhere suggested that they were breeding.

'This is nothing,' said Darryl sheepishly, seeing his guest's startled expression. He waved at the French windows. 'You should see the back garden.'

Stepping gingerly over a tangle of co-axial cables, Lesa looked out of the window at a forest of antennae. There was enough light left for her to see a ten-metre VersaTower topped with a mass of Yagi beam and co-linear antennae. There was a smaller tower that provided support for a cat's cradle of horizontal long-wire antennae. A number of steel uprights set in concrete blocks supported a weird assortment of steerable satellite receiving dishes aimed at the southern sky.

'Good heavens,' Lesa muttered. 'Don't the neighbours complain?'

'Oh, yes. But I'm a licensed radio amateur so the local authority turns a blind eye. My callsign is G1LXP – my ham friends call me the Licensed Ex-Pirate. I won't repeat what the neighbours call me. I live alone so there's no one else to complain.' He gave a disarming smile. 'That's why I bought this house. So I could live like a slob.'

Lesa gazed around the room. There was so much equipment it was impossible to see the original decor. 'Does it all work?' she inquired.

The question seemed to surprise Darryl. 'Well of course it all works. I haven't got room for anything that doesn't work.'

'Darryl,' she said slowly. 'I don't know how much these things cost but there must be at least a million pounds' worth of equipment here.'

'More like two million,' he admitted, tipping a pile of *Byte* computer magazines off a chair and offering it to Lesa.

She sat. 'How can you afford all this on your pay?'

Darryl grinned enthusiastically. 'That's the advantage of living in England's Silicon Valley. It's nearly all stuff that's been junked by the big companies.' He pointed to a hard disk that was connected by a ribbon cable to one of the IBM computers. 'That's a five-hundred-meg hard drive. They cost two thousand pounds new. I got it in a job lot for a tenner. All that was wrong with it was a dud stepper motor control chip costing a couple of quid. That big monitor I rescued off a skip in the Guildford Science Park. It's a Super Megascreen. One of five in the country. Four thousand lines resolution. List price new – sixty thousand dollars. A melted transformer in the main power supply and a blown protection diode. Luckily the tube was okay. It cost me four pounds to fix. And my VAX,' he pointed to a floor-standing cabinet, 'I found on a rubbish tip. It's old and it took a lot of fixing, but it's one of the fastest mini-computers around. Watch the big screen.' He threw a master switch and sat in a well-worn broken swivel chair in front of the giant screen. Several hard disks began whining up to operating speed. All the smaller computer monitors came alive with flashing standby prompts. Lesa watched as Darryl typed in an entry on a keyboard. He paused and polished his spectacles as though he was giving himself time to think.

'Lesa . . . you mustn't tell anyone about what I'm going to show you.'

'Why not?'

'I could lose my amateur radio licence and get done for God knows how much by the French for infringing copyright.'

'I'll keep quiet,' Lesa promised.

He fixed his owlish gaze on her. 'Do you swear?'

Her curiosity was aroused so she checked an impulse to snap back. Instead she replied mildly, 'Yes, Darryl – I swear.'

The answer seemed to satisfy him. He turned back to the keyboard and typed out another command line. A disk drive light on the VAX computer winked rapidly as the program loaded. An options menu appeared on the giant monitor. 'We'll start off with something simple,' he said, moving a scroll bar down the screen to highlight an option. He tapped the keyboard's enter key. Nothing happened at first. The hard disk clucked like a chicken and its light winked rapidly. 'Come and sit nearer,' he suggested.

They altered their positions so that Lesa was sitting in front of the giant monitor. The static from the intimidating screen tugged at strands of her hair, pulling it forwards. She brushed it back and glanced at Darryl who was sitting to one side with the keyboard across his knee. He was making a clear space on the bench to operate a computer mouse.

The screen turned dark blue. Superimposed on the blue were delicate spiral patterns of a lighter blue covered by flecks of white. Lesa knew it was a satellite picture but that was all.

'Plankton blooms off Chile,' Darryl explained. 'I grabbed that image last night. It's now stored on disk. Pretty, isn't it?'

Lesa thought it was one of the most beautiful satellite photographs she had ever seen. She knew enough about picture analysis to first sit back and allow her consciousness to absorb the whole image without concentrating on one particular area. As she did so, she became aware of the subtle variations of hue in the lighter blues. There were spirals within spirals.

'Variations in the bloom density,' said Darryl in answer to her question. 'And the spiralling is caused by the currents. You can learn more about ocean currents from a picture like that than a research ship on the spot.'

'Do you have a scaling graticule overlay?' Lesa asked.

Darryl laughed. 'No need to mess about with acetate overlay sheets any more. Let the VAX do all the work.' He tapped a key and a grid pattern of squares appeared on the screen. 'There you go. Each square covers ten degrees. The software even generates the right distortion into the grid to compensate for the curvature of the earth. See those islands?' He clicked a button on the mouse. A pointer appeared on the screen. He moved the pointer with the mouse to indicate a pattern of islands and clicked the mouse again. The monitor flickered. The pattern of islands jumped at Lesa to fill the entire screen. The grid pattern was still there. 'The whole screen now covers one degree,' Darryl continued. 'About a hundred kilometres. Each square is one kilometre. That's more of a track than a road.'

Lesa followed the mouse pointer that was picking out a dark line that traversed the largest island. 'And that must be a town or village and a harbour,' she said excitedly. She pointed to an irregular blotch on the island's east coast. Static from the screen tingled her fingertip.

'That's right.'

'Can you zoom in closer?'

Darryl clicked the mouse again.

Lesa gasped. What she was looking at was the equivalent of an aerial survey picture taken from a height of about thirty thousand feet. It was possible to make out the irregular streets of the shanty town. The contrasting mosaic patterns were the roofs of buildings. The natural harbour was formed by a wide break in the protective arm of a reef where several fishing boats were at anchor. 'That's amazing, Darryl.'

He shook his head. 'Not really. That's maximum resolution. You could put a viewer on that and you wouldn't see any more – just scanning lines.'

Lesa understood. With photographs the resolution went down to molecular or granular level depending on the quality of the film. With television pictures, the limiting factor was the number of lines the screen was capable of displaying.

'Even so,' said Darryl, 'they're the best pictures I've ever cribbed. A new French satellite. Real state of the art stuff. The most advanced optical remote sensing package in the world and they're launching another one next year that'll be even better.'

'Can you improve on that picture in any way?'

Darryl nodded. 'I've done some mods to the monitor. I can double its scan rate to give eight thousand lines.'

'What's the point if the information's not there on the original picture?' Lesa queried.

Darryl blinked in surprise. 'I didn't think you understood the problem.'

'Don't patronize me, Darryl.'

Darryl sensed the ice in her tone. The lovely eyes that turned on him were hard and relentless. She suddenly smiled and the tension was gone. 'Well? How can you improve the resolution of that picture?'

He swallowed nervously. 'I've written a piece of image-enhancing software that interrogates the information in each line and generates averaging pseudo-lines between the real lines.

'Show me.'

Darryl tapped a function key on his keyboard. The screen gave a momentary glitch as it synchronized to the new scan rate. Lesa gave a little gasp of surprise as the image suddenly sharpened. Now it was possible to discern individual buildings and even larger vehicles, but her attention was drawn inexorably to the boats in the harbour. She studied them for some moments, her delicate features drawn into a frown of concentration. 'Fantastic, Darryl,' she breathed, not taking her eyes off the screen. 'Absolutely amazing.'

He looked pleased. 'Of course, because the pictures are digital, it's relatively easy to play around with the contrast – change all the colour values and so on. It took me about three months to write the control program and another three months to debug it.'

Lesa laughed. 'No wonder you always look so flaked out at work. I thought it was an energetic love life.' She immediately regretted the joke because Darryl looked away in embarrassment. She added quickly, 'Sorry, Darryl – I had no idea you were so clever. Why on earth do you go on working for Sky? With your abilities you could get a job with one of the big companies.'

He smiled diffidently. 'I don't have a degree. I used to drive my parents up the wall because I spent all my time messing about with an old Commodore computer instead of studying.'

'Okay then. So why not set yourself up in business on your own account instead of working for Sky? You could make a fortune.'

He looked alarmed. 'I could never do that, Lesa. Those pictures are copyright material. All I'm doing is grabbing them off air from the satellite's down-link to Paris. If I started using them, the satellite's owners would do their nut. They'd have me extradited, cart me off to the Bastille and guillotine bits off me until I confessed.'

Lesa laughed. She liked Darryl's wry sense of humour.

'And there's the problem of control over the satellite. All I can do is nick pictures that someone else has commanded. I never know what pictures I'm going to get.'

'Could you obtain pictures legitimately?'

'Sure. By taking out a subscription with the satellite's owners.'

'Money?'

Darryl nodded. 'I don't know how much, but it's bound to run into thousands.'

Lesa thought fast. She had an idea that really needed carefully thinking through but she could not resist sounding it right away. 'Listen, Darryl. Why don't we set up a satellite survey business?

There's no end of work around. That week I worked for Jack Kelly when his secretary was off sick I spent typing letters turning down work.'

Darryl's owlish eyes seemed to pop in surprise behind his spectacles. 'For Christ's sake, Lesa. I know nothing about running a company and nor do you. Where would –'

'Of course we don't! But we could learn! Who's always moaning about lack of initiative in this country? Who's always going on about people not prepared to take risks?'

'What about capital?'

Lesa began to get angry. 'We don't need capital! This is your capital.' She waved her hand at the racks of equipment. 'And what you've got up here,' she tapped her head, 'except you're too scared to use it.'

It was Darryl's turn to show irritation. 'I need my job. I've got a crippling mortgage on this place. I can't afford to take risks.'

'You can't afford not to!' Lesa countered. 'What are you going to do with your life? Spend it working for peanuts for Sky?'

'I've got plans –'

'And that's all they will be unless you do something positive. This is the only life you're going to get, Darryl. It's not a dress rehearsal for another one. In thirty years' time you'll still be making plans and doing nothing about them. Except by then it'll be too late.'

'Be practical, Lesa – you need capital to start any business.'

Lesa looked at the Gucci copy watch that she kept pinned to her blouse. 'Oh hell – is that the time? My parents will kill me.' She jumped to her feet.

'I'll run you home,' Darryl offered.

Lesa opened her handbag and took out a notebook. 'What's the name of the satellite?'

'SPOT.'

'What?'

'My French is lousy. SPOT stands for *Système Pour l'Observation de la Terre*.'

58

Carrie was making toast and David was munching a Ryvita when Lesa dropped her bombshell on her long-suffering adoptive parents.

They gaped at their daughter. Lesa always broke shocking news at breakfast before her parents' customary two cups of coffee each had prepared them adequately for the day or her surprises.

Lesa forced herself to adopt a belligerent stance by staring back at them in turn as if she enjoyed disputes. 'Well? What's so unusual about someone setting up a company?'

'It's unusual for seventeen-year-old girls,' said David, feeling that he could use something stronger than Sainsbury's coffee. 'In fact you can't become a company director until you're eighteen.'

'You mean I've got to wait six months?'

'Fraid so, darling.'

'Damn!' She glared angrily at her parents as if they were personally responsible for the Companies Act.

Carrie cleared her throat. 'What did you have in mind, Lesa? A boutique or something?'

'A boutique! My God, you two just don't understand anything about me, do you? You never have and you never will!' She stormed out of the kitchen, slamming the door behind her.

'That explains all the business management books she's been getting out of the library,' David observed, buttering another Ryvita.

'You know,' said Carrie thoughtfully, 'that young lady's going to either fall flat on her face in life or be a dazzling success.'

David nodded his agreement and added, 'And I know which option I'll put my money on.'

## 59

Lesa spent her Saturday afternoon in Guildford giving her Midland Bank Griffin savings account a near-fatal hammering. Pale blue leather shoes, a white silk blouse, a pale blue worsted suit, matching gloves and a handbag. She studied her reflection in the shop's fitting room mirror, trying desperately to view her body with clinical detachment and failing miserably. Ko's lessons at the camp had never really sunk in. Lesa had discovered that the only way she could live with her guilt about her sexuality was to treat her body as a tool and looked after it accordingly. Nothing more. She never could take a pride in something that she knew men lusted after. And those men that did were worthy only of contempt. She was preparing her body now as a woodman would sharpen an axe before venturing into a strange forest to fell a tree and she loathed herself for what she was doing.

'Marvellous,' said the sales girl. 'You look like a business woman about to step into a TV commercial.'

Lesa smiled, showing nothing of her emotions. 'That's the general idea.'

'With your skin and make-up, the hat would be a mistake. It would hide your face. And besides – it makes you look like an air stewardess.'

Lesa removed the hat. 'I thought exactly the same.'

'Much better,' said the sales girl admiringly. 'What wouldn't I give to have skin like yours.'

'Try turning vegetarian.'

## 60

On Monday morning Lesa persuaded Carrie to phone Sky Surveys to say that she wouldn't be in to work because she was feeling sick. Carrie listened to her daughter singing in the shower and decided that she didn't *sound* sick. Nor did she *act* sick by spending an hour changing and making herself up. And she certainly didn't *look* sick when she came down the stairs looking like something out of *Vogue*.

'Good heavens, Lesa! You look stunning.'

Lesa was pleased. Since the big row over her refusal to stay on at school, she and her adoptive mother had settled down to a loving relationship largely because Carrie had seen the sense in David's advice that the only way they could hope to hold on to Lesa was if they treated her as an equal. Tough advice to follow, especially when you're convinced that a loved one is throwing their life away; but it had worked.

'You know,' said Carrie seriously as Lesa did a pirouette, 'I wouldn't be in the least surprised if one day I saw your photograph on the front of a magazine.'

'The *Police Gazette*,' Lesa joked.

'Let me guess. A job interview?'

'Yes – sort of.' A car hooted outside. Lesa gathered up her new handbag and gloves. 'That'll be my taxi – yes, it is. Goodbye, Carrie. Wish me luck.'

'Taxi?' Carrie queried as Lesa opened the front door. 'To go to a job interview?'

Lesa treated her reflection to a quick, final inspection in the hall mirror. To Carrie it was a perfectly natural gesture. She had no inkling of the sickness that was churning in Lesa's stomach as her adopted daughter headed down the drive to the waiting car. 'I don't want to get this outfit messed up using public transport,' Lesa called out over her shoulder.

Carrie watched the graceful figure sliding into the back of the saloon car taxi. The driver had jumped out to hold the rear door open because he wanted to get a closer look at those legs.

'Traffic's not too bad this morning,' he said as he turned the car out of the Flower Walk. 'Should be at Heathrow in an hour.'

Lesa settled back in the seat cushions, closed her eyes and fought back the rising wave of nausea. 'One more step, Neti,' she whispered to herself. 'One more tiny step but we're getting there.'

## 61

'I was worried about you,' said Darryl the next day during their lunchbreak. 'I called your mother but she said you were sleeping.'

Lesa lay back on the grass. It was a warm, sunny day. The misery of the previous day when she had been forced to use her body to impress men was already fading to a bad memory. 'Good old Carrie,' she murmured.

'Who's Carrie?'

'My mother. My adoptive mother.'

Darryl looked owlishly down at her. All he knew about this strange girl was that she was the most determined and single-minded person he had ever come across. For a month she had bullied him until he had eventually agreed to set up an earth resources surveillance company with her. It was crazy. She was only seventeen!

'Actually I was in Paris,' said Lesa sitting up and opening her handbag.

'Paris! What were you doing in Paris?'

Lesa smiled at his alarmed expression. 'I went to see the owners of SPOT.'

Darryl flopped back on the grass. 'Oh no. And you showed them some screen shots I suppose?'

'Oh yes.'

'Lesa – what have you done!' Darryl wailed. 'They'll be round to blow off my kneecaps!'

'Actually they're very charming, helpful people.' *Except the one who stared at my legs all the time.* 'Their director of operations complimented you on your resolution. They were most impressed and wanted to know how you had broken their encryption. I couldn't help them on that but I've done a little deal with them.'

'Let me guess. You're to blow off my kneecaps for them?'

Lesa unfolded a letter and showed it to Darryl. He blinked at it. 'It's in French.'

'That's probably because SPOT's owners are French. They have this touching emotional attachment to their language. They're a commercial concern – they're in business to make a fast franc, but I don't think I would have got anywhere with them if I didn't speak some French. They've given us written permission to use SPOT-originated images in our pre-launch promotional material free of charge. Once we've started trading, we have to negotiate a subscription deal with them.' She brushed the letter playfully against his nose. 'What this means, young Darryl, is that we'll have to save our pennies to pay for the printing of a promotional package using the best covers in the world that'll have every organization in Europe that requires optical remote sensing services beating a path to our door.'

## 62

David drained his third cup of coffee and looked around the restaurant to catch the waiter's eye. They had just finished a pleasant lunch together in the Café de Paris – the best and most expensive restaurant in Guildford.

'This is on me, David,' said Lesa. Before he had a chance to object, she continued, 'If I was still at school, I wouldn't be able to do this.'

'If you were still at school, young lady, I wouldn't let you wear skirts as short as you do. Why do you do it?'

'Do what?'

'Wear such short skirts. You seem to have no time for boys, so why? What are you trying to prove?'

Her voice went cold. 'It's called capitalizing on one's assets.'

'It's called being a brazen little hussy.'

Lesa's hard stare dissolved into a slow smile. There were times when she felt that David could read her mind; it alarmed her that any man could have even a hint of an insight into what she perceived as the black pit of emotions that she barely faced herself. But then David wasn't any man — he was the one person to whom she had told the story of that terrible day in the South China Sea. What she had never told him was that she re-lived those moments each day of her life and that her every action was shaped around her blind obsession to destroy the bull-chested man and his three companions.

'Actually, David, you're not far wrong. What I have to ask you is pretty brazen.'

'Ha! I thought this was more than a celebration of you scraping yourself and my car through your driving test. Okay. Break it to me gently.'

'You once told me that you and Carrie had set aside six thousand pounds for me when I'm twenty-one.'

David nodded. 'Hopefully it'll be a lot more than that in three years.'

'I'd like some of it now.'

He had been half-expecting this. 'How much?'

'About four thousand.'

'I know: to set up this company you've got a . . .' He was about to say 'bee in your bonnet about' but wisdom intervened. The only thing one could predict about Lesa's temper was that it was unpredictable. Instead he finished the sentence with '. . . got a thing about?'

'Yes.'

'Tell me about it.'

Lesa talked for ten minutes, outlining her plans and hopes and aspirations as she wanted David and the world to perceive them.

David was silent for some moments when she had finished talking. He stared down at his coffee cup that the waiter had just refilled. 'Lesa . . .'

'Yes?'

'God — whatever I say, I'm going to sound like a heavy father. This is all wrong what you're planning. Now is the time of life when you should be using your freedom to enjoy yourself, form relationships. To learn about people.'

'You mean boys?'

'Well — yes.'

'You of all people should know just how unlikely that is.'

162

David could think of nothing to say that would not alienate her still further.

'Will you help me?' Lesa pressed.

David raised his eyes and wondered how much self-esteem Lesa had sacrificed to arrange this lunch and plan what she had to say. Also he knew that he could refuse that exquisite face nothing.

'How about getting work?' he asked.

'No problem. Sky are turning down contracts every week. Darryl and I have been building up a database of likely customers for a mail shot.'

'Don't do that. You'll spend a fortune on a presentation folio and it'll be binned along with all the other junk mail. Lay on a full-blown presentation at an hotel with a buffet and everything. That way you'll get to know your potential customers on a personal basis right from day one. Believe me, darling – I know what I'm talking about.'

'I could do with your help, David.' Her face softened into a smile. 'Your PR knowledge would be invaluable.'

'Lesa,' he said seriously, 'nothing would give me greater pleasure. But the real help is money – right?'

'Yes.'

'And you and Darryl have agreed on a fifty-fifty split on the company's shares?'

'Yes. His contribution is the free loan of two million pounds' worth of equipment plus his talent. My contribution is all a bit hazy. I'll be the salesman, secretary, cover analyst and general dogsbody.'

'And you'll be putting up the working capital?'

'Yes.'

'Have you got a name for the company?'

'Systemation.'

'Sounds snappy. Premises?'

'We'll use Darryl's house for as long as we can get away with it. After two years we should have enough behind us to look for somewhere more suitable. We'll need high ground to give us a good window on the polar low earth orbit remote sensing satellites that'll be operating from next year.'

'You seem to have thought of everything.'

Lesa sighed. 'I hope so, David.'

He thought for a few moments and came to a decision. 'I'll have to square it with Carrie,' he said slowly, 'but I reckon you'll need the lot right away. There's a thousand and one expenses connected with registering and launching a company. Carrie's also got some money of her own earmarked should you ever get married. She has dreams of a lavish wedding for you because we couldn't afford one when we got tied.'

Lesa's expression was serious. 'I don't think I'll ever get married, David.'

'No,' he agreed sadly, 'I don't think you ever will either.'

'Maybe I will, to my company. That way you'll live to hear the splatter of tiny bankruptcies.'

David laughed and raised his wine glass. 'To Systemation.'

The presentation at the Hog's Back Hotel, just west of Guildford and one of the highest hotels in southern England, was a success although it came perilously close to being a disaster. It was attended by over a hundred representatives of the country's mining, geological and construction interests. An influential permanent under-secretary and two members of his staff at the Department of Trade and Industry also attended – largely because they were unable to resist the temptation of a flight in and out of London in an Alan Mann helicopter that Lesa had chartered at a special rate.

The plan had been for David to conduct the presentation. He and Lesa had worked for hours over the wording so that everything important would be conveyed in the ten minutes that David had insisted was the maximum time for a speech before people became bored.

Two hours before the guests arrived, he sprang the surprise he had been saving. He took Lesa to one side and said, 'This is your show, Lesa – you've got to deliver the presentation.'

She stared at him in horror. 'But I can't!'

'Why not?'

'Because I can't!'

He put his hands on her shoulders. 'Because you're scared of men looking at you? Come on – be honest with me, Lesa.'

She looked away. David was one person she couldn't lie to.

'You've got to do it, Lesa. It's your show. It's what you've worked for. I know what you're fighting against. Believe me, if you can go through with this, you will have taken a step towards beating it.' He turned her chin so that she had to look into his kindly eyes. For a moment the anger he saw nearly weakened his resolve. 'Give it a try, Lesa.'

'It doesn't look as if I have much choice, does it?'

Two hours later the gathering fell silent when Lesa stepped onto the podium. The sudden quiet nearly unnerved her. She read slowly to avoid making a mistake and in so doing got her timing just right.

The guests listened with interest and made approving noises at the breathtaking live feeds from SPOT via the dish and receiver that Darryl had rigged up in the hotel's car park. The date and time of the presentation had been Darryl's idea; it was no coincidence that SPOT had a particularly good window on the United Kingdom at the precise moment when Lesa logged into the satellite to display its images on the projection screen. No one questioned her statement that development of the remarkable image enhancing system that they were witnessing had cost two million pounds.

'She's brilliant,' a senior executive from ICI whispered to David and Carrie, not knowing who they were. 'Any idea how old she is?'

'About twenty-five, I think,' Carrie whispered back, wondering what the executive would think of the unbent truth – that the elegant young woman he was paying such close attention to was eighteen.

For the first two years of the fledgling company's life Lesa had her own room at Darryl's house. For two years they worked up to eighteen hours each day, seven days a week, rarely taking breaks and having virtually no social life. They would both work on cover analysis, spending hours in front of the giant screen until their eyes ached. When SPOT was unfavourably placed, Lesa would write professional-looking reports for Systemation's customers, preparing the text on a word-processor and typesetting them using a desk top publishing system, while Darryl serviced their equipment and experimented with new imaging techniques to take advantage of the many new remote sensing satellites coming into service.

Lesa's particular interest in the Far East coincided with a huge increase in piracy in the Pacific Basin as a result of China's 'open door' policy aimed at increasing trade with the West. It was piracy on a scale that made the Spanish Main raiders of previous centuries look like street-corner muggers. In 1988 cargoes totalling one hundred million pounds were hi-jacked in the South China Sea. The identities of the seized ships were changed and re-registered by corrupt officials in flags of convenience countries. A concern destined to become the world's largest insurance company – the Chinese People's Insurance Company – became one of Lesa's biggest customers after she provided evidence that led to the recovery of a five-thousand-tonne coaster and its two-million-pound cargo of plywood. The retainers paid out by the company financed Systemation's SPOT subscription charges enabling Lesa to devote most of her free time, which was little enough, to the search for the luxury cruiser whose details were etched so deeply into her consciousness that she had no need to refer to her drawings. Many of her searches were detailed examinations of images held on Systemation's hard disks. If Systemation had had the resources, she would have logged into SPOT more often for up-to-date covers. There was always the nagging worry that she might locate the cruiser on a week-old image but not be able to find it in real time due to the access charges she would incur with SPOT. As it was, Systemation was having to struggle to survive. The turnover was healthy enough but, despite a favourable contract with the owners of SPOT, the subscription payments for use of the satellite were a heavy burden, made worse early in 1989 when there was a sudden upsurge in the numbers of Vietnamese refugees fleeing across the South China Sea to Hong Kong.

Her first inkling of the new exodus was on a Sunday morning when Darryl was visiting his parents. The picture had been taken an hour earlier. There was something unusual on the edge of the image. What she saw when she did a first-level enhancement caused a sickness to churn in her stomach. It was a large sampan some twenty miles off Hong Kong. Her fingers trembled as she clicked the mouse pointer to count the numbers of her countrymen and women crowded onto the half-swamped craft. She gave up when the counter was registering seventy – there could be that number again below. She called the Royal Hong Kong Police, explained who she was, and gave them the sampan's position – impressing on the inspector the urgency of the matter. He called her back two hours later and confirmed that the sampan had been taken in tow.

It was the first and last time that the police were co-operative. Hong Kong had had enough; the dependency could no longer cope. By March 1989 the majority of new arrivals were being treated as illegal immigrants.

June 1989 brought the horror of the massacre of students in Peking – the month in which Chinese communism lost its hold on the future but not on the present. It was Darryl who identified the pit outside the city as a mass grave. It was he who insisted that the image would have to be sold to the highest bidder. 'Our first duty is to survive,' he told Lesa, and she was forced to reluctantly agree.

The world exclusive on the dreadful picture was auctioned for ten thousand pounds. The money enabled Systemation to survive – but only just.

## 65
## 1991

A lucky break occurred in the spring: Lesa was logging plankton blooms in the North Atlantic off Boston for the United Nations Bureau of Fisheries Research when a ship showed up in the same position on two consecutive orbits of SPOT. It was still in the same position on the third orbit.

'Darryl. We've got a ship in trouble.'

Darryl checked Lesa's findings and confirmed that the three covers showed no appreciable movement of the ship other than would be due to windage and drift. Twenty-thousand-tonne ships at sea do not drift unless they are having serious engine problems.

'I think we'd better run some high-level enhancing on these covers before we sound the alarm,' he suggested.

After thirty minutes the VAX computer had extracted all the information it could from the pictures and displayed the results on the giant screen. Darryl zoomed to maximum readable enlargement. He and Lesa spotted the anomaly at the same time and arrived at the same conclusion.

## 66

Drew Hawkins, an Environmental Protection Agency officer at the American embassy in London arrived two hours later, bemused by the fact that Systemation's address turned out to be a semi-detached house in Woking.

He studied the enhanced covers. Although no expert on photo analysis, he conceded that Lesa and Darryl were right – the ship was definitely using her derricks to lift containers from her hold and was dumping them in the sea. Conclusive evidence showed when Darryl converted the prints to thermal images that depicted the containers in false colours as blotches of crimson. There was one patch of crimson a length away from the ship.

'They're hot,' said Lesa cryptically. She compared the images with a colour chart. 'About sixty degrees celsius. My guess is that whatever's in those containers is as radioactive as the core of a nuclear reactor.'

### 67

The embassy official phoned them the next morning. Lesa took the call.

'We're very grateful to you for blowing the whistle on this one, Miss Wessex. The ship was arrested by two coast guard cutters last night with three containers still in her aft hold. The *Milandos*. Panamanian-registered of course. According to her manifest she was sailing in ballast from Brest to Boston. We think she's a ship we lost track of two months ago when she left Singapore.'

'Glad to have been of service, Mr Hawkins,' said Lesa, trying to think of the best way of capitalizing on this latest contact.

'We'll need you to give evidence, Miss Wessex.'

Lesa had visions of having to visit America leaving Darryl to soldier on alone. 'That's going to be difficult. There's only the two of us here.'

'You'll be able to give sworn depositions at the embassy. And you'll be able to recover your expenses.'

### 68

Lesa duly supplied a deposition together with photographs and supporting documentation. She also included an invoice for fifteen thousand pounds plus VAT for professional services rendered.

'They'll never wear that,' Darryl declared.

A month later a cheque arrived for the full amount.

'That's it,' said Lesa resolutely. 'Whenever we're slack, we'll become bounty hunters.'

Darryl knew better than to argue with his partner. He rarely won disputes and subsequent events tended to always prove Lesa right. This was no exception. Her decision came at a time when illegal dumping of hazardous industrial waste at sea was becoming big business on a large enough scale to attract the interest of organized crime. During the next six months Systemation provided evidence of six illegal dumpings at sea, resulting in a big jump in the company's turnover.

By the following spring conditions in Darryl's house had become intolerable with filing cabinets filling the hall and the two downstairs rooms crammed with equipment. Lesa's bedroom also had to serve as her office. There were ways around the problem of entertaining clients but the inevitable clash of their personalities led to their first major row which came close to ending their partnership. It had started with Darryl objecting to Lesa's noisy exercises late at night.

'Why the hell do you have to spend an hour every bloody night kicking the wall when you know I'm trying to sleep?'

The argument that followed was bitter and protracted. It ended with Lesa saying that they would have to find proper premises.

With the aid of a £750,000 mortgage that their bank willingly supplied, they purchased Whitefriars Farm on the south-facing slopes of Hog's Back, within a kilometre of the Hog's Back Hotel where they had held their launch presentation.

After a lot of persuasion, Guildford Borough Council eventually agreed to the property's change of use. Once purchased, Lesa launched a successful appeal with the Department of the Environment against the restrictions that the Council wanted to impose on the erection of satellite receiving dishes near the farmhouse. She argued that four million houses in south east England now had their own Amstrad dishes bolted to their walls to receive DBS television from three Astra TV satellites and that Systemation's dishes would hardly be seen from the main road even though her dishes were much bigger than Amstrad's Sugar bowls.

It was an ideal site with uninterrupted views of the sky from horizon to horizon. The ten-bedroom bargate stone farmhouse had ample accommodation for offices and analysis rooms. Also Darryl had plenty of laboratory space to develop new microwave sensing equipment that the company would need if they were to remain competitive into the twenty-first century.

The magnificent views and the quiet were conducive to the intense concentration that Systemation's work demanded. Lesa decided to improve the view by having the lake at the foot of the slope cleaned and stocked with fish.

'A waste of money,' Darryl complained.

'We can sell the fishing rights to the highest bidder,' Lesa countered. 'not to angling clubs but to individuals. That way we make a lot more money and we have a pleasant scene to look out on.'

Lesa sprang another surprise the day after the lake-cleaning contractors had finished work. It was a warm summer's evening. Darryl was about to drive home when Lesa collared him as he was climbing into his Mercedes.

'Come and see what I've bought,' she said excitedly, grabbing his arm.

'Can't it wait until tomorrow?' he complained. 'I'm knackered.'

'No – it can't. Come on.'

Still protesting that he was tired, Darryl allowed himself to be dragged past his miniature forest of satellite dishes down to the lakeside where a man was leaning out of a Range Rover, cautiously reversing what appeared to be a miniature horsebox close to the water's edge. Darryl groaned. 'Don't tell me you've bought some ponies, Lesa.'

She looked blankly at her partner. 'Why would I want to do a crazy thing like that? What use are ponies?'

'Ready, miss?' inquired the man.

'Fine,' said Lesa happily. 'Can I let them out?'

'Go ahead.'

Darryl watched in bewilderment as Lesa released the latches on the rear of the box and lowered the ramp to the ground. She peered inside and clapped her hands in delight. 'Oh, they're beautiful!' She made noises to encourage whatever was in the box to emerge. Two magnificent white birds with impossibly long legs fluttered out of the box like agitated ballerinas and splashed into the water. They beat their wings to stretch them after their journey and stood looking suspiciously about them. One of them chanced a quick drink, lifting its slender bill to the sky to swallow.

'Storks!' breathed Darryl.

'Storks!' echoed the man indignantly, closing the box. 'They're not storks – they're cranes. Finest sarus I've ever bred. I've clipped their primary wing feathers, miss. Not too much – they'll grow in a few months. They can still fly but the effort will put them off. It'll give them a chance to get used to it here. They'll be a bit nervous at first but give them time and they'll soon get to know you. Keep the fish stocks up and they won't want to leave.' He climbed behind the wheel of his Range Rover and started the engine. 'I'll call back next week to see how they are and I'll bring a couple of sacks of winter concentrates. Cheers.'

The Range Rover moved off leaving Darryl and Lesa contemplating their latest acquisitions.

'Aren't they magnificent?' said Lesa happily. 'And before you start whingeing, I bought them with my own money and the lake's overstocked anyway.'

Darryl shook his head. 'Why, Lesa? You're such a practical girl and yet you do daft things like this. Most people would be happy with a budgie.'

She smiled and kissed him on the cheek. 'In Vietnam we believe that cranes are the souls of people sent from heaven to bring good luck.'

'Not good luck for the fish though,' Darryl observed as one of the birds suddenly jabbed its bill into the water and gulped down a small carp. 'Well – I'm off home. I shall leave you to contemplate your foolish ways. Hey, do you reckon they'd have some meat on them by Christmas?'

He had to duck as Lesa stooped and hurled a clod of mud at him. He reached the converted farmhouse and looked back at the lake. To his surprise the two birds had allowed Lesa to draw near and reach out her hands to touch them.

## 70

Lesa was right about the cranes bringing good luck. Two months after they had moved into their new premises, Sky Surveys went into liquidation. Lesa took on three of their photo analysts and a secretary. She also bought the cover library for a knockdown price together with all her old employer's office furniture.

'We've come the full circle,' Darryl observed as the furniture was unloaded from a truck.

Lesa shook her head. 'Just the first revolution, Darryl.'

There were setbacks but on the whole Systemation prospered thanks to Darryl quickly developing the hardware to take advantage of the awesome power of SPOT 9. The new satellite was launched into a polar orbit from Andoya on the Norwegian coast. As it orbited the earth from pole to pole, so the earth rotated beneath it, and so every square centimetre of the earth's surface passed beneath its two-metre diameter staring eye during each cycle of orbits. SPOT 9 was more than an optical satellite; its remote sensors could see into infrared at the low end of the spectrum, right up into microwave frequencies at the top end of the spectrum. Systemation was the only company that could utilize its formidable powers to the maximum. Towards the close of the twentieth century, the United States Department of Environmental Protection was employing Lesa's skills to nail illegal dumpers and shop hi-jackers on a regular basis.

So effective was her evidence that it became necessary for elaborate precautions to be taken from early on to conceal her identity and the name of her company on her depositions and affidavits. Drew Hawkins, who was now her control at the US embassy, had even furnished her with false passport cards with fictitious identities for use when visiting different countries to deliver such depositions and affidavits on behalf of the United States Environmental Protection Agency; therefore her reaction when he warned her that her Hong Kong cover had been compromised was one of disbelief.

'Nonsense,' she said dismissively to the embassy official over lunch in London. They were celebrating the recovery of a United States bulk carrier, *Eastern Bonanza*, that had been seized by pirates a day out of Jakarta bound for Japan with a ten-million-dollar cargo of hardwood. There had been twelve such celebratory lunches during the ten years of their partnership.

'It's true, Lesa,' said Hawkins earnestly. 'We know that Hugo Sukarno has got a description of you. And he's discovered your Hong Kong cover name – Liz Collins.'

Lesa raised her eyebrows at the mention of Hugo Sukarno. His Hong Kong-based Sukarno Shipping Company had been linked with several illegal dumpings of toxic industrial waste at sea but the wily racketeer had always successfully pleaded his innocence by citing the complex web of worldwide companies registered in off-shore tax havens that leased and re-leased his ships. He had convinced several courts that as a ship owner, he could not be held responsible for the activities of those who leased his ships.

Lesa toyed with food. 'Have you got any concrete evidence for this, Drew?'

Hawkins felt in his pocket and pushed a slip of paper across the table. Lesa unfolded it and studied the neat columns of Cantonese kanji characters.

'That's a photocopy of a document found on one of Sukarno's men when the Hong Kong People's Police pulled him in for questioning yesterday,' he explained. 'We've got an agreement with the police that they pass on everything about Sukarno. It's a description of you, Lesa: height, colour of eyes; everything. As far as they're concerned there's nothing incriminating about someone being in possession of a description of a girl. They accepted his explanation that it was a description of a hooker he had once met who had pleased him and that he was anxious to meet again.'

Lesa smiled. 'There must be millions of women throughout Asia who are the same height as me with the same colour eyes.'

'How many have a tattoo of a half moon on their left forearm and always wear a brooch watch in addition to a cheap, old-fashioned digital watch on their wrist?'

Lesa's smile faded.

Hawkins leaned forward across the table. 'Tell me exactly what happened on last month's trip to Hong Kong.'

'I faxed you a report.'

'Go over it again.'

'Well – I gave Judge Wu Peng an affidavit on the dumping by the *Aikido Warrior* and left him a set of nested zoom-in covers showing the dumping taking place.'

'Who else did you talk to?'

'No one apart from immigration officials and a taxi driver. I arrived at Kai Tak at eleven o'clock and took a taxi to the judge's apartment in Kowloon. He let me in. He was alone. He made me coffee, took my affidavit, and I caught the midnight return flight to London. I didn't stay overnight because I didn't want to be away from the office for too long.'

'Did you wear a short-sleeved dress?'

Lesa thought for a moment. 'Yes, but I wore a jacket . . . But I remember taking it off because it was warm in his apartment.'

'So Judge Wu saw your tattoo?'

'I suppose so. Why?'

Hawkins nodded knowingly. 'That's how Sukarno's got hold of your cover name and description, Lesa. From Judge Wu.'

'That's absurd. He's the most incorruptible man I've ever met.'

'How corrupting can having one's fingernails pulled off be, I wonder?'

Lesa stared at Hawkins. 'What the hell are you driving at?'

'And not just his fingernails: Judge Wu's body was found three days ago in his apartment when his cleaner called. He had been tortured to death.' He took hold of Lesa's hand and held it tightly when she tried to pull it away as he knew she would. 'Listen, Lesa. Don't scoff at me over this. I know I'm sounding melodramatic, but I know what these people are like. Your life's in real danger if they find out who you are. You're a number one target because you've damaged a billion-dollar racket. Don't make any more trips to the Far East until we or the Chinese have nailed Sukarno.'

# SOUTHERN ENGLAND December 31 2000

Lesa, her parents, Darryl, and most of Systemation's twenty employees left the party and gathered at the upstairs office windows of Whitefriars where they could see across southern England as far as the South Downs. It was a perfectly clear night. A television was on in the background, relaying the closing moments of the twentieth century from the capital cities of Europe. Darryl was trading jokes with Carrie. He had changed little and had the same owlish, hollow-cheeked expression although his taste for expensive clothes had nearly banished the impoverished look that he had favoured when Lesa had first met him. In all other respects he was the same dependable Darryl with an ability to forget minor inconveniences such as eating and sleeping when working on a problem in his lavishly-equipped laboratory.

Big Ben started chiming midnight. On the first stroke of the hour the caretaker put a torch to the mountain of faggots that had been built on the highest point of Whitefriars' grounds. The flames roared up the kerosene-primed bonfire, hurling sparks into the night sky and throwing dancing patterns on the clusters of satellite dishes that were staring at the moon like pagan monoliths. Points of light answered from across the landscape, and the giant bonfire on the Devil's Dyke forty kilometres to the south burned sharp and clear in the frost-bitten air.

The guests linked arms and started singing 'Auld Lang Syne' but Lesa continued staring out across the landscape that was now alight with hundreds of flickering points of light. Smoke from their bonfire curled like ectoplasm across the lake. A pair of arms encircled her waist from behind.

'Must be quite a sight from the air.' It was David's voice. Lesa agreed and fell silent. She covered David's hand with her own. She liked the feeling of closeness with him. He was the only man who could touch her without unleashing the black monster that was always waiting to well up inside her. Her long, slender fingers closed over his hands and he could feel the tips of her nails pressing into his skin like warning daggers.

'Of course,' he went on, 'I still think we should have celebrated a year ago. I know the year 2000 was the last year of the old century but it doesn't seem right. What's the matter, darling?'

Lesa shivered. 'Oh nothing . . . I just feel I've failed.'

'Failed? You own fifty per cent of a company valued at five million and you call that failure?'

'You wouldn't understand.'

'Oh, Lesa . . . Lesa . . . listen to me. I'm not as clever as you, but I'm not stupid. Do you think I don't know why you've done all this? Why you've specialized in the Far East? All those trips to Shanghai, Macau and Hong Kong?'

She made no move but he felt her body go rigid. Her nails dug even harder into the backs of his hands. When she spoke, her voice was a whisper. 'You've known? How could you know?'

'Because I remember your expression all those years ago when we first met – when you told me your story. I've still got an English transcript of the tape. Whenever you've driven us to despair, I've read that transcript and it's always helped us to understand.'

They stood in silence for some moments, watching the bonfires flickering like distant fireflies in the night. Lesa's gaze was fixed on the brightest light – the bonfire on the Devil's Dyke. It was a brilliant star shining out of the darkness like a beacon that seemed to be reproaching her.

*I'm sorry, Neti. I've tried and tried. Please forgive me. Please!*

'Will you give up now?' David asked as though he were reading her thoughts. 'They must be scattered all over the world by now.'

It was as if he had given Lesa an electric shock. 'No!' she said with sudden vehemence. She turned to face him – her eyes ablaze with a quiet but consuming passion. 'That's something I'll never do until I've killed every one of those animals!'

# PART THREE
# Diem

Never-flinching labour proved lord of all.

*Georgics*, Virgil

# 1

# HONG KONG

There are few experiences in air travel to match a night arrival at
Kai Tak airport. Whereas most airports serving the world's major
capitals are sited several kilometres outside their respective cities,
Kai Tak is located almost in the centre of Kowloon's bustling
metropolis.

Lesa gazed out of A340 airbus's window at the apartment blocks
that were passing within five hundred metres of the starboard wing.
Her previous Kai Tak arrivals were scant preparation for the shock,
when glancing up from a book or newspaper, of seeing buildings so
close to. She could see a couple having what looked like a heated
argument in a living room that was actually higher than she
was.

'Your first trip to Hong Kong?' inquired a voice at her elbow.

It was the serious-looking young man in the seat beside her. Since
leaving London twelve hours previously Lesa had avoided being
drawn into conversation with him by reading or watching movies
on her Sony Viewman. She had sampled some of the hundred
movies in the British Airways flight library but the problem with
watching a movie on the screen set into the back of the seat in front
of her was that the young man had attempted, in a friendly way, to
make it a shared experience by passing comments on the action.

She turned her gaze from the crazy neon splendour of Kowloon
and regarded the young man. It was the first time she had really
looked at him.

Hitherto the young man's only brushes with fear in his cloistered
life had been on the ski slopes of Cortina or on the even steeper
slopes of his company's sales graphs. But this time, when his eyes
met those of this extraordinarily beautiful girl at his side, he knew
fear. Real fear. A fear that uncoiled in his guts like a malignant
serpent to crush whatever resistance his soul might offer up to
counter this terrible dread. The dark eyes bored into his very being,
dispassionately turning over the complexities of his character, his
ambitions, his likes and dislikes. He saw nothing of her face – it

was a blur. He saw nothing of her lithe body clothed in a skintight Lorietta travel suit with its tiny conditioner clipped to her waist. All the details about her that he had covertly assimilated during the long flight from London were burned out of his consciousness while her awesome stare held him skewered and helpless like a butterfly pinned to a display panel. The dreadful sensation lasted only for a few seconds until she spoke.

'No,' she said simply in perfect English. 'I've been to Hong Kong before.'

He was saved from making a reply by the airbus thumping down on the runway and voiding 150 banshee tonnes of reverse thrust into the night.

2

The Chinese immigration officer fed Lesa's passport card through his reader without bothering to look at her. There was a pause while the system searched for a satellite gateway to the EEC central police computer in Paris. Once through, everything that was known about the girl plus the information on the card's magnetic strip was merged with the data on the People's Immigration Service computer and scrolled onto his concealed monitor. There was no flashing cursor bar on the screen to indicate unpaid fines or serious unspent criminal convictions, and the hologram picture that the Paris computer mapped onto his screen was a good match with the girl standing before him.

Her name was Lesa Wessex. Nationality: British. Occupation: company director. Born: South Vietnam, August 3, 1970. International Credit Rating: 8 – not rich, but by no means poor. Other information: entered Hong Kong as refugee 1985. Closed camp detainee. Repatriated to United Kingdom 1985. Two previous visits to Hong Kong since then but none during the last five years. Distinguishing marks: tattoo on left forearm and scar on left shoulder. Pleasure was the reason for this visit according to the box she had marked on her landing card – the same reason she had given for all her previous trips.

Closed camp detainee? That single sentence was a book. This time the immigration officer looked at Lesa's face. During ten years working at the same desk only a handful of women had instantly captivated him with their striking beauty. Lesa Wessex was one of them. She had that timeless loveliness that came to some women in their mid-thirties and stayed with them through two decades and sometimes even longer. Her bone structure lacked the slightly oval look of the Vietnamese. Her lengthened chin line and large black eyes, watching him with lynx-like suspicion, possessed a European quality. Obviously mixed blood and certainly much taller than was average for a Vietnamese woman. The laser beam she had broken when she had first stepped into the screening booth indicated her height as 1.7 metres, and the piezo-electric pressure sensor under the carpet tiles gave her weight as below normal. The pheromone sensor above her head was showing red. It was convinced she was a woman and so was the immigration officer.

'Your forefinger for identification please,' he requested.

Lesa pressed her right forefinger on the identification pad. She now knew that the machines could not match her prints with her other passport cards; the machines were designed to match the digitalized fingerprint information on the passport card with the holder's actual prints to ensure that the holder was *bona fide*.

'And the other hand please.'

Lesa rested her left forefinger on the pad. Her travel suit tightened across her breasts as she did so. The official reflected that it would be pleasant to detain her in the booth for as long as possible.

'May I see the tattoo on your left forearm please, Miss Wessex?'

Lesa frowned. 'You've never wanted to see it before.'

The immigration officer gave her a bland smile. 'New regulations. Every day there are new regulations.'

She deflated the air seal on the cuff of her travel suit and pulled back the sleeve to permit the officer a brief glimpse of the crescent moon tattoo. He gave no indication that he knew what it meant. 'Thank you, Miss Wessex. That appears to be in order. Where will you be staying?'

'Kowloon. The Waterfront Sheraton.'

'Ah, yes. As from the beginning of the year it is being run jointly with the People's Leisure Bureau but its excellent standards are the same, of course.'

Her reply was a withering stare.

The official smiled diffidently and returned her passport card. 'Enjoy your stay in Hong Kong, Miss Wessex.'

He watched her walk away from the screening booth towards the baggage reclaim hall. She moved with the sensual grace of a panther

– thigh muscles flexing with independent motion beneath her body-hugging travel suit with its conditioner humming away on her belt. He thought thoughts of an overt sexual nature until he realized that a girl so much taller than him would cause him to lose much face with his peers – especially a girl who bore the mark of the ninja; a girl who was a Clanswoman of Death.

He reached for his telephone.

### 3

The airport terminal doors hissed open and Lesa walked into the shower-room heat and humidity of a Hong Kong spring night. She turned up her conditioner. It was some seconds before she felt the drop in temperature of the coolant circulating through her travel suit's micro-mesh tubing. The unit's battery was nearly discharged by the time she found a taxi.

The diminutive, smartly-dressed young man in the grey cotton suit who watched Lesa boarding her taxi was an unlikely-looking killer. He was known as Sammy Lunn. It wasn't his real name. He didn't know what his real name was but everyone had called him that since boyhood days when he had cancelled bad debts for Hung Wai. Cancelling bad debts the Triad way that is – usually by cutting off an arm with a single blow from a short-bladed machete that was easily concealed down one trouser leg. Sammy quickly tired of such crude methods of killing. He turned to more scientific means that exploited his skills in electronics such as his unpatented invention, the telephone bomb – a gram of explosive in the earpiece of a telephone that was detonated by body heat when the victim placed the handset against his ear. Very often the handset contained one of Sammy's bugs that had provided the evidence that led to the victim's death sentence.

Hung Wai and all the other Triad bosses had been mopped up in a huge police operation the day after the British had formally handed over Hong Kong to China. The police must have been planning the operation in collaboration with their forthcoming new administrators for weeks. In twenty-four hours they enthusiastically settled old scores by arresting close on ten thousand Triad members and shipping them off in fleets of buses across a border that had ceased to exist. They were never seen again. It was a smart move by the Chinese. They had rid themselves of a major problem in one fell swoop without getting themselves bogged down in years of tedious disputes with lawyers.

The few Triads that escaped the net promptly saw the wisdom in shutting up shop and becoming law-abiding citizens. Sammy was one of the lucky ones; he became a messenger clerk for Hugo Sukarno. His new boss was quick to appreciate and exploit his employee's many talents, such as his ability permanently to silence talkative crewmen thus deterring others who might be inclined to be over-communicative with the new regime.

There had been an occasion when one of Sammy's clever little bombs had blown the bottom out of a rusting old tramp-steamer in mid-Pacific enabling Hugo Sukarno to claim the insurance on a cargo it wasn't carrying and on the ship, as well as getting rid of a crew who were proving troublesome. Sammy was a smiling, talented and likeable young man with a burning ambition to become rich, who could merge effortlessly into a crowd, and who would kill without compunction. He was a most useful member of Hugo Sukarno's team.

Sammy's orders, which he had just taken on his Klipfone, were not to kill the lovely Eurasian woman he had just watched boarding a taxi, but to follow her and make frequent reports. No doubt he would be ordered to kill her in due course. He was rarely assigned women, especially women as beautiful as this one.

He experienced a little thrill of sexual excitement as he pressed the self-starter on his motorscooter and followed the taxi at a discreet distance.

4

The view from Lesa's top-floor balcony across to Victoria was breathtaking. A billion points of light shone out from the mighty castellated wall of skyscrapers – dominated by the angular Bank of China building – that now stretched from Kennedy Town to North Point. Beyond the line of buildings was the humped outline of Victoria Peak, rising to three hundred metres, its slopes speckled with lights from the millionaires' apartment blocks facing the harbour. Under the British such building had not been allowed. Things were different under the Chinese with their more prosaic attitude to bribery.

Despite the near-panic that had gripped Hong Kong in the

aftermath of the Peking student pogrom of June 1989, the transition to Chinese rule had made little difference to the former colony. That atrocity had been carried out by the old guard in its death throes. China was now ruled by younger men, many of whom had not been born until after Mao's death. One thing had not changed and that was the frenetic pace of tearing down buildings and replacing them with larger, even more extravagant edifices. The process of constant destruction and constant renewal had accelerated dramatically under the new order. The immigration restrictions imposed by the British had acted as a check on new building because of the shortage of labour.

The easing of controls under Chinese rule had ended that shortage and the special administrative status of the former colony with its favourable tax concessions had resulted in the new industrial tycoons of the north flooding in to throw up blocks emblazoned with the names of their concerns to tell the world that they had arrived. Many of the giant neon displays adorning the buildings like nuclear fireworks could be altered from a keyboard so that medium-size businesses on the way up could temporarily short-circuit the route to the top long enough for their public relations staff to take photographs for calendars which they then showered on the rest of the world. To the Chinese, the business of keeping up with the Wongs was heavy spiritual stuff that the ethos of communism was not allowed to impede, with the result that, contrary to the deep misgivings citizens had about the new order, Hong Kong had become the monied Manhattan monster of the Mandarin moguls.

Lesa tipped the bellhop and unpacked in a hurry. There was much she had to do before she could even think of taking a long, hot soak. She peeled off her travel suit, yanked out its now discoloured disposable lining and dumped it down the garbage chute. The conditioner power packs went on charge. She stepped onto the balcony in her underwear, set up her powerful night monocular on a tripod, and trained it through the leaves of the balcony's hibiscus plants across the water to the new giant Hung Hing Marina on Causeway Bay. The light-intensifying instrument had been developed for the observation of wildlife at night. Lesa's experienced eye picked out the numbered concrete mooring jetties which she compared with the SPOT 10 photographs spread out on the table beside her. The images had been grabbed two days previously when the satellite had been directly over Hong Kong.

What she had seen in them was the reason for her being in Hong Kong now.

Jetty 10 . . . Jetty 10 . . . There it was. She dipped the monocular beneath the glare of the marina's security lights and started a slow pan along the length of Jetty 10. The low, oblique angle and the tangled maze of masts and rigging of the hundreds of luxury yachts and pleasure junks made it difficult to pick out individual craft. She glanced at the SPOT pictures. She was looking for Berth 10D. Her long, slender fingers eased the instrument to the left, occasionally making minute adjustments to the electronic focussing rocker control to compensate for the distortions caused by the steamy, humid night air.

Berth 10A – a large luxury junk. Berth 10B – a steel-hulled Dutch motor-sailer. Berth 10C – a ten-metre Hartley trimaran with a rotund young mop-haired Polynesian in shorts at work in the cockpit rubbing down varnish work with an orbital sander. Berth 10D . . . The monocular stopped panning. Lesa's body stiffened involuntarily. An icy chill stole through her, causing a prickling sensation at the back of her neck, bringing out her flawless skin in goose pimples and hardening her nipples despite the heat of the night. She was looking at the boat that she had last seen nearly twenty years previously when, with blood streaming from the bullet wound in her left shoulder, she had stood in the half-swamped sampan and watched the hated craft disappearing into the haze.

There had been a number of changes over the years – some that had puzzled her when she had first found it on the SPOT images, such as the new canopy over the wheelhouse. But there had been no mistaking the rounded after deck and the long, raked pulpit rails that enclosed the flared bow. Even the motorboat hanging from the transom davits was the same. Now that she could see the hull in profile, she knew for certain that her long search was over. Two young Chinese in jeans and T-shirts were sitting on the foredeck playing two-handed mahjongg – probably crewmen. There were lights on in the forward saloon. She zoomed the monocular to maximum magnification so that she could read the name. *Rasputin*, registered in Odessa.

Odessa?

That was unexpected. It had never occurred to her that the boat might be Soviet-registered. Her meticulous searching over the years had concentrated on the pleasure areas of capitalism. She panned the monocular so that the saloon windows filled her field of view. She could see shadows moving against the curtains.

She had found the boat. But after eighteen years, had she also found the three Europeans and the redheaded woman?

Light flared across the lens. She loosened the zoom and saw that a figure had appeared in the doorway. The light was behind him, spilling across the afterdeck. She knew from the figure's outline and slight build that it could not be the bull-chested man or the redhead. Maybe it was one of his two henchmen. The figure crossed the deck and leaned on the rail. It was a man. He was wearing smart white slacks and a loose sweatshirt. Relaxed and self-assured. Probably the motor-yacht's owner. A ring flashed on his fingers as he unwrapped a cigar and put it in his mouth. She tightened the zoom. He was Chinese-looking. Another metallic flash. Possibly a lighter. Light flickered on the man's face. The shock blurred Lesa's vision momentarily but she knew that she had not been mistaken. The intervening years had changed him little.

It was Diem.

## 5

Diem leaned on *Rasputin*'s rail and inhaled on his cigar. He felt good. Another six months working for Alexi Hegel and he would have saved enough to buy the *Rasputin*. That much Hegel had promised him. That much Hegel owed him. He had served the bull-chested Soviet particle physicist well all these years. Even to the extent of getting rid of the body of a Chinese prostitute that he was certain Hegel had murdered.

The change in Diem's fortunes had started on this very yacht back in 1985 when Lesa had jumped over the rail at the exact spot where he was now standing.

## 6

## SOUTH CHINA SEA July 1985

They were all too preoccupied to notice Diem. The bull-chested man gave a bellow of rage after Lesa had dived over the rail. He yelled at his companions in a language that Diem didn't understand and raced up the steep companionway onto the bridge.

The long-haired man shouted at the redhead, pointing down at the sampan and making it clear that they didn't want its painter fouling the propellers. The woman scrambled quickly over the transom and untied the sampan while the bald man clutched a rifle at the rail and scanned the water in search of Lesa's head breaking the surface.

The bull-chested man slammed the throttles open; the diesels opened up – the wash from the propellers churned the water around the sampan nearly sinking it and sending it bucking clear of the motor-yacht's stern. Diem saw Lesa's head for a fleeting second on the far side of the tiny craft just as the powerful eddies from the propellers sent its bow slewing around in a tight semi-circle. Out of self-preservation he rushed to the rail and hung on as the boat pitched while pointing frantically.

'There! She's there! You see?'

The long-haired man seized a rifle. The bald man gave Diem a puzzled look but was distracted by the long-haired man opening fire. The muzzle flashes were bright in the sunlight and the fumes whipped back in Diem's face making his eyes smart; but he kept pointing.

The bald man gave a yell of triumph. He mopped his face with a handkerchief and grinned with pleasure.

The bull-chested man was pointing at the sampan that was now a hundred metres from the cruiser, occasionally dipping out of sight below the swell. He roared encouragement at his men in their efforts to sink it. The rifles continued spitting smoke and lead but most of the shots went wide, provoking the bull-chested man to heap curses on his subordinates.

The long-haired man shouted angrily back.

The bull-chested man swore. He eased back the throttles and

spun the stainless-steel wheel. The group on the after deck clung to the rail as the cruiser heeled and went hard about. It completed its turn. The man at the helm steadied the wheel until the cruiser was aimed at the half-submerged sampan. He opened the throttles, causing the boat to surge effortlessly onto the plane, and strained upwards for a better view. The sampan had disappeared from view beneath the flared bow, and he turned the wheel, trying to guess the craft's position. He looked over his shoulder and swore when the sampan reappeared, dancing like a piece of matchstick in the cruiser's wake. He was about to attempt another ramming but changed his mind when he saw that the boat was now two-thirds swamped. He reduced speed and brought the cruiser onto an easterly course. The sampan was lost to view in the swell as it receded astern. He flipped on the auto-pilot and glowered down at the after deck. His hard blue eyes fastened on Diem and he snarled something, turning the Vietnamese's stomach to water. Diem knew that the leader was giving orders for his execution.

'*Niet!*' said the bald man calmly. He spoke rapidly. Diem was able to pick out the words 'Vietnam' and 'English'. The bald man turned his attention to Diem and said slowly in good English, 'Do you speak English?'

'I speak very good English,' Diem replied. He took great care with his pronunciation, sensing that his survival now depended on this language that he had learned from the GIs.

The bull-chested man's eyes narrowed thoughtfully. He stood and spoke to the long-haired man who dropped his rifle on a beach lounger and took the bull-chested man's place at the wheel. The big man came down the companionway. He was about to speak to Diem but was distracted by the sound of a crying baby. His face tightened in anger. 'Marie!' he bellowed. 'Marie!'

Suzi's crying got louder. The redhead emerged from the forward saloon clutching Suzi protectively against her chest. She had changed into a print dress and beach sandals and was making little soothing noises in a futile attempt to hush the distraught infant. The leader shouted at her again and the woman shrank away, holding the baby even more tightly against herself. She shouted back at the leader; their dispute quickly developed into a vicious row that ended with the leader grabbing her and half throwing her into the saloon. Diem could hear her beach sandals clattering down a companionway.

'Anton!'

The long-haired man at the helm looked inquiringly over his shoulder. His lean, sallow, expressionless features belonged to a face that never smiled. The leader spoke rapidly, obviously giving an order on their course and speed because the helmsman altered course to the west and eased the throttles open. The diesels increased their note to a dull roar and the motor-cruiser rose onto the plane and settled to a steady fifteen knots. Diem thought he heard Macau mentioned in their exchanges but wasn't certain.

The leader turned his attention to Diem and spoke to him in good English. 'Okay. What's your name?'

Diem did not stare back into those cruel ice-blue eyes but bowed his head and looked down at the deck. It would not be sensible to antagonize this man who held his life in his hands. 'Diem Sok, sir.'

'How did you learn English?'

'I used to work for the Americans in Danang.'

'Who were your friends?'

Diem made a dismissive gesture of contempt and glanced astern. 'They were not my friends, sir. Kampuchean filth. They took me a prisoner and forced me to be their guide. I care nothing for what has happened to them.' The betrayal meant nothing to Diem. His companions were dead. His conscience had one master – survival.

'He pointed out the girl for us, Alexi,' the bald man commented. 'We could use him with the Vietnamese site workers.'

Hegel returned his ice-chip gaze to Diem. 'You have any means of identification?'

Diem shook his head and kept his eyes downcast. 'I lost everything in the storm, sir,' he explained.

'How would you like to work for me?'

The Vietnamese snatched at the lifeline and nodded enthusiastically. 'I would like that very much, sir. Very, very much. I will work hard. You will be very pleased with me.'

Hegel suddenly grabbed Diem by his shirt and yanked him close. 'Look at me!' Diem lifted his gaze and saw that everything about the big man was blond – even his eyelashes. 'You say anything about today and you are dead. You understand what I am telling you?'

'I've seen nothing,' Diem agreed.

The big man released him. 'Okay. You will start with cleaning up the deck. Leo! Show him where everything is.'

## 7

Diem worked hard for the rest of that fateful day in the burning sun in a desperate attempt to prove his worth to his new master. He scrubbed down the cruiser's decks, using a pumice block to remove Lin's bloodstains from the teak planking. He feverishly polished fittings and used a wire brush energetically on the anchor. He learned that the boat's name was *Rasputin* and that it was registered in Odessa although he had no idea where Odessa was. A heavily tarnished brass plaque that he cleaned vigorously with metal polish so that it shone in the sunlight told him that the yacht had been built in East Germany. Whilst clearing up the foredeck he found a paperback novel with a lurid cover. The Cyrillic script was meaningless but one of the title pages was printed in English and gave the name of a Moscow publisher.

Land appeared an hour before dusk. Leo ordered Diem into the engine room and told him to clean everything in sight. Diem rubbed frantically at pipes in the stifling heat, his senses dulled by the proximity of the two pounding diesels that stood higher than him on their bearers. The only light was from two portholes virtually on the water line. The engines slowed and finally stopped. He could hear voices, people moving about above his head. Exhaustion triumphed over his fear and thirst and he lay curled up on the sole plates between the engines and dozed off despite the appalling heat. The sleep that followed was untroubled by his conscience. As far as he was concerned his actions that day were born out of the timeless instinct to survive – an instinct that was more sharply defined among the Vietnamese than any other race.

It was dark when he was woken by the harsh growl of compressed-air starters coaxing the engines into life. The engines had been running for an hour when his raging thirst finally goaded him into mustering enough courage to climb the ladder onto the lower deck. The interior of the boat was air-conditioned. The cool air was a heady intoxication after the hell he had endured in the engine room. The companionway was lit with red emergency lights. He passed the open door of an accommodation cabin and saw what looked like Alexi's snoring form sprawled across a bunk. The long-haired man they called Anton was also asleep in another cabin, not making a sound; awake and asleep, Anton was silent. There was no sign of the redhead or Suzi. Diem decided that it would be foolhardy to risk opening the other cabin doors to find out if they were still aboard.

He crept out onto the after deck and looked about him, unsure what to do next. The night was clear. A million stars shone down and the boat's wake was burning a track of luminous phosphorus across the placid sea. Directly astern he could see the distant lights of what he supposed was Macau. He was still tired after his day's work and was tempted to risk sleeping in one of the beach loungers but first he had to find a drink. There was certain to be someone on the bridge. He climbed the ladder, making plenty of noise to avoid the helmsman thinking that he was trying to creep up on him unheard. In the soft glow from the instrument panel and radar screen he could see the bald man – the one they called Leo. He was perched on the edge of the helmsman's seat, holding the wheel with one hand and a cigar in the other. He twisted on the pedestal seat and looked quizzically at Diem.

'Wondered when you were going to show,' he commented, mopping the sweat from his forehead with the back of his arm. 'You did not have to stay down there all the time. Only in Macau.' He spoke in short, staccato sentences, not bothering to construct them properly.

'I didn't realize,' said Diem. 'Please. I am very thirsty, sir. I need water.'

'Drink in galley. I am not a servant. Also you must stop calling me sir. My name is Leon – Leo. You understand?'

Diem muttered a 'thank you' and turned to leave.

'And bring me two Buds. In refrigerator.'

The order was beyond Diem's English. Leo spelt out what he wanted and told Diem where to find the galley. 'And take sandwiches,' he added. 'Plenty of sandwiches. We never eat them all.'

Diem returned to the bridge with the cans of beer for Leo and two packs of sandwiches for himself. He had no idea what was in them but the strange white bread tasted good. He crammed them hungrily into his mouth while listening to what Leo had to say. Little of it made sense but he knew better than to interrupt. His instincts, which had always stood him in good stead, told him that this was a time for listening much and saying little.

From Leo he learned that they were heading back to Kuro – a remote island in the Pacific, some thousand miles to the east, that the Soviet Academy of Advanced Astrophysics had leased from the French Government. On Mount Kuromia in the centre of Kuro the Soviets planned to build the world's biggest optical telescope. The island had been earmarked by the French many years before for anthrax experiments so they had kept the place uninhabited.

'Four linked ten-metre diameter mirrors,' Leo boasted, taking a swig from a can. 'The biggest multi-mirror telescope in the world. It will have ten times the resolving power of the Geck Observatory that the Americans are planning to build in Hawaii. When finished, our telescope will work in . . .' he groped for the right word, '. . . harmony with the American telescope.'

Leo seemed to enjoy talking in his stilted English about the ambitious project. Even if Diem's command of English had been better than it was, the florid little Russian's talk of reflectors and charge coupled devices would have gone over his head. Leo talked affably for several minutes while Diem worked up the courage to ask a few pertinent questions.

'How will I be useful to you?'

The Russian peered at the radar screen to satisfy himself that they weren't on a collision course with a blip that was some ten miles abaft of their quarter. 'Lying Filipinos,' he said contemptuously. 'Last month we recruit a hundred of their Vietnamese boat people. Construction workers, you understand. The Filipinos tell us there are English and Russian speakers among them. We ship them to Kuro. Pay them good money. Give them good accommodation – better than they had in the Philippines – and we find only one speaks English. Not enough. We need at least two – one for the airstrip site and one at the telescope site. So we go to Macau. The Portuguese have many boat people. Many construction workers they said. Some speak English. Some speak French. We negotiate for a week. Do a little sport like today. And we discover that the Portuguese are lying also. They just want us to take some of their refugees off their hands.' He paused and looked sideways at Diem. 'So now we return to Kuro with you as a translator.'

'Who is Alexi?' Diem asked, wondering if he was overstepping the mark with his questions.

'Alexi Hegel is the most brilliant physicist the world has ever known,' Leo replied unequivocally, yanking the tab off the second can of beer and taking a long pull.

The word 'physicist' meant nothing to Diem. 'The other man?' he inquired.

'Anton Pachmann. Alexi's assistant. A Ukrainian. Also brilliant.' Leo took another swig of beer. 'As for me – I am Leon Chernovski – I have learned a little of astronomy on this project but I am a civil engineer.'

'And the woman with the red hair?'

'A prostitute. We pick her up in Macau for sport and we dump her back there with five hundred US dollars to keep her mouth shut.'

## 8

# KURO, WESTERN PACIFIC 1985–86

Three days later the *Rasputin* nosed through a broad opening in the coral reef whose lagoon formed a natural harbour on the western side of the island.

Kuro was a museum of human enterprise and natural forces, both of which had gone wrong, in some cases disastrously so. The French grabbed the island in 1780 – twenty-five square kilometres of jungle surrounding an extinct volcano – as a means of stopping the British or the Dutch doing the same.

A determined party of nineteenth-century settlers cleared some jungle on the relatively flat area in the north and tried to grow fruit. The rain defeated them. The moisture-laden trade winds, having to unexpectedly climb the slopes of Mount Kuromia, didn't merely drop their cargo as heavy rainfall – they dumped it as if from disembowelled water towers.

Two explorers from the Royal Society who came ashore in 1890 were promptly set upon and killed by wild boars. A third naturalist in the party died for his convictions. Or rather, one conviction – that the banded krait was not a poisonous snake.

In the early 1940s the Japanese decided to use the lagoon as a harbour for the repair and victualling of submarines. So that submarines could remain hidden, they built a camouflaged concrete pen that looked like a waterside warehouse plus a few administrative buildings, but abandoned the project when the shifting fortunes of war resulted in their supply of submarines disappearing faster than their islands.

In 1945 the Americans carved an airstrip through the steaming jungle, but the need for it ended the day it was completed when a US bomber dropped its deadly payload over Nagasaki.

In the 1950s the French toyed with the idea of using the island for germ warfare research but gave up in the face of determined opposition from the Philippines. In 1960 a team of Belgian scientists perished during a typhoon when their ship ran aground on the western shores.

Nature fared a little better. The rabbits and goats introduced by the early settlers did well and multiplied. But that success had to be set against the depreciation of the jungle by the creatures' descendants. The settlers' domestic pigs mated with the indigenous wild boars to produce an even more bellicose breed of hybrids that were small enough and fast enough to decimate the rabbit population.

The turning point in the island's uninspiring history had come the previous year, in 1984, when a team of Soviet surveyors made a hazardous landing in their transport aircraft on the abandoned, potholed airstrip. They stayed for three weeks, making test bores in the basalt on the peak of Mount Kuromia, and reported back to the Moscow Academy of Advanced Astrophysics that the site was ideal. After that, securing a hundred-year lease from the French was a mere formality.

Within an hour of his arrival, Diem was shown charts of Kuro. It was roughly rectangular, measuring five kilometres along each side. Mount Kuromia was the island's principal distinguishing feature – an extinct volcano whose flattened peak stood seven hundred metres above sea level. Not high by the standards of extinct volcanoes in the Pacific but high enough to be above the worst of the humidity and make the building of the giant four-mirror telescope worthwhile. The big plus factor was the absence of light pollution from nearby cities.

Leo took Diem to the airstrip on the pillion of a battered motor-scooter where the Vietnamese workers were housed in wartime concrete huts. The Soviet engineer explained that they had arrived the week before in an airlift of chartered DC-3s from Manila. The first priority was to repair and lengthen the airstrip so that it could handle big transports capable of flying in earth-moving equipment and major supplies. Only when the harbour had been improved and accommodation built for the Soviet technicians and visiting dignitaries could a serious start be made on the twenty-year programme of building the telescope.

Once the labour force had clear directives from Diem, they proved eager workers. They were being well-paid in Philippine pesos, not because of largesse on the part of the Russians but because this was a major prestige project that would attract worldwide interest. The last thing the Soviet Union wanted was flak from her political enemies in the form of accusations of using slave labour.

It took seven days' sweated labour in the steaming humidity to prepare the runway to receive a Tupolev transport that flew in from Tashkent, using braking parachutes to land on the short length of patched-up concrete. Diem and his team cheered the landing and the first bulldozer that rolled down the big transport's ramp.

Within six weeks the runway was properly surfaced and lengthened, and construction of the road to the harbour was underway. After that the transports were regular visitors, shuttling in concrete, earth-moving machines, prefabricated buildings and civil engineers to oversee the construction and commissioning of a small nuclear power station three kilometres from the harbour on the west coast.

After twelve months Kuro had been transformed. The harbour grew into a small community that was duly dignified with the name Kurograd. It consisted of a single-storey hotel and a bar, a clubhouse complete with a swimming pool, plus a clinic, a small supermarket and even a savings bank where the workers were encouraged to deposit their earnings. A project office was built and a small residential area consisting of prefabricated bungalows for construction engineers and their families began taking shape along the beach front to the west of the harbour. The largest residence was the bungalow built for Alexi Hegel and Anton Pachmann on top of a hill overlooking the harbour. A TV satellite receiving dish was installed on the same hill, aimed at an Intelsat satellite which provided twelve channels of television entertainment, distributed across the island by means of a UHF repeater. No one had any use for the concrete submarine pen that the Japanese had built so it was used as a typhoon shelter for the *Rasputin*.

Diem earned the trust of his employers. His monthly pay-cheque in Philippine pesos was meagre by the standards of the Soviet workers but it amounted to more money than he had ever had in his life. He saved it assiduously in the bank, not out of thrift but because there was little to spend it on. As the money mounted it encouraged him to save more and spend less in the bar. He proved to be a hardworking, fast learner and even managed to pick up enough Russian to increase his usefulness. Leo arranged for him to have his prefabricated one-bedroom home in the residential area and put him in charge of the gang tasked with blasting the six-kilometre road that snaked around Mount Kuromia's volcanic slopes to the peak. It was slow work: the gradient had to be shallow for the benefit of the heavily-laden trucks that would be climbing to the peak once work on the telescope site got underway.

With the completion of the road, Diem began worrying about his future on Kuro. Over fifty per cent of the Vietnamese workers had finished their contracts and were returned to the Philippines. Most of the heavy work on the preparation of the telescope site was being done by machines operated by Soviet personnel. Diem could see the day looming when he would be of no further use to his employers and that he, too, would be shipped off. The trouble was that he had no passport and would most likely be sent back to Vietnam, a fate he viewed with such misgiving that he summoned the courage to mention his fears to Leo.

'We've got no long-term plans for you, Diem,' the civil engineer admitted. 'Once we've finished with the Vietnamese, you'll have to go home. I'm sorry.'

'But there is much I could do, Mr Chernovski,' Diem pleaded. 'I can fix engines. I've learned much here. No one works as hard as me. I could . . . I could . . .' He cast around desperately. 'I could keep *Rasputin* in good repair. Already it needs a new paint and varnish.'

Leo considered the matter. It was true that Diem was hardworking and conscientious, and that he was proving to be an able mechanic. Several dump trucks were operating thanks to his skills. 'I'll see what I can do,' he promised.

The Soviet engineer was as good as his word. A week later he found Diem on *Rasputin* where the Vietnamese was working in the heat of the confined engine room re-grinding a burnt-out valve in the port engine. Whenever Diem couldn't be found, the *Rasputin* was the best place to look.

'I've had a discussion with Alexi about you,' said Leo, 'and he's agreed that you can stay on as our maintenance foreman for the town.'

Diem was overjoyed. His eyes shone in excitement and he was about to pump Leo's hand when he realized that his own hands were covered in grease. 'I will work extra hard – I promise!'

'I don't doubt it,' said Leo. 'You're to look after all general purpose vehicles and do all the odd jobs that need to be done around Kurograd such as filling in potholes, looking after *Rasputin*, and generally making yourself useful when Alexi needs you. Your bungalow will also have to serve as your workshop and stores.'

Diem could hardly contain himself. The best news was that he would be allowed to carry on looking after *Rasputin*.

'But there's a problem,' Leo continued. 'Because this is a Soviet project, Moscow have ruled that all senior personnel must be Soviet citizens.'

The joy faded from Diem's face.

'Which means,' Leo concluded, 'that we're going to have to fix you up with a Soviet passport. Not easy, but there are ways and means.'

Diem settled happily into his new routine and Kurograd benefited from his diligence. With his staff of three Vietnamese he worked long hours keeping the growing township in good order. There were occasional breaks in his routine when he was required to crew for Leo to take *Rasputin* to Macau, Hong Kong or Manila for regular orders of luxury goods and scientific supplies. Diem became a proficient seaman and navigator. Such trips were possible because Leo had kept his promise and piloted Diem through the bureaucratic labyrinth necessary for him to receive Soviet citizenship, acting as his sponsor.

Diem was immensely proud of his new passport but whatever the future held for him, he prayed that it would not involve having to live in the Soviet Union. At least he was no longer a stateless person.

The trips to Macau, where Hegel had an arrangement with the Portuguese vice and casino baron, Jimmy Pria, were usually to pick up girls for the wild parties that Alexi gave for visiting VIPs in his bungalow.

'It helps keep up the funding for the project,' Leo had explained to Diem on his first trip when they were returning to Kuro with a troupe of six pretty Chinese girls who normally earned their living by working as hostesses in Jimmy Pria's Casino Taipa on the Avenida da Amizade. 'The deputies on the appropriation committees who vote the funds like to pay regular visits to Kuro to see how the money is being spent. Naturally Alexi likes them to go home happy.

This is his boat and he pays the girls out of his own money so there can be no question of misuse of state funds. Simple, eh?'

The Mount Kuromia road was completed in the spring of 1987. A Soviet minister and teams of journalists were flown in for the ceremonial dynamiting of a small hole on Mount Kuromia to mark the beginning of construction work on the telescope site. Afterwards the visitors were entertained at a riotous party in Hegel's bungalow.

Hegel himself was rarely seen. He conducted operations from his bungalow, occasionally summoning senior personnel to conferences by his swimming pool that the Vietnamese had built for him under Diem's direction. More usually it was Anton Pachmann, the Soviet physicist's lank, long-haired, sallow-faced, unsmiling, silent lieutenant, who acted as a go-between when dealing with day to day problems. It was Pachmann who used to give Diem his instructions regarding his trips in *Rasputin*. There were other times when the two Russians returned to the Soviet Union on one of the Tupolev civilian shuttle flights. Some of their absences were quite long. It was not unusual for the bungalow on the hill to be in darkness for several months at a time.

'Design problems with the telescopes,' said Leo when Diem queried a particularly long absence. 'What can you expect? Nothing like this has ever been built before.'

There were more celebrations at the end of 1989 when the excavation of the line of four thirty-metre-square pits in Mount Kuromia's rocky plateau was completed. Each of the huge pits was twenty metres deep. The model of the finished telescope in the planning office showed the four telescopes that made up the system aiming their lattice frameworks at the heavens like the projectors of a science fiction battle-cruiser in a big budget space movie.

About this time there was an increase in Diem's normal work-load owing to the influx of Soviet engineers who were replacing the Vietnamese as the heavy labouring work was completed. Compared with the Vietnamese, the Russians had a high standard of living. Land had to be cleared around Kurograd and more prefabricated, air-conditioned bungalows had to be erected for them. Despite the pressure, he still found time to carry out maintenance work on the *Rasputin*. He was never so happy as when he was sanding, varnishing, and painting. Sometimes he trolled the big cruiser out of its shed into the harbour just to listen to the rich burble of the idling engines while pretending to make adjustments. He dreamed of one day owning such a magnificent cruiser and taking parties of the rich and famous on charter cruises around the South China Sea.

As with any major civil engineering project, there were the inevitable fatal accidents; a Vietnamese worker was crushed to death under an earth grader, and a Soviet crane operator was killed when a jib collapsed; the wife of a Soviet engineer was gored by a wild boar during a cull. The blackies, as the islanders dubbed the jet-black bellicose creatures, were fast and dangerous and didn't take too kindly to being culled even though it was for their own good. The fourth fatal accident was when Leon Chernovski fell from a telescope catwalk.

The Russian civil engineer was the nearest to a friend that Diem had on the island and therefore he was allowed to be a pall bearer at the funeral. He threw a handful of soil on the coffin during the brief civil service that took place at the small plot of land outside Kurograd that had been set aside as a cemetery. After that the only times he ever thought about the Russian were when he needed to use his passport on his trips in the *Rasputin* for Hegel.

The second expansion phase on the tiny island got underway in 1991 with the arrival of the thirty Soviet technicians and their families who were responsible for the intricate task of building the four telescopes. They did not mix readily with the rest of the island's personnel. Indeed they were rarely seen in Kurograd and they built their own small residential area near Mount Kuro's peak. Nothing could be seen of their work because they erected four aluminium and perspex covered protective geodetic domes over each of the pits. Alongside the row of domes was the prefabricated machine shop where the ten-metre diameter floppy mirrors would be built from a lightweight expanded plastics material.

Whenever he had some free time, Diem liked to ride his motor-scooter up the winding mountain road and enter the dome housing the Alpha Telescope to watch the huge latticework slowly taking shape. It was the first telescope and was not due to start observation work until 1999. The entire system of the four linked telescopes with their giant ten-metre diameter mirrors was not scheduled to be fully operational until 2002.

Diem could only wonder at the determination of a people who, in their ceaseless quest for knowledge, were prepared to spend such vast amounts of money and resources. And it wasn't only the Soviets; giant telescopes were being built all over the Pacific by different nations, such as the mighty Geck Telescope on Hawaii, although none rivalled the Kuro Multiple Mirror instrument that Diem's employers were building. The nearest in design concept was the United States' National Optical Astronomy Observatory under construction in Tucson, Arizona.

On one occasion Diem rode up to the telescope site and was surprised at the activity around Dome Beta. According to the wall-planner charts in the project office, work on Beta – the second telescope – was not due to begin yet but the mechanical buckets of two excavators were busy cutting a deep, two-metre-wide trench that led away from the dome. He dismounted from his scooter and watched the excavators emptying their loads of black basalt into waiting quarry trucks. The purpose of the trench puzzled him – he could not recall such a feature on any of the plans.

'As far as I know it's for a new drainage pipe,' one of the Soviet construction workers shouted above the roar of concrete mixers in answer to Diem's question. 'They've decided that the surface water drainage system won't cope.' The engineer grinned and tapped the side of his head. 'Never worked on a project yet where the drawing office didn't chop and change.'

Diem thanked him and entered the Beta dome. He hesitated when he noticed Alexi's Soviet-built jeep parked just inside the sliding doors. His first reaction when he saw Hegel and Pachmann standing on one of the catwalks over the pit was to leave as quietly as he had come. But the two men were deep in a heated argument with their backs to him. The pit beneath them seemed to be the subject of their dispute. Occasionally Hegel thumped the catwalk rail in anger and pointed down. Diem moved into the shadow of a pile of concrete reinforcing rods and tried to make out what they were saying, but they were talking too quickly for his rudimentary Russian. He decided it would be prudent to leave but Hegel suddenly stormed off the catwalk, still conducting the argument over his shoulder.

Diem shrank behind the reinforcing rods, terrified of the consequences if he were seen. The two men paused briefly on the far side of Diem's hiding place to continue their row; it was strange to hear the usually silent, morose Pachmann raising his voice. Diem thought that they would come to blows but they suddenly climbed aboard the jeep and drove off, still shouting at each other.

Diem waited several minutes before he dared emerge. He was about to saunter casually out of the dome when he noticed something odd about the huge excavation. He approached the guard rail and looked down. The excavation was nothing like the pits in the other three domes. It was twice the depth due to a second, slightly smaller excavation having taken place leaving a two-metre-wide step around the bottom of the initial pit. Fresh white concrete lined the base of the secondary pit. Set upright into the concrete was a ten-metre diameter circle of threaded steel studs, each as thick as a man's arm. Obviously the studs were to provide a mounting for something huge, but what? As far as Diem could recollect from the models and drawings in the project office, all four telescopes were to be identical. A harsh voice behind him barking in Russian nearly caused him to lose his balance.

'What the hell do you think you're doing?'

Diem spun around. A senior technician was regarding him; one of the new arrivals. His expression was unfriendly. It was the first time on his frequent visits to the site that Diem had ever been challenged in such an aggressive manner.

'I came to check on the delivery of the Klipfone repeater mast,' he stammered in poor Russian, saying the first thing that came into his head. 'I wanted to make sure all the components were there.'

'It's been checked. Everything's in order. We'll be erecting the mast and satellite up-link dish tomorrow. Anything else?'

'No.'

'Good. Now you must leave. No one is to enter without permission. We've reached the stage where we must avoid contamination. You understand?'

Cement dust was blowing through the open sliding doors but Diem sensed that it would be unwise to mention it. Instead he nodded.

'Next time something needs checking, you telephone the office here and we do the checking. This is a restricted area until further notice.'

Diem mounted his scooter without argument and rode back down the winding road. The new restriction puzzled him. Hitherto the only prohibited area had been the power station, but that was obviously on the grounds of safety. He entered Kurograd, parked his scooter outside the project office and studied the cutaway models and diagrams of the telescope that were provided in the lobby for visiting journalists.

The four pits were shown as being identical.

1995

There was a break in the routine in June with the arrival of a Raisa Class helicopter assault carrier. The warship dropped anchor two miles off the harbour entrance. Two hours later *Rasputin* returned to the harbour with Hegel and Pachmann on board. The motor-yacht was tied up outside the submarine pen and several Vietnamese harbour workers started unloading some crates of drink and a petite Chinese girl who looked barely out of her teens. The crates and the girl were dumped in the back of a truck which a Vietnamese drove up the hill towards Hegel's bungalow. The two men and the *Rasputin* had been away for nearly a year during which time the motor-yacht had been fitted with a new wheelhouse canopy.

Hegel's booming voice carried across the harbour. He had lost some weight during his absence but the way he started berating a senior technician the moment he stepped onto the quay, waving his brawny arms about to emphasize his points, suggested that his temper was unchanged. He glanced across at the warship and dropped his powerful frame into the passenger seat of a jeep. Pachmann climbed in beside him. The vehicle set off along the road that led to the telescope site where the four mountain-top domes gleamed in the sun like a row of planetaria.

An hour later there was activity on the warship. Diem borrowed a pair of binoculars and stood on a chair outside the bar to watch preparations being made around a giant Kamov flying crane helicopter that was sitting on the aft flight deck. The machine stood on four absurd-looking spindly legs that were designed to straddle its payload. In this instance the payload appeared to be a large circular object swathed in tarpaulins. The strange helicopter resembled a grotesque insect about to devour its prey. Diem used the men making the payload secure to gauge the size of the payload. He estimated that the object was at least five metres in diameter and about the same length. The ant-like figures of the men moved clear and the Kamov's turbines began building up to a shrill whine.

Diem watched as the unwieldy-looking machine lifted slowly off the carrier's flight deck. Even at this distance, the dull throb of its twin contra-rotating rotors beating against the humid air caused glasses on the tables to rattle. A crowd of workers and their wives gathered, chatting excitedly and pointing. The cables beneath the helicopter straightened as they took the strain. The note of the hammering rotors deepened and the strange payload, suspended at least thirty metres beneath the machine, swung clear of the flight deck. The machine altered course and as it did so, Diem saw the payload was hollow like a giant doughnut.

'What is it?' he asked an engineer who was watching the strange sight with her husband.

'Probably some sort of support for Beta's mirror,' she replied. 'I've heard that they're going to use a different design on Beta.'

'I thought that all four telescopes were to be the same?'

The woman shrugged. 'It's not my field,' she commented. 'But with such new technology being applied, it is inevitable that one learns as one goes along and makes changes.' She pointed. 'Look.'

The helicopter had reached the telescope site and was hovering over Dome Beta, waiting for its load to stop swinging. Diem refocussed the binoculars and saw that several panels had been removed from the apex of the roof to create a gaping hole. He could see men standing near the rim of the aperture. They were staring up at the improbable doughnut that was suspended above them. The load stabilized and the sky crane lost height and paused in mid-air while the pilot made final adjustments to its position before he completed his delicate task of lowering his machine's burden through the hole. It hovered motionless for five minutes, its rotors thrashing the air, then it rose steadily and winched up its now empty shackles. It tilted its nose down slightly as the pilot altered cyclic pitch and returned to the warship, settling on the flight deck like a dragonfly taking a rest. The warship weighed anchor when the machine had been made secure and set off on a northerly course.

## 14

There was a noisy party that night in Hegel's bungalow. The beat of a hi-fi system and loud female shrieks – probably made by the Chinese girl – carried across the harbour to Diem's house in the residential zone. By 1:00 all was quiet. At 2:00 he was woken by his telephone. It was Hegel demanding his immediate presence at the bungalow.

He set off on his scooter, wondering with some trepidation what the big Russian had in store for him. He entered by the garden gate and skirted the swimming pool, gleaming in the moonlight. The sliding doors to the living room were open. Hegel and Pachmann, wearing shorts, were slumped in easy chairs, watching a pornographic video disc amid the remnants of a party.

'Get rid of the thing in the pool,' said Hegel, scratching his barrel chest, not looking up from the television screen.

'Thing?' Diem repeated, not understanding.

'Use your eyes! Turn on the underwater lights!'

Diem remembered where the switch was and turned it on. The underwater lights turned the swimming pool into a rectangle of aquamarine liquid light. The naked body of the Chinese girl was floating face down near the water filter. The halogen lights gave her flesh a ghostly white appearance in sharp contrast to her long, black hair that fanned out in the water like the fronds of a sea anemone.

'Stupid cow got drunk and fell in,' Hegel muttered. 'Wrap it up in a blanket or something and take it out in *Rasputin* – dump it well out to sea. Use a chain to weigh it down. You'll find a plastic bag with her things in it on my bed. Dump that as well. You can take the jeep. I've told the harbour captain that you'll be taking the boat out to test its engines so you won't have any trouble. Here's the keys.' He tossed a bunch of keys to Diem. 'Make sure you lock everything up when you've finished.'

## 15

The lights that marked the entrance to the harbour were ten miles astern when Diem cut *Rasputin*'s engines. Since the refit the instrument panel had been completely re-designed. The cutout switches were no longer in their usual place and the wheelhouse was now completely enclosed and air-conditioned. The motor-cruiser lost way and rolled in the swell. Diem double-checked the radar screen to make sure nothing was nearby – a pointless action because other ships in this area were virtually unknown – but he did it to be certain that there would be no one to witness his next move. He turned on the after deck lights and opened the wheelhouse door.

The boat's motion had caused the girl's body to roll out of the blanket. She lay on the teak planking, her left arm doubled under her. There were no marks on her body that he could see in the dim lighting so maybe Hegel had been telling the truth about her getting drunk and drowning. Diem went in search of a length of chain. All he could find was a spare kedge anchor and some cable. He tied the cable around the girl's neck as best he could and secured the other end to the anchor. He rolled her body under the rail into the sea. It fell with a dull splash and remained floating in the water, tethered to the boat by the cable. He sat on the deck and pushed the anchor over the side with his feet. By the time he stood up and looked over the rail, the girl's body had vanished. Out of curiosity, he went through the girl's belongings in the plastic bag and was surprised to discover a Klipfone. Prostitutes had to be big earners to afford a Klipfone subscription; maybe she had been – she was pretty enough. He re-packed the articles in the bag, weighted it with a couple of tins of fruit from the galley and tossed it over the side.

He went into the forward saloon and poured himself a generous measure of whisky from the cocktail cabinet to steady his nerves. The business reminded him of events in the South China Sea ten years previously. He rarely thought about what had happened; there was no question of time healing the wound because there had been no wound in the first place. His actions had been motivated by the need to survive. But Hegel and Pachmann had no such excuse. He wondered how such men, who could watch a video disc while a dead girl floated a few metres away, came to terms with their consciences.

Several drawings scattered on the table caught his eye. Half-expecting to hear Hegel suddenly bellowing at him, he glanced fearfully around the saloon before switching on the table light.

The first drawing was a schematic diagram of all four telescopes. Diem had seen similar drawings before. The difference with this one was the number of manuscript amendments that had been made to the cross-sectional dimensions of the Beta Telescope's lower mountings. The curious addition to the excavation was clearly shown as was the huge circle of mounting studs set into the concrete base.

The second drawing consisted of a mass of neat freehand sketches that depicted a curious doughnut-shaped coil. Diem looked amongst the mass of scrawled calculations for the arrowed figures that would indicate the object's dimensions. When he found them he realized that he was looking at sketches of the strange object that the sky crane had ferried ashore that afternoon. There were a series of cross-sectional drawings that showed the intricate pattern of windings that made up the toroidal's curious shape. One of the sketches used a cartoonist's techniques to show energy or matter rushing through the coil's centre. The rapid force lines were then shown passing through a smaller coil that appeared to focus the lines into a tight, coherent beam that stabbed across the paper. Neat little groups of mathematical formulae, some very complex and running across several sketches, were printed in ringed boxes along the path of the lines. Many of the formulae were in Pachmann's handwriting – scribbled fast with bold flourishes as if a blinding demonic passion burned beneath his cold, silent exterior. The only word that Diem could read was carefully lettered in large pencilled characters at the foot of the bizarre sheet. He could read it but he couldn't understand it:

TORUS.

Victor Koniev persuaded the Soviet Academy of Advanced Astrophysics that work on the Kuro Multi-Mirror Telescope was now sufficiently advanced for him to permanently transfer his office as director of the project to Kuro. The academy were reluctant to let him go. Koniev's administrative skills, boundless energy, infectious enthusiasm, and wide circle of influential friends on the various appropriation committees had ensured that there had been continuous funding for the project despite it being nearly two hundred per cent over budget. He assured his fellow academics that there would be a continuation of the central government's funding – especially now that the telescope was nearing completion – so they agreed to his relocation.

He flew into Kuro on 1 July. Most of the island turned out at the airport to welcome him when he stepped from his Tupolev. Although a frequent visitor to Kuro, he ensured that this arrival would receive worldwide publicity. The official welcome was handled by Peter Menkova, the chief engineer and Leo's successor. Hegel and Pachmann were noticeably absent from the airport.

Diem listened to Victor Koniev's speech and wondered what impact this genial, silver-haired scholar would have on his life. The astronomer was certainly very different from any Russian that Diem had encountered previously. Such was his commanding presence that he had only to hold up his hand for silence and it was immediately secured. He smiled warmly at his audience and opened his speech by giving his age as sixty and describing his career, first as a deputy director of the Caucasus Six-Metre Telescope, then chairman of the International Astronomical Union for three years, and latterly director of the Konstantin Tsiolkovskii Orbital Telescope. He went on to announce that Telescope Alpha would be commissioned by the end of the year. Design problems were delaying Telescope Beta, which was employing a novel mirror. Alexi Hegel and Anton Pachmann were to continue in charge of development, but there was no reason why the hold up should affect the completion schedule for Gamma and Delta. He said that he was looking forward to the completed telescope working in conjunction with the United States Geck Telescope on Hawaii. His concluding joke earned laughter and applause: he said that it was a real pleasure to take up his duties on the island when most of the donkey work had been done. To the surprise and appreciation of the foreign journalists present, he repeated his brief address in French and English.

A dissenting note was struck by an American science journalist commenting to a colleague in Diem's hearing: 'I once interviewed Kookie Koniev at a science convention in Tokyo; I can't imagine him collaborating with the Americans. The man's a hard liner.'

A convoy consisting of every vehicle on the island that could be pressed into service took the party up to the telescope site. It was the first time Diem had been there since his warning off in 1992.

Although most of the changes could be seen from Kurograd, the near-completed state of the project surprised Diem. He listened with half an ear to Menkova who was standing on a rostrum, pointing out the various buildings in the compound to the assembled journalists. Where there had been rough ground there was now smooth tarmac with parking spaces picked out in fresh white paint. There was even a helicopter landing pad marked out as a circle. Alongside the row of four domes was the long, single-storey telescope control building where the teams of astronomers would work. It housed the computers and sensing equipment that would process the images of the far reaches of the universe gathered by the four mirrors. All the signs were in several languages for the benefit of visiting scientists and astrophysicists who would be coming to Kuro from all over the world. Heads turned at the sound of an approaching engine in low gear. Hegel's jeep, with the ever impassive Anton Pachmann at the wheel, entered the compound and stopped at the far end of the telescope control building. Pachmann jumped out of the vehicle without sparing the gathering as much as a glance and used a magnetized security card to open an unmarked door.

Koniev and Menkova led the visitors through the main entrance. Inside the central control room batteries of large closed-circuit television screens relayed pictures showing the four telescopes. To save weight the concept of the conventional tube to house each telescope had been abandoned in favour of a lattice work of toughened stainless-steel tubing. Only Telescope Alpha had its monster ten-metre diameter mirror in place.

The party gathered around a working scale model of one of the telescopes and watched dutifully while Peter Menkova demonstrated how hundreds of computer-controlled actuators hooked to the back of the giant floppy mirror maintained its correct parabolic curve – providing continuous compensation for distortions caused by wind, temperature changes and gravity. It was the design breakthrough that had made the ten-metre super telescopes possible. A conventional ground and polished mirror of the same size would weigh sixty tonnes. Even if such a mirror could be built that didn't distort or even crack under its own weight, mounting it would add many millions of roubles to the overall cost, making construction hopelessly impractical.

'Why four telescopes?' a journalist asked.

'For greater accuracy,' Victor Koniev smilingly replied, taking over from Peter Menkova. 'Even with computer-controlled surface curvature systems, the mirrors won't be absolutely perfect. But with several mirrors we can use computers to process the images and average out the errors. Human beings no longer look through very large astronomical telescopes, ladies and gentlemen. The human eye is a very poor instrument for collecting light from distant galaxies. Charge-coupled devices, ultra-fast photographic emulsions, and computers do a much better job. Come – we will now take a close look at the telescopes.'

To Diem's surprise, after visiting Telescope Alpha, the party was shown along the connecting tunnel to Telescope Beta. Considering the odd modifications that had been carried out to Beta, he had not expected it to be included in the itinerary. Everything in the dome appeared normal – there was nothing to suggest anything unusual beneath the mighty telescope. The exception was that Beta's intricate mirror-mounting was not in place. Instead there was the giant torus, wrapped in brightly-coloured plastic sheeting. The strange device provoked a barrage of questions.

Koniev smiled and held up his hand. 'It's an electromagnetic coil, ladies and gentlemen. The biggest in the world. In their quest for perfection, Alexi Hegel and his team are experimenting with variable magnetic flux fields to control the shape of the mirror. They hope to achieve an even more accurate curve than the system being employed for the other mirrors. It's a most exciting concept that will, I'm sure, fully justify the delay in getting this telescope working.'

Diem, like everyone else, accepted the story. It was plausible and it made sense.

## 17

That evening Diem joined a group of workers at a table outside the bar for their customary game of poker. There was something different about the bar but he wasn't certain what it was. The first hand was being dealt when the bartender came out and told them to stop.

'Sorry, comrades. No gambling,' he said.

The group looked nonplussed.

'But we always play at this time,' Diem protested.

'Not any more, gentlemen. I'm sorry but that's the rules.' The bartender was a genial Georgian who looked unhappy about the situation.

'What rules?' Diem queried.

'Our new boss has decreed that the gambling is a decadent Western practice and must stop. If you want to play poker, do it in your house. You can't do it in public.'

There was a chorus of protests.

'I'm sorry, gentlemen. Our new leader may be light-years ahead on the scientific front, but politically he's out of the ark.' The bartender grinned at his crestfallen customers. 'And you can forget I said that.'

Diem suddenly realized what was different about the bar: all the Coca Cola and Pepsi signs had disappeared.

Later that night he thumbed his television remote control to watch Cable Network News and was greeted with a blank screen. It was the same with the Stag Channel and all the American-originated channels. All were off the air, including the Japanese channels, leaving only a bland diet of old movies dubbed into Cantonese from the Hong Kong and Canton uplinks. He checked with his neighbours in case his television was on the blink. They reported the same thing. He called the engineer in charge of the UHF repeater and got a recorded announcement saying that on the orders of Victor Koniev, until further notice, certain PacSat TV channels would no longer be relayed.

Diem went to bed reflecting that the smiling new boss hadn't wasted time in making his presence felt.

Victor Koniev's arrival coincided with an increase in the frequency of Diem's errands for Hegel in *Rasputin*. But the trips to Macau to collect girls ceased.

. 'The Chinese screw up everything,' Hegel had bitterly remarked. 'No more girls. And the casinos now belong to the state.'

Diem had made no reply. He suspected that the curtailment of Alexi's favourite form of relaxation had more to do with the arrival of Koniev than the Chinese takeover of the former Portuguese colony in 1997. Even Hegel and Pachmann's fishing trips in *Rasputin* had become a thing of the past.

Hong Kong became Diem's principal destination. The cheap, good quality clothes he could buy there accounted for his increasing taste for the good life. He now favoured smart shorts and T-shirts and expensive sandals. His one luxury purchase out of his steadily mounting savings was a genuine gold Rolex Oyster Perpetual. The cargoes he ferried back to Kuro were scientific instruments, engineering components manufactured by specialist machinists in accordance with Anton Pachmann's detailed drawings, and large quantities of computer equipment. On one occasion he and his crew of two Vietnamese made a hazardous return to Kuro overloaded with several tonnes of packing cases lashed to *Rasputin*'s broad after deck. Among the cases was a satellite television receiving system that he was required to install in the grounds of Hegel's bungalow because the big blond man had nothing but contempt for Koniev's censorship of the island's television.

Diem had once questioned Hegel over why the usual supply system of transport from the Soviet Union wasn't used to bring in scientific instruments. 'Because we can't get the quality and precision we need from home, that's why,' Hegel had snapped back.

Diem had made no reply. Of late the Soviet physicist's temper had been getting worse. He was spending longer hours than usual locked in his laboratory with Pachmann. Both men had red-rimmed eyes from lack of sleep and were now rare visitors to the bar. When they did put in an appearance, Hegel was loud in his criticisms of Victor Koniev, saying that the stinking little party creep was driving him like a dog.

2002

It was gone eleven when Diem rode his motor-scooter up to Hegel's bungalow with a parcel strapped to the pannier. He had just returned in *Rasputin* from Hong Kong. According to the manufacturer's agent he had collected the parcel from, it contained the very latest magnetic flux density analyser. Diem had no idea what such a device was but heeded the agent's advice and handled it with great care. On arrival back at Kuro, he decided not to entrust the instrument to anyone but to deliver it personally. On the way to the house he passed a noisy group of American and Canadian astronomers who were holding a party at the barbecue site; Kuro had many such visitors now that Alpha and Gamma were working. The sounds of their revelling faded as he climbed the hill. He wondered if his late visit was such a good idea when he saw Koniev's car parked outside the bungalow.

Diem stopped his engine and could hear Koniev's voice raised in anger. He had half a mind to leave and come back later but his curiosity got the better of him. He parked the scooter out of sight and crept up to the gate that led to the swimming pool. He could see three figures seated around an aluminium table on the terrace. Had they been talking more quietly it would have been impossible for Diem to make out what they were saying above the racket made by insects. As it was, every angry word carried clearly through the hot, humid night. As usual, the silent Anton Pachmann made no contribution to the argument.

'Alpha and Gamma are working and producing good results,' Hegel was saying. 'Surely that's taking the heat off you?'

'It's making it difficult for me to justify the research and development budget,' Koniev countered. 'I can't go on manipulating the figures for much longer.'

'Another million and another six months should see it perfected,' said Hegel quietly. After seventeen years, Diem knew the volatile Soviet physicist well enough to recognize a danger signal.

'You can't have either,' said Koniev evenly. 'The torus beam is ready for testing and you know it is. You've had nearly twenty years.'

'Okay. So what difference will another six months make?'

Diem was a stationary target for the swarms of mosquitoes but he dared not slap at them, especially when he heard a blackie snuffling about in the nearby undergrowth. The bad-tempered creatures had poor eyesight but keen hearing. It was best to keep perfectly still. Eventually the unseen creature stumbled off into the darkness enabling Diem to concentrate on the conversation he was overhearing.

'You don't need another six months!' Koniev was shouting. 'The torus is working. It's time for a test firing.'

'That's what the latest of your little spies has told you, is it?'

'Spies? What spies? I don't know what you're talking about.'

'Don't give me that shit, Victor. The latest is Menkova. The first was a pathetic attempt to plant a pretty little Chinese girl on us. A hooker who could afford a Klipfone – a real amateur. Anton overheard her in the toilet talking to you. She didn't even have the sense not to use your name.'

'What happened to her?' Koniev demanded stiffly.

Hegel shrugged. 'She went for a dip without bothering to learn to swim. Tragic. Body never found.' Hegel's voice rose. It was only a matter of time before he lost his temper. 'So you listen to me, Koniev – *I'm* the one who's in charge of the torus beam – not you and your clique of string-pulling Moscow toadies –'

'And *I'm* the one who has made it possible! Without me and my like-minded, string-pulling toadies, as you so insultingly call us, to cover your profligate spending there would be no torus beam. It's thanks to *my* foresight and my planning that we now have the beginnings of an umbrella defence system to compensate our great nation for the damage done by our woolly-minded liberal leaders – men who have persistently weakened our defence by their willingness to enter into international agreements and not carry out research of this nature.'

'Crap,' said Hegel succinctly. 'You know what, Koniev? You sound like something out of a bad movie. Moscow's full of shitty little social-climbing party creeps like you. You're not even a scientist – just an oily little scumbag that's made it to the top by getting itself invited to the right parties.'

Koniev stood suddenly. Diem pressed himself back into the

shadows of the shrubs. 'I don't give a damn what you think of me, Alexi. The important thing is that I'm in charge here and what I say goes. You will select a suitable defunct satellite from the list I've provided and you will carry out a test within the next fourteen days. You will agree to that otherwise both of you will be flown out of here on the next transport under arrest. Do I make myself clear?'

Diem braced himself for the inevitable explosion. No one ever threatened Alexi Hegel, it was unheard of. But instead of losing his temper, Hegel's response was astonishingly mild. It was as if he had suddenly tired of the whole business. 'Okay, Comrade Koniev. You're the boss. You'll have your test firing.'

'Thank you,' said Koniev stiffly.

'In the meantime,' Hegel continued, 'I don't have to listen to your sanctimonious nationalist crap, so kindly get your loathsome presence off my premises before I kick it off.'

Diem melted behind the cover of the shrubs when he heard Koniev's approaching footsteps. The administrator yanked the gate open, jumped into his car and slammed the door. The glow from the instrument lights on his face revealed his tight-lipped anger. He started up the engine and drove off.

Diem tucked the parcel under his arm, entered openly through the gate and approached the two men sitting at the table. In answer to a question from Pachmann he heard Hegel say, 'Sure we'll go ahead with a test firing. But we'll choose a target satellite that will shaft that little shit for good.' He looked up and gave an uncharacteristic, good-natured grin when he saw Diem. 'Hallo, Diem. Is that my flux density analyser?'

'The Hong Kong suppliers were so concerned about its safety that I thought I'd best bring it straight to you,' Diem replied, placing the package on the table.

'You're a good man,' Hegel rumbled as he slid the package across the table to Pachmann. 'How much have you got saved up in that account of yours in Hong Kong?'

Diem was taken aback. He had never told anyone about the convertible currency account he had opened. Over the years he had been steadily transferring his funds from Kuro's saving bank to the Hong Kong account which paid a higher rate of interest. 'Hong Kong account?' he said nervously.

Hegel gave a friendly smile. 'I've had enough shit for one night,

Diem. You're a fool if you haven't taken advantage of all your trips to Hong Kong – and you're not that. So how much?'

'Nearly all my pay over the past ten years,' Diem replied cautiously, not sure how Alexi would react but too scared to lie.

'A convertible account?'

Diem nodded and avoided meeting the Russian's eye. Pachmann had produced a penknife and was cutting through the parcel's wrapping paper. Hegel chuckled.

'How much in US dollars?'

'About forty thousand dollars.'

Hegel threw back his head and laughed. 'Should go a long way towards buying *Rasputin* when we've finished with it.'

Diem's eyes widened. To own *Rasputin* would be a dream come true. He would make a fortune taking charter parties on cruises around the South China Sea. 'That is something I would love above all else, Alexi,' he said seriously.

Hegel nodded and watched Anton unpacking the instrument. 'I reckon we'll be through here in another six months, Diem. Maybe even less.'

Fifteen minutes after her discovery of the motor-yacht, Lesa was distastefully examining her reflection in the hotel suite's full-length mirror. She was wearing a transparent silk blouse without an underslip, and an immodestly short two-way stretch skirt that would not prevent her kicking if she had to. Just to be sure, she aimed a couple of practice swings at the wall-mounted conditioning control panel. No problem. She bowed her head and composed herself. Relaxing as Ko had taught her – trying to clear her mind of personal emotions – preparing herself to use her body to conquer the enemy by whatever means the circumstances were likely to dictate.

Lesa began to fret. She had been fifteen minutes sitting in the back of a taxi in the new cross-harbour tunnel and there seemed no sign that the snarled-up traffic was going to move.

'How long do they usually last at this time of night, for God's sake?' she demanded.

The taxi driver shrugged and eyed his lovely but agitated passenger in his mirror which he had tipped down to get a better view of her legs. He saw her pull a Klipfone from her handbag and stab angrily at the buttons.

'No good in tunnel, miss,' the taxi driver advised.

'I'm trying to get through on an auxiliary channel. Don't you have feeder antennae in the tunnels?'

'All channels taken over by emergency services, miss.' As the taxi driver spoke, two ambulances confirmed his statement by howling along the opposite carriageway going in the wrong direction.

Lesa swore softly and thrust the Klipfone back in her handbag. She realized she was getting agitated and made an effort to calm herself.

She had been gone from the hotel for nearly an hour when the taxi finally dropped her outside the security office of the Hung Hing Marina.

'I've an appointment on the *Rasputin*,' she told the berthing clerk. 'Berth 10D.'

The clerk eyed her curiously. This one was a little older than the usual marina maids that hung about waiting for wealthy yacht owners to invite them aboard. And she had class – real class. Her smile and the glimpse of her breasts as she leaned across his counter turned his stomach to water. 'Sorry, miss. *Rasputin* left thirty minutes ago.'

Lesa controlled herself. Her heart started hammering at the news but she managed an indifferent smile. 'A cruise round the islands perhaps? A fishing trip?'

'I couldn't say, miss.'

She leaned forward even more provocatively but he was too unnerved by the ice in this extraordinary woman's eyes to allow his gaze to take advantage of the improved view. 'Surely you can tell me where they've gone? It's most important.'

'I don't know, miss. Mr Sok never tells us his movements.'

Lesa realized that she had not known Diem's full name. She thought fast and adopted a different tactic. 'I believe the owner of the trimaran in Berth 10C is an old friend of Mr Sok's. I'm sure you won't mind me having a word with him. He might have a message for me.'

The clerk hesitated. The girl knew the berth numbers. She didn't look like a casual caller or a hooker on the make. He scribbled out a visitor's pass and handed it to her. 'Okay, miss. You can go through.'

Lesa thanked the clerk, showed her pass to the security guard and strolled along the rows of moored yachts until she came to the trimaran. The name across the transom, printed in white letters on the varnished mahogany, was *Sparkle*. The mop-haired Polynesian was carefully brush-varnishing the cabin door. Lesa was surprised at just how much varnish work there was. No fibreglass appeared to have gone into the craft's construction.

'Hi,' she called out.

The young man looked up in surprise. His usual cheerful expression faded when this exotically-dressed woman with the intimidating gaze captured his attention and held it. The hypnotic eyes toyed with him and then relaxed. Despite her sudden, unexpected smile he unaccountably found that he lacked the courage to let his gaze roam over her body. He wiped his hands on a clean rag. Despite being a little overweight, he vaulted nimbly onto the pier and shook Lesa's hand. 'Des Gibson. You wanna charter my trimaran? Very fast, very light, very stable. Special rate this week because I'm broke.'

Lesa laughed politely. 'I was wondering what had happened to the *Rasputin*. I was supposed to meet Mr Sok.'

'Can't help,' said Des sorrowfully. 'He comes and goes. Never tells me what he's doing.' He brightened. 'But maybe we could catch them. They only left about an hour ago.'

'Without an engine?'

Des looked indignant. 'This is a Richard Hartley design. All marine ply. Very light. Very fast. Every nail I banged in myself. We'd overhaul *Rasputin* in an hour if we know where it is headed.' He dug in his pocket and produced a grubby card which he pressed into Lesa's hand: *Des Gibson Charters. Island cruises. Yacht racing. Fishing trips. Scuba diving. Cheapest rates in Hong Kong.*

'Perhaps another time, Mr Gibson. Is Mr Sok a regular visitor here?'

'Six or seven times a year. Usually leaves loaded up with crates and booze.'

'Is that his full name? Diem Sok?'

'I think so. He's not friendly. But he doesn't have to be. Me – I'm friendly with everyone. Have to be, else no business.'

Lesa thanked the cheerful Polynesian, insisted that he accept a handsome tip, and walked nonchalantly back to the security gate. She sat at the marina's terrace restaurant and ordered a coffee. The other customers regarded her speculatively. Feeling self-conscious in her ludicrous get-up because she guessed that few Hong Kong hookers could afford a Klipfone subscription, she punched the UK international code and waited for the instrument to bleep – indicating that it had accessed a satellite and found a routing. She entered Darryl's number. He answered immediately.

'Hallo, Darryl. Are you in the office?'

'I was just about to go home. How's Hong Kong?' The one second delay before he answered suggested that her call was being bounced around the world via two satellites. She would have to be careful not to interrupt him.

'Hot and sticky. Darryl, listen carefully. On my desk there's a set of copies of the maxi images of a motor-yacht relating to the case I'm working on. Can you see them?'

A long pause before he answered. She could hear him shuffling about in the background. 'Okay. The boat marked in highlighting ink in a harbour or marina on Hong Kong Island?'

'That's the one. It left the marina about forty minutes ago. See if you can find it.'

'Hold on. I'll find out which low orbit satellite is best placed. Dark at this time in your neck of the woods so it'll have to be infrared. Yeah – SPOT 9 should be okay. Do you want me to log in?'

Lesa suppressed an urge to yell at him. God – he could be infuriating. 'Yes, Darryl. Right now, please.'

'Hold on.'

Keys tapped on a keyboard. The one-second time delay was maddening. Then, 'Sorry, Lesa. All SPOT 9's infrared sensors are in use.'

'All three of them?'

She could hear him tapping on a keyboard. 'Looks like it. I can't get in. Yeah – I've got a "system busy" message come up. I could try a geosync.'

She thought quickly. The infrared sensors on all the geosynchronous satellites could not resolve small craft. They were hard-pressed to detect anything much below one thousand tonnes. 'No – don't bother, Darryl. Thanks for trying. It'll be getting light here in seven hours. Do you mind going in early and taking an optical scout around for me? It's vital I find that boat.'

'Okay, Lesa. I've got some work to do so I'll stay over in the flat.'

'One last thing, Darryl. The boat's called *Rasputin*. Registered in Odessa on the Black Sea. Dig up everything you can for me on it and fax it to my hotel, please. And call me Klipfone direct when you find it. Got that?'

'I can't Klipfone you, Lesa – you've got a call re-direct on. Your answering machine's been gobbling up memory all day. There's twenty odd numbers on the log screen.'

Lesa remembered initiating a call re-direct. It meant that her Klipfone would accept local calls from within Hong Kong but international calls would be re-directed to her answering machine. The idea was to prevent her being woken in the middle of the night by callers who didn't know that she was in a different time zone. 'Hold on, Darryl.' She punched buttons on the handset and checked her command that was displayed on the handset's tiny screen. 'Okay

– I've instructed acceptance of calls from your number. We'd better check it. Give me a call now.' She cleared the channel and switched the call alarm from audio to visual. A bright light flashed on the handset a few seconds later.

'Okay – that seems all right,' said Darryl. 'I'll start digging for info on *Rasputin* now and I'll call you as soon as I've got an optical on it. In the meantime, you get some sleep.'

Lesa felt a surge of warmth towards him. It meant a lot to her having someone as dependable and trustworthy as Darryl looking after her affairs when she was away. She blew him a kiss and cleared the line. She pushed the Klipfone back into her bag, finished her coffee and was about to leave when a well-dressed, distinguished-looking man of about sixty approached her. He looked nervous and ill-at-ease.

'Excuse me, but I heard you speaking English. This is our first trip to Hong Kong.' He gestured to a table where a heavily made-up middle-aged woman was sitting. She smiled seductively at Lesa. 'I promised my wife a special treat. A nice young girl. It's what she –'

Lesa told him in blunt terms exactly what he could do with his wife.

'Oh, I'd like to,' said the man unhappily. 'But she prefers women.'

Lesa stormed off the terrace, her checks burning. Someone whistled at her. She calmed down in the back of a taxi. Well what did you expect, Lesa? You go out looking like a hooker and someone thinks you *are* one. She managed a smile at the recollection of the respectable-looking man and his unfortunate choice of spouse.

Harry Dysan looked at the hologram image of Lesa Wessex on his monitor and drooled. Jesus – the kid was gorgeous. Kid! She was thirty plus! He checked the hologram's date; taken a year ago. It was unbelievable.

Harry, he told himself, for this baby you're gonna have to smarten up. Systemation were a hi-tech outfit. They would be certain to have video conferencing. No way was he going to talk to this lady looking like a slob. A sexist slob, his conscience reminded him as he showered, shaved and dragged a comb through his hair.

He slumped in front of his terminal and tried to look like an exciting male. It came to life, waiting for him to do something exciting. He called Lesa Wessex's Klipfone number. The call was blocked and re-routed to her office. A video recording of her lovely face appeared on his screen. Harry hit the recording key to capture the image. She smiled warmly, apologized for her absence and said that she would return the call as soon as possible. A list of Systemation numbers appeared at the foot of the screen in case the caller was trying to contact her on a business matter.

Harry cleared the channel without leaving a message and replayed the message. Klipfone calls re-directed, huh? Well there were ways round that little problem. He called the Federal Communications Commission office in Jacksonville and identified himself to the duty officer who made loud protests in answer to Harry's request. Nothing short of a national emergency would persuade the FCC to interfere with the worldnet Klipfone system. It took a directive from Gus Whittaker's office to make the FCC official unbend.

'Go ahead and make your call, Mr Dysan,' the official said sulkily when he called Harry an hour later. 'The subscriber's re-direction command has been over-ridden. But only for thirty minutes.'

# 22
## HONG KONG

Lesa felt good the following morning. Jet-lag had never troubled her. Her circadian rhythms had a happy knack of readjusting to a new time zone after a long sleep. She sat in an easy chair on her balcony, enjoying the sun before it got down to business, and eating a light breakfast of toast and ginger marmalade with plenty of coffee.

Her Klipfone shrilled. She snatched it off the trolley, expecting to hear Darryl's voice. Instead she got an American accent:

'Miss Wessex?'

That anyone other than Darryl had got through to her meant that this had to be a local call. It worried her that someone knew her whereabouts. On the other hand it could be someone local calling her who had no idea that she was in Hong Kong. Best to put a brave face on it and find out more. 'Yes. Good morning. Who's this?'

'Miss Wessex. My name's Harry Dysan. I represent a large concern that would like to hire your services.'

'If you call our office direct, Mr Dysan, or our agents here, they'll be able to give you all the details and our terms of business.'

'By "your" I mean you personally, Miss Wessex.'

'Doing what?'

'I can't discuss it over the phone, Miss Wessex. I think we should have an eyeball meet . . .'

'Sorry, Mr Dysan,' Lesa broke in. 'I don't freelance.' To her surprise the caller talked through the interruption.

'. . . ing to discuss the matter.' Only when he had finished the sentence did the caller respond to her interruption. 'We're talking somewhere in the region of a half a million dollar contract, Miss Wessex.'

Lesa sat up. This sounded like an international call. 'I don't think you heard me, Mr Dysan. I *don't* freelance. We have an agent here in Hong Kong. Charlie Foy Services. You get in touch with him. He'll fix everything up, okay?'

'At a guess we'll need your services for . . .'

'Sorry. You'll have to call Charlie Foy,' Lesa interrupted again.

She listened carefully. Again the caller talked through her interjection.

'. . . about three weeks' work. Could we eyeball discuss this? It's very urgent.'

Lesa's mind raced. The way the mysterious Harry Dysan talked through her interruptions meant that there was a time lag which also meant that his call was via a satellite. It most certainly was not a local call; she felt it was essential to find out more about him.

'All right, Mr Dysan. If you've got so much money to splash out. How about lunch at one o'clock at the Club Volvo?'

'S..ry, Miss Wessex. I'm busy the rest of the day. How about breakfast this time tomorrow?'

The suggestion confirmed Lesa's suspicion that this Harry Dysan was calling international. Probably from America. If she was using an ordinary telephone she would know for sure because they displayed the number of the incoming caller. 'Very well, Mr Dysan. I'm staying at the Waterfront Sheraton, Kowloon.' The 'call waiting' tone buzzed in her ear. 'Breakfast tomorrow. I have to go now, someone else is trying to get through. I'll look forward to meeting you tomorrow.' She cleared the channel without waiting for a reply.

The second caller was Darryl. 'I've just found the *Rasputin*, Lesa. I've got her up on the screen now. Ten knots. Twenty-two degrees north, heading due east into the central Pacific. She's clearing the southernmost tip of Taiwan now.'

'Where's she heading for?'

'If she holds her present course, there's nothing for two thousand miles until she reaches Hawaii smack in the middle of the Pacific Ocean.'

'What info have you dug up on her?'

'Nothing.'

'What!'

'There's nothing in Lloyds. The Soviet shipping computer is off-line at the moment so I've drawn a bit of a blank all round.'

'Damn! For Christ's sake, Darryl! There's got to be another way of skinning the cat.'

'I'll think of something,' Darryl promised. 'In the meantime what do I do about this tracking?'

'Stay with it.'

'You mean stay logged in to the satellite?'

'Yes.'

'Are you crazy? The access charges are clocking up on the screen like there's no tomorrow. I've got to log off now.'

Lesa closed her eyes and thought hard. Darryl was right. Satellite surveillance was designed for grabbing images for subsequent analysis at leisure – not for lengthy surveillance operations in real time. The access charges would be crippling. 'Okay, Darryl. Log in every hour on the hour and report back. Do me a favour and check my answering machine log.'

'I'm looking at it now.'

'Any United States numbers on it?'

'Yeah. There's one. Called in just over an hour ago. Didn't leave a message.'

'Find out whose number it is.'

'Hold on.' She could hear Darryl's fingers clattering on his keyboard as he accessed directory inquiries. Then: 'Lesa?'

'Yes?'

'Subscriber is a Harold Dysan. Titusville, Florida.'

'Thanks, Darryl. Is anyone else in the office?'

'Mike's here.'

'Ask him to try Klipfoning me. I want to check that the call re-directing is working.'

'Hold on.'

She heard Darryl relaying her instruction. A few seconds passed before he came back. 'It's working fine, Lesa. Mike just got shunted into your answering machine.'

'Thanks, Darryl. Call me when you have something.'

Lesa cleared the channel and studied the touch buttons on her Klipfone, trying to remember the key combination to replay the last conversation but one. Her first attempt got a recording of the conversation she had just finished with Darryl. She got it right on her second attempt. She replayed her conversation with Harry Dysan several times, listening carefully to her interruptions and the delay in Dysan's response to them. She convinced herself that the American was dangerous.


## 23

'Lesa! My angel! How lovely to see you!' Charlie Foy drove his bulk across the floor of his ornate office and hugged Lesa. It was like being embraced by an oriental Michelin Man. Charlie Foy was fat enough to warrant the invention of a new word next up the scale from obese. He was by no means the richest man in Hong Kong but he was most certainly the largest. The division between each of his chins formed an echo of his warm, beaming smile – a smile that cloaked a shrewd and calculating brain. He knew about everything that was going on in Hong Kong. 'I'm fat,' he was fond of declaring, 'but not so fat that I can't keep both ears to the ground.' Luckily Charlie Foy was a good friend to Lesa but there were many who regarded him as a dangerous enemy.

'I'm fine, Charlie,' said Lesa, sitting in the offered chair. She turned down her travel suit's conditioner now that she was in an air-conditioned building. Her host busied himself at a coffee dispenser. 'How's business?' she asked.

'Oh. So so,' Charlie replied. 'Things are getting better now that the talent is coming back. They flocked out in 1997, discovered that there's nowhere else quite like Hong Kong for making money – so now they're drifting back from Vancouver and Brisbane and San Francisco. Fools. They did not realize that when wealth and dogma are locked in a battle to create a social structure, wealth will always win.' He chuckled richly and placed a strong, black coffee on the table beside Lesa, wheezing as he straightened. He lowered his mountain into a specially-made swivel chair and regarded his guest intently.

'So you're still making obscene millions out of the new order?' Lesa asked.

Charlie's huge girth quivered when he laughed. 'Definitely obscene millions the way they're breeding, my angel – quite obscene. As for our new lords and masters, they're not too bad now we've had a chance to get used to each other, although they seem a little slower in getting used to us. There's now a People's committee running the stock exchange. Naturally we are most anxious that they should be kept fully informed on every little detail and have everything at their fingertips, therefore each member of the committee receives about fifty kilos of papers and reports each week to digest and give decisions on. And naturally we want to make them feel at home, therefore they get showered with irresistible daily invitations to all the most glamorous parties and receptions.' Charlie paused and frowned. 'It's strange, my angel, but they don't seem to be taking their duties seriously. They're forever delegating their awesome responsibilities back to us members of the exchange.' He lowered his voice. 'They actually seem happy to let us run things the way we've always run them. Can you believe that?'

Lesa burst out laughing. 'You're impossible, Charlie.'

Charlie grinned mischievously. 'An old mandarin solution for dealing with over-industrious emperors. So tell me, what brings you here without you tipping me off first? I'll be thinking next that you no longer love me.'

'I'll always love you, Charlie. I'm here on a private visit.'

'Ah.' He looked sharply at her. 'Under your own identity?'

'Yes.'

The fat Chinese stirred his coffee slowly. 'Well that might help. I most certainly pray that it does. I've heard a whisper that Hugo Sukarno is looking for a woman who just happens to match your description. Heaven only knows who he's bribed to keep an eye open for you.'

'I heard about Judge Wu,' said Lesa casually. She smiled. 'Perhaps I should pay Hugo Sukarno a visit? Save him wasting time looking for me.'

'Don't even joke about it,' Charlie admonished. 'He is an extremely dangerous man. You've caused him many problems.'

Lesa changed the subject. 'Actually, Charlie, I've come to you for some help.'

'Ah.'

'I'm after information. There was a motor-yacht in the Hung Hing Marina yesterday: the *Rasputin*. Registered in Odessa. I'd like to know who the owner is and where he or she lives.'

Charlie raised his eyebrows. 'A Soviet motor-yacht? Well – there are many wealthy Soviets now. I do business with them.' He scribbled on an electronic memo pad with a gold stylus. 'You've tried getting information from the Soviet data bases?'

'Their computer is always down.'

'Typical. Hung Hing Marina? Mmm. I know one of the directors. I'll call you as soon as I have something.'

Lesa finished her coffee. She stood, kissed Charlie on the cheek and turned up her conditioner so that her suit would be cool by the time she left the building. 'Thanks, Charlie – I love you.'

Charlie eyed the lovely figure in the body-hugging suit. 'Lesa, my angel,' he said wistfully, 'if only that were true and not a mere pleasantry.'

## 24

Sammy Lunn allowed ten minutes to pass after Lesa had boarded her taxi before walking breezily into the lobby of the hotel as if he owned the place. He was wearing a respectable charcoal-grey business suit – always a good idea when dealing with hotel staff. His face was cheerful and there was a bounce in his step as he approached the desk.

'You have a Miss Lesa Wessex staying here,' he informed the receptionist. 'An old friend. I wish to send her some flowers and would be grateful if you could give me her room number please.' He had a high denomination banknote in his pocket in case it was needed. Luckily it wasn't, which meant he could use it to top up his expenses. Provided he got results, of course. With Hugo Sukarno, it was better to be honest if one didn't get results. He thanked the receptionist for the information and bounced out of the hotel, whistling cheerfully.

He was back twenty minutes later in an entirely different garb, clutching a small tool-box. He had changed into a red one-piece suit and a peaked cap used by a fire protection and security company as the uniform of its maintenance personnel. It was complete in every detail down to a lapel badge bearing his photograph. This time he took the lift to the top floor and sought out the floor manager who was reading a newspaper in his cupboard-sized office.

'Fire Protection Services,' he announced. 'I've come to replace the smoke detector in the bathroom of room thirty-twelve.'

'Outside contractors,' the floor manager grumbled as he led the way along the carpeted corridors. 'It means I'll have to stay with you while you work.'

'No problem,' said Sammy cheerfully. 'It'll only take a couple of minutes.'

The floor manager passed his magnetized card through the lock on Lesa's door and pushed the door open. He watched disinterestedly as Sammy stood on the shower stool and unscrewed the smoke detector from the bathroom's false ceiling. He deftly disconnected the alarm wires and took a new detector from its box.

'New model,' Sammy explained. 'Much more reliable. Soon we'll replace all the smoke detectors with these.'

Sammy wasn't lying when he said that it was a new model. It was much more than a ubiquitous smoke detector; it still worked as one but it had a number of unusual features. The glass centre stud, no larger than a thumbnail, was the business end of a surgical Panasonic miniature television camera fitted with a wide-angle lens. The bulk of the unit behind the bezel that would be out of sight when the detector was installed consisted of a low-power UHF television transmitter. The neat thing about the gadget was that it was activated by artificial light and therefore active only when someone was in the bathroom thus giving the battery a useful working life. A bug detector scanner would detect the presence of the transmitter only when the bathroom light was on. The power output of the transmitter was a mere forty milliwatts; not enough for the pictures to carry beyond the room, particularly with the antennae in the confined space behind the bathroom's false ceiling, but sufficient to reach a higher-powered repeater transmitter near the bedroom's balcony – provided Sammy could plant such a transmitter.

He tightened the screws, stepped down from the stool and slipped the repeater up the sleeve of his suit while returning his tools to the tool-box. He straightened and grinned at the floor manager.

'Okay. All finished.'

They were about to leave the room when Sammy whistled and said, 'Hey. Look at that view! Mind if I take a look?' Before the floor manager could object, he marched across the bedroom and pulled open the sliding door that led onto the balcony. His glance quickly took in the tubs of hibiscus plants and deemed them suitable. 'This is something else,' he breathed, stepping onto the balcony and gazing at the Victoria skyline.

'Come on! I've got better things to do than stand around while you gawp at the view,' the floor manager muttered irritably behind him.

Sammy pushed the repeater firmly into the soft peat in one of the plant tubs. He turned and beamed. 'Okay, all done. Let's go.'


# 25

Hugo Sukarno's penthouse office had one of the best views of the whole of Victoria and Kowloon, on the top floor of Victoria Peak's most prestigious apartment block. From here Sukarno could watch the coming and going of his merchant ships. He was a slim, darkly handsome Indonesian in his early fifties dressed in slacks and a rollneck sweater.

Sammy watched his boss anxiously as he trained his 150-millimetre telescope through the haze to the Waterfront Sheraton Hotel five kilometres distant.

'What's she doing now, boss?'

Tiny motors whirred in Sukarno's artificial hands as he made adjustments to the instrument's focus and zoom. He could do much with his hands – even use chopsticks.

'Still sketching,' said Sukarno, not looking up.

Forty years previously his parents had arrived in Hong Kong as legal immigrants. His father had been a production manager with Jakarta Electronics. His stern, disciplinarian attitude towards his son – every dollar that went into Hugo's pocket had to be earned and earned hard – instilled two powerful driving ambitions in the boy: the first was to make money – real money; the second was to outshine his father.

His father's favourite grouse about the cost of disposing of toxic waste prompted the young Sukarno to buy a sampan and a clapped-out Evinrude outboard, and set himself up in business disposing of drums of hazardous toxic waste from the sweat-shops of Kowloon. Sukarno's fees were half those charged by the legitimate disposal companies. One drum at a time to start with, hidden under fishing nets, until he made enough money to buy a hundred-tonne motor-junk. He never knew what the chemicals were that had destroyed his hands. The yellow sludge burst from a corroding drum as he was rolling it up a plank. If anything the loss of his hands was offset by an increase in his hard-nosed business acumen. By the turn of the century he owned, through a network of leasing companies which he also owned, a merchant fleet whose earnings were out of all proportion to the fleet's tonnage. The loyalty of his skippers and crews was guaranteed by paying them generously and making them part-owners of their ships. Sammy dealt with any employee who was less than loyal.

The method his ships used was simple: pick up a load of waste in one port, sail to another port, dumping the waste on the way, and pick up a legitimate cargo for the return. A London-based company owned by Sukarno would then invoice for the disposal of the waste and issue the necessary certificates. It was a billion-dollar industry that was now being systematically destroyed by the evidence of a tall, beautiful Eurasian-looking girl with a crescent moon scar on her left forearm.

'She's gone inside,' said Sukarno, looking up from the telescope.

Sammy turned on a television and switched the receiver to the same channel as the repeater he had planted two hours earlier. A co-axial lead snaked from the television to a beam antenna that was clamped to a balcony rail and aligned with the hotel. The two men watched the glowing blank screen intently.

Several minutes passed.

'I tell you, boss,' said Sammy. 'All this is unnecessary. She's got to be the girl. She's just as that judge said. Height – looks – everything.'

Sukarno nodded. 'I'm sure you're right, Sammy; I have great faith in you. But you know me well enough by now to know that with any problem, I like to be a hundred per cent certain that the solution is the right one. And with the solution I have in mind for this particular problem, I want to be a hundred and ten per cent certain.'

The television screen suddenly flickered and cleared to show an oddly distorted colour picture of an hotel bathroom viewed from above. The wide-angle image resembled the picture obtained when using the back of a spoon as a mirror but much more detailed and distinct. The recording light on the video recorder came on automatically.

'Will we have sound, Sammy?'

'No, boss. Just the pictures.'

The two men watched in silence as a lovely young woman wearing a silk bathrobe appeared immediately below the camera. She used tissues to carefully wipe off her make-up before unpinning her hair. It fell in a glorious cascade of ebony about her shoulders.

'Beautiful, eh, boss?'

Sukarno nodded. 'Yes, Sammy. You were right – very beautiful indeed. But also curious.'

'How's that, boss?'

'She's not looking in the mirror. A woman in the privacy of her bathroom and she doesn't use the mirror. I find that very strange.'

Sammy didn't take his eyes off the television. Watching a woman who had no idea she was being watched was sexually very exciting. His excitement mounted as she untied her bathrobe and slipped it off her shoulders. There was a tantalizing glimpse of her breasts as she turned towards the door but there was nothing tantalizing about the view both men had of the tattoo on her arm; it showed up clearly for several seconds as she hung the bathrobe from a hook, took a Klipfone from a pocket and placed it on the dresser.

'Top left-hand drawer of my desk,' said Sukarno quietly.

Sammy crossed the thick pile carpet without taking his eyes off the television screen. He opened the drawer and took out a bundle of banknotes.

'I'm sure I don't have to spell out how I want that spent, Sammy.'

Sammy grinned. 'No, boss.'

'And there will be the same amount again when the job is done.'

## 26

The Klipfone shrilled just as Lesa was drying off in the warm air blowing through the shower stall's grilles. It was Darryl.

'Hi, Lesa. I've got an update on that motor-yacht.'

'Hold on, Darryl.' Lesa left the bathroom, pulling on her robe. She sat on the bed. 'Okay – go ahead.'

'The Soviet shipping registration database is still down so I've not been able to find out anything about the boat's ownership, but I picked it up on SPOT 10 about ten minutes ago. It's still heading east but it's altered course slightly on a route that could be taking it to Kuro.'

The name rang a vague bell. Something she had read in the *New Scientist*. 'Kuro? What's that?'

'A volcanic speck about a thousand miles almost due east of Hong Kong. It's doing about twenty knots so it'll probably get there around midnight your time tomorrow.'

'What's so special about Kuro?'

'It's the site of the Ten-metre Multi-Mirror Telescope that the Soviets have been building for the past eighteen years or so.'

A icy chill stole through Lesa's veins. The massacre of her family had taken place eighteen years ago. For a few moments she lived again the terrible seconds when Neti had tried to escape from the motor-yacht. 'Thank you, Darryl,' she said calmly. 'Find out what you can about Kuro and fax it to me.'

She went back onto the balcony. She felt more comfortable after her shower, and the heat of the afternoon was in retreat as the sun sank towards Lantau Island. She resumed her drawing of the Hong Kong skyline but her fingers skilfully shading in the skyscrapers had to work alone, without direction from her brain. Eventually they ceased functioning as Lesa gazed sightlessly across the harbour. She made no attempt to shut out the harsh memories – to do so would be a betrayal of her loved ones.

The Klipfone's buzz broke through the agony of the colour movie film that was running in her mind.

'Lesa! My angel!' said Charlie Foy ebulliently. 'I've been doing a little arm-twisting on your behalf. *Rasputin*'s marina dues are paid by the Soviet Academy of Advanced Astrophysics against a bank account in Manila. It's been an on and off visitor to Hong Kong since 1985 or thereabouts – usually skippered by one Diem Sok. Soviet passport. No standard telephone number or Klipfone number listed for him and the *Rasputin*'s Klipfone number is unlisted. Sorry, my precious, but that's all I've been able to dig up.'

'That's fine, Charlie,' said Lesa, her mind racing. 'You've been wonderful. I don't know how to repay you.'

'I can think of several ways, my angel, but I fear that you would reject them out of hand were I to broach them with you.'

Lesa laughed politely and thanked Charlie again. She remained sitting very still when she had finished the conversation. Her attention focussed on a flock of cranes flying in loose formation towards the fish ponds in the New Territories, their wings beating effortlessly in the golden light of the setting sun. 'We're getting there, Neti,' she whispered to the graceful birds. 'It's been a long time, but it's nearly over now.'

# PART FOUR
# Lesa and Harry

Meanwhile time is flying – flying, never to return.

*Georgics*, Virgil

# 1

## HONG KONG

Harry Dysan's room in the Waterfront Sheraton was nothing like as luxurious as Lesa's room four floors above. The only pleasing view it had to offer was Harry's reflection as he admired himself in the bathroom mirror. Following a refreshing sleep after his long flight, he had showered and dressed himself in a ruinously expensive Heads tropical suit in white Drexon carbon fibre – as indestructible as his good looks, or so he thought. Matching Dodds lightweight chukka boots – ones that really fitted, unlike his Italian shoes – and a spotless new Joe Moran shirt completed the ensemble.

You'll knock her out, Harry, he told his reflection as he applied a final squirt of *Monsieur Rochas* aftershave. She'll be like putty in your hands.

Satisfied that he had achieved near perfection with a hairbrush, he called Lesa Wessex on the hotel's internal telephone and informed that divine voice that he had arrived to allow her to claim her first prize of breakfast with him. She gave him her room number and told him to come up right away. 'The door will be on the latch, Mr Dysan. I'll be on the balcony, so come right in.'

Harry's step was jaunty as he walked along the hotel corridor and became even jauntier when he caught sight of himself in a full-length mirror. He found Lesa Wessex's room and pushed the door open. Lace curtains were billowing around the sliding doors leading to the balcony and he walked towards them, rehearsing a witticism under his breath; he promptly forgot it when he came face to face with Lesa.

No hologram could do justice to the smiling vision that rose from her chair and shook his hand. She was about his height, which was wholly unexpected; her hair, black as a coal face, hung straight down – a perfect frame for her Eurasian features; her eyebrows were evenly-shaped semi-circles that gave her eyes a permanently quizzical look as though she were gently mocking him. She was wearing a high-necked silk bathrobe that tended to exaggerate her height. Her fingers when she shook hands felt strangely delicate as if any undue pressure from him would break them.

'Mr Dysan? How do you do? I'm Lesa Wessex. Please sit down.'

'Very pleased to meet you, Miss Wessex,' Harry mumbled, managing to kick the laden breakfast trolley as he lowered himself into a chair that Lesa had pulled up for him.

'Coffee?'

'Yes please. Black, no sugar.'

The deep black eyes remained fixed on Harry during their opening exchanges of inconsequential pleasantries as they drank coffee. He had an uncomfortable feeling that this beautiful creature was playing a game with him; waiting for him to make a wrong move or say something out of turn before pouncing on him.

'Naturally,' said Lesa carefully, 'I'm interested in your mention of a quarter of a million dollar contract for three weeks' work.'

'That's the figure we have in mind, Miss Wessex.'

'But I was disappointed that you were not interested in my suggestion of lunch at Volvos.'

Harry smiled. 'I daresay we can put that right, Miss Wessex.'

'I doubt it, Mr Dysan.'

Her calm, matter of fact tone sounded a warning bell in Harry that was cancelled by her benign smile. 'Oh? Why's that?' he asked.

'Volvos is a nightclub. They no longer serve lunches.'

Harry laughed. 'I guess I've not been here long enough to be familiar with Hong Kong.'

'Especially as you only arrived here late last night and that you're staying in this hotel. I checked with reception, Mr Dysan.'

Harry felt that his defensive smile was useless against this woman. Her black eyes seemed to be advancing on him like the twin nuclear muzzles of an Eisenhower tank.

'In fact I've carried out several checks since you called me, Mr Dysan. For example, I learned from Arnold Salter at the Environmental Protection Agency that you tricked him into revealing my identity to you. The Federal Communications Commission were not so obliging but I did manage to discover that only in exceptional circumstances can Klipfone call re-directions be overridden. During your call to me yesterday I could tell from the time delays that it was via two satellites – that means it was an intercontinental call – probably from your home in Florida. Am I correct?'

Harry nodded sheepishly. The black eyes were boring into him. 'You're correct, Miss Wessex.'

'Then why did you try to mislead me?'

'You cover your traces well, Miss Wessex.'

'So you've uncovered them. Congratulations. Why?'

'It was imperative that I meet you.'

'So we're now meeting. Who do you work for?'

'I can't say just yet.'

Lesa rose to her feet and held out her hand. 'Good day to you, Mr Dysan.'

Harry stood automatically. 'You're making it very difficult for me, Miss Wessex.'

'Perhaps you would like me to make it easy?'

The strange question puzzled Harry. Uncertain how to respond he said, 'Well – yes.'

Lesa moved too quickly for him to see her spring at him. Before he could recover his balance he was spun around and thrust into the bedroom. What felt like all sixty floors of the People's Bank of China fell on him. Stars exploded on his retinas as he hit the carpet and something akin to a meat skewer drove through his temple. He struggled to free himself of the weight that was pinning him to the floor but he was unable to move. He was out of condition, out of breath, out of practice, and out of luck. The only thing he wasn't out of was pain; pain he had plenty of; the sort of pain that comes from having one's neck screwed up in a clamp and one's teeth forced to unpick the pile of an expensive carpet in order to breathe.

'I'm sure I'm now making it much easier for you to talk,' Lesa's voice informed him. 'You can either give me your last will and testament verbatim which I will commit to memory and pass on to your next of kin, or you can answer my questions. Which is it to be?'

'Answer questions,' Harry managed to choke. It came out as, 'Arther questhogs' because he was forced to talk into the carpet.

'Pardon?'

'Arther questhogs for chriffake!'

She twisted his head to one side, affording him a close-up view of the inside of a female thigh that was mouth-watering in its perfection. Under normal circumstances he would have considered that the closeness of such a view meant that he was in heaven. Under these present circumstances the considered collective opinion of his senses was that he was in hell.

'Your real name?'

The appalling pressure on his temple eased sufficiently to allow his brain to perform some sort of recall. 'Harry Dysan *is* my real name – please, Miss Wessex – you're killing me.'

'That's right – I am. Who are you working for?'

'The United States Government.'

'Which department?'

Normally Harry would not divulge information until his dying breath. But the circumstances were such that he was convinced this *was* his dying breath. 'The National Security Agency,' he blurted out.

The pressure suddenly returned to its former level of agony. Exploding stars became entire galaxies going super novae. 'Tell the truth, Mr Dysan, otherwise you'll force me to hurt you a little.'

'For chrissake – that *is* the truth!'

The sudden easing of the pressure was orgasmic bliss. The terrible weight on him shifted and he was rolled over onto his back. The cruel meat skewer that had been boring through his temple suddenly returned but with reduced intensity. He looked up into Lesa Wessex's large round eyes framed by her long jet-black hair. She was sitting astride him, her knees pressing painfully into his biceps and her silk bathrobe had fallen open to reveal black lace underwear. She was breathing gently, an arm outstretched – his temple and forehead lightly gripped between her fingers and thumb.

'The NSA?' she queried.

'I'm telling the truth, for God's sake!'

Lesa was undecided for a moment. She jumped nimbly to her feet and stood back, re-tying her bathrobe. It was some moments before Harry realized that he was free to move.

'Okay, Harry – you can get up now.'

He climbed groggily to his feet and looked worriedly at Lesa. Suddenly she was smiling – a lovely radiant smile; her manner was warmth and charm.

'You see, Harry? I made it easy for you to talk, didn't I?'

'You certainly did,' he said shakily. 'Who taught you that little trick?'

'A long story, Harry. May I call you Harry? You must call me Lesa. Shall we finish our breakfast and talk business?'

Harry allowed himself to be led back to his chair. He watched Lesa warily as she buttered a hot muffin for him. 'I'm sorry I had to do that, Harry, but I had to be certain. This may sound melodramatic but I've been warned that I could be in danger.' She sat opposite Harry and crossed her legs, giving him another glimpse of her thighs but this time under circumstances in which he could appreciate them. 'So – do you now feel like telling me everything?'

Harry smiled. 'I guess I'd better. Okay – I'll start at the beginning.'

He talked for ten minutes, starting with a full account of his examination of the PacSat 19 and ending with the concern expressed by Gus Whittaker although he didn't mention the general by name.

'So why the big secret?' Lesa wanted to know when he had finished. 'If the Soviets have developed some sort of neutron projector or whatever, presumably they know about it anyway?'

'It might not be the Soviets,' Harry answered. 'It could be the Chinese. Whoever's got it, it could give them one helluva bargaining chip. One side having that sort of umbrella protection could upset the whole delicate process of disarmament and put it back twenty years. We have to be certain before we take this any further. We know there's a beam. My job is to pinpoint likely sites and turn the matter over to the powers that be for detailed investigation. Nothing more. It's a very fragile situation, Lesa.'

Lesa wiped her fingers on a napkin. 'It sounds like a fascinating project.'

'Will you take it on?'

Lesa looked pensive. 'Quarter of a million dollars for the work. Correct?'

'Correct.'

'And another hundred and twenty-five thousand if the site is found.'

Harry allowed a face-saving pause. 'Okay.'

'We have a deal,' said Lesa shaking hands with Harry. He found it difficult to believe that these same delicate fingers could inflict such pain.

'A deal, Lesa.'

'But I've some very important unfinished business here that I must get out of the way first.' She picked up a large hotel envelope and took out a satellite photograph of Kuro that Darryl had faxed her. The envelope also contained several articles on Kuro that Darryl had managed to unearth. 'That's Kuro. Ever heard of it?'

Harry's nerves had steadied sufficiently for him to concentrate. Ye gods, she was weird. 'Yes – it's got to be the most photographed island in the Pacific. It's where the Soviets have built their multi-mirror telescope.' He pointed. 'That complex must be the telescope.'

'I wish to pay a visit to Kuro before I can start on your project, Harry.'

'Why?'

Lesa shrugged. 'I've heard that they've developed some imaging techniques which might be useful to my company. My problem is getting there. It's a thousand miles east of here. The next charter flight from here isn't for another month when Kowloon Airways are flying out a party of British and French astronomers.'

'What about a private charter?' Harry suggested.

Lesa's ironic laugh suddenly brought home to Harry what strange but delightful company this extraordinary woman was. There was no sign of the ferocious lynx that only a few minutes ago had had him in fear for his life.

'I called them this morning,' Lesa replied. 'The only aircraft available is tomorrow – a Skyliner twenty-seat executive jet for which they require the princely sum of six thousand US dollars to fly me to Kuro and back, and another two hundred dollars an hour stopover charges.'

'I guess my expenses will go to that,' Harry commented.

Lesa frowned, guessing what was coming next. 'What do you mean?'

Harry felt that it was time to establish some sort of control over the situation. He stood. 'Get changed, Lesa. I've not been to Hong Kong before, so let's pay Kowloon Airways a personal visit instead of phoning them.'

'No!' said Lesa sharply. 'I don't want any handouts.' What she really meant was that she did not want to end up owing Harry Dysan any favours.

Harry feigned a look of surprise. 'Who said anything about handouts? I'm going to charter a flight to Kuro to take a look at the place. If there's room on the aeroplane, this passing ego in the night would consider it a great privilege if you'd think about stringing along.'

For a moment Harry regretted the flippant remark but Lesa's face relaxed. And then she laughed.

## 2

Sammy Lunn's luck was in. Kowloon Airways booking office at Kai Tak airport had a wide reception desk laden with racks of colourful brochures detailing their scheduled helicopter and light aircraft trips around Hong Kong. He would be able to browse through them within earshot of Lesa Wessex and the stranger with her without arousing suspicion. He was relieved; when he had realized that the taxi he was following on his scooter was heading for Kai Tak, his worry had been that Lesa Wessex was about to leave the country before he had had a chance to carry out his mission. Mr Sukarno would have been most displeased.

'I'm very sorry, sir,' Sammy overheard the booking clerk saying as he approached the brochures, 'but we have no aircraft available for private charter until tomorrow.' The clerk turned his head to check his wall-planner. 'And that's a Skyliner twin-jet executive aircraft. Very expensive. On Friday we'll have –'

'I'll take the Skyliner,' Harry interrupted, handing the clerk an Amex charge-card. 'We want to fly to Kuro.'

An American, thought Sammy, wondering who the man with Lesa was.

'Ah, yes – Kuro. The big telescope,' the clerk nodded, slotting the Amex card into a reader and watching the screen while the machine dialled into a satellite link. 'It will have to be daylight arrival and departure, sir. The telescope authorities don't permit night movements. Hot gases from jets cause air distortion.'

'Daytime is fine.'

'Also we have to get advance permission for a visit in case they are carrying out calibration work, but it's usually okay. With the minimum twenty-four-hour stopover charge, charter fees and taxes, that comes to eleven thousand five hundred US dollars, sir.' He looked questioningly at Harry, his finger poised over the reader's keyboard.

'Fine,' said Harry as if spending that sort of money was part of his daily routine. He pressed his forefinger on the fingerprint identification panel set into the desk.

The clerk entered the information on the keyboard. He had to wait five seconds for authentication of the amount and verification of Harry's identity.

'That seems to be in order, sir. What time would you like to leave?'

Harry looked questioningly at Lesa. Sammy risked a glance at her: few women could wear a skintight travel suit the way she could wear it. His fertile mind toyed with many imaginative ways in which he could turn earning his fee into a pleasure.

'As early as possible,' Lesa said. 'It might be a long day.'

Sammy could not help noticing that she seemed to be irritated by something. He sensed that she was resenting the way the American seemed to be in charge.

'Thank you, sir,' said the clerk, handing Harry the charter confirmation that had rolled out of a printer and his Amex card. 'Please come to this desk at eight tomorrow morning. Take off will be at eight thirty. I'm sure you will enjoy your trip. The Skyliner is very modern. Only six months old.'

Harry thanked the clerk and he and Lesa left. Sammy didn't bother to follow them. There was no point now that he knew their movements. He finished perusing the brochures. The wall planner gave the last two registration letters of the only Skyliner owned by Kowloon Airways – Foxtrot Victor. Sammy returned the brochures to the rack and sauntered out of the booking office. He had a busy day in front of him. First a telephone call.

### 3

The security guard responsible for Kowloon Airways maintenance area picked up his telephone. The display told him it was an airport number calling him.

'Admin office,' said the voice curtly. 'Have Fire Protection Services called to replace the faulty smoke detector in the compound toilets yet?'

The guard checked the log. Everyone entering the maintenance area was logged in and out and times recorded. 'Nothing here – only employees.'

He heard a muffled curse at the other end. 'Damned contractors. Okay. We'll give them until midnight. Make a note on the log for whoever's on duty to notify the office if they haven't called by then. Fire Protection Services. Faulty smoke detector in the compound toilets. Got that?'

The security guard made a note on the electronic pad.

'Okay – it's entered.'

'Damned contractors,' the voice muttered again and hung up.

## 4

It was eleven at night when Sammy stopped his van outside Kowloon Airways maintenance area. He jumped out and walked quickly into the security office before the guard had a chance to come out to him. He was wearing the same uniform he had used when planting the television bugs in Lesa Wessex's hotel room. He sprawled tiredly across the counter as though he had had an exhausting day. That way he could see the guard's battery of closed-circuit television monitors. The guard on duty was not the one he had spoken to that morning.

'Fire Protection Services,' Sammy announced, yawning. 'Faulty smoke detector somewhere.'

'Compound toilets,' said the guard looking up from his log. He pointed through the window to a small brick building beyond a group of parked aircraft. 'Over there. You should've been here hours ago.'

'Don't you start,' Sammy complained, scribbling on the visitors' pad. 'I've had a terrible day. Van's been playing up. Clapped-out bloody thing keeps stalling. It's time I was given a new one.'

The guard made sympathetic noises. 'Another hour and you would've been in trouble.' He pressed the button that opened the barrier and watched Sammy climb into the van. The engine started on the third attempt, got halfway across the floodlit compound and stalled. It took another three attempts to get it started again. Clouds of smoke billowed from the exhaust. The vehicle stalled again beside the Skyliner. He chuckled to himself when Sammy gave up tinkering under the bonnet and walked angrily into the compound toilet clutching his tool-box, leaving the bonnet open. Normally the guard would not have permitted a vehicle to stop so close to an aircraft, especially when it blocked his view and the field of one of the cameras, but he did not have the heart to go after Sammy to tell him to shift it. He scanned his bank of television monitors and went back to reading his newspaper.

Sammy waited three minutes in the compound toilet. He returned to the van and pretended to tinker with the engine. The sleek shape of the Skyliner twin-jet was less than six metres away. Through the windows of the security office he could see the guard reading his newspaper.

The bomb Sammy had made that day was small enough to be housed in a fifty-gram tobacco tin with holes punched in it to let the barometric detonator 'breathe'. He snatched the device from its hiding place in the van's engine compartment, tore off the protective covers from the self-adhesive pads, and darted towards the Skyliner. He ducked under the nose and reached up into the dark recess of the nose wheel compartment, his fingers searching for a small flat surface that would be clear of the nose wheel when it was retracted. He found a horizontal bracing strut on the left-hand side of the compartment that was ideal and jammed the bomb against the upper surface of the strut. The adhesive pads gripped immediately, holding the tin firmly in place. Sammy returned to the van, tinkered for another minute, and slammed the bonnet shut.

He waved in acknowledgement to the guard when the barrier opened and drove out of the maintenance area. He had every reason to be pleased with himself: he had defeated a whole host of security arrangements to successfully plant a bomb consisting of twenty grams of Niroxal explosive. Deadly stuff. It had a detonation velocity ot twelve thousand metres per second. The advantage of planting the bomb where he had was that the nose wheel compartment was not pressurized. When the aircraft reached fifteen thousand feet, well out over the sea, the contacts on the aneroid bellows would complete the battery circuit to trigger the detonator. Twenty grams of Niroxal would be enough to blow the nose off Skyliner Foxtrot Victor and rupture the pressure hull.

Sammy reckoned that the chances of the executive jet or anyone on board surviving such catastrophic damage were nil.

5

Hugo Sukarno's face was expressionless as he watched the Skyliner taking off from Kai Tak airport. He panned his telescope to keep the executive jet centred in his vision. The nerve-activated motors in his artificial hands whirred softly – stopping and starting in response to the signals from his malignant brain.

The thirty-second separation between take offs that the over-loaded airport was forced to apply meant that an A300 airbus began accelerating from its holding point the moment the Skyliner's tyres left the runway. Sukarno tracked the Skyliner until it drew level with Causeway Bay and turned due east towards Clearwater

Bay. He took his eye from the telescope and regarded Sammy. 'When?'

'Hard to say, boss,' Sammy replied confidentially. 'As soon as it reaches fifteen thousand feet. That depends on its flight plan.'

# 6

## SOUTH CHINA SEA

Lesa was unhappy about the situation with Harry Dysan. Letting him charter the Skyliner had been a mistake. She cursed herself for her lack of judgement in permitting him to take over to the extent that he had. She should have chartered a boat; it would have been slower but at least it would have got the American out of her hair. She hated any form of dependency on others unless it was someone she could trust implicitly such as her parents or Darryl. At least the single seats each side of the executive jet's aisle meant that he could not sit next to her. She could ignore him without seeming to be obviously rude.

The Skyliner banked left shortly after take off. The pattern of over two hundred sub-tropical jade islands that made up Hong Kong tipped towards her: Bluff Island; Joss House Bay; Basalt Island. She knew them all; she knew every inlet and every anchorage from her hours spent before the giant monitor at Whitefriars Farm, sifting through hundreds of satellite photographs of the sea.

The seat belt signs went out. Harry changed seats and sat behind her.

'Better view on this side,' he observed cheerfully over Lesa's shoulder. 'Have you ever flown on an executive jet before?'

'No.'

'Weird isn't it? Just like a big jet but everything's in miniature. Miniature doors, a miniature galley.'

He broke off when the flight deck opened and their Chinese stewardess emerged. She was petite like a piece of Dresden china. Her smile looked as if it had been painted in place with make-up.

'Even the stewardess is a miniature. Let's hope the drinks are full-size.'

The Chinese girl reached automatically for the passenger address interphone and suddenly realized the incongruity of using it to address two passengers. 'Captain Elliot says that our flight time to Kuro will be two hours precisely,' she said brightly. 'We will be flying at a height of ten thousand feet. If you would like to visit the flight deck, you will be most welcome. In the meantime, if there is anything you need, please ask.'

'A scotch and water,' said Harry promptly. 'With plenty of ice.'

Lesa turned in her seat and looked disapprovingly at him. 'At this time in the morning, Harry?'

He smiled dismissively. 'My body clock's still on Eastern Standard Time.'

'You drink like that and your body clock's going to stop prematurely.'

'You sound like my ex.'

On the flight deck a pleasant but synthesized female voice advised Captain Grahame Elliot that the Pacific Ocean ATC had loaded a revised flight plan into the Skyliner's flight management computer. Would he please study and acknowledge. The central monitor was displaying:

COURSE REQUIRED: 100 DEGREES. COURSE ACTUAL: 95 DEGREES.
FLIGHT LEVEL REQUIRED: 11. FLIGHT LEVEL ACTUAL: 07.

Less than a metre away, almost immediately under the pilot's feet, was Sammy's ingenious homemade bomb. The priming mechanism inside the tobacco tin consisted of a miniature concertina-like metal bellows. The air inside the bellows was sealed at atmospheric pressure. As the Skyliner climbed, so the air pressure in the nose wheel compartment dropped, causing the bellows to expand thus closing the gap between two electrical contacts. At take off the gap had been twelve millimetres. At the Skyliner's present cruising height of seven thousand feet, the gap was ten millimetres.

Elliot touched the confirmation box on the screen three times to activate it. It changed colour, indicating that the revised course and height requirement requests were being acted upon. The Skyliner's power increased to eighty-five per cent. The control yoke moved towards him of its own accord and the Skyliner began climbing at a steady two hundred feet per minute – the real and artificial horizons showing a five degree turn to the right.

The bellows in Sammy's bomb responded to the increasing height by closing the gap between the detonator contacts.

Elliot was flying 'hands off'. Control of the Skyliner was handled by the Sperry Avionics flight management system – the whiz words for autopilot – except that the old autopilot systems were concerned only with maintaining an aircraft's course, height and airspeed whereas the modern systems provided total systems management, to such a degree that the conventional instrument panels of the previous century had disappeared altogether to be replaced by a series of flat screen displays that showed graphic representations of the old instruments as and when they were required. Triple redundancy transponders on the aircraft maintained a continuous telemetric link through the Pacific Air Navigation satellite with the regional air traffic control centre at Manila. In effect all civil aircraft in the region were under the control of the ATC computers in Manila although all required course changes had to be acknowledged by the pilot. It made them feel wanted. Only in an emergency would Elliot grab full control of the aircraft by pulling down the overhead guarded red handle between his seat and the empty co-pilot's seat.

The Skyliner reached eleven thousand feet and completed the five degree turn to bring it onto its designated course. The climb indicator and the turn indicator were no longer needed therefore they were cleared from Elliot's primary flight screen. He settled down to his daily struggle with the *South China Post* crossword puzzle.

The gap between the bomb's detonator contacts was steady at seven millimetres.

'Now listen,' said Lesa seriously in answer to Harry's question. 'You're the one who wants to see Kuro. I'm just stringing along for the ride, remember?'

'It was a polite question,' said Harry, aggrieved.

'And you got a polite answer, Harry. Once I've got my business out of the way, I'll give your job my undivided attention . . . provided I'm free to do so.'

Harry frowned at the odd statement. 'Well I won't stop you. I don't understand.'

'I meant exactly that – if I'm free to work on your project, I will do so.'

'You're not making sense.'

Lesa's answer was to put on the binaural sound headset, select Wagner from the control panel, and recline her seat. She'd made her point. Harry consoled himself by ordering another whisky from the Dresden china stewardess.

'A warming drink by the harbour?' the Pan Am skipper drawled into Elliot's headphones. 'Eight letters beginning with em? Okay, Kowloon Foxtrot Victor – we'll give it some thought.'

Elliot thanked him. He retuned his HF radio and listened to a couple of Qantas flights arguing about an umpire's decision during a recent test cricket match. He considered taxing them with ten down – only six letters – the Aussies ought to be able to cope with that, when the synthesized female voice requested an altitude change from flight level eleven to twelve – twelve thousand feet. Elliot sent the necessary acknowledgement and the Skyliner began climbing another thousand feet. The stewardess entered the flight deck and sat in the co-pilot's seat.

'It seems strange only having two passengers,' she observed. 'Any idea who they are?'

'Not a clue. Do me another coffee?'

Harry surreptitiously watched Lesa's profile. Her face was perfectly relaxed. Her slim body in the grey travel suit was stretched out tantalizingly in her seat. There was so much he wanted to know about her. He wondered about her aloofness, guessing that it was a defence mechanism. At first he thought that perhaps it came from living in England until he remembered an English secretary that he had had a brief affair with two years previously, a girl with a sexual appetite that was frightening. The English and their so-called reserve was a baseless generalization.

'What are you staring at?' Lesa suddenly asked without opening her eyes.

'You.'

This time she opened her eyes. She slipped her headphones off and looked quizzically at Harry. He expected a blast of verbal paraquat. Instead she gave a knowing smile. Harry decided that he would never understand her, even if she gave him the chance, which was unlikely.

The Skyliner trembled as it encountered the beginnings of some clear air turbulence.

'Shit!'

The jolt was unexpectedly severe. The stewardess dived into the galley, returned with a clean cloth and gave it to Elliot who dabbed it ineffectually at the coffee he had spilt in his lap. Another jolt made her grab at Elliot's seat back.

'Do you want another one, skipper?'

'No I don't. Christ – look at the mess.' He lifted the interphone off its hook and said automatically, 'This is Captain Elliot, ladies and gentlemen. We're running into a spot of turbulence. It won't last long, but in the meantime it would be best if you returned to your seats and fastened your seat belts.'

Lesa had experienced severe clear air turbulence before but she did not realize just how severe this was because there were no other passengers to heighten the effect with their inevitable gasps of dismay. She stared up at an overhead locker, noting how the pounding caused the moulded casing around the door to twist and distort. A glance at the wing was a mistake – it was almost flapping.

'Well the consensus of opinion on this flight deck is that the answer's "Mulberry",' said the Pan Am skipper. 'That's a Roger on your CAT. The opinion of this flight deck is that if you had a real airplane, maybe you'd be given a real flight level.'

Elliot thanked the Pan Am skipper for the opinions of his flight deck and cleared the frequency.

The instrument faces on the master flight screen had increased in size to make them easier to read during their appalling hammering. The only time Elliot had seen that happen before had been on the simulator. The aircraft's sensors would be radio-ing the pounding the Skyliner was receiving to the ATC computers which any moment now should be ordering a change of altitude. Nothing happened. Although the turbulence would not harm the aircraft, there was no point in subjecting the airframe to such punishment if it could be avoided. Elliot picked up his comms handset and punched out the frequency that would give him a real human being to talk to. He muttered a curse when the jolting caused a keying error, obliging him to cancel and start again.

'Good morning, Manila. This is Kowl Air Foxtrot Victor. Charter flight one-nine-five requesting flight plan deviation. Over.'

'Good morning, Foxtrot Victor,' the air traffic control officer in Manila responded. 'Go ahead.'

'We're experiencing sustained scat, Manila. Requesting flight level zero five. Over.' At five thousand feet Elliot would be able to complete the flight under manual control. He would enjoy that. Opportunities to get some real flying time in his logbook were rare.

'Negative, Foxtrot Victor,' the officer replied. 'We can give you flight level one-six. Over.'

Elliot was tempted to point out that he would be at the top of his descent in forty minutes and under Kuro control, but he had to accept their ruling. Maybe there were a lot of light aircraft movements at the lower altitude although there was nothing abnormal on his radar display. He acknowledged, waited for the revised altitude to appear on the screen and sat back to let the computers do all the work. Engine power increased to eighty-five per cent.

The Skyliner nosed up thirteen thousand feet and kept climbing.

The bellows in the bomb swelled. The contacts moved closer together.

Six millimetres . . . five millimetres . . .

The turbulence suddenly stopped.

Lesa breathed an inward sigh of relief. She saw Harry looking at his watch. 'Half way,' he observed.

Sensing that he was about to make another attempt at conversation, Lesa unfastened her seatbelt and caught the stewardess's eye. 'I'd like to take the captain up on that offer to visit his front office,' she announced.

Elliot beamed at his visitor in genuine pleasure. He waved his hand at the right-hand co-pilot's seat. 'Please, Miss Wessex. Help yourself.'

In the narrow confines of the flight deck Lesa's thighs brushed against his shoulders. 'I promise not to touch anything,' she joked as she settled in the seat.

With many women, the remark would have earned a *double entendre* from Elliot but he sensed that with Lesa Wessex, such a comment would not be appropriate. Instead he chuckled. 'Damned computers won't even let me fly it, so you've got nothing to worry about.'

'Is that why you don't have a co-pilot?'

'Not for two-hour flights. If the company had their way I think they'd like to do away with me as well.'

Lesa looked down through the side window. There was no cloud but a layer of heavy haze completely obscured the sea. The horizon was an indistinct smudge that meant it was impossible to judge where the sea ended and the sky started. She was all too familiar with such conditions over the South China Sea and Eastern Pacific. 'That turbulence was bad,' she observed.

'Probably a vortex from another jet,' Elliot explained. 'They're not fully understood, but they can hang around for hours after a jet has passed by if the conditions are right. Not so usual at this low altitude though. We're now on a slow climb to sixteen thousand feet. Just passing thirteen thousand five hundred feet.'

'Where are we now?' she asked.

Elliot touched the pad that provided Lesa with an illuminated display of the Western Pacific. 'Use the plus and minus touch areas to change the scale to zoom in and out.'

Lesa studied the display with professional interest. Darryl had once built an experimental receiver to intercept the plan position displays from air navigation satellites. They had both decided that the computer-generated images were of little use.

'Flight level one-four,' announced the synthesized voice.

'Fourteen thousand feet,' Elliot translated.

Four millimetres.

The climb indicator pointer was showing a rate of climb of two hundred feet per minute.

Lesa followed the projected line of the Skyliner's flight path across the display to Kuro. 'Have you ever flown to Kuro before?' she asked.

'About three times a year now that the telescope is working. Last trip was a month ago. Party of astronomers.' He looked speculatively at his lovely passenger. 'Is that your line, Miss Wessex?'

'No – my business is the reverse – looking at earth from above: remote sensing. I wouldn't mind squeezing in an hour's deep sea fishing while we're there if we've got time. Do they ever have any suitable boats in the harbour?'

Elliot shook his head. 'Can't say I've ever noticed.'

The contacts nudged closer together until the gap between them was three millimetres.

'You've never seen a large white motor-yacht there?'

'No. Wait a minute, though – yes – there was such a yacht on the last trip. It probably put in for refuelling.'

The door to the passenger cabin opened. 'Can I get you anything before I close the galley?' the stewardess asked brightly.

'Not for me,' Elliot answered. 'Miss Wessex?'

'No,' Lesa replied absently, trying to think of a way of pumping the pilot for more information without arousing his suspicions.

The stewardess left the door open and began tidying her tiny domain behind the flight deck.

'Who's in charge there?'

Two millimetres.

'I don't have any dealings with the technical side,' Elliot admitted. 'Flight operations on Kuro are looked after by a guy called Peter Menkova. Seems okay. Whenever I've been there I've dropped my passengers and picked up a returning group. A thirty minute turn round.'

One millimetre.

'Flight level one-five,' the synthesized voice stated.

'Another thousand feet and we'll level out,' said Elliot. 'We're just over half way. Kuro's now our nearest land for five hundred miles around.'

Half a millimetre.

The stewardess entered the flight deck and leaned across Elliot to retrieve his coffee cup.

At that precise moment the contacts completed the detonation circuit and Sammy's bomb went off.

By positioning it on the left-hand side of the nose wheel compartment, Sammy had unwittingly placed his deadly package where it would cause the most damage. The twenty grams of Niroxal exploding beneath Elliot severed all the pilot's control and power lines despite their armoured sheaths, and detonated with sufficient force to rupture the Skyliner's hull and drive a thirty-centimetre length of nose wheel steering link into Elliot's stomach. His gasp of agony was obliterated by the roar of air driving into the flight deck like an express train. The flight deck door was ripped off its hinges. It struck the stewardess on the side of her head, killing her instantly. She died with her painted smile intact. The tremendous inrush threw the aircraft's nose up, hurling Lesa backwards in her seat. With the sudden agony in her ears threatening to burst her head open, she snatched blindly at her seat harness. The only way to stop the straps flaying her alive was to grab the buckles and snap them shut across her waist. In so doing she saved her life because the Skyliner suddenly pitched forward into a steep dive. Coherent thought was impossible. Her ears were ringing from the explosion's terrible report, a hurricane-like blast of air was tearing at her, and the air was filled with a maelstrom of whirling papers and radio headsets. Through the confusion she saw Elliot clutching at his stomach. Blood was spouting through his fingers, atomizing to a nightmare spray of red that splattered across his horror-struck face and the bulkhead behind him.

'What do I do?' Lesa tried to scream. But opening her mouth gave the mounting typhoon of raw energy the necessary leverage to tear at her cheeks and rip the words into oblivion. She saw that Elliot was making a superhuman effort to raise his left arm. He was pointing. There was a guarded red lever set into the roof panel. It was the largest control of them all and centrally located where it could be reached by either pilot. It was obviously important. Had Lesa been able to focus her eyes properly she would have seen that the light track around the lever was flashing urgently. She forced her hand up to the lever and looked questioningly at Elliot.

She screamed again at the top of her voice, 'This one?'

It was impossible for him to see her face because it was being lashed by her hair but he managed what Lesa took to be a nod. She yanked the lever down.

The display panels before her came alive. She saw that the digital altimeter was winking rapidly towards seven thousand feet. The sea was now visible – filling her entire field of vision through the forward windows. Her mind wrestled with the problem of getting Elliot into her seat and realized that it would be impossible. The pilot's head was lolling sideways towards her – his eyes listless. Blood was welling from his mouth and being turned to spray like the blood voiding from the terrible wound in his stomach. He seemed to be mouthing something.

Lesa abandoned trying to make out what Elliot was saying. She forced herself to shut out the hideous cacophony and concentrated on the illuminated displays. One was a graphic representation of a diving aircraft. A flashing fingerprint highlighted the touch-sensitive area of the display – she touched it. Nothing happened. Elliot was watching her. He forced his arm up again. Lesa could see that he was holding up three fingers. She thumbed the touch-sensitive area again using three fingers and then realized that Elliot meant her to touch it three times. Her thumb jabbed the defined area three times and the graphic displays changed. The largest, directly in front of her, was a pictorial representation of a robot holding a control column. She jabbed frantically at it until it started flashing. She saw a movement out of the corner of her eye that wasn't part of the crazy cyclone of whirling debris. It was Harry lying sprawled on the floor, clinging to the seat supports. Somehow he had managed to half crawl, half slide forward. He looked up at Lesa. The blood from a deep cut on his temple would normally have streamed down his face, instead it was being syphoned straight out of the wound by the dervish hurricane.

She was about to yell at him to get back when the sensation of the Skyliner's steepening dive made her forget him. Only the left-hand digits of the maddened blur of racing numbers on the altimeter were changing slowly enough to be read. Lesa instinctively grabbed the control yoke and hauled it into her stomach. The nose came up sharply causing the air-speed to drop. Her weight seemed to double, making her arms leaden and forcing her body into the seat cushions. The sea disappeared from the forward windows to be replaced by sky and the tumbling altimeter digits went into reverse. The howling noise that was punishing her eardrums slackened off. To her horror, the sea appeared above her head and she realized that the Skyliner was upside-down. She looked at Elliot for guidance and saw with a terrible sick feeling that the pilot was dead.

Lesa had pulled the Skyliner out of its dive too sharply with the result that it was about to loop.

'Neti!' she sobbed as the airspeed began building again and the altimeter resumed its downward plummet. 'What do I do? What do I do?'

The sea reappeared. This time it was horribly close and the left-hand altimeter digit winked ominously from five to four.

*Four thousand feet! Neti! Neti! Help me!*

This time Lesa drew the control yoke towards her with greater care. Air was still roaring into the flight deck but everything loose had been smashed or blown into the cabin with the result that it was possible for her to think more clearly and concentrate on what she was doing. She gave a little gasp of surprise when the horizon suddenly appeared – scrolling downward like a badly adjusted television picture. Pushing the yoke forward stabilized the line. With a shock she realized that the Skyliner was now flying level – something that would have been impossible had the aircraft been carrying a full load of passengers and baggage. Another factor working in Lesa's favour was that the aircraft was carrying minimum flight plan fuel. Had Elliot survived he would have initiated the correct ditching procedure and dumped what fuel there was. As it was, even if Lesa had known how to lighten the aircraft, dumping the relatively small amount of fuel in the tanks would not have made that much difference to the Skyliner's handling characteristics.

The altimeter was reading 3,200 feet and dropping slowly. Lesa was able to take in the other instruments: the hand on the climb indicator was pointing down. Engine power reading was zero per cent. Airspeed was dropping back from the five hundred knots it had peaked at when she pulled the aircraft out of the dive.

Harry was struggling to his knees and had to hang onto the back of Elliot's seat to prevent himself being blasted back into the cabin. His dazed look took in the level horizon.

'We're going to have to ditch!' Lesa yelled.

Harry saw Lesa's lips moving and pushed himself closer to her so that she could shout in his ear.

'We're going to ditch!' she yelled again. 'Can you fly?'

Harry shook his head and tried to focus his eyes on the instrument display. Blood from his cut temple splattered over Lesa's left arm.

Two thousand feet. Airspeed 420 knots and falling.

Lesa discovered that she could reduce the airspeed by drawing gently back on the yoke, but that forced the nose up and set off an alarm that flashed insistently until she eased the yoke forward again.

1,500 feet. Airspeed four hundred knots.

'Flaps!' Harry shouted. 'They'll bring the speed down!'

Lesa touched the box marked FLAPS. A row of illuminated graphic symbols appeared showing the aircraft's flaps in different positions from clean to fully extended. Sensing that it would be unwise to extend the flaps fully, she selected five degrees.

One thousand feet. Airspeed 340 knots.

The sea was very close now. Lesa could pick out individual waves.

'It's working!' she shouted and selected ten degrees' flap.

One thousand feet. Airspeed three hundred knots.

Lesa felt a surge of exhilaration. The Skyliner was flying level. She applied another five degrees' flap and watched the airspeed indicator drop to 260 knots.

Eight hundred feet.

Lesa fought against mounting panic until her intuition told her that without power the aircraft could not possibly maintain level flight.

Another warning sign started flashing. This time it was the main gear symbol that showed a diagram of the aircraft's tricycle undercarriage. She was about to touch the control when she heard Harry shout something.

'What?' she yelled.

'Land clean!' Harry shouted. His words were obliterated by the noise. With an effort he raised his voice and bellowed, 'Land clean, Lesa! Land with the gear up!'

Lesa saw the sense in the suggestion and snatched her hand away. It would be best to hit the water with as few obstructions as possible sticking out of the Skyliner's fuselage. She lowered the flaps fully and watched the air-speed drop to two hundred knots. Somewhere she had read what aircraft touchdown speeds were. She suspected that any speed when ditching on water would be too fast.

The Skyliner's nose sank and airspeed began building. Only by pulling the yoke further back could she correct the situation.

Five hundred feet. 180 knots.

And then back to two hundred knots when the nose dropped again.

Goddam it! she wanted to scream out. How do I stop it from diving all the time? By now she had hauled the yoke all the way back against its stops. Sweat was trickling into her palms despite the gale screaming through the flight deck.

Four hundred feet. 180 knots.

At this height she could see that the aircraft was going to hit the water at an angle to the main swell. She had no doubt that ramming the Skyliner into one of those slow-moving walls of water would be the equivalent of flying into the side of a mountain. She gingerly eased the yoke to the left and was rewarded by the aircraft banking accordingly.

'Get back and strap in!' she screamed in Harry's ear.

'I don't want to leave you!'

'There's nothing you can do! Get back!' Harry moved out of her vision but she dared not take her eyes off the sea that was now a blur. Centring the yoke levelled the wings. The Skyliner was now flying parallel to the main swell.

Three hundred feet. Two hundred knots.

The sea was now a blur of grey nothingness streaking beneath the nose and completely filling Lesa's view. As near as she could judge, the Skyliner was going down at an angle of about fifteen degrees. Her instincts screamed at her that their chances of survival depended on hitting the water level. At the angle it was now, the Skyliner would be certain to break up on impact.

Eighteen years earlier, after diving into the sea to escape from the *Rasputin*, Lesa had been threatened by a shark. As the dreaded fin had closed in, she did not realize that her next act was one that many had found to be effective when dealing with sharks about to attack. She had done it out of desperation and because she could think of nothing else: she had put her head underwater and screamed.

Fate played its hand again. With the Skyliner within three hundred feet of a fatal nose dive into the sea, against all her instincts, Lesa pushed the yoke forward and steepened the dive. The sea came racing up towards her. At one hundred feet, she suddenly hauled the control yoke back. The nose came up and she caught a fleeting glimpse of the horizon. The airspeed suddenly dropped to 170 knots. Without really knowing what she was doing, Lesa had flared the aircraft at exactly the right height resulting in its belly hitting the water, spreading the force of impact and so preserving the airframe in one piece.

What happened next she would later recall as a mosaic of disconnected images. The impact threw her against the seat harness. Water came boiling into the flight deck from nowhere with terrible sudden-ness like an unleashed monster. It didn't behave like water; it was something solid and terrifying – a blind malignant entity of unimaginable strength seeking to pummel her defenceless mind and body into total submission by the ferocity of its attack. The monster seized her fingers and tried to tear them away as she fought with the release mechanism on the harness buckle. Then the monster hurled her against the bulkhead, driving the air from her body with the force of a maddened bull charging into her. The mighty surge spun her around and tossed her through the door into the rapidly flooding cabin, her flailing arms and legs crashing into the passenger seats with a force that she did not feel. The smiling face of the dead Chinese stewardess flashed past her like a mechanical ghoul hurling itself at a ghost train. The water was churning around her waist. Something grabbed at her arm, enabling her to fasten her fingers onto a seat back and pull herself upright. It was Harry.

'I've got the door open,' he gasped. They staggered against each other as the weight of the engines tilted the cabin down by the tail. Plastic cups and seat cushions danced around them. Lesa saw the sea surging through an opening in the hull. It was the emergency exit. Somehow Harry had managed to get it open. A fully-inflated fireproof escape tunnel with curved up ends was flapping against the side of the hull, threatening to tear loose. It was bright yellow like a grotesque banana. 'Get in!'

Too dazed to resist, Lesa allowed Harry to push her into the tube. He jumped in after her, tumbling over the raised ends. Surprisingly there was no water inside. The wind and the swell swept them clear of the stricken jet; its tailplane was half submerged, dragged down by the weight of the engines, but the flight deck was clear.

'A life raft!' Lesa shouted. 'Surely there's a proper life raft?'

'Well I didn't see one,' Harry answered, lying on his stomach and focussing on the Skyliner. 'I didn't have time to read all the instructions on the door. I don't think there was anything about a life raft.' He pulled off his shoes and jacket.

'What are you doing?' Lesa demanded.

'Going back in. There's got to be an emergency radio in there.'

Before Lesa could stop him, Harry had dived into the sea. Three strong over-arm strokes took him into the flooded doorway. He half swam, half crawled into the cabin and disappeared. Lesa lay on her stomach and used her hands to paddle the escape tube nearer the Skyliner. Bubbles suddenly erupted from around the half submerged nose causing the fuselage to settle lower in the water.

'Harry! It's sinking!'

The nose sank until the aircraft was floating level but two thirds submerged. The tailplane was sticking up like a rigid windsurfer sail. It was no longer lifting to the gentle swell. There was a sudden procession of debris swirling through the open exit: cushions, papers, seat covers, plastic cups – all came surging out of the Skyliner, propelled by the rush of air being driven out of the cabin as the aircraft sank further. By now there was less than a hand's breadth of a gap between the water and the top of the exit, and even that disappeared momentarily as the swell rode right over the fuselage. Perhaps he had become caught on something; perhaps at this very moment he was fighting for his life.

Without hesitation, Lesa dived into the sea and swam to the opening. She reached it just as a great gout of bubbles erupted through the opening – the exit was now completely submerged. Lesa tried diving underwater but the buoyancy of her travel suit forced her to the surface. Her second attempt was equally futile. She tore open the main waist-seal, kicked off the lower half of the garment and yanked off the top. The cold against her body caused her to give a shuddering gasp. She took a deep breath, jack-knife dived beneath the surface, and opened her eyes underwater. To her horror she saw that the exit was now a metre beneath the surface and still sinking. With only the drag of her bra and panties to impede her, she swam down easily, and pulled herself into the cabin. All she could see in the gloom were the patches of light from the windows. She twisted around when something caught her eye and came face to face with the stewardess's macabre painted smile. Her lungs were bursting. It was hopeless. She backed out through the exit, kicked to the surface and sucked a heady draught of air into her lungs.

There was no sign of the escape tube. For a moment she was seized by a wave of panic. Then the swell dipped and she saw a flash of bright yellow. It was only a few metres away. It turned in the wind so that she could see right through it. There was no sign of Harry. All that was visible of the Skyliner was the tip of the tailplane and a small area of the upper fuselage over the flight deck. She was about to take another deep breath and dive down again when a hatch opened and Harry's head and shoulders appeared.

'Harry!'

He heard the cry, looked around in alarm and spotted Lesa in the water. 'Why aren't you in the tube?' he demanded.

'Because I'm looking for you!'

'But I'm not lost, you stupid bitch!'

'Don't you call me a stupid bitch!'

The incongruity of trading insults in their present circumstances was lost on Lesa but not on Harry. He burst out laughing which infuriated her further. 'Get into the tube!' he yelled.

Lesa swam to the tube and clambered over the raised lip. She smarted with embarrassment when she realized just how inadequate her underwear was. When she looked up, Harry had disappeared.

Her valise and handbag appeared on the fuselage followed by his head and shoulders.

'Where would madam like her bags?'

'Oh for Christ's sake stop behaving like a stupid ass!'

'Catch!'

Harry tossed over the valise and she caught it. He climbed onto the roof and threw her handbag followed by his travel bag. She paddled the escape tube nearer and glared up at him.

'Well, come on then! Or are you going to let it sink under you?'

'I think madam should adjust her dress before entering the dining room,' said Harry solemnly before sliding into the sea.

Lesa looked down and saw that her breasts had spilled out of her bra. She angrily hitched the garment back in place and moved out of the way as Harry pulled himself over the lip.

'You were supposed to find a life raft!' Lesa scolded. 'Not go looking for baggage! That was a stupid thing to do! Against my better judgement – I went after you.'

'This *is* the life raft,' said Harry simply.

'What?'

'It's an escape chute and raft all in one. Neat. I didn't realize it until I looked down on it. There she goes.'

Lesa followed his gaze. A swirl of bubbles and then there was nothing left of the Skyliner except the debris that was now spreading over a wide area. Streams of bubbles bursting to the surface marked where the aircraft had finally sunk. Both of them allowed their thoughts about Elliot and the stewardess to pass unsaid.

'First things first,' said Harry, looking around the interior of the tube. 'Move your ass, sweetheart.'

To Lesa's fury he actually slapped her on the bottom. She would have flown at him but her attention was caught by what he was looking at – a sign in orange letters stencilled on the raised lip of the escape tube that read: EMERGENCY SUPPLIES. PULL RED TOGGLE. Harry pulled the red toggle. A seam split open and several packs tumbled out onto the inflated floor.

'Concentrated food, first aid,' said Harry sorting through the packs, 'fruit juice, hot drinks, fluorescent light packs. Even some fishing tackle . . . Ah – a SARAH beacon.' He held up a cylindrical device.

'A what?'

'An automatic search and rescue and homing radio beacon.' He read the instructions printed on the side of the device, unscrewed the cap and extended a telescopic whip antenna. He leaned out of the tube, found a hook and attached the radio to it.

While his attention was diverted, Lesa opened her valise and was delighted to see that the maker's claims about the case being waterproof were correct; all the contents were dry. She wrapped a towel around herself and immediately felt better.

'Harry.'

'It's got a battery life of a hundred hours. Should be long enough for someone to find us.'

'Harry.'

'Yes, sweetheart?'

'Thanks for getting my things.'

'That's okay, sweetheart.'

'And, Harry. If you ever slap me like that again I'll probably kill you. And if you don't stop calling me sweetheart I will anyway.'

Harry met her gaze. He recalled the same expression from the previous day in her hotel room and realized that she was not joking. He nodded. 'Message received and understood, Lesa. So which button did you accidentally press to get us into this mess?'

His flippancy irritated Lesa. 'I didn't press anything,' she retorted. 'There was a loud bang and this terrible inrush of air, and then the aircraft went out of control.'

'No smoke or fire?'

'No.'

'Well – I've heard of birds causing catastrophic damage to aircraft,' Harry commented.

'This wasn't a bird strike, Harry,' Lesa said adamantly. She went on to explain about the length of metal that had embedded itself in Elliot's stomach.

Harry looked seriously at her. 'I know from the lengths that the EPA went to to protect your identity, and you admitted to me, that you're in danger. Could it have been a bomb?'

'How could anyone have planned a bomb in time? You chartered the plane yesterday and we flew out first thing this morning. And you saw the security compound: electrified fences, closed-circuit TV cameras.'

'True,' Harry conceded, not convinced. 'Well – maybe it was metal fatigue. A section of skin ripping out at four hundred knots would cause a helluva lot of damage. Or it could've been a compressed air cylinder blowing up. Was there any indication of automatic distress signals being sent when the aircraft went out of control?'

Lesa shook her head. 'I don't know,' she admitted. 'Nothing like a radio symbol came up on the instrument panel.'

Harry thought for a moment. 'Okay. There'll be an alert on from the moment the transponders on the aircraft stopped squawking. The signals from the beacon will be picked up by a satellite so all we can do is sit tight and wait.'

'My Klipfone's dry,' said Lesa, reaching for her valise.

'Waste of time. In this part of the world, we're certain to be out of range of any ground repeaters. We'd better make ourselves more comfortable.' He discovered the drop down transparent panels that sealed the ends of the tube to keep out the elements. He smiled at Lesa when he had made the panels secure. 'Better?'

'Better,' Lesa murmured. It annoyed her the way this friendly American kept taking command. She was about to say something when shock set in. She shivered. The covered raft's insulation ensured that its interior remained chilly despite the sun beating down. Harry looked at her in concern.

'Are you okay, honey?'

'Yes!'

Harry broke open a small packet and shook out an aluminium foil body heat conserver shaped like a sleeping bag. 'You'd better get into this.'

'I'm perfectly all right!' Lesa snapped.

Harry shoved his gaunt face close to Lesa. Despite her undoubted superiority when it came to violence, this was one battle he was determined to win. Her eyes snapped fury when he had the temerity to place his hand on her forehead. 'You are not all right, Lesa. You've been through a helluva stressful time and now your body's screaming "enough". You're losing heat fast so I'm going to get you into this thing if I have to half kill you to do it.'

All the fight went out of Lesa; to her surprise and Harry's relief, she allowed him to help dry her properly and pull the foil sheath around her so that she resembled an oven-ready chicken. She watched him reading the instructions on a can of malt beverage. He broke the reagent seal on the base of the can and passed it to her when the reacting chemicals had heated it up. She sipped cautiously. It tasted hot and sweet.

'Okay, honey?'

She was tempted to say something cutting but the look of genuine concern in his eyes stilled her tongue. Besides, it was pleasantly warm in the conserver and the drink took away the taste of seawater.

# 8
## KURO, WESTERN PACIFIC

Harry was right when he said that there would be an alert on from the moment the Skyliner's transponders stopped transmitting. Peter Menkova was parking his jeep outside the tiny air terminal hut to greet the expected arrival of the Skyliner when he saw the duty communications officer waving frantically to him from a window. He ran into the building.

'An alert from Manila ATC, sir,' said the communications officer. 'The flight from Hong Kong disappeared five minutes ago in grid square AJ4567 – two hundred miles and ten miles due west of us. They're picking up a distress beacon in square AJ4568. As we're the nearest, they want to know if we can get a helicopter out to them.'

Menkova grabbed the handset. He remembered to speak in English. 'Hallo, Manila? This Menkova on Kuro. We can scramble a helicopter immediately but we might have a boat in the area. Stand by, please.' He took the handset away from his mouth and spoke to the communications officer. 'Diem's on his way back from Hong Kong. Find out his position.'

The officer dialled up a frequency on the communications console and transmitted *Rasputin*'s selcall code. It was some seconds before Diem's voice answered.

'Hallo, *Rasputin*. This is Kuro. An executive jet *en route* from Hong Kong to Kuro has disappeared in grid square AJ4567. Distress signals are being received from AJ4568. Give your position please. Over.'

'AJ4558. Over.' Diem answered when he had checked the motor-yacht's fix.

'AJ4558,' the officer relayed to Menkova. The two men located Diem's position on a chart and scaled off the distance from AJ4568.

'Hallo, Manila,' said Menkova into the handset. 'Our boat is one hundred miles west of the position. It will take it four hours to reach the area so we're sending a helicopter out now which will be there in two hours. Any specific instructions? Over.' He listened intently and passed Manila's requirements to the communications officer. The helicopter was to pick up any survivors and return them to Kuro. Meanwhile *Rasputin* was to head for the area, collect any wreckage it found and rendezvous with two helicopters and a frigate which were already on their way to the scene.

Five minutes later a Kamov light helicopter took off from Kuro and headed west, nose down for maximum speed.

## 9

# WESTERN PACIFIC

From the darkness came the sound of singing. Dance music. People laughing and shouting. She saw the wretched figure of a half naked young girl lying in the bottom of a sampan, bilge water awash around her skinny body. The girl lifted her head and stared uncomprehendingly at the blaze of lights.

It was a shallow draught cruise liner like the pictures of Mississippi river boats. On the lower state deck were women in beautiful evening dresses dancing with partners in white tropical suits. There was a long buffet laden with food at one end of the dance floor and a small band at the other, where a man in a tuxedo was singing into a microphone. The entire apparition was less than a hundred metres away and was passing by like a bejewelled dowager duchess. She heard someone screaming. It was the girl, now awake and waving a shirt frantically at the passing ship. But it took no notice; the singer continued singing; the band continued playing. The night mist gradually absorbed the ship like a wraith returning to its secret lair but the girl's screaming went on and on. Then a voice was calling her name.

'Lesa! Lesa!'

A friendly voice. A voice fraught with anxiety. A voice she knew she could trust. But it was a man's voice therefore how could she possibly trust it?

She opened her eyes and the wretched young girl and the ship, the music and the revellers and the cold and the night were gone. For a fleeting moment she was back in a dank-smelling paint locker with Lin's arms around her, feeling his warmth as he moved in her. Her eyes focussed away from the screen of the past to now and she saw that it wasn't Lin. It was Harry.

'Lesa? Lesa – what's wrong?'

He wasn't touching her. He had learned that lesson. For a blind, irrational moment she wished that he was. She needed warmth – close human animal warmth to bridge the cold gulf between the past, when a young man had briefly made love to her because she had wanted him to, and this bleak prison cell of the present, built up ever since she had been raped and her family murdered.

'I must have been dreaming,' she mumbled, struggling up. Harry made no move to help her but he smiled his relief. 'You sure were, honey. You've been asleep for an hour. Who was Neti?'

'Neti? Oh – a friend.'

*Betrayal! Tell him! Tell him the whole story!*

'What happened to her?'

For seconds she teetered on the edge of indecision. This good-natured man deserved to be told; it was because of those terrible events that he was here in this present mess.

Harry had no idea what her uncertainty was about. He decided to cheer her up. 'Hey – I've found something for you!' He unfastened an end panel and felt around on the outside of the tube. 'Yep. Nice and dry.' He turned around and showed Lesa her Lorietta travel suit. He had even recovered the belt with the conditioner still attached. 'Will it be okay, do you think?'

Lesa smiled gratefully and took the garment from him. The material felt soft to the touch. He had taken care to dry it evenly. 'Oh yes, thank you, Harry. A dipping in seawater won't hurt it. The material's indestructible.'

He laughed. 'Like my pants. Look at them. Smart, huh?'

'All it needs is a new lining,' Lesa continued, not interested in the fate of Harry's suit. 'I've got plenty of those.' Harry's recovery of the travel suit was inconsequential considering their circumstances yet she was touched by the gesture. She found herself regretting her harsh treatment of him when they had first met.

'So tell me about Neti.'

She hesitated. The only other person she had ever told the story to had been David Janson. 'She was my best friend twenty years ago when I was a kid in Vietnam . . .'

'Younger or older than you?' he prompted gently.

'About three years older . . .' She closed her eyes and saw a vivid picture of herself and Neti dancing with the cranes. She could even hear the beat of their wings as they rose briefly into the air when performing their strange courtship hops. But the beat was wrong. It was too regular, with a mechanical quality. 'Listen!' she exclaimed.

Harry listened. He was about to say that he couldn't hear anything when Lesa scrambled to the end of the raft and yanked up the panel. She paddled the raft around in a semi-circle and pointed to the hardening dot that was moving towards them.

It was the Kamov helicopter from Kuro. They had been in the water for two hours and ten minutes.

## 10

*Rasputin* was the first surface craft to get there. It arrived on the scene two hours after Lesa and Harry had been winched to safety. A US navy helicopter was already hovering over the area where the Skyliner had gone down but keeping a good distance so that the downwash from its rotors did not disperse the debris anymore than the wind and swell was already doing. Another helicopter was about a mile distant, using its dipping side-scan sonagraph equipment in an attempt to locate the aircraft on the floor of the Pacific which was two miles deep at this point. The observers in the first helicopter directed the *Rasputin* over the radio. After an hour's hard work by Diem's three-man Vietnamese crew using gaffs and nets, there was a small mountain of sodden seat cushions, seat covers, plastic cups and other debris piled up on the after deck.

'What do I do now?' Diem asked the pilot of the first helicopter.

'Wait until the frigate shows and hand over the debris,' the pilot advised.

'How long will that be?'

'Could be nightfall.'

Diem fretted. On board was another of the precious flux density analysers that Alexi needed as a matter of urgency. It was beginning to look as if the delay would make him a day late in returning to Kuro. He wondered what Alexi would say.

## 11
### KURO, WESTERN PACIFIC

What particularly infuriated Victor Koniev was that despite being the director of Kuro Multi-Mirror Telescope, he did not have a magnetized card to unlock the door to Alexi Hegel's laboratory at the far end of the telescope control building. There was no bell and no windows. He had telephoned Alexi to say that he was on his way and now he was fuming outside and having to resort to beating on the door with his fist. Luckily there was no one around to see his humiliation.

Eventually the door was opened by Anton Pachmann.

'Yes?'

Koniev controlled his temper. 'I've come to see Alexi. He is expecting me.'

Pachmann grudgingly admitted Koniev and led him along a corridor into Hegel's tidy research suite. The bull-chested physicist was wearing only shorts, tinkering with a one-tenth scale model of the torus coil that was suspended from the ceiling. He gave Koniev an indifferent glance and continued to work.

'Good afternoon, Victor. To what do we owe the pleasure of this visit?'

Koniev looked around the laboratory. It was only his third visit. He noticed that his directive that the labels be removed from non-Soviet-built equipment was being flouted yet again. Sitting on a workbench was a Hughes plasmascope bearing the Hughes logo. 'You gave me an undertaking to reduce your dependency on foreign-built equipment,' he said stiffly, pointing to the offending piece of test equipment.

Hegel shrugged. He was in no mood for an argument with Koniev. 'I said where possible, Victor. You find us a home-built plasmascope that works as well as that one and we'll be happy to use it. Won't we, Anton?'

Pachmann gave a cursory nod without looking up from some drawings he was studying.

'What is the point of the Soviet Union making the biggest

breakthrough in the history of physics if we have to use American equipment to achieve it?' Koniev demanded.

Hegel's icy blue eyes regarded Koniev. 'What the hell do you want out of this project, Victor? A working plasma beam or a political platform for you and your little clique of scheming loonies in the Kremlin?'

It wasn't difficult to goad Koniev into losing his temper. One had only to pour contempt on the ideals of his Lenin Reform Group. What was harder was equating the silver-haired, usually genial and smiling, distinguished-looking man whom visitors saw with the fuming bigot now confronting Hegel.

'If it wasn't for me there would *be* no project!' Koniev shouted. '*I* was the one who recognized your talent; *I* was the one who spent hours persuading endless committees that we should build this telescope; *I* was the one that spent countless hours manipulating the accounts so that you had the funding you needed. If it wasn't for me there would be no torus beam.' Koniev realized that he was ranting and forced himself to calm down. He added in a more moderate tone, 'And as I think you know, Alexi, it is your incompetence and stupidity that has nearly wrecked the entire project.'

The accusation caused even Pachmann to look up from his drawings. Hegel's grin that the outburst had provoked remained in place but his voice was dangerously quiet when he spoke. 'Now what are you going on about, Victor?'

'I'm talking about last month's test firing of the torus beam.'

'What about it?'

'The target satellite you used was *not* Soyuz 560!'

Hegel shrugged. 'You were in the control room. You saw the sighting images. You gave the order to fire.'

'Because I stupidly accepted your word that the target satellite was Soyuz 560! I'm not an expert on satellites, God damn you!'

'Okay,' said Hegel easily. 'So which satellite did we zap?'

Koniev opened his briefcase and tossed a photograph of a satellite down in front of Hegel. It showed a large communication satellite in orbit. It was normal in all respects except for a jagged hole at one end near the antennae clusters. 'The new director of the Konstantin Tsiolkovskii Orbital Telescope is a member of our movement. I asked him to take some high-resolution pictures of Soyuz 560 for this month's meeting of the executive committee meeting. He found that it was undamaged so he checked the other defunct satellites in the same arc of the Clarke belt and he found that one. PacSat 19! A commercial satellite!'

Hegel passed the photograph to Pachmann who studied it with professional interest. After all, it was evidence of the success of nearly twenty years' research.

'I don't see what you're so upset about,' said Hegel. 'Show that to your precious committee. If they're all as ignorant as you, they won't know what satellite it is.'

The answer infuriated Koniev. 'I can't show them that! And there's worse. Two weeks ago the satellite was Hoovered by the Americans!'

'So what's the problem?'

Koniev could scarcely credit the physicist's indifference. 'The problem, my dear Alexi, is that thanks to your monumental incompetence, the Americans must now know about the beam before we're ready to show our hand!'

'It looks like meteoroid damage,' said Pachmann, speaking for the first time.

Hegel nodded. 'Precisely. The Americans are doing exactly what we're doing, and what the French are doing in the Hoover Programme. Large geosynchronous satellites are stowed in the bay of a shuttle and released into a low earth orbit so that they burn up within a few hours on re-entry into the atmosphere. Simple. PacSat 19 no longer exists.'

'And nor does our evidence of what we've achieved,' Koniev retorted.

Hegel was tiring of the argument. 'Listen, Victor. You were the one who pushed us into a test firing before we were ready. Anton and I had to work twenty hours a day to meet your deadline. Any mistakes made are your fault. Anyway, why maintain secrecy any longer? We've proved the torus beam works. What's the point of keeping up this silly secret weapon melodrama any longer? It's time to publish our results.'

Koniev stared at Hegel in undisguised contempt. 'You may be a brilliant physicist, Victor, but you're a political cretin if you can't see the value of a working torus beam as a political weapon.'

This time Hegel came close to losing his temper. Until now he had enjoyed toying with Koniev's volatile temper. 'Now listen to me, comrade. Anton and I have been working for the best part of twenty years on this thing. We've proved that our theories work. We've got a working prototype to demonstrate to the whole world. Not to just a handful of your turn-back-the-clock cronies.'

Koniev's scalp went back. 'I'm *not* interested in a prototype. We must have an operational system working in time for the elections in three years if we're to convince the Soviet people that our candidates can offer them the best chance of peace and security from a position of strength and a return to the basic principles of the founders of our state. We will conduct another test firing one month from today with members of the executive committee present. This time *I* will select the target and supervise every aspect of the test firing!' Koniev seized the photograph from Pachmann and stuffed it back in his briefcase. 'Three weeks, Comrade Hegel – May the first. I think that will be a most appropriate date for the test, don't you?' Koniev turned to the door. 'One last thing – I shall require a key to these laboratories. I want it on my desk within three hours. That's an order.'

'Dear God, how I loathe that man,' Hegel muttered when Koniev had left.

'Which makes two of us,' Pachmann commented.

'Well he's not getting a key. To hell with him. Right now he needs us more than we need him. I'll tell you something, Anton – I'm tired; I'm tired of this God forsaken hole; I'm tired of taking orders from that tinpot commissar; I'm tired of this thing now that we've got it working, and I'm tired of the idea of having to wait for recognition until it suits Koniev.'

'Which makes two of us,' Pachmann repeated expressionlessly.

Hegel shot a glance at his colleague. Even after over twenty years' collaboration, he never knew what the impassive physicist was thinking. 'Okay. What's stewing in that devious little mind of yours?'

'Now that the torus beam works, I think it's time we demonstrated our achievement to the whole world by selecting a more ambitious target than a dud satellite.'

'What sort of target?'

Pachmann rummaged through some papers and handed Hegel a drawing. The older man looked at it in surprise. His eyes met Pachmann's bland gaze. 'You're not serious?'

'I'm perfectly serious,' said Pachmann evenly. 'There's a launch scheduled for the twenty-ninth of April.'

284

'Could it be done? Right under the noses of Koniev and his buddies in the control room?'

'Dummy data feeds to his console wouldn't be too difficult to rig. They could be removed later. We could be sitting at the real console at the back of the control room looking at the real target while we fed a dummy target to Koniev and his dummies. Today is the ninth of April. That gives us twenty-one clear working days till May Day. It will be hard work but we could do it.'

Hegel chuckled. 'It would certainly finish Comrade Koniev and the more ambitious of his power-mad little friends. We'd be killing two birds with one stone.'

'Certainly killing one bird,' said Pachmann with clinical mildness. 'And a large one at that. An unfortunate accident as a result of Comrade Koniev's willingness to cut corners with new, untried technology. We would, of course, be most profuse in our apologies. Koniev and his little group would be finished and we would have demonstrated to the world what we've achieved.'

Hegel stared at his colleague, then his eyes dropped to the drawing. He was silent for a few moments and then he gave a rich, booming laugh as the implications sunk in. 'You know something, Anton? You're an evil little bastard!'

The drawing was of a United States space shuttle.

## 12
### HONG KONG April 9

Hugo Sukarno watched the English language television news without speaking. Sammy gave his employer an occasional worried sidelong glance but wisely remained silent.

'Kowloon Airways have named the survivors as Lesa Wessex, a business woman from the United Kingdom, and Harry Dysan, a researcher from Florida,' a newsreader was saying. 'They had been staying in Hong Kong as tourists and were flying out to Kuro on a day trip when the Skyliner came down in the Pacific just over an hour out from Kai Tak. We have this report from Johnny Harding.'

The picture cut from the studio to a shot taken from a helicopter of a net load of wreckage being winched up from *Rasputin*. 'This is all that's left of Kowloon Airways' Skyliner executive jet, Foxtrot Victor, that came down in the Pacific just after ten forty-five this morning,' intoned an unseen reporter. 'A helicopter from Kuro, where the jet was heading, was on the scene within two hours of the alert to pick up the two survivors. The charter jet's crew of two went down with their aircraft. Two helicopters and this motor-yacht are now scouring the area for more wreckage in the hope that it might contain a clue as to what caused the crash. They will be joined in the search this evening by a frigate from the People's Liberation navy which is on its way to the scene. This is Johnny Harding, two hundred miles west of Kuro, reporting for RTHK.'

The picture cut back to the newsreader. 'Accident investigators are now on Kuro interviewing the survivors,' she concluded. 'We'll bring you more on that story when we receive it.'

Sukarno muted the television's sound and regarded Sammy with a stony expression while unwrapping a cigar.

'I'm sorry, Mr Sukarno,' said Sammy awkwardly. 'I did my best.'

A contributing factor to Hugo Sukarno's success was that he rarely berated an employee when that employee had done his or her best. He had no idea how Sammy had planted the bomb and wasn't interested; that Sammy had succeeded in doing so was a remarkable achievement. To Sammy's immense relief he nodded and lit the cigar. 'You had bad luck, Sammy. It looks like there's going to be a major investigation so it might be a good idea if you used your earnings for a holiday in Singapore or somewhere. I certainly don't want you coming here. You know where to find it.'

Sammy was incredulous. 'You mean you're going to pay me, boss?'

'I said, you know where to find it.'

Sammy crossed the office and opened the desk drawer. The second half of his fee was there – a neat bundle of banknotes which he slipped gratefully into his pocket. 'Thank you very much, boss,' he said, giving a polite bow.

Sukarno drew slowly on his cigar and exhaled a cloud of smoke while continuing to watch the silent television. 'I still want her dealt with, Sammy, so spend your vacation doing some serious thinking. Do I make myself clear?'

Sammy nodded emphatically. 'I won't fail next time, boss.'

The Indonesian smiled indulgently. 'No, Sammy. Not a second time. That would be most inadvisable. But there won't be a second time. Not for a while.'

'Why is that, boss?'

'For the time being I think it would be advisable to leave Miss Wessex alone.'

Kuro's medical officer was delighted to have something to do. Doctor Valentina Lenka was young, charming and efficient. She subjected Lesa and Harry to a meticulous medical examination in her clinic, refusing to accept their assurances that they were okay until she had satisfied herself that they were indeed none the worse physically for their harrowing experience. Nevertheless, mindful of the effects of delayed shock, she over-ruled the protests of her patients and gave them both a substantial sedative. Sleep, she assured them before they went under, was the best medicine. Her motives were to give Lesa and Harry a chance to fully recover before they had to face the team of accident investigators and journalists who had arrived on a flight from Hong Kong that afternoon.

Lesa was woken at seven o'clock the following morning by Harry's snoring in the bed beside her. It wasn't loud snoring, it was just that she wasn't used to sharing a room with men who snored, or to sharing a room with anyone, for that matter. There was a moment of disorientation at the strange surroundings before the events of the previous day slipped into place: the dimly-lit room was laid out like a miniature but well-equipped hospital ward. Some thoughtful person had even provided a large vase of glorious hibiscus blooms – probably locally grown. Early morning light was sneaking around a Venetian blind. Her bed, like hospital beds the world over, was hard. She swung her feet to the vinyl floor and discovered that she was wearing a pair of good-quality pyjamas although she couldn't remember changing into them. A tray contained a large selection of self-chilling cans of fruit juice and two cool draughts cleared her head of any residual drowsiness. She was pleased to discover her valise on a bedside chair. It contained a change of underclothes and two disposable linings for her travel suit. The travel suit itself was on a hanger alongside Harry's clothes and appeared to have been correctly steam-cleaned. Even the conditioner batteries had been recharged. The best find of all was her Klipfone. What she thought was a closet turned out to be a bathroom; a ten-minute shower, a brisk towelling off and she felt able to tackle anything the world could throw at her with the possible exception of Harry's snoring. Only when she had changed into the travel suit did she inflict an unkindness on Harry by dribbling ice-cold orange juice onto his bare chest. He turned over and stopped snoring.

She opened the Venetian blind and stepped out onto a small veranda with a table and chairs. She had only vague recollections of the place from the previous day. Now she was able to take a good look at her surroundings: the clinic overlooked an empty harbour. There was no sign of *Rasputin*. The only sign of life was a bar on the opposite side of the dusty road where the owner or manager was opening shutters and setting out tables and chairs. The low, early morning sun was below the far side of a stunted mountain. The peak of the mountain was crowned with four lattice frameworks that supported the mirrors of the Kuro telescope. Only when she saw a truck skirting the concrete apron around the telescope did she realize just how massive the construction was.

She wondered if Kuro had a Klipfone satellite repeater and was rewarded by a SYSTEM STANDING BY message when she switched on the miniature handset. She called Darryl's number.

'Lesa!' he said delightedly when he answered. 'What the hell's been happening? I've been worried sick about you. What's all this on the news about you being in a plane crash? I've been trying to call you, and your parents are going mad because all their calls are being shunted into your answering machine.'

Lesa gave Darryl a brief, heavily abridged account of events over the past twenty-four hours and assured him that she was fine; no, she didn't know when she would be returning home, and would he please call David and Carrie and tell them that she was okay because she didn't feel up to having to provide a lot of explanations over the phone.

The tiny township was nearly wide-awake with a few light trucks buzzing about when she finished the conversation and cleared the channel. She sat very still for some moments until she heard an approaching engine. A jeep was skirting the harbour. It had probably left the bungalow that she could see perched on a low hill on the opposite side of the harbour. Despite the warmth of the morning, a chill stole through her and her pulse quickened. Although there was no sign of *Rasputin*, she was certain that she could sense the presence of the men who had massacred her family. The sensation was more of a sickness. A sudden nausea, so alien in its intensity that it both puzzled and frightened her. The jeep got to within two hundred metres of where she was sitting and turned up a side road that appeared to head off into the interior. All she saw of its occupants was a glimpse of two hands gripping the steering wheel and a hairy arm resting on the passenger door. She couldn't be a hundred per cent certain but from the way the low sun caught the arm for a second, it looked as if the hairs were pure blond.

'Very soon now, Neti,' she whispered when the sickness had passed. 'Very soon.'

Harry's dishevelled pyjama-clad figure emerged on the veranda. There was a dressing on the cut on his temple, he needed a shave and his hair was standing on end. He was a walking bad start to anyone's day.

'You'll have to marry me,' he announced, slumping into a chair.

'Oh? Why's that?'

'You've spent the night with me. My family will insist that only marriage can restore my honour.'

Lesa's scorching reply was interrupted by the arrival of Dr Valentina Lenka in her Lada. Harry had imagined that Russian women doctors would be large, formidably-muscled, matronly types armed with suppository tubes around their necks instead of stethoscopes. Valentina Lenka refused to fulfill his stereotyped image by virtue of being a petite brunette in her mid-twenties.

'You both look fine,' she said cheerfully, unlocking her office. 'The bar over the road will be sending your breakfast across. There's a horde of journalists and air accident investigators staying at what passes for an hotel here – I do hope you feel up to facing them. If you don't, I can always order them off the premises.'

'I think we can face them,' said Lesa, smiling. She jabbed a thumb at Harry. 'Of course, whether or not they're up to facing this one is another matter.'


# 14

Anton Pachmann sat in front of the television set in Hegel's living room and used the remote control box to tune the satellite receiver into the NASA Information Channel – one of the channels that was no longer distributed on Kuro following Koniev's ruling on what should be re-broadcast to the island's inhabitants. Once he had a clear picture and sound, he pressed the store button so that the frequency was held in memory. Most of the time the channel carried rolling captions giving up-to-date information on the agency's activities interspersed with documentaries and special features. The diet was aimed at educational organizations and news services rather than a mass audience although the live television feeds of broadcasts from the space station, and particularly shuttle launches, often attracted sizeable audiences even though shuttle lift-offs were now routine. The incredible spectacle of an orbiter riding away from Canaveral or Vanderberg on a column of fire and thunder was one that would never pall.

Pachmann watched the cycle of caption cards and called Hegel into the room from the kitchen when the card appeared that he was waiting for. Hegel didn't like being disturbed during his culinary duties when it was his turn to thaw out a meal.

'I haven't got time to watch television when I'm cooking,' he grumbled.

Pachmann gestured at the television. In terse NASA jargon, the card stated:

SHUTTLE LAUNCH NUMBER: 323.
LAUNCH VENUE: CAPE CANAVERAL.
ORBITAL VEHICLE: COLORADO.
LAUNCH DATE: APRIL 29.
LAUNCH TIME: 0600 EST.
CREW:
    MATT GOSLING – COMMANDER.
    PAUL BALDWIN – PILOT.
    STELLA RICHARDS – PAYLOAD MASTER.
DESTINATION: 37,000 KILOMETRE CLARKE ORBIT.
    MISSION PROFILE: HOOVER PROGRAMME. CONTINUATION OF ORBITAL DECOMMISSIONING OF 42 NON-FUNCTIONING GEOSYNCHRONOUS SATELLITES IN EQUATORIAL ARC 130–133 DEGREES EAST.
MISSION DURATION: 100 HOURS.

'Convenient,' Anton commented impassively. 'It means that the shuttle will be virtually directly overhead on May the first.'

## 15

The questions seemed endless. For three hours the polite, unsmiling accident investigators, armed with video cameras and recorders, battered away at Lesa and Harry in turn in the clinic's day room. They were questioned separately like criminal suspects under interrogation, and were sometimes asked the same question repeatedly in different guises. Sometimes even the journalists present joined in.

No – Lesa did not know if it was a bomb. She said that she had no idea what a bomb going off in an aircraft was like. No – she hadn't seen any birds before the bang. No – she had not seen any feathers. No – she couldn't remember what all the instruments were saying. Her offer to draw the instrument panel was not taken up. The investigators weren't interested in what they thought Lesa was capable of drawing. They wanted facts and, as the chief investigator made clear, despite Lesa being so close to the source of the disaster, he was disappointed that she had been so unobservant. After which Lesa began to get angry, and the questioning degenerated into a heated argument that ended with Valentina Lenka bundling the inquisitors and the journalists out of the room.


## 16

By contrast, Victor Koniev was all smiles and public relations charm when he visited Lesa and Harry after lunch. Naturally, he had a photographer with him. He shook hands warmly with them, commiserated with them over their shocking ordeal and announced that because they had come to see his wonderful new telescope, he personally would take them on a conducted tour.

It wasn't often that Valentina had two patients to care for. She was reluctant to let Lesa and Harry out of her sight but she had to concede that they were fully recovered and that there was no good reason why they should not leave her clinic.

'Kowloon Airways are sending out a jet to fly you back to Hong Kong tomorrow,' Koniev explained to Harry and Lesa as they bumped and ground up the hot, dusty winding road to the telescope in Koniev's Lada. 'There are no visiting astronomers on the island at the moment so there's plenty of room in the hotel for you tonight. I expect Doctor Lenka has told you about our rules for visitors.

They're posted up in the information centre. Vehicle lights to be fitted with cowls to prevent light pollution – not that that affects you of course. But the safety rules do: visitors must stay within the confines of Kurograd and the two designated bathing beaches. If you want to visit the telescope or the airport, don't hesitate to thumb a lift. We're all very informal here. What you must not do is go wandering off. The jungle is infested with poisonous snakes and then there are the blackies, of course.'

'Blackies?' Harry questioned.

'Wild boars. Very wild, Mr Dysan. They're small and extremely bad-tempered.' The vehicle slowed to negotiate a hairpin bend. 'Ha – we have a good view of the telescope from here.'

Lesa paid the genial Russian scant attention as he droned on about the construction of the giant telescope. Her interest was directed at the changing coastline that came into view as they cleared the tree line. The only part she could not see properly was where the concrete roof of an industrial building showed above a rocky bluff to the west. Harry studied her covertly and wondered for the hundredth time why she was interested in Kuro. It certainly wasn't the telescope. Even when Koniev drove into the spacious compound adjoining the massive concrete apron her attention remained fixed on the western coastline.

'There we are, ladies and gentlemen,' said Koniev with a prac- tised, proud wave of his hand when they got out of the car. 'The largest optical telescope in the world.'

Lesa turned up her travel suit's conditioner and squinted up at the telescope. It was certainly impressive. The four giant hexagonal steel frames supporting the ten-metre mirrors were mounted on a massive slab of concrete measuring one hundred metres by twenty metres and standing five metres above ground level. Koniev kept up a steady commentary as he preceded his guests up a flight of steps that led to the top of the apron. They leaned on the guard rail surrounding the circular pit that housed the nearest telescope. Even Lesa was sufficiently captivated by the awesome construction to forget her interest in the island's coastline. The size of the telescope was truly colossal and was best conveyed by a technician wearing a safety harness who was dwarfed by the lattice framework he was sitting astride. He was at the rim of the mirror taking measurements with a stress gauge.

Harry took off his sunglasses and cleaned them. They were

constantly misting up in the soul-sapping humidity which was, as far as he could judge, nudging one hundred per cent. Florida could serve up similar conditions on occasions but they seemed to be the norm here, and it was still only April. He envied Lesa, looking cool and graceful in her body-hugging travel suit with its conditioner humming softly on her belt.

Koniev called out a greeting in Russian. The man acknowledged him. 'This is the Alpha mirror,' Koniev explained. 'It's been in use the longest and has provided a wealth of information on the most distant galaxies – those that are so far away that their recessional velocity is close to the speed of light.' He spoke to the technician again in rapid Russian. The technician seemed to agree and talked into a miniature boom microphone attached to his safety helmet. 'I think you will find this interesting,' Koniev murmured.

There was a whir of hidden motors. Like the synchronized guns of a battleship, the four telescopes began turning as one, accelerating rapidly to a remarkable speed to the apparent unconcern of the technician who was being spun around. Lesa and Harry instinctively stepped back from the guard rail as the mighty framework glided by. 'Don't worry,' Koniev laughed. 'There's a good safety clearance.'

'I'm surprised they can turn so fast,' said Harry in genuine amazement.

'That's made possible by the lightweight construction,' Koniev replied. 'As you can see, the mirrors are a mere third of a metre thick. They may look rigid but in fact they are remarkably flexible.' He went on to explain how the curvature of the mirrors was constantly maintained and corrected by hundreds of computer-controlled actuators attached to the backs of the mirrors. 'In an hour of good seeing conditions it is possible to move to as many as thirty different observation positions – the older telescopes can take many minutes to move to a different position. The degree of computer control we have means that the telescopes do not have to be equatorial-mounted to compensate for the earth's spin like the older telescopes. Ah – they are now elevating.'

The giant lattice frames of tubular steel began tilting upwards until all four eyes were aimed directly overhead. At this angle Harry and Lesa could see directly across the diameter of all four of the remarkable mirrors. Harry pointed. 'Why the hole in the second mirror?'

'Ah, yes – the Beta mirror,' said Koniev. 'Come – I will show you.'

Harry and Lesa accompanied the Soviet scientist to the guard rail surrounding the second mirror. It was identical to its three companions apart from a perfectly round metre diameter hole in the centre.

'This mirror has been fraught with problems,' said Koniev, gesturing expansively. 'Its curvature is maintained by a variable flux magnetic coil to give even greater accuracy. Unfortunately an error developed early on in the coil that led to a permanent distortion in the centre of the mirror. Our designers have removed the centre portion and are at present working on a method of welding in a new section. The idea is to save the several million roubles it will cost to replace the entire mirror but I fear that is what we will have to do in the end. However, even in its present state, Beta is still capable of collecting thirty times the light of the Mount Palomar Telescope.'

'How did you get all the materials here?' Lesa asked. 'There must be thousands of tonnes of concrete in this apron alone. Surely it wasn't all flown in?'

'Ah, but it's not solid,' said Koniev in a patronizing tone as though he were addressing a school kid – an attitude that did not endear him to Lesa. 'Even so, everything was brought in by air transport. We costed out extending the harbour and opening up the reef to take large ships and calculated that air would be the cheapest in the long run. The reef virtually surrounds the island and makes any civil engineering projects very difficult and expensive.'

'It didn't stop you building over there,' said Lesa, pointing to the concrete building whose roof was visible above the bluff.

'Ah, yes – our little power station. It provides all our needs. Nuclear, of course, but perfectly safe.'

'Perfectly safe, but built a long way from everything,' Lesa commented acidly, meeting Koniev's bland smile with a frosty stare.

'My dear Miss Wessex, on Kuro nothing is very far. It is a very small island.'

Lesa decided that she did not like this smiling, silver-haired man. Apart from his patronizing attitude, which was bad enough, he was yet another male who made no attempt to disguise the fact that he mentally undressed her whenever he looked at her. 'If everything is flown in,' she continued, 'why is it that Kurograd is built around the harbour?'

'Historical reasons, my dear Lesa. There were already some buildings there put up by the Japanese. It seemed the natural place to build. Also, the harbour is visted by small ships from time to time, and quite a few of our personnel enjoy sailing. Our chief designer has his own motor-yacht. He used to live on it when the project first started nearly twenty years ago.'

'Interesting,' Lesa commented, sounding anything but interested. 'What happened to it?'

Harry shot a sidelong glance at Lesa. He thought he knew her well enough by now to know that her seemingly casual questions had a definite purpose.

'The *Rasputin* was on its way here when it was diverted to the scene of your unfortunate crash. Its last radio report was that it was having to remain in the area to help round up wreckage. It should be back tomorrow. Come – I will show you the control room.'

Lesa and Harry dutifully followed their guide down the concrete steps. They entered a long, low, air-conditioned building and passed through an entrance lobby into a large, windowless room that housed a host of control consoles. Two technicians were working at one of the consoles. They had opened a number of inspection ducts set into the floor and exposed a mass of wiring looms and fibre optic tracks. Their work appeared to annoy Koniev who snapped a number of sharp questions at them in Russian. Their answers did not satisfy him but he was suddenly all public relations smiles again when he realized that the exchanges might embarrass his visitors. For a few moments Lesa saw the ugly side of his nature which tended to confirm her low opinion of him.

'Our chief designer,' he said dismissively. 'Forever ordering alterations. Always getting the technicians to try out something new. Sometimes I think that the telescope will never be finished.'

'Like works of art,' said Lesa. 'They are never finished – merely abandoned.'

Koniev gave a booming, hearty laugh. 'Quite so, Miss Wessex.'

One of the technicians caught Lesa's eye and gave a broad grin, making it difficult for her to keep a straight face by pulling a face at Koniev behind his back; obviously his minions didn't have much time for him either.

'It looks more like the control room of a power station,' Harry commented, oblivious to the facial exchanges between Lesa and the technicians. 'Not a bit like I imagined.'

Koniev laughed. 'You're not the first person to have said that, Mr Dysan. Those cabinets over there are the computers that control the mirrors and the telescope's orientation. The principal telescope officer sits at that central console and initiates the settings required by the astronomers who have their own observation desks. As you can see, each desk has its own terminals and screen for reading the processed images from the spectrum analysers.'

'And no one ever actually looks through an eyepiece any more?' Harry queried.

'Correct,' Koniev confirmed. 'A second is long enough for a computer to obtain a hundred images. With modern high-speed satellite data links, it is not even necessary for astronomers to be here to use the telescope, but they are human; they enjoy their expenses-paid trips to a Pacific island even if Kuro does not have the more decadent attractions of Hawaii.'

Despite her reservations about Koniev, Lesa enjoyed the thirty minutes spent in the control room. She took a professional interest in all the imaging equipment and lingered a long time over a set of stunning close-up thermal images of Jupiter that had been grabbed the previous evening. She was surprised when Koniev had to refer a number of her questions to one of the technicians. They were fairly basic queries concerning the line resolution of images obtained from charge-coupled devices. That Koniev was unable to deal with the questions puzzled her and certainly irritated the Soviet physicist. But the moment passed and he was once again all smiles.

'You seem better versed on the subject than our usual casual visitors, Miss Wessex. Come – we must leave these men to get on with their work.'

'Casual visitors!' Lesa muttered angrily under her breath to Harry as they followed Koniev back to the car. 'I'd casually throttle the little creep if I had the chance.'

'Now then,' said Koniev affably, 'is there anything else I can show you?'

'How about the power station?' Harry suggested.

Koniev shook his head sadly. 'I'm very sorry, Mr Dysan. Author-ized personnel only. Even *I* have to get clearance from the station supervisor before visiting there.'

Lesa spotted the jeep she had seen that morning. It was parked at the far end of the control room building. She pointed. 'What's down there, Mr Koniev?'

'That's our chief designer's laboratory suite.'

'Can we take a look?'

Koniev opened the rear door of his car. 'I don't think that would be advisable. Like all geniuses, Alexi Hegel can be difficult. He doesn't like visitors.'

'Hegel?' Harry queried, pausing as he followed Lesa into the car's baking interior.

'Why, yes. You've heard of him? He is extremely well-known of course.'

Harry sat beside Lesa and tried to remember where he had heard the name before. He recalled reading several articles about the telescope and seeing a television documentary, but that had been a few years ago whereas the name Alexi Hegel was fresh in his mind. His memory wasn't that good so it must have been something he had come across recently.

Lesa looked quizzically at Harry. 'What do you know about him, Harry?'

'A genius,' said Koniev over his shoulder. He started the engine and drove out of the compound. 'He came up with that ingenious design of the floppy mirror which has made Kuro's ten-metre multi-mirror telescope possible.'

'Where does he live?' Lesa asked.

'Have you noticed the bungalow on a hill on the other side of the harbour?'

'Yes.'

'That's his house. He shares it with Anton Pachmann, his assistant. But they're hardly ever there now. They've got beds in the laboratories.'

The car started down the long, winding descent to Kurograd in low gear.

'Surely their work-load has decreased now that the telescope is virtually finished?' Lesa queried.

Koniev chuckled. 'My fault, Miss Wessex. I've given them a deadline to sort out the design problems with the Beta mirror.'

'Look out!' Harry yelled.

Koniev slammed on the brakes and hooted impatiently at the belligerent-looking wild boar that was standing in the middle of the road, confronting them. The creature was smaller than the domestic pig it was descended from. It was jet-black apart from a white patch on its back, had none of the fat associated with domestic pigs, and sported a pair of long, wicked-looking tusks. The creature's head-lowered stance suggested that it knew how to make good use of its formidable weapons if it had to, or indeed, even if it didn't have to.

'A blackie,' said Koniev, sounding the horn again. 'It's rutting time now which means they can be a nuisance.' The boar gave an angry bellow and charged at the Lada and would have crashed into the car had not Koniev discouraged its enterprise by gunning the engine and holding his finger on the horn. The animal's hoofs scrabbled on the hot top and it veered off into the undergrowth at a remarkable rate of knots. 'It looks as if another cull is called for,' the Russian commented as he engaged the clutch.

## 17

'Koniev is a phoney,' Lesa declared that evening as she and Harry were finishing a tasteless hamburger dinner at one of the bar's outside tables. At night Kurograd looked almost attractive, bordering on the romantic. Moonlight sparkled across the harbour and couples strolled around the quay. In the bar a group of noisy engineers were watching a football match.

'How do you mean?' asked Harry, downing his third whisky.

'I asked him a few simple questions about imaging techniques and he was sunk.'

'Your training is the opposite of his,' said Harry.

Lesa frowned at him. 'What do you mean?'

'Your discipline is sitting in space looking at the earth; his discipline is sitting on earth looking into space.'

'In his job he should know all there is to know about imaging.'

'Probably a good administrator,' said Harry, trying to catch the waiter's eye. He waved his hand around. 'Must be, to get this lot going.' He noticed that Lesa's gaze had returned to the darkened bungalow on the hill. She had been watching it all evening. 'Lesa.'

His tone caused her to look questioningly at him.

'Don't you think it's time you told me what all this is about?'

'What all what is about?'

'Why you were so keen to get to this Godforsaken place.'

'I've already told you, Harry – I'd heard that they had developed some imaging techniques here that might be useful to my company.'

'Crap.'

Lesa's expression hardened. 'Are you accusing me of lying?'
'Yes.'

Harry had an anxious moment when he thought that Lesa was going to fly at him despite the number of witnesses there would be to his untimely demise.

Her voice was charged with suppressed hostility when she spoke. 'So why do you think I should lie to you?'

'Because I don't believe that the techniques of astronomy can be applied to remote sensing. Sure, you were interested in the control room – anyone would be – but not sufficiently interested to trek half way around the world. Besides, if you take a look in the information centre, you will see that full details on all the techniques developed here are being published in scientific journals.' Harry paused and smiled uncertainly. Lesa had such control over her emotions that it was difficult to tell if he had annoyed her. He guessed that he had. 'If you want to get mad at anyone, Lesa – get mad at your enemies – not your friends.'

Her resentment towards any form of male dominance welled up. 'Don't run away with the idea that you can consider yourself a friend, Harry,' she snapped. Almost before she had finished the sentence, she regretted the sharpness of the reply. 'I'm sorry, Harry. It's just that I don't make friends easily. When I do, it takes me a long time to recognize them as such.'

'So tell me about it,' Harry invited.

She shook her head. 'Not yet, Harry. Sometime, maybe. But not yet.'

## 18
### April 11

It was 2:00 when Lesa rose from her bed in the hotel and looked out of the window. The bar was closed. A few regulars were inside watching a video movie – as well they might; the offerings on the television channels were abysmal political services, she had discovered. Several all-night fishermen were sitting on the harbour wall and a couple were sitting close together on a bench. The bungalow was still in darkness; the occupants would be unlikely to return now.

She fitted a new lining into her travel suit, pulled it on and turned up the conditioner to maximum because tropical temperature inversion had made the night suffocatingly hot. She rubbed some insect repellent provided by the hotel onto her face and felt prepared to face the hazards of the night. Earlier she had found a supply of candles and some matches in the dresser drawer. Obviously the combination of typhoons and overhead cables supplying Kurograd from the mysterious power station on the west coast meant that the electricity was subject to power cuts. That was the odd thing about the Soviets: technically they were one of the most advanced nations on earth and yet they were slow to adopt conveniences such as uninterruptable power supplies or stand-by generators. She slipped a candle and a box of matches into the pouch on her belt and left the room.

There was no one in the hotel lobby to see her leave. Fortunately the main entrance was not kept locked. With its predominant population of professional middle classes, petty crime was probably a rarity on Kuro. Most cars were left unlocked with their keys in the ignition. It took her fifteen minutes to skirt the harbour and find the road that led up to the bungalow. The mosquitoes sensed her blood and descended in swarms but the travel suit and insect repellent defeated them.

The only entrance to the bungalow appeared to be a side gate set into an overgrown hibiscus hedge. It was unlocked. She pushed it open and waited in the shadows, watching and listening. She turned down her conditioner in case its humming could be heard but restored it to full power when she realized that it was unlikely to be audible above the racket the insects were making. The moon broke out, illuminating a steerable satellite television receiver antenna mounted on a sandbagged tripod. That Kuro was only twenty degrees north of the equator was borne out by the dish's angle – it was pointing nearly straight up. The system puzzled her because it was the only privately-owned satellite receiver she had seen on the island. Beyond the metre diameter dish was a small swimming pool. The filter pump was running, probably on a time-switch, but the pool looked neglected and unused. She cautiously approached the black, staring windows, ready to flee if an infrared intruder alarm detected her body heat. A careful circumnavigation of the bungalow revealed that all the windows were locked.

She returned to the back of the premises and studied the roof, wondering if she could break in by removing some shingles. A heavy, long-handled swimming pool vacuum-cleaning appliance leaning against an outhouse gave her an idea. She moved it half a metre to put it into a favourable position. It would have to be a fastidiously tidy householder to notice that a pool cleaner had been moved such a small amount. The scatter of aluminium chairs and general mess on the terrace suggested that the occupants of the bungalow were anything but fastidious. She gave the handle a firm push, and the end of it thumped into the middle of a window pane beside a side door; but not hard enough to break the glass. A harder push resulted in the handle bouncing off the glass. Oh, well, it would have to be a particularly hard gust of wind. Her third swing broke the pane with a shattering crash that she was certain would be heard all over the township. It prompted her to dive for the shadows of the hibiscus hedge and wait, her heart pounding. Minutes passed and no one came to investigate the noise. She emerged from her cover and inspected the damage. As she had surmised, she had broken a kitchen window. She moved the pool cleaner handle out of the way and reached through the jagged hole to slip the catch. The window opened outwards. Taking care not to disturb broken glass on the window-sill, she wriggled into the kitchen and crouched cat-like on the work top before dropping lightly to the floor. A savage little demon of fear that knotted in her stomach gave way to a sense of foreboding as she straightened. There was more than the animal-sweat smell of men pervading the bungalow; this was a presence – a force that had marked the place like a cat uses glands in its cheeks to mark its territory and warn off enemies. Her hand trembled as she lit the candle.

Twenty years ago the kitchen would have been considered ultra-modern by Western standards. All the fixtures and fittings were the best quality that the 1980s had to offer: a Miele washing machine, a Smeg cooker and hob, and pine-fitted units. In the flickering light of the candle she saw that everything looked well-worn and shabby, and she was right about the occupants being untidy – the sink was piled high with dirty dishes; a trash bin was overflowing with empty self-chilling lager cans. She used one of the cans as a base for the candle which she held high while she looked around for clues as to the identity of the bungalow's occupants. But there was nothing – not so much as a faded photograph tacked to a wall or even a message board.

Her crawling sense of foreboding was stronger in the living room but she forced herself to ignore it. The discarded video discs scattered on the floor around the television and the crate of lager suggested that the room was used for watching television and little else, and it hadn't been used for that for some time if the layer of dust and dank smell were anything to go by. She used the television receiver's remote control to switch the set on and scan through the satellite channels to learn something of the occupiers' viewing preferences, in the same way that visitors to houses in earlier decades had made deductions about the characters of their hosts by studying titles on bookcases. Only four channels were properly tuned in – the Stag Channel, two other channels also offering non-stop near-pornography and, surprisingly, the NASA Information Channel. Lesa watched the rolling caption cards for a few seconds and then switched the set off, carefully replacing the remote control on the coffee table in exactly the same position as she had found it. She looked around the room for more clues. There were no photographs in frames, and nothing but bottles of spirits in the sideboard.

By contrast the first bedroom she explored was neat and tidy. The shoes and tropical casual clothes in the wardrobe provided a clue as to their owner's slight stature but that was all. There were no private papers in the dresser drawers. She was careful to leave everything exactly as she found it.

She pushed open the door of the second bedroom and the terror leapt at her from the darkened interior. Her instinct was to turn and flee and keep running until she was back in her hotel room but she stood her ground. It was as if the evil of the room's occupant was a living entity that had remained there in his absence.

*This is his room, Neti! It's got to be! I can feel him! I can smell him!*

The sudden sting of hot wax spilling onto her hand from the candle helped restore rational thought. She put the candle down on a dresser and allowed her body to relax as Ko had taught her. A few moments of silent contemplation returned her heartbeat to normal and made rational thought possible. Her search of the room was methodical and thorough. The clothes in the wardrobe and tossed on the bed were for a large man. She forced herself to touch the shirts in order to find their size labels. Those so marked were intended for a 140-centimetre chest: a big man.

The dresser proved more interesting. The hairs in the hairbrush on top of the dresser were blond. In the bottom drawer was a photograph album containing a series of date-captioned pictures of the telescope during various stages of construction. All of them were taken from the same position. The photographs started in 1985 when the site was a level area of mountain top strewn with rocks and tufts of stunted grass clung to the basalt soil. The later photographs showed men working earth-moving machines but none included anyone close enough to be recognizable.

Her fingers were searching carefully through the contents of the last drawer when they encountered a bulky envelope. Inside was a set of Polaroid colour photographs. She tipped them onto the bed and picked them up by the edges. For one ghastly moment she thought the terrified girl with the lovely long black hair was Neti. The similarity was in the look of agony in the naked girl's eyes – exactly the same expression as that worn by her last memories of dear, beloved Neti. Lesa's instinct was to stuff the dreadful photographs back in the envelope, but she steeled herself to look at each one; it had been much the same eighteen years ago when she had forced herself to watch the unspeakable horror that Neti was suffering. On that occasion she had made herself a witness out of loyalty to Neti. On this occasion, not only was it her duty to the wretched girl so that someone should know about and experience revulsion at what had happened to her, but also because the obscenities might contain a clue as to the identity of her tormentors.

There were two men – that was obvious. But never at the same time, which meant that they had taken it in turns to take the pictures.

Also, they had been careful not to show much of themselves. A hand, the back of a shoulder, a close-up of genitals; never a face or even the back of a head. She saw from the matching floor-covering that the photographs had been taken in the bungalow's living room, with one exception: a medium shot of the girl sprawled on her back, lying over the edge of a swimming pool. It was the most terrible picture of them all because a hand had grasped hold of the girl's hair and was holding her head underwater.

Lesa stared blindly down at the macabre pictures in the light of the flickering candle and was unable to stop the tears that rolled down her cheeks. She slipped the last photograph into her pouch and left the room as she had found it. After wriggling carefully through the kitchen window, she closed the broken frame and positioned the handle of the swimming pool cleaner so that it looked as if it had fallen through the shattered pane.

Silent tears were still coursing down her face as she walked back to the hotel. She didn't know if they were for Neti or the unknown girl. Perhaps it didn't matter. All that mattered now was that she find these vermin and kill them.

### 19

Had Lesa not been the mistress of her emotions that she was, she would have been quiet and withdrawn at breakfast. As it was she fooled Harry by making cheering and witty conversation that belied the sickness she was feeling. Today was the culmination of eighteen years of searching and of nursing a hatred that was as bitter today as she drank her orange juice as it had been eighteen years previously when she had stood in the swamped sampan and watched the white motor-yacht vanishing into the haze: today was the day of vengeance. Tomorrow she might be on her way to Soviet prison to face trial and a long term of imprisonment. If she could use her cunning to escape detection, she would do so. But if she failed it would be of little consequence to her. So long as she succeeded in her primary objective.

'Did you find out what time our return flight is?' she asked Harry, taking her eyes off the deserted bungalow for a moment.

'Four o'clock. Koniev is sending a car to pick us up at three thirty. Looks like we've got most of the day to kill together.'

Lesa smiled and said nothing.

'Have you thought about what you want to do when you get back to Hong Kong?' he asked.

'No,' said Lesa truthfully. 'Go home as quickly as possible, I suppose. I've left my partner to struggle on alone. He's very capable but I don't like being away for too long.'

'The air accident investigation team Klipfoned me this morning. They want to interview us in Hong Kong. Clarify a few points.'

Lesa grimaced. 'They're like a dog with a bone.'

'I'd like to go back to the UK with you, Lesa.'

'What's the point? You've told me what you want to look for. I'll scour within a radius of two thousand five hundred miles centred on Hong Kong for an unusual construction site and fax you weekly reports with covers showing likely finds.' The brisk way Lesa handled the conversation gave no hint that she was preoccupied with other matters.

'I'd like to go back with you; I'd like to see how you work.'

'It's boring and repetitious. It means spending hours at a terminal getting a sore bottom.'

Harry chuckled. 'I'm used to that.'

Lesa returned her gaze to the bungalow. 'Well I can't stop you, Harry.'

'Okay. That's settled. So what do we do today? How about a lazy day on a quiet beach?'

Lesa gave him a dazzling smile. 'What a lovely idea, Harry. Unfortunately I don't have any beach wear and I wouldn't be seen dead in the stuff on sale in that shop. Besides, there's something else I need to do today – I want to spend it in meditation. It's very important to Buddhists and I haven't done any for such a long time. I do hope you understand.' Lesa gave the statement just the right amount of flippancy to fool Harry into thinking that the matter was important and private. She had chosen her words carefully; in particular her use of the word 'need' which conveyed much more than 'like'.

Lesa had guessed correctly in assuming that Harry would be out of his depth with religion, particularly with a religion about which he knew nothing. His reaction was exactly as she calculated it would be; by trading on the respect that most Americans have for other people's beliefs she had caused him to be slightly embarrassed at having forced her to reveal what he took to be her innermost convictions.

He said hurriedly, 'Sure I understand, Lesa. I'll leave you alone.'

## 20

It was a lucky chance that led to Harry looking up at the precise moment that Lesa strolled past the crowded little general store that served most of Kurograd's needs. He returned the paperback to the shelf and moved nearer the window, pretending to be interested in plastic souvenir models of the telescope. Instead of heading for the road that skirted the harbour, she took the steep turning that led to the airport and the telescope. He slipped out of the shop and crossed the street to where he was hidden by a parked van.

Lesa's unhurried pace, which was perfectly natural in the rising heat of mid-morning, ensured that she attracted little more than a passing glance as the people of the township went about their business.

The change from town to jungle was dramatic. Half a kilometre up the steep road took Harry past a scattering of the prefabricated houses whose occupiers had to fight an unceasing battle to prevent the jungle climbing through their windows. The power lines supplying Kurograd, buzzing softly in the humidity, were out-decibelled by the deafening birdsong. It occurred to him that astronomers on Kuro who had to work at night would get little sleep during the day. A sign bearing the symbols of a spitting snake and a charging boar marked the boundary of Kurograd. Beneath the symbols was a message in several languages saying that proceeding beyond the sign on foot was forbidden.

The continuous bend in the road helped keep Lesa just out of sight. After thirty minutes he found that he had to increase his pace to bring her into view again. She was walking faster now. Harry began to sweat; he wasn't used to exercise and he envied Lesa her water-cooled travel suit. He wondered why she was making this trek. Perhaps she wanted to find solitude for meditation well away from the town? The possibility made Harry feel guilty about following her. On the other hand solitude could be found in Kurograd itself. She could just as easily have sat on the harbour wall because few people ventured out when the sun got high.

His Dodds chukka boots occasionally kicked loose stones but the increasing birdsong racket meant that his clumsiness was unlikely to be heard by Lesa. After two kilometres of steady walking uphill, his shirt was drenched with sweat and his knee joints were aching. Adding to his discomfort was the need to stay out of sight by keeping to the side of the road, brushing against the encroaching hanging vines where he was prey to just about every variety of stinging and biting insect that the jungle harboured.

Harry hung back at a fork in the road to see which direction Lesa would take. The right fork was signposted with a logo of the telescope. The left fork had a properly metalled surface and as yet was unmarked but it was the direction taken by the powerlines. She hesitated for some moments before deciding to take the unmarked left fork that headed in a westward direction.

The going became easier. The road sloped gently downwards, towards the coast and became straighter because it was routed away from Mount Kuromia, which also meant that Harry had to slow his pace to increase the gap between himself and Lesa. He heard a vehicle reach the fork. Perhaps it was heading up to the telescope; but the engine note got louder. Fearful of being set upon by hordes of snakes, he crouched in the undergrowth and waited until the truck had passed. There was no sign of Lesa when he emerged from his hiding place. He waited some minutes, guessing that she was making doubly certain that it was safe before returning to the road, but she failed to appear. He broke into a jog that after two minutes provoked a river of sweat down his spine, and stopped at the top of a rise, keeping close to the jungle to avoid being seen. There was a cool, welcoming breeze off the sea but he was too surprised by the panorama before him to notice. The road led down to a group of concrete flat-roofed buildings about a kilometre away. The largest building was a windowless cube like an automated manufacturing plant. He guessed that its roof was the roof that could be partially seen from the telescope site. It had to be the power station, but what puzzled him was the absence of step-up distribution trans-formers and the inevitable mass of cables and giant insulators normally associated with even small power stations such as this one.

There was no sign of Lesa. He retraced his footsteps and came to a track that crossed the road that he had not noticed in his anxiety to reach the top of the rise. The track was little more than a narrow opening in the jungle on each side of the road. A peppering of hoof marks in the soft ground suggested that the track was not man-made.

There was no sign of human footprints around the entrances on either side of the road, but then on seeing the soft ground, if Lesa had used the track, she would have been careful to walk on the undergrowth.

Harry stood in the middle of the road and thought hard. The sun beating down and the raucous uproar of the birds of paradise were not conducive to rational thinking. Lesa had vanished – no doubt about that. The jungle was an impenetrable wall of foliage flanking each side of the road which meant that she must have taken to the track. The question was, which side? He tossed a mental coin and entered the jungle to the south side of the road.

The span of Harry's life to date was marked by a dismal catalogue of mistakes; his drinking; his blazing rows with his wife that had led to their divorce; and, more lately, his working alone. They were more monuments to misfortune than incompetence. But this latest mistake, his decision to set off along the track, could definitely be attributed to the latter. The difference between this mistake and earlier mistakes was that on this occasion enlightenment came much sooner.

Five minutes after he left the road, to be precise.

The snorting and snuffling behind him suggested several things to him all at once: that he was being followed; that whatever it was that was doing the following was not human; that it was moving fast; that it sounded most displeased with having the smell of Harry's sweat polluting its environment. This time Harry made a sensible decision – he broke into a run.

The track was not designed for a creature of his height. Vines and prickly leaves slashed at him as he crashed through the dense undergrowth. At one point he tripped on a hidden root and risked a quick, fearful glance over his shoulder as he recovered his balance; he was horrified to see not one, but two of the creatures coming for him. They were fifty metres behind and closing the gap fast but not fast enough to deprive them of the energy required to let rip angry, snorting bellows of porcine rage. They were blackies – a friendly-sounding name for a decidedly unfriendly animal. The leader had small black eyes and large white tusks and his companion was similarly equipped.

Panic added to Harry's speed. Bent double he tore through the jungle and came to a broad, artificial-looking clearing. The nearest of the two creatures was only five metres behind him when he spotted what appeared to be two pipelines supported at either end of cross-arms on top of a procession of concrete columns set out along the centre of the clearing. The pipes were roughly the diameter of a man's leg and suspended some three metres above the clearing's carpet of dead and decaying vegetation. Under these conditions Harry's brain was operating in top gear, several moves ahead of his body.

Normally there would have been no chance of him reaching the overhanging pipeline but he leapt for it just the same. The adrenalin in his blood added thirty per cent to the strength in his thigh muscles with the result that his fingers closed thankfully around the nearest of the two pipes. He jack-knifed his knees into his stomach but was too late to avoid the jarring blow that tore into his right calf. In panic he realized that his grip on the pipe was imperilled by the sweat on the palms of his hands. Also the pipe's large diameter made a safe purchase virtually impossible. He felt a little more secure after making a huge effort to hook his left leg over the pipe. He looked down into the glaring gimlet eyes of the two wild boars and saw unbridled hate, drooling saliva, four ten-centimetre-long tusks – one of them stained red – and his own blood dripping from his right leg onto the floor of the jungle. The beast gave an enraged bellow, leapt for Harry's flailing foot, and luckily missed. The second creature snorted its fury and trotted a few metres away. At the exact moment it began its charge, its attention was distracted by a loud cry. It skidded to a halt, throwing up a cloud of decaying vegetable matter. Both creatures turned to confront a figure that had emerged from nowhere and was standing further along the clearing.

'Lesa!' Harry gasped, by now nearly hanging upside-down in his determined exertions to get both legs over the pipe.

'Stay where you are!' she snapped, not taking her eyes off the blackies.

'I wasn't planning on going anywhere,' he assured her.

The leader of the two beasts gave a snort of fury, lowered its head and charged straight at Lesa. Harry's half-inverted position made it difficult for him to comprehend fully what happened next, but it seemed that she made no attempt to move as the maddened creature hurled itself towards her. It was within a metre of her when her leg swung up in a graceful high kick. Harry wasn't certain if the blackie had jumped into the air at the exact moment that Lesa's foot lashed out but there was a sudden loud crack. The creature performed a mid-air somersault, crashed to the ground and lay on its side, its belly heaving as its tortured lungs pumped squeals of agony into its throat while its thrashing legs pedalled impotently at nothing. On its side the creature was transformed from a fearsome, ravening beast to a pitiful wreck. Lesa took careful aim and drove her foot into the animal's exposed testicles. Its belly stopped heaving and its squeals ceased the instant her foot made contact. She followed through by uttering a loud cry and rushing at the second boar. It was undecided for a moment; it gave a mighty bellow and looked as if it was about to charge, but changed its mind and went crashing off into the undergrowth. She listened for a few moments to make certain the creature was unlikely to return and contemplated Harry doing his impersonation of a two-toed sloth.

'That's the first time I've ever seen a pig chase another pig,' she commented. 'If I were you, I'd stay up there. You may well find the offence those animals took at your presence in their domain is nothing compared to my anger at being followed.'

Harry dropped to the ground and gave a yelp of pain when his right leg took his weight. He sat down suddenly and yanked up his trouser leg that was soaked with blood. The blackie's tusk had left a deep gash in his calf. He swore and grimaced. 'Jesus Christ – look at that.'

'If you *will* go around provoking the wildlife, don't go expecting any sympathy from me. I'm not pleased about this.'

'Well I'm not exactly over the moon myself,' Harry retorted, trying without success to stop the bleeding. 'Christ only knows what sort of infection that thing's given me. Jesus – it hurts.'

'Let it bleed,' said Lesa shortly. 'Actually, you can count yourself lucky that you weren't electrocuted. Not that that would have been any great loss.'

'Electrocuted?'

She nodded at the two pipelines. Harry followed her gaze and his eyes popped in surprise. He had thought at the time that the pipeline had felt odd but he had been too preoccupied with other matters to pay it close attention. It wasn't a pipeline but a cable made up of hundreds of twisted strands of thick uninsulated aluminium wire. There were two of the massive conductors, separated by three-metre long cross-arms on top of the row of squat columns that were planted at regular intervals along the length of the clearing. What held his attention was that the conductors were hanging from giant ceramic insulators that shone with porcelain whiteness in the dappled sunlight filtering down through the overhead canopy of foliage.

'I imagine,' said Lesa drily, 'that had you managed to touch the other conductor with your foot during your ridiculous contortions, we'd be able to send your mortal remains home in a small urn.'

Harry levered himself backwards on his hands and leaned against the concrete column. Blood was still coursing freely from his wound. 'Okay – I'm sorry. But for chrissake do something about this mess before I bleed to death.'

'Take off your shirt.'

Harry wriggled out of his shirt with some difficulty because it was wringing wet with sweat. Lesa handled it with disdain and ripped a sleeve off.

'That cost four hundred dollars,' Harry moaned.

'Obviously worth more than your life,' was Lesa's unhelpful reply as she sank her fingers painfully into the flesh around the gash. Harry yelped but was relieved to see that the bleeding stopped. Lesa knelt before him, pressed her lips to the wound and sucked. She spat out some blood and repeated the treatment. Harry was tempted to make a jocular remark about what a distant observer might make of the scene but decided that it would not be a smart thing to do. He looked across at the motionless boar.

'Did you kill that thing?'

'Well it's not moving so I expect I did.'

After two minutes of sucking and spitting she straightened and wiped her mouth on the remains of Harry's shirt.

'Did you know I was following you?'

'From just after we left Kurograd when you started playing football with stones.'

'Christ – I'm surprised you heard me.'

'I'm not deaf,' she retorted, smoothing the shirt-sleeve across her thighs. 'I gave you the slip but then you went and got yourself into this stupid mess. Hold your finger there.'

Harry pressed his finger where she indicated. 'Where were you heading for?' he asked.

'I was curious about the power station because it wasn't included in our tour. And then I was planning a stroll up to the telescope.' She bound the shirt-sleeve loosely around his calf above the wound having first wrapped a stone in the material so that it would press against the artery when the tourniquet was tightened.

'Why?' Harry insisted, knowing that he was asking for trouble. He met her gaze and saw the suppressed anger smouldering in her black eyes.

'None of your damn business!' She thrust a stick into the layers of the makeshift bandage and twisted it sideways. The shaft of pain from the sudden tightening made Harry arch his back against the column. He opened his eyes and saw for the first time that the gap in the foliage above the clearing had been closed by strain cables which pulled the crowns of the more slender trees together. There were hundreds of the thin, almost invisible wires. He drew Lesa's attention to the cables but she wasn't interested. He saw something else: a small closed-circuit television camera clipped to the underside of one of the cross-arms. There was one on each column and they were trained along the powerlines, but doubtless their angle of vision was wide enough to see Harry and Lesa. He groaned.

'Oh shit.'

'I'm not hurting you,' Lesa snapped. She jumped to her feet and stood surveying him in a threatening stance with her hands on her hips. 'I'll be gone about two hours. Slacken off the stick every ten minutes or so. The bleeding should get less and less each time that you do . . .'

'Lesa —' he began.

'If I'm not back in two hours, you'll have to make your own way back to Kurograd.'

Lesa heard the men before Harry. She suddenly wheeled round and stared back along the boar track that led to the road. She was about to vanish into the jungle when two men appeared holding carbines.

'No one is to move,' said the taller of the two men, levelling his rifle at Lesa. His English was stilted but correct. 'You're both under arrest.'

'TV cameras and infrared intruder sensors,' said Harry, pointing to the instrument underneath the cross-arm. 'Probably set so that the body heat of a boar is not enough to trigger them off but a person will.'

Lesa stared at the approaching men and rounded on Harry. There was none of the usual tight control over her emotions now. 'Damn you, Harry Dysan!' she raged. 'Damn you to hell!'

## 21

Alexi Hegel swore roundly at the dead spectrum analyser. 'You sure it's not something stupid like the main fuse?'

'It's definitely the CRT,' Pachmann replied.

'What about the spare?'

'That *is* the spare.'

'Shit!'

Pachmann gestured at the open ducting in the control room floor where he and Hegel had been re-routing cables to their control console at the back of the room. 'We're going to need a replacement if we're to check the screening on that lot.'

'It's got to be checked,' said Hegel savagely. 'Any spurious emissions getting into the main ignition circuit and triggering it prematurely could blow us all to glory.'

'Well it's still under guarantee,' Pachmann pointed out.

Hegel pulled his Klipfone from his pocket. The instrument looked vulnerable in his ham-like fist. He called the laboratory test equipment supplier in Hong Kong and explained the problem. The supplier agreed to replace the faulty spectrum analyser provided it was returned. Hegel resisted an impulse to swear. The whole point in dealing with Hong Kong suppliers over the years had been that they were an efficient, eager-to-please source of top quality laboratory equipment that could be obtained without the bureaucratic red tape involved in getting supplies from the Soviet Union; all such purchases went through the contingency fund that Koniev had devised and did not show up in the detailed quarterly returns that went to Moscow. It was a system that had worked well for nearly twenty years.

While Hegel was talking, Pachmann put a call through to Kuro airport.

'Okay,' said Hegel, winding up his Hong Kong conversation. 'We'll get it back to you as fast as possible.' He cleared the channel and swore again. 'When the hell is Diem due back?'

'Not until tonight,' Pachmann replied smoothly. 'I've just checked with the airport, Alexi. There's a flight leaving for Hong Kong in thirty minutes. If we can get this thing packed up properly, we should be able to get it on the plane and we can radio Diem to turn back to Hong Kong for a replacement. That'll take four days. In the meantime we can continue with the re-routing work and test the whole job when we're finished instead of in stages.'

Hegel's scowl relaxed. Pachmann's greatest strength was his ability to remain calm and think clearly when things went wrong while Hegel tended to lose his temper. Without Pachmann's quiet help the torus beam would still be a science fiction dream and not the reality that it was today. 'Okay – let's get started,' he muttered.

## 22

Lesa sat in the clinic between the two men who had arrested her and Harry in the jungle. She was dispassionately watching Valentina Lenka finish spraying Harry's wound with an enzyme-enriched plastic film that would speed healing. Nothing about Lesa's mask-like expression betrayed that she was seething with resentment at the way the American had ruined her plans.

*What plans, Lesa? You have no proof that Alexi Hegel and the man who was in charge of the* Rasputin *on that dreadful day are the same person. Even if he was, would you recognize him after eighteen years? You didn't even know if he was at the telescope. Even if you had met him face to face and it was the same man, would you have killed him there and then?*

*YES! YES! YES!*

Such was her desperation that she even considered making a break but the two guards were alert; an escape bid would be doomed to failure.

'All finished,' said Valentina, dropping her disposable instruments in an RF crucible. 'The stitches will dissolve and the dressing will peel off easily in about ten days.'

Harry thanked her and pulled on the trousers and shirt that Lesa had purchased for him from the supermarket. One of the guards had insisted on accompanying her on the short trip.

'They fit,' said Harry cheerfully, wincing when he tried walking.

'Thank you for everything you've done for us, doctor,' said Lesa standing up but making no attempt to help Harry.

The doctor smiled. 'See you in five years when the ban is lifted.'

Lesa and Harry were escorted out to the waiting car and had to sit in the back, crushed uncomfortably between the two guards. Koniev's instructions to his men had been explicit – on no account were they to let the two miscreants out of their sight until they were aboard their flight. Koniev had been waiting for Lesa and Harry at the clinic. He had delivered a brief but stern lecture about their stupidity in venturing into the jungle without permission and had ended by saying that the rules that applied to guest astronomers applied to them: they were banned from visiting Kuro for five years.

There were no formalities at the airport. Harry and Lesa were shown aboard a waiting Kowloon Airways executive jet Skyliner, the twin of the ill-fated Foxtrot Victor. They were the only passengers. The stewardess said that they could sit where they liked. Lesa deliberately let Harry go first. He selected a window seat near the tail, assuming that Lesa would sit with him and was hurt, though not surprised, when she pointedly chose a seat several rows in front of him.

'I'm sorry, ladies and gentlemen,' said the stewardess over the passenger address system, 'there will be a few minutes' delay while we wait for some late cargo.'

Lesa fastened her seatbelt and watched the restricted view from the small window. A jeep scurrying along the perimeter road caught her attention. It was about half a kilometre away and moving quickly. It veered off the road towards the jet, flashing its headlights, and passed out of sight behind the tail. She changed seats in an attempt to see what was going on but obviously the jeep had stopped directly behind the waiting jet. There was the sound of the Skyliner's hold door being opened and closed. An airport ground crewman wearing a radio headset spoke into a boom microphone and the Skyliner's engines increased to a muted whine. The aircraft began to roll, turning towards the holding point, and the jeep came into sight. It had moved clear and the driver was talking casually to the ground crewman. They were less than ten metres from where Lesa was staring at them.

The shock was such that it seemed as if she were momentarily separated from her body. The whine of the engines, the cool draught of scented air from the overhead vents, the feel of the narrow seat – all faded into oblivion in the dominating proximity of the blond man. He had changed little in eighteen years; the same bull-chest, the same incredible steel-blue cruel eyes, the same blond hair. The hair on his arms and even his eyebrows were of such bleached whiteness that they seemed to gleam in the burning sun. The man looked up. For a terrifying instant it seemed to Lesa that his hard blue eyes were boring into her like a grotesque rape instrument. He threw back his head and laughed just as he had laughed eighteen years ago when he had toyed with her breasts and compared them with those of the redhead.

The Skyliner accelerated, sweeping the dreadful scene aside, leaving Lesa trying to choke back little gasps of terror. By that one look the bull-chested man had revealed to her just how facile and useless were her carefully nurtured poise and sophistication, her so-called iron will. Over the years she had nursed such a blind determination to exact vengeance that it hadn't occurred to her to consider what her feelings might be when she eventually came face to face with the perpetrator of the massacre. That she might be paralysed with fear, unable to lift so much as a finger, had been a thought too awesome to contemplate and yet that was exactly what had happened. It was of no consequence that she was aboard an aircraft, unable to reach the man even if she had wanted to; she had been too terrified to move. Her emotions had been a devastating betrayal of Neti and Lin and the others.

As the jet banked to the west, Lesa's fear gave way to a black cloud of depression as she realized that she would be unable to return to Kuro and so redeem what she perceived as her supreme act of despicable treachery.

## 23

# HOOVER PROGRAMME SIMULATION
# CENTRE, HOUSTON, TEXAS April 12

Only the lightest of touches were needed to control the shuttle's manipulator arm. The sensors in Stella Richards' glove control translated the movements of her fingers to the mechanical fingers on the end of the Canada arm. She aimed the grab at the satellite's solar panel mounting bracket and seized hold of it. It wasn't a real satellite but a computer-generated hologram that possessed all the characteristics of the real thing; there was a noticeable resistance due to the instrument's three-tonne mass as she eased the arm down towards the shuttle's open hold. Once she had got the satellite moving, she exercised skilled judgement in her timing of a nudge in the opposite direction so that the satellite came to rest floating in the open cargo bay.

'Neat,' complimented the programme director's voice.

Stella made no answer. The next step in recovering the defunct satellite was the most tricky of all – it had to be secured so that it didn't bounce around in the shuttle's cargo bay during manoeuvring. She released the manipulator's fingers and withdrew the arm carefully without touching the satellite. Even a gentle knock would be enough to send it drifting slowly out of the hold. The mechanical fingers closed on an inflatable collar. Fitting it around the satellite was rather like putting a diaper on a baby without waking it. Once it was in position, she steered the arm to the collar's air valve. Instead of watching what she was doing through her work station's aft windows that overlooked the shuttle's yawning cargo bay, this delicate part of the operation required her to concentrate on the closed-circuit television monitor beside her that was showing a picture from the camera on the end of the Canada arm. The mechanical fingers closed on the toggle and broke the air seal. The collar inflated, gripping the satellite firmly in position in the shuttle's hold. Stella relaxed. Stowing the satellite had required two hours of sustained concentration. She felt mentally and physically exhausted.

'How's that, Jim?'

'Looking fine, Stella,' the director's voice answered. 'Okay – tomorrow we'll tackle AstelSat 10. Five tonnes and there's a couple of isotope modules to be removed first so it's going to be a long day.'

Stella glanced at her watch. April the twelfth. Lift off was scheduled for April the twenty-ninth. The mission profile called for the recovery of forty-two defunct satellites. That meant working her ass off over the next three weeks to complete the mission preparation programme.

## 24

## SOUTHERN ENGLAND April 13

'If you wish to use our computer terminal facilities,' said Lesa politely to Harry, 'you're perfectly welcome to do so. But I think one hundred and fifty dollars an hour in addition to our fee is reasonable, don't you?'

Darryl was surprised. Normally Lesa was all charm when dealing with customers. He wondered what had happened between them in the Far East that might account for her uncharacteristic behaviour. He had read stories of lifeboat survivors who ended up hating each other, but from the detailed account that Lesa had given upon her return to work that morning and the earlier news reports, they had been in the life raft for only two hours.

'Perfectly reasonable,' said Harry easily, thinking that Lesa looked even better in a skirt and blouse than she did in that wretched travel suit. 'So which terminal do I use?'

'The only one that's going spare is the one in this office,' Darryl pointed out, nodding to a computer terminal work station near Lesa's desk.

'I won't be any trouble to you,' Harry promised.

Lesa considered. 'I'm sure you won't. I'll be working in the imaging room most of the time on your project so I won't be using this office. Okay – help yourself, Ha – Mr Dysan.' She gathered up some papers and caught Darryl's eye as she stood. 'We'll leave you to carry on. Have you made arrangements for your accommodation?'

'I thought I'd book into the Hog's Back Hotel across the road,' Harry replied.

Darryl was about to point out that the flat wasn't in use but he guessed that Lesa would not welcome the suggestion.

'You'll find it very comfortable and the views from the bedroom windows are spectacular. Many of our clients stay there. Have a word with my secretary – she'll look after all the arrangements.'

Darryl followed Lesa into the outer office.

'So what's he done to upset you?' he asked as he closed the door.

'Nothing,' said Lesa curtly.

'I can't imagine that he'd dare make a pass at you.'

'You can be a real pain at times, Darryl. Whatever Mr Dysan did or did not do, I don't want to talk about it, okay?' She gave him that sudden smile, as lovely as it was unexpected, that could disarm a battleship. 'Sorry I wasn't in this morning but I had lunch with my parents. They've been worrying themselves needlessly since they heard the news about the crash. I had to go and see them and they're always keen to hear all about Hong Kong. I hope you've been looking after my cranes properly?'

'They mugged me for my pizza yesterday,' said Darryl sorrowfully. 'It's dangerous eating lunch by the lake these days with those damned birds hanging about, and the anglers are complaining about raids on their keep nets.'

Lesa laughed at her partner's expression. 'I'll be saying hallo to them if anyone wants me.'

'The anglers or the cranes?'

Lesa's answer was a rippling laugh over her shoulder as she left the room.

Darryl moved to the window so that he could watch her walking down to the lake and reflected that it was good to have her back.

Harry sat at the terminal in Lesa's office. It was a desktop Cray like his own machine at home – a formidable piece of hardware. Systemation didn't do anything by half-measures.

He contemplated the blank screen and experienced a feeling of emptiness. For a few days he had actually experienced the pleasures and pitfalls of working in partnership with someone instead of toiling alone at a goddam terminal. That it had been an uneasy partnership with Lesa was his own stupid fault; he had spent so long working alone that he no longer knew how to relate to people – how to moderate one's own behaviour to take account of the whims and needs of others. On Kuro Lesa had wanted to be alone for a while and he had stupidly followed her and loused everything up. Since then the beginnings of any warmth towards him had been abruptly shut off, and that was no more than he deserved. He shook himself out of his reverie. There was work to be done. Alone.

He felt round the back of the system case, disconnected the keyboard and voice input socket, and waited two minutes before plugging them back in. This simple but often overlooked precaution caused the terminal to default to maker's factory settings; he didn't want any cunning chunks of software lurking in the depths of the machine's memory busily logging all his keystrokes and screen output for someone else to examine later at their leisure. Sure enough the screen came up with the message:

DO YOU REQUIRE INPUT/OUTPUT LOG TO BE ACTIVE? Y/N.

He answered N and felt more comfortable with the machine.

The next step, logging into his computer in Florida, required some care. The sensitive nature of the information in his computer files, including lists of passwords that gave him legal and illegal access to hundreds of official databases all over the world, meant that the protection level provided had to be complex. He entered his telephone number on the keyboard. Finding a clear satellite channel and logging in to his home machine took less than ten seconds. There was no confirmation of what computer he had accessed or where it was located. The single word on the screen said:

PASSWORD?

Harry checked the day of the month. The twelfth. One and two added up to three – that meant entering the third anagram of Jelly Roll Morton's name. Jelly Roll Morton was his least favourite twentieth-century jazz musician.

FINGERPRINT requested the screen.

Harry pressed his forefinger on the machine's identification pad. A second passed and the screen displayed:

ARE YOU HAROLD DYSAN? Y/N.

Harry answered N and he was in. That last little idiosyncrasy had been his idea; it had fooled two National Encryption Agency experts when they had tested his machine's security.

There was a string of messages waiting for him. He checked quickly through the originators to see if any were urgent. As expected, there was no message from Gus Whittaker even though he must have seen the news about the loss of the Kowloon Airways Skyliner. All the messages could wait until he had dealt with the problem of Alexi Hegel. There had to be a reason why the name of Kuro's chief designer was preying on his mind. Unearthing information on the Soviet scientist would be no problem – he could go into any number of specialist databases on the world's top physicists but the most sensible place to start would be his own database. He tried to recollect the correct spelling of Hegel's name from the publicity material in the information centre on Kuro and gave up. His fingers snazzed on the keyboard:

PHONETIC MATCH HEY?GIRL?

The screen answered instantly with:

HEY THERE, GEORGIE GIRL.
FIRST LINE OF SONG 'GEORGIE GIRL'. MOVIE THEME SONG —

He impatiently hit the next key before the information finished scrolling onto the screen.

Bingo.

ALEXI HEGEL.
TAPE TRANSCRIPT. CONVERSATION HAROLD DYSAN — STEVEN KRANTZ, DEPUTY PROJECT RESEARCH DIRECTOR, TEXAS PARTICLE ACCELERATOR CENTRE.
VENUE: POMPANO BEACH MARITIME RESEARCH STATION.
SUBJECT: HOLE IN PACSAT 19.

Harry stared at the screen. He suddenly remembered Steven Krantz mentioning Alexi Hegel and cursed himself for his monumental stupidity in not following it up. He called up the transcript. It was all there — the entire conversation including his Cray's attempts to identify the various sound effects on the original tape.

KRANTZ:     It came from outer space.
DYSAN:      What did?
KRANTZ:     Whatever drilled this hole. No — drilled is the wrong word. Whatever vaporized this hole. We are not alone.
DYSAN:      Just what the hell are you driving at, Mr Krantz?
KRANTZ:     Call me Steven. Or Steve. I'm easy.
DYSAN:      What do you mean, it came from outer space?

(SYSTEM MESSAGE: UNIDENTIFIABLE EFFECTS. PROBABLY VENDING MACHINE FOLLOWED BY KRANTZ DRINKING OR SWALLOWING)

KRANTZ:     As I said — whatever made that hole wasn't of terrestrial origin. Firstly — we're still a hundred years off that sort of technology anyway. Maybe a lot less than that if Alexi Hegel hadn't stupidly

323

given up his work on plasma physics. Secondly –
the angle of the hole means that whatever made
it wasn't on earth.

(SYSTEM MESSAGE: HEGEL – PHONETIC SPELLING PROVIDED. VERIFY
CORRECT SPELLING WITH ORIGINATOR)

Harry read the transcript and wondered how it was that he had
ignored a vital clue. He tried to recollect his frame of mind at that
time and gave up. He looked up Steven Krantz's Klipfone number
and caught the young scientist as he was driving to work.

'Hi there, Mr Dysan. Lucky you, in England. It's nudging thirty
here and the car's air-conditioning is acting up. Have you found the
little green men that caused our hole yet?'

'I think you've got the wrong colour there, Steve. Listen, when
we were looking at the satellite, can you remember saying that we're
still a hundred years off the sort of technology that could make that
hole – maybe a lot less if Alexi Hegel hadn't given up his work in
plasma physics?'

'Sure I remember saying that,' said Krantz easily. 'I'll stand by
it too. Why?'

'So what's so special about Alexi Hegel in the world of plasma
physics?'

Krantz whistled. 'Hey – you really ought to do some reading up.'

'I intend to,' Harry answered tersely, 'but a little background
from you to start me off would be appreciated.'

'He's before my time but what he did is folklore in my field. Just
trying to think of a way of putting it in layman's terms . . . About
twenty-five years back he and his assistant built a torus coil at the
Pavel Alekseyevich Cherenkov Institute near Moscow. My old
professor was a witness at the third demonstration. No one knows
what the design of the coil was – Hegel was secretive about the
whole thing – he promised to publish but never did. Hold on – I'd
better concentrate on this intersection.'

Harry heard the faint sounds of traffic from a highway over six
thousand miles away.

'Sorry about that,' said Krantz.

'About Hegel's torus coil,' Harry pressed.

'The story goes that Hegel pumped about half a megawatt through
his coil and produced a strong enough magnetic field to focus a

plasma into a beam. It lasted a few milliseconds but there was enough energy expended to melt a hole in a lead shield . . .'

Krantz's words had a numbing effect on Harry. The shock dulled his hearing for a few seconds as he tried to comprehend the implications of a crazy, impossible, unwelcome theory about Kuro that was taking awesome shape in his head. Meanwhile Krantz's voice droned on in his ear.

'. . . Hegel had a dream about building an ion drive that could accelerate a spacecraft to near C speeds so that the Soviet Union could send a manned mission to Proxima Centauri. That's our nearest star after the sun. It's a low-magnitude red dwarf in constellation Centaurus which is now known to possess a planetary system.'

'What do you mean by near C speeds?' asked Harry, forcing himself to concentrate on what Krantz was saying.

'Three hundred thousand kilometres per second – the speed of light,' Krantz answered. 'Unfortunately Hegel was unable to solve the mathematics involved in putting a power station into orbit and letting off atomic bombs to provide the plasma. He didn't get the funding he wanted so he gave up the whole thing in a fit of pique and got himself involved in the design of very large telescopes. A crazy waste of talent. But there you are – people do crazy things.'

'Steve,' said Harry slowly, 'I don't know how to thank you for your help on this.'

'Hey – you'd better check me out on all of this,' said Krantz worriedly. 'I know that millions have been wasted trying to duplicate Hegel's torus but it's all before my time. I'm only quoting what I can remember my professor saying and what I've picked up in science journals. My memory isn't the best in the world, as my wife reminded me on our first anniversary.'

Harry chuckled. 'Even so, you've been a great help.'

'You've got me thinking now,' Krantz complained. 'Tell you what: I've got a quiet day ahead of me. I could do some ferreting for you on Alexi Hegel and what he's up to and dump the lot in your mail-box.'

Harry thought fast. Krantz would know his way around the scientific databases. His expertise could save a lot of keyboard research time. 'Thanks, Steve – that would be great. A dump will be fine but could you also Klipfone me with a rundown?'

'I'll call you on my way home,' Krantz promised.

Harry thanked him and cleared the channel. He sat in thought for some moments. He remembered Victor Koniev's tight-lipped anger when he and Lesa had been discovered in the jungle. If the Kuro telescope project was being used as a cover for another project, then Koniev had to be involved up to his neck. He logged into the World Reporter database that contained literally several million articles from the world's newspapers and magazines. Entering ?KURO produced a listing of well over two thousand articles. The summaries showed that they ranged from progress reports in *Nature* about the construction of the giant telescope to a recent story in the *National Inquirer* claiming that astronomers on Kuro had seen flying saucers landing on Mars. In addition there were transcripts of TV commentaries about the telescope. The project appeared to have received more press coverage than any other undertaking in the history of Soviet research. That in itself undermined Harry's improbable theory.

He scrolled idly through the listings and realized that he couldn't possibly read them all. Entering ?KURO ?KONIEV narrowed down the field to less than a hundred articles. He ran his eye down the columns and stopped at a name he recognized. Five years ago Jonathan Praad had written a two-thousand-word profile on Victor Koniev for the *Aristotelian*. Praad was a larger than life, hard-nosed New Jersey based science writer whose ego-pricking style attracted storms of writs and threatening letters that he used to wallpaper his office. Praad's two thousand words would tell Harry more about Koniev than the information extracted from a hundred databases. He called up the article, dumped it to Lesa's printer, and logged out of World Reporter.

The article provided a better insight than Harry had expected. Its opening sentences must have had battalions of libel lawyers licking their lips. Praad's view was that Victor Koniev's considerable achievements in the scientific field were best measured against the fact that academically he was a fraud, but as an administrator he had a persuasive ability that ensured successful funding for those projects that he had enthusiasm for. The world of science would be a better place if there were more Victor Konievs around because scientists needed money therefore they needed egotistical wheelers and dealers of his talent. There followed a long list of all the projects Koniev had been associated with, all of which had benefited enormously from his boundless energy and enthusiasm provided he wasn't allowed to become involved in the actual research.

The hard-hitting writer went on to say that Koniev should have been an American rather than a Russian; in America administrative talents were recognized as such and were rewarded accordingly, but not in the Soviet Union where scientific ability was accorded a higher status. As a consequence Koniev had applied his abilities to high-prestige projects in the hope that the glory would rub off on him. The latest was his crusade for the building of a giant optical telescope – the ten-metre multi-mirror on Kuro. When finished it would be the largest in the world. What was remarkable about the Kuro telescope was that fifteen years earlier Koniev had persuaded the brilliant particle physicist Alexi Hegel to take over the design of the instrument. Using a man of Hegel's talent to solve what were basic engineering problems had been condemned at the time as a lunatic waste of talent. And yet Hegel had gone along with the project despite a bitter enmity between the two men that stemmed back from the days when Koniev, as chairman of the powerful Soviet Science Endeavour Appropriations Committee, had blocked Hegel's request for funding to build an ion drive. Koniev had aroused Hegel's wrath by describing the physicist's plans to send cosmonauts to the stars as ill-considered pie in the sky. 'Real scientists of Hegel's calibre,' Praad wrote, 'have the morals of a Hamburg hooker when it comes to getting their hands on money. All too often they show a remarkable willingness to climb into bed with anyone who has access to funds for a pet project. That being so, the mystery is why Hegel, who is not an astronomer despite his interest in space exploration, threw in his lot with Koniev on the Kuro telescope.'

Praad's article went on to outline Koniev's unfashionable left-wing views and political activities. In 1987 he had used his position to deliver a speech roundly condemning the Soviet leadership for their dilution of the simple principles of Marxism to bring about a short-term solution to the problem of a populace that was demanding more consumer goods. Koniev's 'guns before butter' theme had not endeared him to his political masters but Praad's guess was that Koniev commanded wide support because there had been no attempt to remove him. Either that or he was regarded as a harmless crank. Koniev had followed a hard line over what he had described as the American assimilation of Soviet culture. He was chairman of the Lenin Reform Group – a band of leading dissidents against creeping imperialism, who were vehemently opposed to the government for refusing to match US spending on star wars research.

Harry was intrigued by a photograph taken of a band of protesters at the opening of a giant McDonald's near Red Square. Koniev was clutching a bullhorn and a placard which, according to the caption, condemned this latest piece of fast food imperialism in the capital of the motherland. Harry reflected that despite Praad's low opinion of him, at least Victor Koniev had the courage of his convictions.

He skimmed quickly through the rest of the article: Praad concluded that Koniev was an arrogant administrative and financial genius eaten up with bitterness at not having achieved the status in the scientific world that he craved. The irony was that these were the exact qualities that were making the Kuro Mutli-Mirror Telescope possible. The real purpose of Koniev's open door policy in welcoming foreign journalists to Kuro was to enhance the prestige of Victor Koniev rather than Soviet science. In the long run, the man should not be judged by his motives, however suspect, but by the fact that Kuro was a considerable achievement only made possible by Koniev's impossible ego, his arrogance, iron will, and capacity for hard work. Qualities he shared with Hitler. The last photograph was a small inset showing Koniev and Hegel standing before the telescope; the construction site was hidden under four protective domes.

Harry sat silently with his thoughts for some moments when he had finished reading Praad's profile. The more he thought about it, the more the whole business made ghastly sense. He put the article in his pocket and went in search of Lesa. He found her sitting on a bench by the lakeside dictating letters into a recorder. It was a warm, spring afternoon and the sun shone on her long black hair hanging straight down her back. So far as Harry could judge, the only treatment it received was a regular brushing. Two cranes standing guard either side of her moved away at his approach causing her to turn around.

There was an open-ness about Harry Dysan that Lesa admired. You knew where you stood with him. He had been genuinely upset at his stupidity that had led to their expulsion from Kuro. He knew nothing about her interest in the island and, to his credit, he had not pried once she had made it clear that she was not prepared to discuss the matter. Nor had he made a pass at her although there had been plenty of opportunities. Because she did not have to be on the sexual defensive with Harry, she felt that she had their relationship firmly under her control. It was that above all else that gave her confidence in her dealings with him.

Harry neared the bench with some trepidation, but instead of scowling at him as he expected, she smiled – that lovely, radiant smile.

'Harry,' she said, inviting him to sit beside her, 'I owe you an apology. I've been a real bitch these last two days. I'm so sorry.'

Harry gave a dismissive gesture. 'My fault for being such a nosy slob . . . Lesa – you won't believe this but I think I've stumbled on the site where the beam was fired from.'

Lesa looked dismayed. 'Damn – I was looking forward to that nice fat contract.'

'You'll still get it,' said Harry seriously. 'Because you found it.'

'I did? Where?'

'Right under our noses. On Kuro.'

Lesa stared at him. 'Where on Kuro?'

'The telescope. Or at least, one of them. The Beta mirror.'

Lesa was tempted to laugh out loud but she knew Harry well enough by now to know that he was no fool. 'Now hold on, Harry – you're saying that a major scientific enterprise, which has had the world's press sniffing round it for twenty odd years, is a front for your beam site? Don't you think you're being just a little bit fanciful?'

'I don't think the telescope's a front in that sense. It's working as a telescope, sure enough, but I think the construction has provided a nice cover for building the beam projector, or whatever it is.'

Lesa looked doubtful. 'That's crazy, Harry. Why would the Russians build such a politically sensitive installation where they would have no control over it?'

'Their lease on Kuro gives them all the control they need. Besides, not building it in the Soviet Union means that the international disarmament inspection teams can't demand access to see it. Also the telescope provides ideal cover. A construction out in the wilds of Siberia or somewhere would be certain to be spotted on satellite pictures and suspicions aroused.'

'But the place has had the press crawling all over it for nearly twenty years,' Lesa argued. 'Look at all the facilities there are for them.'

'Which makes the cover even better,' Harry pointed out. 'And don't forget that no one can just drop in on Kuro.'

'We did.'

'No – if you remember, that booking clerk in Hong Kong said that they would have to get permission for the visit. You can bet that if a visit hadn't been convenient, the Russians would have trotted out an excuse as to why we couldn't go. And there's not that much freedom of movement on the island – look what happened to us when we strayed from the approved beaten track.'

Lesa thought for a few moments. Some of Harry's points made sense – especially the one about hiding the construction. Unaccounted for, large-scale building work anywhere in the Soviet Union would have been spotted by any number of remote sensing agencies, civilian and military, and questions would have been asked of the Russians as to its purpose. 'A damned expensive cover if you ask me,' she commented. 'Building a billion-dollar telescope on a remote island.'

'Not so expensive if they were planning to build such a telescope in the first place. There's another reason for building it on Kuro: I don't think the Soviet Government know about it.'

'That's absurd, Harry. The cost would have to be borne by the government.'

'A telescope that size has never been built before therefore the costing could easily be manipulated to absorb the cost of building a beam projector. Especially if they've got a boat to ship in specialized supplies, which they have.'

This time Lesa couldn't help smiling. 'Now I know you've flipped, Harry.'

Harry grinned and pulled the article from his pocket. 'Read that. If Jonathan Praad is right, the real looney in this business is Victor Koniev.'

Lesa skimmed through the piece. The photograph at the end of Alexi Hegel jumped off the page. The hard eyes bored into her, renewing her fear – a fear that was overshadowed by her sense of shame therefore it was a fear she knew she could master. Ever since leaving Kuro she had been desperately trying to think of ways of returning to the island but a solution eluded her. Now, she knew not how, it might be possible to turn this crazy fixation of Harry's to her advantage. She picked up her recorder and stood. 'There might be something in what you say, Harry. Let's take a close look at Kuro.'

They returned to the offices and sat at an unused work station in the main analysis room. Each station, with its intimidating metre-square monitor, was surrounded by high screens so that the image analysts could hold conferences around their monitors without disturbing other colleagues.

Careful preparation was the key to the economic use of SPOT 12. Harry watched with interest as Lesa entered the keyboard commands that would train the satellite's telescope precisely on the remote island and grab a series of images the instant she accessed the instrument.

'How long will you be logged into it?' Harry asked.

'Sixty seconds should be long enough.'

Harry tried mentally calculating the amount of information that would flow from SPOT 12 into Systemation's mass storage system in that sixty seconds and gave up. Satellites were very different from databases – one didn't use a satellite for real-time browsing.

'Good – no one else is using it,' said Lesa, reading the system information that appeared on the screen. 'We're right at the head of the queue . . . Okay – we're in. An hour after dawn out there so the light should be just right.'

Harry expected a picture of Kuro to appear on the screen but all that showed was a string of report messages. 'Okay – fine,' said Lesa, logging out of the satellite. 'That minute should have given us ten images that will have cost us a total of fifty thousand francs . . . and that's what we've got.'

The screen suddenly exploded into a rich blue with the now familiar rectangular shape of Kuro near the middle of the screen. Lesa used a tracker ball to centre the image. Harry blinked in surprise. It was all there: an oblique view of Kurograd and harbour; the roads; the power station on the coast that he had caught a glimpse of, and, on top of Mount Kuromia, like four sparkling jewels in a crown, were the four awesome mirrors of the mighty telescope. The brilliant natural colours and the sharp contrast due to the long shadows from the early morning sun conspired to give a vivid three-dimensional effect to the scene as though they were hanging in a balloon about ten thousand feet above the island.

Lesa spotted the anomaly in the harbour and zoomed to plus-twenty magnification. Her face remained quietly impassive as she studied the moored motor-yacht.

'That's either a passing millionaire or it's *Rasputin*,' said Harry.

'It's *Rasputin*.'

'How do you know?'

'I think there was a picture of it in the information centre,' said Lesa dismissively. She rolled the tracker ball to centre the strange power station. The movement of the image produced a sensation of flying. Harry looked at the complex with interest.

'It's bigger than I remember.'

Lesa's practised eye converted the image and the telltale shadows into three-dimensional topography in her mind. She pointed. 'That's because you could see the smaller building. It's a water distillation plant. Kuro probably needed a lot of freshwater when the telescope was being built. But the main power station containment building has been extended by cutting into the hillside. You couldn't see all of it from the road.'

'Looks like one building to me.'

'Look carefully and you'll see that the concrete roof is a slightly different colour where it's been let into the hillside. See?'

Only when Lesa used a screen mouse pointer to highlight the boundary of the discoloration could Harry see what she had spotted immediately.

'Different curing rates of the concrete,' Lesa commented. 'One half of the roof cast during different weather and humidity conditions from the other half. It can show up for years afterwards. Concrete takes about ten years to cure to full hardness.' She drew a box around the building with the mouse and clicked it. Dimensions appeared on the screen that showed the building to be two hundred metres long by fifty metres wide.

'I'm no expert on power stations,' said Harry, 'but doesn't that strike you as somewhat large for a power station serving a small community?'

'How about power for the telescope?'

'It doesn't need much. Remember Koniev telling us that the mirrors were so well-balanced that they could be turned by washing machine motors?'

Lesa nodded. 'That's right – he did.' She picked up an interphone and touched a number. 'Darryl. Station Ten. Can you spare a few minutes?' She replaced the handset and looked at Harry, her face sombre. 'Darryl's the expert on power stations.' She produced an electronic notepad from a drawer and began sketching. Harry saw that she was drawing the power line in the jungle where they had been caught. Her fast, confident strokes with the stylus resulted in a realistic drawing of the low columns with their cross-arms and giant ceramic insulators that supported the two massive power conductors. She was adding dimensions to the sketch when Darryl appeared.

'What's the problem, folks?'

Harry stood so that Darryl could sit in front of the monitor. 'Ah – I recognize that,' Darryl remarked. 'Kuro.' He looked questioningly at Lesa. 'So what can I do for you.'

'Take a look at that power station and tell me what you think.'

Darryl gave the screen a casual glance. 'A Soviet one-gigawatt power station. The smaller building is a two-hundred-tonne per day distillation plant. So what?' He was about to say something else but his face froze and he turned back to the monitor to examine the image more closely. 'Why the hell have they built themselves such an enormous generating capacity? Are they expecting to turn the whole island into a metropolis or something?'

'You tell us,' said Harry phlegmatically.

Darryl zoomed out and did a quick count of the prefabricated houses in the residential area. 'Probably about four hundred dwelling units on the island overall. So what sort of population are we looking at? A thousand?'

'About that,' Lesa agreed.

Darryl did a rough mental calculation. 'Okay. Allowing fifty kilowatts per day per unit because they're probably all running air-conditioning flat out – hot spots on the thermal images will show that – and allowing another fifty kilowatts per day per head of population because the Russians are getting as bad as the Americans at using energy, I'd say they've given themselves an over-capacity in the order of nine hundred per cent. And those are generous consumption allowances. We're talking about a gigawatt of power – a thousand million watts. Enough to drive a city.'

'Would they be producing that all the time?' Harry asked. He noticed that Lesa was putting the finishing touches to her sketch by drawing in trees. Her artistic talent surprised him. He wondered when she was going to stop surprising him.

'It's unlikely,' Darryl replied. 'That containment building is a fairly standard design. It's designed around four two-fifty megawatt type twenty PWRs, each one driving two Tumanski seawater steam turbines. You can't close down pressurized water reactors but you can run them well under capacity. I could verify that by running thermal imaging checks on the outfall pipes, no problem. But that won't explain why they've built such a huge generating capacity in the first place.'

'This is the power line I told you about,' said Lesa, sliding her drawing in front of Darryl. She had included a rough sketch of a man standing by one of the columns to give an idea of scale.

Darryl gaped at the picture in astonishment. 'Are you sure you've got this right?'

'It's correct, isn't it, Harry?'

'Dead accurate,' Harry confirmed.

'Three metres high?'

'That's right,' said Lesa defensively.

'And the diameter of those conductors? Forty centimetres?'

'Give or take about five centimetres.'

'That can't be right. They must be out of proportion.'

'Now see here, Darryl; when I draw a picture, I get it right.'

Darryl turned his attention back to the monitor and studied it intently. He zoomed in on the road where Harry had followed Lesa out of Kurograd and he pointed to the silvery lines strung out like cobwebs on wooden poles alongside the road. 'That's a standard eleven-kilovolt supply to Kurograd – right?' He rolled the tracker ball and picked out similar lines leading from the power station. 'And those are the eleven kay vee supply lines to the airport and the telescope. That's the total power distribution needs of the entire island taken care of. So what the hell is that massive thing?'

'That's what we're asking you,' said Harry.

Darryl frowned at the sketch. 'Are you sure it wasn't a pipeline?'

Lesa arched her eyebrows. 'A pipeline on insulators?'

'Hell – I don't know what to make of it. The normal way of keeping losses down when distributing vast amounts of electricity is to step up the voltage to several kilovolts so that the current is next to nothing then step it down to usable voltage and current ratings at its destination. With the short distances involved on Kuro, that's not necessary. This weird power line is obviously high tension

334

but with a phenomenal current-carrying capacity if the size of those conductors is anything to go by.'

'A gigawatt?' Harry ventured.

'Easily. But if I was running a power line like this, I would run it through a clearing, well away from trees.'

'It *is* run through a clearing,' said Harry. 'But the tree canopies had been pulled together with cables.'

Darryl looked surprised. 'Roughly where did you find this power line?'

After a brief discussion, Harry and Lesa agreed on the likely location of the strange power line and pointed it out to Darryl. The technician keyed in some image-enhancing software and zoomed to about a thousand feet above the jungle. No one spoke as he began a diligent search. He entered a keyboard command and the colours of the jungle changed to a curious mottled effect. He pressed a key and the colours changed again.

'And again,' said Lesa peering closely at the screen.

Darryl punched the key a second time to change the mottling effect to a pattern of different hues.

'Got something,' Darryl muttered.

Harry looked at the screen and could not see anything amiss even when Darryl pointed out a series of uniformly-coloured patches. It was only when he drew a line across the screen that Harry realized that the patches formed an approximation of a straight line that traversed the jungle from the power station in the direction of the telescope. Darryl boxed one of the patches and called up a menu onto the screen. Harry watched with great interest as the computer went to work on a chlorophyll spectrum analysis of the patch. The seconds ticked by, indicative of the enormous computing power that the Cray was bringing to bear on the problem. A list of likely trees appeared on the screen. At the top of the list was the message:

EUCALYPTUS – PROBABILITY 95%

'I'd say a hundred per cent,' Darryl commented. 'That's what they've done: planted eucalyptus to fill any gaps in the cover. A nice, fast-growing tree.'

'Why didn't they just bury the power line and be done with it?' Harry queried.

'A power line of that capacity is going to require frequent inspection,' Darryl replied. 'Anyway – they have buried it where it leaves the tree line on Mount Kuromia. See?' He pointed to a line of discoloured vegetation that led from the jungle and up the side of the mountain to the Beta Telescope.

Lesa smiled at Harry's bewildered expression. 'Digging a trench and then refilling it with broken-up rock changes the drainage pattern of the soil where the trench was, which in turn has a long-term effect on the vegetation,' she explained.

Harry nodded and could only marvel at the expertise of these two. It occurred to him that earth resources analysts were the modern day equivalent of Sherlock Holmes.

'There's nothing particularly clever about all this,' said Darryl, guessing what Harry was thinking. 'We've only found these anomalies because we were looking for them on the basis of your ground intelligence. That island would stand up to normal inspection.'

Lesa gave Darryl a warm smile. 'Thanks, Darryl. You've been a great help.'

'Anytime,' said the technician standing up and moving away. 'Give me a shout if you need me again.'

Lesa looked speculatively at Harry when they were alone. All he needed now was gentle pushing along the path she was making for him. 'Ground intelligence is the key,' she said slowly.

'How do you mean?'

'Do you think all this adds up to proof that the Russians are up to something on Kuro?'

Harry could picture Gus Whittaker's wrath if he received a report based on his findings to date. 'No,' he said flatly. 'Now supposing you tell me what's churning under those lovely black tresses?'

'I think we should go back to Kuro and take a close look inside that telescope.'

'I can see a thousand problems.'

'To which I can offer a thousand solutions.'

'Problem number one is that we've been banned from Kuro.'

'Solution number one is that we make a night landing on a deserted beach,' Lesa countered, pointing out several breaks in the reef. 'Next.'

'Problem number two is that we don't know what we're looking for.'

'Solution number two is that we take someone along who's an expert on these matters.'

Harry looked at Lesa's quizzically raised eyebrows and laughed. 'Problem number three is that you're mad.'

'Let's get problem number two out of the way first.'

There was another problem that Harry lacked the courage to voice to Lesa: he wondered why she was so keen to return to Kuro.

Steve Krantz was indignant.

'I don't think I'm hearing this right,' his voice yelled in Harry's ear. 'At a moment's notice you want to tear me away from my wife, whom I love deeply, and my two children, whom I love deeply, and come jetting to England – all expenses paid – on a project that's bound to be crazy because you won't say what it's all about.'

'Yes . . .' said Harry, thinking fast.

'Okay.'

'It'll be a chance for you to do something for your country.'

'I said – okay.'

Harry was thrown for a moment. 'What was that?'

'I said, okay,' Krantz muttered patiently. 'Include me in. When do I start?'

'Grab the next flight to London,' said Harry. 'Call me when you've fixed a ticket and we'll meet you at the airport.'

Harry cleared the channel and went in search of Lesa. He found her at the work station downloading detailed images of Kuro onto a printer. It was early evening; all the other employees had gone home. He told her about Steve Krantz and that he was on his way to England.

'These will make superb maps,' she explained when Harry asked her what she was doing. 'Also I've checked every centimetre of the coastline. The only radar installations are at the airport. Darryl says they're approach systems and aren't designed or set low enough to see close inshore.'

'You'd think they'd have some sort of coastal surveillance system,' Harry observed.

'Why risk setting up radar systems when they're not supposed to have anything to hide?'

'They've got TV cameras and infrared warning systems along that power line.'

'That's because it's vulnerable. Trees falling across it and so on. We know where the power line is so we give it a wide berth – simple. I've also found a boat you can charter to get us in close to Kuro,' Lesa continued. 'Des Gibson Charters. I met him in Hong Kong

337

before we ran into each other. He's got a trimaran. Low, fast, all-wood construction which makes it a lousy radar reflector.' She looked questioningly at Harry, confident that he had walked into her trap.

## 25
April 14

Within an hour of his arrival in England, Steve Krantz was introduced to an unchanging English tradition by being caught in an anti-clockwise traffic snarl-up on the M25. It took two hours to cover fifteen miles on the orbital motorway between London airport and Guildford. By the end of the journey he had got the full story from Lesa and Harry. Instead of being doubtful about the enterprise, the clandestine nature of the operation appealed to the boyish streak in his nature although the scientist in him had doubts.

'But I have to be straight with you, Harry,' he admitted as Lesa turned her Audi onto the A31 that led to the Hog's Back. 'Even though I've seen the damage to that satellite, I still can't believe that it's actually been done. There's a side of me that's screaming that beam weapons are too akin to science fiction for me to swallow.'

'Despite the billions we've spent?'

'Throwing billions of dollars at a problem doesn't always solve it, as we've discovered.'

'What about throwing Alexi Hegel at the problem?'

Krantz grinned broadly. 'That's why I'm here.'

The test firing of the torus beam was scheduled for midday when any corona radiating from the giant coil would be difficult to see against the sunlight. According to Hegel, it was to be a random sky firing at no target – a rehearsal for the targeted firing scheduled for May the first. Victor Koniev was told that the purpose of the test was to evaluate energy dissipation rates of the torus coil under full load. The real reason for the test was because Hegel wanted to ensure that his control console at the back of the control room that he and Pachmann had re-wired was in working order.

Countdown for the test started at eleven when Hegel and Pach-mann took their seats at their desk. Koniev and Menkova filed into the dimly-lit control room and sat at their consoles, unaware that the information being fed to their monitors and instrument panels was under Pachmann's control.

'I'm ready for your lights, gentlemen,' said Koniev genially, glancing around the room. Four green lights appeared on his central monitor indicating that everything was ready for the first phase to begin. Koniev put on a headset and touched the talk pad that was linked directly to the superintendent at the power station. 'One hundred per cent power please,' he requested.

In the power station's control room, the white-coated superin-tendent sounded the alarms that ordered all out of the distribution room. Next he slid his forefinger the full length of the master touch control that initiated a series of checks by the other ten technicians in the control room. In the concrete and lead-lined reactor building hydraulically-operated seawater valves were opened and the huge main pumps started up, ramming six tonnes of seawater per minute through the heat exchangers. Electric motors whirred softly as they fed fuel into each of the four reactors. For several minutes none of the instruments in the telescope showed any change in the power being received from the power station.

Koniev placed his finger on the telescope public address pad. 'All personnel to clear from the gantries and apron.' He repeated the request three times in accordance with his own standing orders regarding the conduct of tests. The order was not strictly necessary because the closed-circuit television cameras covering the concrete apron around the four mirrors showed that the entire area was empty, but Koniev was a stickler for safety precautions.

'We're closing the switch now,' the power station superintendent advised.

Pachmann keyed in a closed-circuit line so that he and Hegel could see the contacts closing on the monster switch in the power distribution room. The gold-plated tongues of manganese alloy interlocked their surfaces tightly together forming two continuous conductors that would not break down under the enormous one-gigawatt load which would shortly be placed on them. The design, construction and testing of the mighty double-pole switch had been a four-year programme in itself.

'Switch closed and locked,' the superintendent's voice reported.

'Target alignment of Alpha please, Alexi,' said Koniev.

Hegel touched out the controls that turned Alpha's mirror to the target area. The computer-controlled actuators that adjusted the mirror's focal length provided Koniev and Menkova with a sighting screen picture of a blank portion of sky. The picture in front of Hegel and Pachmann was supposed to be the same; in fact it was an image of an old geosynchronous Pacific weather satellite dating from the 1960s, poised in equatorial orbit over Borneo, that had ceased functioning in 1970. In the control room's darkened interior, Hegel could afford to give Pachmann a delighted grin. Everything was working perfectly: the picture they were receiving on their sighting screen was from the Delta mirror and was aimed precisely at the torus coil's true target. The Alpha mirror that was providing Koniev and Menkova with their sighting screen was half a degree out of true alignment. Pachmann had done his job well.

There was little to report from the power station while the superintendent and his staff concentrated on increasing the output before their eight turbines. At eleven forty-five, fifteen minutes before the firing, the digital meters were showing that the coil was receiving fifty per cent power.

'Initiate arming,' Koniev ordered.

'Arming initiated,' Pachmann responded.

Deep beneath the Beta Telescope was a pressure vessel with a volume of less than a quarter of a cubic metre – about the volume of a domestic refrigerator. The chamber's inner lining was made of titanium alloy with a wall thickness of half a metre. The intermediate lining, after the lead shielding, consisted of a one-metre thickness of carbon fibre, and the whole chamber was encased in a two-hundred-tonne mass of reinforced concrete. Inside the container was a miniature atomic bomb – the warhead of a modified hundred-millimetre nuclear contact detonation artillery shell with the propellant charged removed. It was the latest Red army 'clean' shell with an explosive yield equal to one hundred tonnes of trinitrotoluene – better known as TNT. Leading directly from the centre of the detonation chamber was an armoured tube that formed part of the torus coil. On Pachmann's command, the telescopic sleeves that housed the detonator plunge began closing.

'Seventy-five per cent power,' the superintendent reported, confirming the evidence of the meters in the control room.

'Ignition in seven minutes,' said Pachmann, not looking up from his console.

'Eighty per cent.'

'Three minutes.'

Outside the telescope something extraordinary was happening. Under the influence of the awesome magnetic flux being generated in the hollow core in the torus coil, the air inside the coil was becoming ionized and was being ejected through the centre and into the sky as a beam of weak plasma that would have been visible had the test been conducted at night. Air rushing in to replace the air being sucked through the torus coil created a miniature gale on top of Mount Kuromia.

'Two minutes to ignition,' said Pachmann. Unlike Hegel his face was devoid of expression.

'Abort level C passed,' said Hegel.

The worst that could happen at this stage was a power failure. Up to abort level B Pachmann could shut down the nuclear device. At abort level A, the system was committed to detonation of the nuclear shell.'

'One minute to detonation.'

'Ninety per cent.'

Koniev shifted uncomfortably in his seat. At this point his pride in the achievement of building a working torus beam was tempered by an anxiety that there might be a power failure. The principle of the beam was simple even though building one that worked had eluded physicists for several decades. No amount of armoured pressure vessels could contain the force of even a small atomic bomb. The idea of the torus coil was that it would suck up the energy of the explosion as it occurred and hurl it into space as a beam of plasma. A power failure at the crucial moment would mean that the pressure vessel would explode, taking the entire telescope and the top of Mount Kuromia with it.

'Thirty seconds and counting . . .'

'Ninety-five per cent power.'

'Abort level B passed.'

'Twenty . . .'

Pachmann glanced at Hegel and saw that the big man was staring at the sighting screen picture of the old weather satellite.

'Fifteen . . .'

'You have one hundred per cent power. Good luck, gentlemen.'

The scream of the artificial hurricane could now be heard inside the building.

'Ten . . .'

Koniev turned round to give Hegel a quick thumbs up sign and was disconcerted by Hegel's answering grin.

'Abort level A passed.'

Hegel rested a finger on a key pad. It was one of Pachmann's more simple innovations; pressing it at the right moment would generate a convincing bright glitch of light on Koniev's sighting screen.

'Five . . . four . . . three . . . two . . .'

The flash from the sighting screens lit up the control room at the same instant as a dull rumble reached through the concrete floor. From the centre of the Beta mirror a beam of energy possessing the power of a hundred tonnes of TNT lanced into space. Its duration was less than a second. Seismic recorders throughout the Pacific would detect the shock but it would be too little to show up against the background seismic 'noise' from the earth's tectonic plate movements.

'Cut power! Cut power!' Koniev ordered the superintendent. The meters in the control room showed an immediate collapse of the flux field in the torus coil. He turned his swivel chair and beamed at Hegel. 'How was that, Alexi?'

'Brilliant,' Hegel answered, looking at his sighting screen. The ancient weather satellite had ceased to exist. It had been completely evaporated. 'One hundred per cent successful.'

'Excellent. Excellent, Alexi. A pity we did not have a target lined up.'

'A great pity, Victor,' Hegel agreed sagely while avoiding Pachmann's eye.

'This gives me great confidence for our test firing on May Day, Alexi. There will be a number of important colleagues from Moscow present. I must confess that I am greatly looking forward to our unveiling of what we have achieved here.'

'That makes two of us,' said Hegel with uncharacteristic honesty. He grinned broadly at Pachmann who, for once, managed to muster a semblance of a faint smile.

Lesa stopped at Berth 10C in the Hung Hing Marina. 'This is it,' she announced to her two companions. '*Sparkle*.'

Krantz stared askance at the ten-metre trimaran despite its sleek, modern appearance. In the United States multi-hulled craft had fallen from favour because they occupied double mooring space and were charged accordingly by marina operators. As a result, *Sparkle*, with its broad, flat decks spanning the outer hull, looked decidedly alien to his eyes. 'That!' he echoed.

'Looks okay to me,' Harry commented, running his eye over the trimaran's lines, noting the lightweight carbon fibre mast that was taller than the masts on many much larger yachts in the marina. It was swivel-mounted at the base and provided with its own winch in the centre of the main hull which suggested that it could be easily raised and lowered. He liked the hydraulically-operated roller reefing on the neatly-folded spinnaker booms and the self-steering gear above the cockpit. The gaps between the three hulls where they emerged forward from beneath the deck were strung across with trampoline-taut safety nets. It was a well-equipped, well-found craft, in excellent repair, that could be sailed comfortably and fast by one man on long ocean voyages.

'A giant pedal boat is *okay?*'

'The Polynesians were sailing all over the Pacific in trimarans before the Pilgrim Fathers set off from Plymouth,' Harry answered curtly.

Lesa jumped nimbly into the cockpit and rapped on the saloon door. 'Anyone at home? Mr Gibson?'

The door opened and the plump Polynesian whom Lesa had met on her last visit to Hong Kong poked his tousled mop of hair out. He blinked in the sunlight and gave a broad grin of pleasure when he saw Lesa.

'Hallo, Mr Gibson. I'm Lesa Wessex. Remember me? I called

you from England last Saturday about chartering your boat for an extended cruise.'

Des Gibson emerged from the saloon and pumped Lesa's hand. He was wearing shabby shorts, a peaked cap – pushed back at a rakish angle – and a permanent smile. 'Sure I remember you, Miss Wessex. Please – you must all come aboard.'

He ushered his guests into the surprisingly spacious, well-fitted saloon and fished cans of self-chilling beer from a locker. Krantz was mollified by the air-conditioning and the modern galley complete with a freezer. Maybe a long voyage on this strange boat wouldn't be so bad after all.

The deal was concluded between Harry and Des Gibson over the second round of beers: for $850 per day, to include all food and provisions, *Sparkle* was theirs for as long as they wanted it. 'I've no other bookings,' said Des with disarming honesty.

'What's your cruising range?' asked Harry.

'Distance no object,' said Des cheerfully. 'In this boat, we can go anywhere. *Sparkle* is like all trimarans – can sail very close to the wind. Philippines; Taiwan; Indonesia. Even Hawaii. Take ten – twelve days to get there. *Sparkle*'s fast. No centre keel – no drag.'

'We have in mind a round trip of about two thousand miles,' said Lesa carefully.

Des beamed. 'No big problem.'

'And I'll need a separate cabin.'

'Separate cabin for'ard, Miss Wessex. Very comfortable. Very clean. No big problem.'

'How do you navigate?' Krantz demanded suspiciously. 'By the stars?'

Des looked startled. 'No bloody fear. Not clever enough.' He pulled aside a curtain opposite the shower room compartment to reveal a drop-down flap desk. On a rack against the side of the hull was a host of satellite navigation equipment; echo sounders, a radar set, a high-power, all-band Icom transceiver, and even a fax machine. 'Got everything,' he said proudly, showing white teeth when he grinned. 'Business people like to keep in touch on long trips.' Operating in eastern waters meant that he had been able to take advantage of the plentiful supply of cheap but good quality electronic equipment available.

'Okay – it's a deal,' Harry said, catching Lesa's nod of approval. 'How soon can we get going?'

346

Des cocked his head on one side. 'Today Thursday. Need four days to get *Sparkle* ready. Say we leave early on Tuesday? April twenty-second?'

'That's fine,' said Lesa. 'That'll give us time to get some supplies.'

'So maybe you tell me where we're going?' Des queried.

'Eastwards, I guess,' said Harry. 'But knowing us, we probably won't make up our minds until we're at sea.'

Des grinned and nodded. He liked charters by people with money and time to spare. They were rare. These days there were too many in a hurry. They wanted to sample the pleasures of real sailing but they demanded the precision scheduling of motorized craft.

The shuttle *Colorado* thumped her main gear down on the Shuttle Landing Facility runway at 17:33 – three seconds behind schedule – and needed virtually the entire length of the five-kilometre stretch of concrete to roll to a standstill. Packed in her cargo bay was an entire airlock module from the space station. The vital component had been giving problems therefore Boeing's designers wanted the entire unit returned to earth for detailed examination. The three-man and two-woman crew disembarked and a tug hauled *Colorado* to the reception facility for removal of her cargo. It had been one of the shuttle's shortest missions – a mere twenty-four hours. Once the spacecraft was under cover, technicians began the exhaustive checks and preparations for its next mission. They worked fast because they had to pack the fifteen-day turn around programme that was now the norm for hard-working shuttles into eleven days.

*Colorado* was scheduled to lift off from Pad 39A on April the twenty-ninth.

Lesa was surprised at the amount of storage space there was in *Sparkle*'s outer hulls. There was sufficient headroom for her to stand upright as she helped Des guide the pack containing the Zodiac four-man inflatable boat through the hatch. Des pushed the pack into place so that it was wedged securely between the frames. The tubby Polynesian was capable of remarkable contortions without losing his peaked cap. He helped Lesa scramble back onto the broadside deck.

She peeled off her T-shirt and flopped out in the sun, looking decorous in a white one-piece swimsuit. 'I'm not doing another stroke,' she declared.

'Hey!' Harry yelled, passing a carton of lager to Krantz. 'Mutinous crew, Des! Make her walk the gangplank!'

'Tell him I'm too exhausted to walk anywhere,' Lesa muttered.

'Just about finished anyway,' said Des, fastening the outer hull's watertight hatch. 'You rest, miss. You work twice as hard as them two.'

Harry sat on the broad aft mattress in the cockpit and marked off the items they had stowed aboard on an electronic memo pad. They had spent the first two days while Des had prepared *Sparkle* buying a quarter of a million dollars' worth of equipment from Hong Kong's galaxy of suppliers. A similar spree in America in the same amount of time would have been impossible because no one city could have met all their needs. The previous day had been spent familiarizing themselves with their purchases.

Krantz dragged the last box of frozen meals into the galley and tried to make room for them in the freezer. They had all been working non-stop in the heat of the morning, loading up *Sparkle* with enough supplies to last a three-week cruise. Des walked a little way along the quay and squatted down to eye *Sparkle*'s trim. Correct balance of the multi-hull was essential because it lacked the several tonnes of keel of a conventional yacht to provide stability.

'Pretty nice trim,' he announced. 'We can leave now. Forecast good.'

'What about freshwater?' Krantz asked, emerging from the saloon. 'We haven't taken any on board.'

'Two tonne already in tanks,' said Des simply.

'Fuel?'

'Four hundred litres plenty. We only need diesel for harbour. We go everywhere with the wind, like the wind.'

They completed the customs formalities and cast off at noon. Des used the craft's Volvo Penta stern drive diesel to take them across the paths of the antique bottle-green Star ferries plying back and forth between Kowloon and Victoria – yet another tradition of Hong Kong that the new Chinese masters had left untouched. The presence of a modern diesel cheered up Krantz when he investigated the engine by lifting an inspection hatch in *Sparkle*'s cockpit floor.

He joined Harry and Lesa sunning themselves on the port-side deck. They were leaning against the saloon coaming watching the jewel-like islands of Big Wave Bay slip by. It was a magnificent day; a light breeze blew from the north east and a cloudless blue sky was marred only by the whine of jets climbing away from Kai Tak airport at two-minute intervals. Lesa was wearing dark glasses so Krantz wasn't sure whether or not it would be safe to admire her. The previous day she had caught him gazing at her and had fixed him with a stare of such withering contempt that he decided not to try the same thing again unless he was at least two hundred per cent certain he could escape detection.

'Shouldn't we be doing something?' asked Krantz, stretching out beside Lesa.

She lowered her sunglasses. 'Like what?'

'I don't know. Hoisting the main brace or something? I thought life on a sailing boat was all work and no rest to take one's mind off being seasick?'

'There'll be plenty of work soon enough,' Harry murmured lazily.

'Problem, Mr Dysan, sir,' Des called out from the cockpit.

'What's that, Des?'

'You make up your mind where we go now?'

'Due east.'

'Where east?'

'A thousand miles east, Des. Little island called Kuro. Good game fishing I've heard.'

Des glanced around to ensure that no shipping was near before disappearing below and reappearing with a large-scale chart of the Pacific. He spread it out over the stainless-steel helm and studied it intently. 'Ah, yes, I find. Very small island.'

'Sure you won't miss it?'

Des grinned. 'Got satellite navigation. Know position to within ten metre.'

'How did we manage before satellites were invented?' Krantz asked of no one in particular.

'How indeed,' Lesa replied, closing her eyes and enjoying the warmth of the sun. 'If it wasn't for satellites, we wouldn't be here now.'

'North east trades a little problem at this time of year,' Des called out. 'Best we tack south east on three-hundred-mile leg, then claw north east on three-hundred-mile leg. Take us through Balingtang Channel north of Philippines. Then we do long tacks in Pacific.'

'You mean we can't sail straight there?' asked Krantz.

'Not in sail-boat. We go up then we go down. Big zig-zag. No problem. Re-setting sail something to do.'

Krantz groaned. 'I knew there'd be a snag,' he complained.

'So how many sea miles to Kuro, Des?' asked Harry.

'Twelve, maybe thirteen hundred mile.'

'How long's that going to take us?'

'Five, maybe six day.' Des pointed to an isle on their port quarter. 'Nam Kwo Chau. Last Hong Kong island. We sail now. Miss Lesa – you unhitch spinnaker booms like I show you.'

Glad of something to do, Lesa released the shrouds securing the twin booms and attached the ends of the booms to the push-pull flexible control lines that led under the side deck back to the servos in the cockpit. She swung them out so that they and the mast formed a giant inverted T. Next she attached lines that hung down from the mast to the corners of the triangular spinnaker sails that were furled tightly around the booms.

'Okay, Des.'

Des watched the booms swivel in response to his adjustments of the two miniature joysticks on the helm control panel. He gave Lesa a thumbs up sign and cut the engine. *Sparkle* lost way. Two small hydraulic winches on the foredeck began turning. Harry and Krantz turned their attention from Lesa to watch the spinnakers unwinding from their booms. They began filling with wind when they had reached a height of a metre. Such was the responsiveness of *Sparkle* that she immediately picked up speed.

Krantz was sitting on the saloon roof where it was easier to keep Lesa's lithe form under observation. The sudden acceleration as the sails reached half way up the mast caused him to slide off his perch and land beside Harry. 'Jesus,' he muttered, 'methinks this thing doth goeth somewhat I declare, Mr Christian.'

'That's enough sail,' Des called out. 'You make good first mate, Miss Wessex.'

'I bet she would,' said Krantz, keeping his voice low. He looked speculatively at Harry. 'Have you and she . . . ?'

'No,' said Harry abruptly.

'There's hope for both of us. I've heard that sea voyages can do strange things to women.'

'She'll do strange things to you if you try anything,' Harry warned.

'Funny girl. Have you noticed that tattoo on her arm?'

'Yeah.'

'And what about that watch she wears?'

'What about it?'

'I reckon the Smithsonian would like to get their hands on it – quite a museum piece. I wonder why she wears it?'

'Why don't you ask her?'

'I have this suspicion that asking such a question could be fraught with uncertain danger.'

'Not uncertain,' said Harry lazily. 'Certain.'

'We now make ten knots,' Des bragged. 'Pretty damn good on short sail, huh?'

'Pretty damn good!' Lesa laughingly agreed when she was drenched with spray.

Harry looked up at her. She was standing legs slightly apart, bracing herself against the motion of the deck, holding a mast shroud with one hand, and facing into the wind. Her long black hair was streaming out behind her. She looked like an avenging Circe; a Homeric enchantress speeding across the wine-dark sea to exact a most terrible retribution on her enemies.

The pressure hoses on the radio-controlled mole completed their task of washing out residual radio activity from the detonation chamber. All the water sucked out of the chamber was pumped into a deep well and the pumps themselves were finally flushed clean with seawater. By nightfall the team of ten technicians working in the chambers beneath the Beta Telescope had completed all the operations on their check lists. The torus was ready to receive another nuclear shell from the small underground arsenal that had been dug into the cliff face at the power station.

# CAPE CANAVERAL, FLORIDA April 24

In the massive, cube-like Vehicle Assembly Building, built in the previous century to assemble Saturn rockets to take men to the moon, the space shuttle *Colorado* was hoisted nose-up into the air and attached to the huge cigar-shaped fuel tank and two solid fuel boosters. The entire ungainly contraption was held in place by the service tower which was in turn mounted on a crawler. In three days, when all the assembly checks were completed, the sections of the Vehicle Assembly Building door would open and the crawler would emerge to begin its three-kilometre per hour journey across the reclaimed swampland to launch pad 39A.

South of the Batan Islands the continental shelf dropped quite suddenly from a depth of two hundred metres to five thousand metres. Lesa held the helm tightly, feeling the movement of *Sparkle*'s rudder through her fingers, while watching the echo sounder's gas plasma display. She tried to picture in her mind the awesome five-kilometre gulf between the trimaran and the abyssal plain of the Pacific's floor and decided that it was something best not thought about. It was better to concentrate on the gyro-compass and keep *Sparkle* on her true easterly heading. Behind her Des was stretched out asleep on the aft mattress. Harry and Krantz were lying on the safety nets where they could catch the down draught spilling off the spinnakers while not seeming to mind the occasional drenching they received when a swell broke across them.

Lesa picked up her new waterproof Klipfone, one of several purchases in Hong Kong, and called Darryl. He sounded pleased to hear her voice. Before leaving England, Harry had reluctantly briefed him on the purpose of the mission at Lesa's insistence.

'I'm coping fine,' he said in answer to her query. 'I'm getting used to not having you around. Your signal's a bit noisy.'

'That's because the call's going through the boat's system. We're out of range of terrestrial repeaters. Darryl – I'm so sorry I've left you to hold the fort so much.'

'Don't worry about it – so long as you're having fun.'

'Anything happening at our destination?'

'I took a quick look an hour ago. All quiet on the western front. I found your boat too. You're making good progress.'

It was a comfort knowing that Darryl was looking, god-like, down on them even though he was on the other side of the world. She dealt with a few routine queries that he had on slow-paying customers and then said goodbye.

The sailing-yacht thrashed on through the hot, lazy afternoon, her twin spinnakers pregnantly rounded with the brisk trade wind. A lone albatross caught Lesa's eye. The seabird was pacing *Sparkle* on the trimaran's quarter, hoping for a meal of fish guts to be tossed into the sea which it had come to expect from the fishing boats of Basco. Lesa reached forward and turned up the contrast on the plan position indicator so that she could see the screen in the bright sunlight. Three days' sailing had taken them seven degrees east of Hong Kong, a distance of over four hundred miles made good although their zig-zagging tacks into the north easterly trades meant that they had covered the best part of seven hundred nautical miles overall.

The albatross tired of waiting for a meal and wheeled away towards the dark fringes of the Batan Islands on the northern horizon.

'We're nearly half way, Neti,' Lesa whispered to the departing bird. 'I won't fail you this time. I swear on my life.'

Hegel stood in front of his living room television receiver and flicked through the satellite's transponders. He stopped when he came to the NASA Information Channel. This time the usual captions were now scrolling from left to right along the foot of the screen. The picture itself was a live feed from a fixed, unmanned camera in the Vehicle Assembly Building at Cape Canaveral showing a shuttle being prepared for its roll-out. A lapsed time indicator in a corner of the screen was showing sixty-eight hours and ten minutes to lift off.

He picked up a Klipfone. 'No change,' he said curtly into the mouthpiece.

'I'm standing by,' Pachmann's voice answered.

Hegel stood a small UHF transmitter on the floor and connected its input to the satellite receiver's auxiliary output. He switched the transmitter on.

'Getting something,' said Pachmann. 'Lot of noise on the picture. Where's the TX unit?'

'On the floor.'

'Try standing it on the coffee table.'

Hegel dragged the coffee table near the television and stood the transmitter on it. 'How's that?'

'Fine,' said Pachmann. 'Nice and sharp. Still inside the building. Kind of them to tell us how long we've got.'

Hegel considered that enough had been said over the air and refrained from further comment. He glanced at the television screen.

*Colorado* was now sixty-eight hours from lift off.

In the control room on Mount Kuromia, Anton Pachmann turned down the contrast on his monitor and watched the technicians working on the up-ended shuttle. Hopefully NASA would be providing a live television feed from the shuttle two days after lift off. It would be interesting to see the consternation aboard the spacecraft when the torus beam zapped a hole in its wing.

The fine weather continued to hold but the unfavourable winds forced Des to beat a long way north east to within two hundred miles of Okinawa. 'Best way, Mr Dysan, sir,' he assured Harry, spreading a chart out on the saloon table. 'You see? We make another hundred mile on this tack then we turn on long fast run south to Kuro. No big problem.'

Lesa entered the saloon and sat beside Des. 'Sorry, miss,' said Des sheepishly. 'Little longer to get to Kuro than I think.'

'Well there's no rush,' said Lesa. 'When do you expect us to get there?'

Des eyed the chart. 'Two, three days. Wednesday night. Maybe early Thursday morning – May first.'

Lesa looked levelly at Harry. 'I think it's now time to give Des a few more details about our fishing trip, Harry.'

Harry nodded. 'We've been less than honest with you, Des. We're not interested in the game fishing around Kuro. We're really journalists.'

Des grinned. 'I guess right. All the time I'm saying to myself, why do you want to sail so far for fish? Plenty of fish right here.'

'The Russians have built a big telescope on Kuro,' Harry continued. 'They've let reporters in to cover the telescope construction, but not to check on the effect their work has had on the wildlife. They've made lots of promises they would disturb habitats as little as possible, but we want to find out for ourselves. We want to make a clandestine landing, get some recordings and get out. You understand?'

Des nodded delightedly. The idea of being involved in a secret operation had considerable appeal. 'Now I know why you bring Zodiac boat and all that gear. It all makes big sense.'

'The idea is me and Miss Wessex go ashore at night in the Zodiac, stay ashore twenty-four hours or thereabouts, and radio video pictures to Mr Krantz who stays here on the boat with you.'

'And we have rods out pretending to be fishing!' Des finished. 'It is very simple.'

'Let's pray that it stays as simple as it sounds,' said Harry with feeling. He caught Lesa's eye. For once her superb control failed her and she looked away.

# CAPE CANAVERAL, FLORIDA

It was a few minutes after 10:00 Eastern Standard Time when the doors of the Vehicle Assembly building began opening, lifting section by section until there was sufficient clearance for the four-thousand-tonne crawler to emerge onto the gravel crawler-way and begin its six-kilometre journey to the raised ramp near the coast that was Launch Pad 39A.

The ungainly contraption was a hundred metres clear of the building when the executive jet bringing the shuttle's crew from Houston began its final approach.

'They're shaving it a bit close,' Stella Richards commented to Matt Gosling.

'Forty-eight hours for fuelling and final check-outs? Yeah – they'll do it,' said Gosling, peering out of the aircraft's window. 'When I started in this game, the damn thing could be sitting out there for several weeks with the humidity playing hell with the electronics.'

'Those were the days, eh, Matt?'

'No, Stella,' said Gosling seriously. 'These are the days.'

Responsibility for smartening up Kurograd before the arrival of the VIPs fell on Diem's shoulders. For two days he and his team laboured in the heat to make the scruffy little prefabricated township look as respectable as possible: they whitewashed walls and ran out of paint; they tried to clean up the years of guano that encrusted the harbour walls and burned out their power tools. They weren't helped by Victor Koniev pouncing on them every two hours with loud complaints about their lack of progress. The administrator's popularity could be judged by the fact that the citizens of the township paid lip-service to his demands that they clean up the place. As soon as his car disappeared in the direction of the telescope, they went back to their fishing from the harbour wall and drinking in the bar.

'Who's coming?' Diem asked the bartender as he and his assistants trooped back into the bar after Koniev's second haranguing visit that morning.

The barman shrugged. 'Big shots from Moscow I've heard.'

'I thought the official opening wasn't until next year?'

'It's not. Friends of Kommissar Koniev's as far as I can make out. Any friend of Koniev is an enemy of mine. Oh shit – the crafty little swine!'

Diem twisted on his stool and groaned. Koniev had turned his car around and driven straight back into the township. He looked far from happy.

# CAPE CANAVERAL, FLORIDA April 29

At 05:00 local time, shuttle commander Matt Gosling, pilot Paul Balchin and payload master Stella Richards rode the elevator up the launch gantry to the service structure's 'white' room. They assumed responsibility for the *Colorado* from the handover/ingress team the moment they completed the formalities. Gosling was first into the narrow corridor of the crew access arm. He climbed through the shuttle's hatch and eased himself onto the flight deck and into the left-hand seat. Balchin strapped himself into the right-hand seat, and Stella Richards occupied the payload master's seat behind the two men. Movements in the up-ended spacecraft required care. By the time she had fastened her seat harness, Gosling and Balchin had completed the communication voice checks with launch control.

There was little for Stella to do once she had checked that her communication headset was working. She disregarded the discomfort of lying tipped backwards; her mind was on the coming barmitzvah of her sister's eldest boy. She pulled a memo pad from her breast pocket and added some names to the guest-list that she was helping her sister compile while she listened with half an ear to the exchanges between the two men and mission control. Then there was the vexed question of a suitable present for a thirteen year old that she and her husband had argued over. By the time she had narrowed the choice down to either a windsurfer and sail or a camcorder there was a jolt as the crew access arm was retracted.

'*Colorado* – you have main engines gimballed to launch position,' said the voice of the launch controller.

'That's a roger,' Gosling confirmed.

Stella returned the electronic pad to her pocket and concentrated on the closing seconds of the launch countdown. All she could see of the outside world from her position were rectangles of the dawn sky through the forward windows.

'*Colorado* – APU start-up is go. You're on internal management.'

'Roger, control,' Balchin replied. 'SSME ignition start sequence initiated.'

'Confirmed, *Colorado*. Five . . . four . . . main engine ignition . . .'

The dull rumble sounded like an approaching subway train. It rose steadily to a deep roar as all three main engines cut in.

'Three . . . two . . . one . . .'

The shuttle lurched alarmingly as though it were about to topple. By now Stella accepted as normal the offset thrust from the engines, designed to keep the incandescent gases away from the giant external fuel tank, and which caused the entire airframe to rock sickeningly. The acceleration was gentle – slower than the start of an elevator. The difference was that it was constant.

'You've cleared the tower,' advised the launch controller.

The red light on the remote control TV camera came on, indicating that a wide angle picture of the flight deck was being relayed to the NASA Information Channel. Stella wondered if her husband had set the alarm to watch the launch.

'Launch Control. This is *Colorado*. Initiating roll manoeuvre,' Balchin reported.

The Atlantic Ocean appeared in the windows. The spacecraft had reached a height of twenty-five kilometres and was flattening out her climb and twisting onto her back. Despite the padding in her coveralls, the awkward position and the acceleration conspired to make the seat harness straps cut into Stella's shoulders. It was the least comfortable part of the mission.

The roar of the rocket engines suddenly diminished.

'Launch Control. *Colorado*. We have solid rocket booster burnout.'

'Roger, *Colorado*. SRB burnout confirmed.'

Small separation motors fired to steer the two now spent boosters away from *Colorado*. They would parachute back into the Atlantic for recovery by a NASA ship. The three main engines continued their long burn. The shuttle, now 150 kilometres above the earth, was draining the fuel from the external tank – clinging to the giant cylinder like a parasite greedily draining life and blood from the underbelly of a bloated host body.

'One and three engines close down,' Balchin reported.

The roar became even more muted. *Colorado* had reached a safe altitude that guaranteed her ability to remain in orbit in the event of a major systems failure. All the spacecraft had to do now was maintain a steady burn on one engine that would take her up to the

363

geo-stationary orbital height of 37,000 kilometres – a height that was beyond the design capabilities of the earlier shuttles. It would be a long, slow climb lasting several hours. Stella closed her eyes and dozed. She ignored the TV camera's glowing red light. She had no idea how big the worldwide audience was for the NASA Information Channel. A million? Maybe, maybe not. It seemed unlikely that there was enough interest in a shuttle launch these days to attract a million watchers but she hoped that her husband and children were among them.

There were two watchers on the other side of the world who followed the launch with avid interest. Alexi Hegel and Anton Pachmann sat before the big television in Hegel's bungalow and studied the tracking station shots of *Colorado* relayed from automatic cameras.

Hegel spread some cut-away technical illustrations of the shuttle out on the floor in front of the television. 'Okay – so where exactly do we hit the thing?'

Anton knelt beside the big man and pointed to a wing. 'Right in the centre of the wing where there's only frames and struts and hardly any avionics. If we hit the centre, we avoid damaging the main gear and the elevator controls. Naturally, a wounded shuttle making a return to earth will attract worldwide attention. We will get massive publicity.' He sat back on his heels and looked levelly at Hegel. 'No matter what we say by way of apology or talk about accidents, there will be a tremendous row. You must ask yourself if that is really what you want.'

Hegel gave a deep, booming laugh. 'A row that finishes Koniev for good and gives me worldwide publicity for what I've achieved? Oh yes, Anton – I fancy that that will do me very nicely.' He clapped his partner on the back. 'Don't worry, Anton. We have our stories ready. Shortages of funds so that we could not perfect the sighting system. And Koniev's insistence that the test went ahead when I said that the torus was not ready is on record. Not even Menkov will be able to deny that.'

There was shooting: the sharp *crack crack* of rifle fire.

Lesa scrambled to her feet and staggered to the opposite rail. The redhead saw her and yelled. Lesa launched herself into the sea, managing to convert her hurried fall into a semblance of a dive that took her deep beneath the surface. She felt and heard a round whack into the water. Two more smacked the water in front of her when she surfaced. One of the rounds, its energy spent, actually brushed against her leg as it sank. She gulped down a hurried gasp of air and jack-knife dived to go as deep as possible just as a fourth round tore through her left shoulder.

The searing stab of pain and the shooting jerked her fully awake. That she had been escaping the heat of the afternoon by lying asleep in her cabin in *Sparkle* with the air-conditioning running flat out was of no consequence; that she was naked had no influence on her reactions; her weeks of training with Ko in Sham Shui Po Closed Centre were forgotten; in the few seconds that it took her to dash from her cabin, she was once again a terrified fourteen-year-old at the mercy of a gang of Europeans who had massacred her family.

Harry braced himself against the cockpit coaming, centred the shark's dorsal fin in the rifle's sights and squeezed off a fourth shot. This time his round punched a neat hole through the fin. The shark swam on, unconcerned.

Des gave a lusty cheer and clapped Harry on the back. 'You getting better, Mr Dysan.'

'Okay – my turn,' said Krantz. He was about to take the rifle from Harry when the saloon door burst open.

'What the hell do you think you're doing!' Lesa screamed.

The three men turned and gaped at her in surprise. She was standing in the doorway clutching a curtain across herself. The expression in her eyes was a mixture of fury and terror.

'What does it look like?' Harry answered. For an anxious moment he thought Lesa was going to fly at him. 'Taking pot shots at sharks until the wind picks up. Does it bother you?'

Lesa suddenly felt foolish and vulnerable. She pulled the curtain protectively around herself. 'I was asleep. I didn't know what the noise was.' She slammed the door shut and rushed blindly back into her cabin, threw herself down on her berth and clutched the sides of the mattress with sufficient force to tear the foam rubber. Gradually the terror subsided and gave way to anger. For a few blind, panic-stricken moments the treacherous past had thrust aside her carefully nurtured poise and sophistication to seize control. How could she hold any hope of avenging Neti and her family when she kept betraying them so?

For some seconds she ignored the muted buzzing of her Klipfone. Eventually she forced herself to pick up the instrument and make her voice sound natural when she spoke.

It was Darryl, agitated. 'Something's happening at your destination. Two aircraft have arrived.' As previously agreed, Darryl avoided mentioning Kuro by name even though Klipfone conversations were supposed to be a hundred per cent secure.

'So what?'

'These aren't ordinary transports, Lesa. They're a pair of Tupolev executive jets – one in civilian markings and the other with military markings.'

'Have you checked the registrations?'

'Yes.'

'And?'

'Top brass. It could blow your cover if I gave you any more information.'

Lesa considered. 'We'll have to chance it,' she decided.

'Okay. The civilian jet is from the General Administration flight pool and is available to deputies, and the military jet is the personal transport of General Zworkin.'

'Who's he?'

'Acting Commander in Chief of Soviet Land Forces.'

'There's top brass visiting the place all the time, Darryl. It means they'll be distracted.'

'It means that they might be stepping up their security,' Darryl retorted.

'How about the *Rasputin*?'

'Still in the harbour,' Darryl replied. 'Listen, Lesa – you've got to be careful.'

Lesa ended the conversation with her thanks and a promise to

367

keep him posted. She cleared the channel. There was the sound of the spinnaker's hydraulic winch turning above her head and feet moving about on the deck. She felt the gentle surge of the trimaran picking up speed, signalling that the wind had returned. She changed into shorts and a T-shirt and made her way through the saloon to the cockpit. The rifle had disappeared. *Sparkle* was thrashing along at a steady fifteen knots under a full spread of sail. Des had thrown in the self-steering gear and was helping Harry and Krantz unpack the Zodiac inflatable boat. Des gave her a sheepish smile but Krantz and Harry concentrated on spreading the boat out on the deck.

'I'm sorry about my little outburst just now,' she said awkwardly.

Harry looked up in surprise and wondered how much the apology had cost her. He knew Lesa well enough by now to know that she hated losing face. He shrugged. '*I'm* sorry, Lesa. Guess I didn't think about your nerves.'

'You didn't spend your childhood in Vietnam,' Lesa replied, resisting an impulse to snap back at Harry for his patronizing tone.

Harry caught her gaze and for an instant saw in her troubled eyes a side of her that she was always careful to keep hidden. The lowering of her guard lasted perhaps a second, and was quickly restored by her lovely smile.

'How are we doing now, Des?' she asked.

The Polynesian grinned. 'Hundred miles west of Kuro, Miss Wessex. This wind keep up, we'll be there by nightfall.'

Lesa smiled. 'Good timing, Des.'

There was an explosive hiss of gas when Krantz opened the valves on the Zodiac's compressed air bottles. The boat was spread out on the deck like the blackened, dried skin of water buffalo. The crinkles smoothed out of the vinyl until the craft was fully inflated. Lesa helped the three men lower the boat over the side and make it secure to the outer hull on a short painter. The tiny craft, dancing in the trimaran's wake, was a vivid reminder of the time on Tao's motorized junk when she had watched the frail sampan that was later to become her salvation leaping from wave to wave during their escape across the South China Sea. Nor was that the only image that sprung fleetingly to her mind: there was the disconcerting picture of Harry's lean body bending over to make sure that the Zodiac was safe; for a moment he was Lin; the same build, the same white shorts. And when he turned to look at her, the same ready smile. With a little shock she realized that had Lin lived, he would have been about the same age as Harry.

## EARTH ORBIT

Stella Richards was woken by the vibration from her wrist alarm. Usually she was awake before the buzzer went off but the previous day's concentrated work using the Canada arm had been particularly difficult. Hoovering two satellites had taken longer than expected with the result that her normal eight-hour work period had been extended to twelve hours.

She unzipped her sleep restraint bag and slid back the sleeping berth's privacy panel. Getting out of bed in the weightless conditions aboard the shuttle required more care than effort. On her first mission she had managed to crack her head on several occasions as part of the painful process of learning that mass and weight, or rather, weightlessness, were not the same things.

A gentle push sent her across the lower accommodation deck to the washing station. The same amount of energy that went into the push was required to stop her at her destination. Careful to keep her back to Paul Balchin in case he was only pretending to be asleep, she pulled off the loose T-shirt that she favoured on shuttle flights and gave herself a brisk rubdown with a hot towel from the dispenser. Changing the rest of her underwear meant returning to her berth, closing the panel, and performing intricate gyrations in the confined space. She emerged wearing a pair of baggy, unglamorous pants that always irritated the NASA public relations staff during televized live feeds. She didn't give a damn: she was in space to do a job, not take part in a public relations exercise.

After squeezing a breakfast of mashed grapefruit and plain yoghurt down her throat, she disposed of the sachets and steered herself expertly through the hatch to the flight deck to startle Matt Gosling who was dozing in the commander's seat.

'All positioned up for you, Stella,' he commented, waving a hand at the aft windows that overlooked the cargo bay. 'Don't want another pig like yesterday.'

Stella agreed, levered her body upright in relation to the shuttle and pushed her Velcro overshoes onto the mat by her work station.

She looked through the window along the length of the cargo bay. Hovering twenty metres above the open doors was the bulk of IntelSat – a 1980s communications satellite now at the end of its working life. Above IntelSat was the white and aquamarine radiance of the earth. At this height the entire planetary crescent was visible. Moonlight imparted a suffused glow in the wake of the terminator as it edged across the Western Pacific, bringing night to South East Asia.

'Beautifully positioned, Matt,' said Stella appreciatively as she started work.

At one minute past midnight the navigation satellite plotter was indicating *Sparkle*'s position as twenty-five miles west of Kuro. Des worked the roller reef winches to furl the trimaran's sails around her booms. The big yacht lost way and came to a rolling standstill – pitching uncomfortably on the steep swells. Des switched on the cockpit floodlighting and checked the electronic log. Such was the boat's lightweight construction that even under bare poles it was able to make one knot in the gentle but humid breeze.

Krantz and Harry sweated to lift the ten-horsepower Evinrude electric outboard motor through the stowage hatch in the port hull while Lesa went below and tested the mining survey helmets that she and Harry would be wearing. Each helmet was fitted with a voice-command-activated miniature television camera linked to a video recorder that the wearer carried on a belt. Also on the belt was a UHF television transmitter. The equipment was neat and unobtrusive. The moulded belt packs, including lithium batteries, weighed less than five hundred grams. Even the camera was moulded into the helmet.

The plan was for Krantz to remain with Des on *Sparkle* and survey by remote control anything that Lesa and Harry found. He could also direct them by radio to turn their heads towards anything that particularly interested him. That was all Harry and Lesa had to do in connection with using the equipment: merely turn their heads where directed by Krantz. They didn't even have to bother with the camera controls because the tiny Panasonic devices possessed automatic sonic focussing.

'Comms units working fine,' Lesa reported, poking her head through the saloon's roof hatch.

'Okay – fine,' said Harry looking up at her from the Zodiac where he and Krantz were checking the condition of the outboard's batteries. For an instant the single floodlight shining down caught Lesa's expression of suppressed anxiety. It was gone as quickly as it appeared.

'Best give it quick burst,' Des advised. 'Best way of checking battery condition and making sure transom clamps are tight.'

'The meters say the cells are fully charged,' Krantz pointed out, scrambling into the trimaran's cockpit.

'Des is right,' said Harry. He untied the painter and switched the outboard into reverse. The Zodiac purred astern. He flicked into forward, opened up to full power and sent the craft scudding around *Sparkle* in a tight circle, staying within the pool of light from the floodlight.

'Handles like a dream,' he reported, making the inflatable boat secure and rejoining the others in the cockpit.

'So when do we leave?' asked Lesa. She glanced at Harry and didn't like the way he stared at her. 'Well?'

'First a final briefing so we all know what we're doing.'

*Sparkle*'s air-conditioning was able to do its job properly once the saloon hatch was closed and conditions soon became tolerable. The four sat at the table and studied the large-scale prints of Kuro that Lesa had provided.

'What's our position from Kuro now, Des?'

Des twisted around in his seat and checked the navigation display. 'Twenty-three miles due west of your landing beach.'

'It's a fine night,' Lesa observed. 'So if the claims made by the Zodiac's makers are right, we should be there in an hour.' She smiled at Harry and, once again, was worried by his evasive expression. 'What's wrong, Harry?'

'I'm sure Des and Steve won't mind stepping out into the cockpit for a few minutes.'

Lesa's heart quickened. She could guess what was coming. 'Why should they?'

'Because I want you to tell me why you're so anxious to get back to Kuro,' said Harry evenly, spreading his hands palms downwards on the table as though bracing himself for a showdown.

Lesa regarded him in silence for some moments. Krantz made a move to stand but she stopped him. 'It's okay – stay where you are, Steve.' She turned her fathomless eyes on Harry. Her outwardly calm expression belied the turmoil that was churning within her like a malevolent beast. 'No, Harry – that's my business.'

'Then you're not going to Kuro,' said Harry emphatically. 'I'm sorry, Lesa – but I can't take the chance. All we have to do is collect

373

data and get out. Nothing more. I'm probably overstepping my terms of reference on this case as it is. My guess is that you want to return to Kuro to settle an old score. Maybe I'm wrong but I'm not prepared to add to the risks.'

Krantz raised an eyebrow. 'You're not planning on going alone?'

'If I have to,' Harry replied, not taking his eyes off Lesa. He was expecting an outburst from her but to his surprise she merely shrugged.

'Well – it's not that important anyway. I'm happy to stay here.' She had everything worked out in that fertile mind of hers – down to the beguiling smile she gave her three companions. 'You'll make out okay, Harry. I'll be happy to stay and help Steve.' She yawned and rose. 'It's been a long day, so if you gentlemen don't mind, I'm going to grab an hour's sleep. Steve – give me a call when Harry's landed.' She turned her half-smile on Harry. 'Good luck, Harry. I'll keep my fingers crossed for you.' She stifled another yawn and made her way forward to her cabin.

The moment she closed the door her movements became purposeful. She splashed water in her tiny hand basin as though she were washing, sprayed herself with insect repellent, wriggled quickly into her travel suit and plugged a new battery pack into its conditioner. She made sure the unit was working properly and switched it off in case the others heard it humming. Her waterproof Klipfone went into a pouch together with a map of Kuro, as did one of her Hong Kong purchases that the others didn't know about – a PebbleZing catapult with an aluminium handle and wrist brace. The slingshot was just like the one that she had owned when she was a child. Accompanying it was a handful of smooth, slightly flattened pebbles and a pocket torch. A smear of face cream on the hinges prevented the hatch from squeaking when she cautiously pushed it open and scrambled nimbly onto deck. The night was close and humid; *Sparkle* was rolling in the heavy swell but there was hardly a breath of wind.

She glanced aft towards the cockpit. Lights shone out of the saloon windows. To pass the windows by moving aft along the deck was too risky so she slipped silently into the water. The buoyancy of the travel suit enabled her to concentrate on guiding herself along the hull until her fingers encountered the yielding flanks of the Zodiac dinghy before moving to the painter and untying it. A firm push with her feet while hanging onto the Zodiac sent the craft twisting away from *Sparkle*. She hauled herself over the side, sorted herself out and sat on the thwart behind the simple steering wheel. Being electric, it was necessary only to click the switch to start the outboard. The instruments on the simple dashboard became illuminated at the same moment as the outboard emitted a loud whine. The sudden accleration jerked her backwards and thumped the Zodiac's snub prow into a swell causing it to leap clear of the surface so that for one ghastly moment Lesa thought that it was going to flip right over. Obviously inflatable boats needed circumspect application of power to remain upright in a brisk sea.

She eased back the lever and steered away from *Sparkle*'s pool of light. Just before the trimaran dipped below the swell, she saw the saloon door burst open. Des appeared in the cockpit and yelled at her. She glanced over her shoulder; when the Zodiac leapt clear of the next swell she saw that he had been joined by Harry and Krantz. All three were shouting and waving frantically. The Volvo engine coughed into life. Lesa chanced increasing the power while hanging grimly onto the wildly bucking helm wheel. A sudden drenching from a cloud of spray nearly caused her to lose her grip when she chanced a quick glance at the compass in order to bring the craft onto an easterly heading.

At that moment there was a sound that conjured up terrors fuelled by the terrible memories of her childhood – the sharp *crack crack* of rifle fire. She gave a little whimper of fear and hunched over the wheel, pushing the power lever against the stop at the same time. The outboard screamed, sending the Zodiac pounding from swell-top to swell-top like a skimming stone. Luckily the over-rev compensators cut in each time the propeller came clear of the water, otherwise the tortured motor would have torn itself apart.

### 42

Harry fired two more shots into the air and had to grab hold of the coaming to keep his balance as Des started the trimaran's engine and spun the helm.

'Des!' he yelled when he had finished cursing. 'What are our chances of catching her?'

'We can make ten knots on the engine, Mr Dysan.'

'That thing can do twenty-five,' Krantz observed.

Harry ignored the comment. 'What about sails?'

'Not enough wind. We make good time with engines. Maybe twelve knots.'

'Methinks she'll be in Scotland afore ye,' was Krantz's unhelpful contribution.

Harry's reply was crude but to the point.

## 43

It was 01:30 when Victor Koniev, all smiles and bonhomie, escorted his two VIP guests from the hotel to his car to chauffeur them up to the telescope. Mosquitoes swarmed into the car for a ride and a meal the moment the doors were opened and the courtesy lights came on. First Deputy Yuri Salvanis was a slightly-built, nondescript man in contrast to General Zworkin whose figure was not in rapport with the much-reduced, streamlined Soviet land forces that he commanded. General Zworkin was fond of fooling himself that his over-eating was necessary to fuel the nervous energy he was expending to achieve his burning ambition and restore the Soviet army to its glorious strength of the 1980s. Unlike Salvanis he was not a member of Koniev's Lenin Reform Group, nevertheless he was one of its most active, behind-the-scenes supporters, and had connived with Koniev over the diverting of several million roubles of army funds into the Kuro project. As he sat sweating in the back of Koniev's car, he wished that some of the money had been spent on decent air-conditioned ZILs.

'Why,' he demanded testily, slapping at the mosquitoes, 'does the test have to be conducted at this God-forsaken hour?'

'I'm extremely sorry, general,' said Koniev, cursing himself for not specifying a time when he had insisted on a May Day demonstration. It was typical of Alexi Hegel's perverse nature to arrange it for the middle of the night. Hopefully, if all went well, the physicist's services wouldn't be needed for much longer. 'But Hegel said that it would have to be at this time. Like all geniuses, he can be extremely difficult.'

The under-powered car began the climb up the winding road to the telescope.

## 44

Pachmann replaced his Klipfone on the console. 'That was the hotel,' he told Hegel who was sitting at the desk that was to be occupied by Koniev. 'They're on their way.'

The blond physicist nodded. 'Final alignment checks,' he instructed the three technicians.

Had the technicians been able to see the monitor in front of Pachmann at the back of the control room, they would have been surprised at the picture. Instead of displaying the image of an old Soyuz spacecraft that all the other sighting monitors were showing and which they thought the torus was targeted on, Pachmann's monitor was showing something quite different: it was a pin-sharp thermal image from the Alpha mirror that was in no way degraded by the high humidity of the atmosphere that night. The winged object had achieved a good geosynchronous orbit; during the previous hour it had not strayed from the centre of the picture.

It was the space shuttle *Colorado*.

## 45

The headlights of Koniev's car snaking around Mount Kuromia enabled Lesa to make a good landfall because she had seen them from a distance of ten miles. She steered the Zodiac to within a mile of the eastern reef and turned north towards the harbour. She rejected the idea of landing on the beach that she and Harry had decided on; now that she was alone she could do as she pleased. Landing near the harbour was risky but it would save a good deal of walking. Also she didn't want to waste power jockeying the Zodiac through the reef. The fast run of over an hour had resulted in an eighty per cent drain on the outboard's battery pack.

The motor hummed softly. The heat of the night was unbearable now that she was moving at a reduced speed. She turned on her travel suit's conditioner and rejoiced in the delicious sensation as the cooling water circulated through the micro-tubing. Being cool and comfortable was conducive to clear thinking. She prayed that the conditioner's battery would see her through the night's business.

The lights marking the harbour entrance came into sight. Like all the public lights on Kuro, they were cowled to prevent light pollution spoiling the seeing conditions at the telescope, but from the sea they were clearly visible as were the sprinkling of lights from the township.

She steered the Zodiac towards the bathing beach near the harbour wall. Her great fear now was that she would be seen by an all-night angler. She scanned the rocks for the gleam of a fishing rod or a glowing cigarette – the Soviets were inveterate smokers – but there was nothing.

The Zodiac bottomed on sand. Lesa jumped from the craft and hauled it clear of the surf. She could spare neither the effort or the time to hide the boat, but instead she lashed its mooring line to a rock. She scrambled up the rocks and worked her way along to the harbour wall, making sure it was deserted before climbing over the low parapet. The first thing she saw was *Rasputin* moored against the quay. From now on her movements were brisk; peering around, skulking from shadow to shadow and generally acting suspiciously would be a mistake. She walked along the quay as though she had every right to be there. She passed *Rasputin* and saw that the boat was in darkness. She expected to feel a sickness, coming so close to the nightmare craft, but she was surprised by her cool detachment. If an opportunity arose, she would return to the boat to destroy it, but inanimate objects could wait. The sound of laughter from the bar attracted her attention. She could see about a dozen late-night customers sheltering behind the plate-glass windows to escape the heat and the mosquitoes. Hegel and Pachmann were not among them.

Hegel's bungalow was in darkness and there was no sign of his jeep outside. That meant that he and Pachmann were at the telescope, but she had to make sure. The kitchen window she had broken on her last visit had been temporarily repaired with a plywood panel. Doubtless glass was scarce on the island. She managed to spring it out of position without making a sound. This time there was no broken glass to contend with when she scrambled through the opening but there *was* the frightening sensation of Hegel's presence. After a few moments her heartbeat had slowed sufficiently for her to carry out a careful reconnoitre of the premises. As she suspected, the place was empty: Hegel and Pachmann had to be at the telescope.

She sat on the settee in the living room and positioned her torch on the coffee table beside an electronic gadget that she assumed was a video recorder because a red pilot light was glowing on its front panel. The torch provided a pool of soft illumination. If a vehicle approached she could be out of the bungalow and into the shrubbery in a matter of seconds. She pulled her Klipfone from its pouch. The stand-by light was on which meant that the island's repeater was still working. First she put a re-direct on all local calls because she didn't want Dysan calling her and blocking the channels. Darryl's voice sounded tired when he answered. She guessed that he had had little sleep during the previous twenty-four hours. Good old dependable Darryl.

'Lesa! God – it's good to hear you. What's happening?'

Lesa briefly outlined what had happened.

'You mean you're at the destination by yourself!'

'That's right. Listen, Darryl. Do me a big favour and see if you can locate the trimaran. The chances are that they're coming after me. I want to know how much time I've got.'

'Come off it, Lesa – find a wooden sailing boat at night?'

'They won't be far from their last position when you logged in to the satellite,' Lesa reasoned. 'There's not enough wind to sail at any great speed. The chances are they're using the engine so you might pick up a thermal on them.'

'Okay – I'll give it a whirl and call you back in five minutes.'

Lesa blew him a kiss. 'Thanks, Darryl – what would I do without you?' She cleared the channel and set the Klipfone to mute so that it would not make a noise when he called. She was about to pick up her torch when she noticed that the gadget on the coffee table was sporting a stub antenna. It was not a video recorder but some sort of transmitter. Fear knotted in her stomach at the possibility that her conversation with Darryl had been monitored. She was about to flee the bungalow when her Klipfone buzzed.

'I think I've found them but I can't be a hundred per cent certain,' said Darryl. 'There's a thermal anomaly fifteen point two miles west of you – moving east at about ten knots. You've got an hour and a half before they arrive – that's assuming it's them.'

'It's got to be them,' Lesa decided. 'Thanks, Darryl. It's great knowing that you're listening out for me. A query for you before you go,' she leaned forward and directed the torchlight on the front of the gadget so that she could read the maker's label, 'there's a thing in front of me called a . . . Uniden VideoMaster two thousand. It's got a stub helical on top about eight centimetres long and there's an active LED on the front panel so obviously it's switched on. Any idea what it is?'

'A Uniden VideoMaster?'

'That's what it says on the front.'

'Hang on, Lesa – just calling up the Uniden catalogue.'

She could hear the clatter of keys, then: 'Yeah – I've got it . . . it's a gadget for re-transmitting the output from a satellite receiver or a video recorder. Sort of thing used on condominiums and estates to save on cabling costs. Single channel. Ten watts out – fairly powerful. Probably got a range of about ten kilometres. Hold your Klipfone near the antenna for a couple of seconds.'

Lesa did so. The handset emitted a whistle.

'I heard that,' said Darryl. 'It's transmitting all right. Front end overload on your Klipfone.'

'Yes – but what *is* it transmitting?' Lesa wanted to know.

'Is it connected up to a satellite receiver or a video recorder?'

Lesa held up the torch and spotted the co-axial cable that snaked from the gadget to the satellite receiver perched on top of the television. 'Yes – it's hooked up to a satellite receiver on top of the television.'

'Okay,' said Darryl. 'Now switch on the television but don't change the channel on the satellite receiver.'

Lesa located the remote control box, switched on the television and had to hurriedly turn down the volume. The picture that appeared on the screen showed the interior of a space shuttle. The familiar NASA logo was superimposed at the foot of the picture alongside a caption that stated: LIVE FROM THE COLORADO SPACE SHUTTLE. MISSION 323

'Getting anything?' Darryl asked.

'Yes – the NASA Information Channel,' Lesa replied, looking at the picture in surprise. 'Now why would anyone want to relay that?'

'Search me, Lesa. What's it showing?'

'Live pictures from the *Colorado* shuttle. Mission 323. Doesn't seem to be much happening. I don't know what to make of it. But someone has gone to a lot of trouble to set everything up.'

'Hold on, Lesa.'

She could hear sounds in the background. Then Darryl was back. 'Okay – I've got the same channel up. Sparkly picture but it's readable. I'm now getting a picture of a satellite just above the cargo bay.'

'Same here,' Lesa confirmed.

At that moment the picture changed to information on this particular mission. The page of text gave the orbital position of the shuttle and the name of the satellite that was about to be recovered in this phase of the Hoover Programme.

'See that position, Lesa? Hundred and thirty east.'

'What about it?'

'That puts the shuttle virtually right over your head.'

An icy serpent of dread began to writhe in Lesa's stomach even before Darryl had started the sentence. The elements in the equation were almost too stark and dreadful to contemplate but they had to be faced: senior Soviet officials visiting the site of a beam weapon of terrible power and accuracy: a transmitter rigged up relaying pictures from a US space shuttle that was nearly overhead. Who on the island would be receiving those pictures but the operators at the site of the weapon? 'Darryl,' she said urgently, 'listen carefully – run a careful check on the alignment of the telescope mirrors to see if they're aimed at that shuttle and call me back.'

She knew the order would not be easy to carry out but to her immense relief Darryl correctly interpreted the tension in her voice and didn't antagonize her by raising objections. Instead he said calmly, 'Okay, Lesa. It might take about thirty minutes but I'll call the moment I've got something.'

Lesa thanked him and cleared the channel.

She switched off the television, put the remote control box back in exactly the same position as she had found it, rounded up her things and left the bungalow via the temporarily repaired window. She was pushing the plywood panel back into position when she heard a noise above the racket of the insects that made her think a vehicle was approaching the bungalow. She crouched in the shrubbery near the swimming pool and listened intently to the strange whine, trying to make out what the sound was and where it was coming from. Certain now that it wasn't a vehicle, she ran into the road where the noise from the swarms of insects was not so intrusive. The sound was getting louder, becoming shriller: as near as she could judge, it was coming from the direction of the power station. In that instant she knew what the strange sound was: it was the roar from eight Tumanski seawater generator turbines gradually opening up to full power.

## 46

'For chrissake!' Harry yelled at Des. 'Can't your goddam engine do more than three thousand rpm?'

'We're going flat out, Mr Dysan,' Des shouted over his shoulder. 'Not enough power. Engine only designed for getting in and out of harbours.'

*Sparkle* pitched suddenly causing Harry to lose his balance. He staggered backwards and flopped down beside Krantz on the broad seat that spanned the width of the trimaran's cockpit.

'You're going to have to radio Kuro and warn them,' said Krantz.

'Why?'

'Because we could be wrong about the whole thing; because there's a psychotic girl on the rampage on their island.'

'Lesa is *not* psychotic.'

'She's weird, you said yourself that she's dangerous, and you've no idea why she's so hell fire keen to get onto that island. If we're wrong about the telescope, and she achieves whatever it is she's so determined to achieve, we could end up in the centre of a major international row that'll screw my career and yours. You've got to use that radio.'

Harry yanked his Klipfone from his pocket and tried Lesa's number for the tenth time. As on the previous nine occasions, all he got was her answering machine in the UK.

He wrestled with the problem: Krantz was right. Why the hell hadn't the stupid bitch confided in him? 'Des!'

The Polynesian looked questioningly over his shoulder. 'Mr Dysan?'

'How much longer?'

Des glanced at the plan position display. 'Eight miles – we make Kuro in forty, maybe fifty minutes.'

'And there it is,' said Krantz quietly.

Harry followed Krantz's finger. Points of light from the peak of Mount Kuromia could be seen straight ahead – shining out through the night's cloying, misty humidity.


**47**


'Gentlemen,' said Koniev expansively, beaming at his guests sitting attentively at the front row of consoles in the softly-lit control room.

'Tonight you are going to witness a demonstration of the awesome power of the torus beam. For twenty years my hardworking colleagues, under the direction of Alexi Hegel and Anton Pachmann, have laboured in the appalling conditions on this island to ensure that our beloved country retains its power and prestige despite those in Moscow who have consistently sought to undermine –'

'Comrade Koniev,' General Zworkin broke in irritably. He was not in the best of tempers: he disliked having to sit behind a cramped console; he disliked Kuro; he disliked its mosquitoes; above all he disliked no smoking signs almost as much as he disliked Victor Koniev droning on.

'General?'

General Zworkin's comment was terse and to the point. A good translation into English – a translation that carries the full flavour and nuance of what the senior Soviet officer said – would be: 'Cut the crap and get on with it.'

Koniev saw that Hegel and Pachmann, sitting at their console at the back of the room, seemed to be enjoying his discomfort. 'I was merely pointing out, general,' he said stiffly, 'that this weapon will give our beloved country total umbrella protection against missile attack should the need ever arise. On the screen in front of you is a defunct Soyuz satellite. In thirty minutes it will have ceased to exist.' He sat at his master console in the second row. 'I'm ready for your lights, gentlemen.'

Hegel gave Pachmann a sly grin. The space shuttle *Colorado* was still neatly centred on their screen. The cross-hairs were sighted precisely on the spacecraft's port wing. Such was the resolution of the picture it was possible to see the open doors of the cargo bay and Canada arm manipulator that had reached out to grip a satellite. The big blond man thumbed the touch-sensitive control that caused four green lights to appear on Koniev's central monitor indicating that the countdown could begin.

'Thank you, gentlemen,' said Koniev. 'Those lights in front of you, general, mean that we're now ready.'

General Zworkin grunted an acknowledgement.

Koniev picked up his headset and spoke to the power station superintendent. 'One hundred per cent power please.'

Stella Richards peered through the aft windows at the satellite. She switched her microphone to VOX – voice activated – and spoke direct to mission control. 'Houston. Payload master, *Colorado*. Copy?'

'Go ahead, *Colorado*,' Mike Connors, the capcom, answered.

'This package has a more pronounced asymmetric mass than our data on it, Houston. Every time we try to claw her into the hold, she starts to tumble. It's no real problem but it's going to take about two hours longer than the sked. Over.'

'Roger, *Colorado*. We noted that from your pictures. What do you propose? Over.'

'We rotate *Colorado* through ninety degrees and claw the package in sideways. That's the way the thing wants to go so we might as well go along with it. Over.'

There was a pause before Connors answered. 'We concur with that proposal, *Colorado*. Go ahead. Good luck. Over and out.'

Stella turned to Matt Gosling. Her good mood, despite having spent an hour wrestling with a recalcitrant satellite, prompted her to make an uncharacteristic joke. 'Okay, Matt – roll me over and we'll try it once again.'

Matt Gosling laughed. 'Now that's what I call a generous offer,' he commented, reaching for the thruster controls to turn *Colorado* onto her side in relation to the earth.

'Switch closed and locked,' the power station superintendent's voice reported to Victor Koniev. 'One hundred per cent power in thirty-three minutes.'

Anton Pachmann frowned at the target screen. The wings of the shuttle appeared to be getting shorter. He leaned forward, staring at the monitor. Hegel saw the anomaly at the same time.

'What the hell's happening?' he whispered worriedly.

'She's turning about her axis,' Pachmann replied dispassionately, keeping his voice low.

'For God's sake why?'

Pachmann called up the NASA Information Channel that was being fed to their console from the transmitter in the bungalow. With a precautionary glance at the back of Koniev's head he pulled on a pair of headphones and listened for a few seconds before passing them to Hegel. The physicist listened to the voice exchanges between mission control and the *Colorado*. He removed the headphones and regarded Pachmann.

'We'll have to re-align Beta and target on the Soyuz,' said Pachmann.

'No!'

It was an answer Pachmann was expecting. He looked at the monitor; the *Colorado* had stopped turning. It was now sideways on, presenting its profile to the earth. The articulated Canada arm, reaching out of the open hold, was clearly visible. 'Wherever we hit the thing now is going to cause catastrophic damage,' he observed.

'Tough,' said Hegel belligerently.

Koniev heard the whispered argument and turned in his seat. 'Anything wrong, gentlemen?'

'All going beautifully, Victor,' said Hegel sourly.

'You have thirty per cent power,' the superintendent's voice reported.

Lesa was undecided about what to do as she trotted down the road that led from the bungalow. Hegel and Pachmann had to be at the telescope therefore that was her first objective. Or was it? What about the danger that she was now convinced a US space shuttle and its crew were facing at the hands of these maniacs? After a wait of nearly twenty years, the sudden realization that she had a primary duty to the living was hard to accept. Her logical mind dictated that first she had to stop the firing of the torus beam, and then seek retribution for Neti and the others. But how could she warn the shuttle? She could make phone calls but how many phone calls would it take to convince NASA officials to order *Colorado* to make an emergency burn? Even if she could persuade them, how long would it take? Maybe she should call Harry? But Harry had shot at her with a rifle, therefore the hatred she was feeling for him at this moment was such that she doubted if she could talk rationally to him. Supposing she was wrong? Supposing the whole thing was a terrible misinterpretation of the facts?

The insidious whine from the power station decided her: the power station was the key. She had to get to it first.

A Skoda saloon outside the harbour captain's office became the victim of Kuro's first car theft. The owner had even obligingly left the keys in the ignition. She turned the little car around and drove at a moderate speed out of the township to avoid drawing attention to herself. Once she had rounded the bend that she had walked along on that fateful day when Harry had followed her, she dropped into low gear and gunned the engine hard. She had reached the T-junction when she realized that her Klipfone was buzzing impatiently. She stopped the car and took the call. It was Darryl. There was a strained note in his voice.

'Lesa – listen carefully. I'm logged permanently into SPOT. Right now the Cray's still processing the results but the prelims don't look too good. It looks certain that the Beta mirror is trained on the space shuttle. There's an error factor of plus or minus five per cent on the alignment readings, but the nominal reading says that the mirror is aimed smack at *Colorado*.'

'Okay, Darryl. I'm on my way to do something about it now.'

'You'll have to be quick. The infrared images are showing a huge increase in warm water from the power station's outfall pipes and it's still shooting up. I'm running colour temperature comparisons against the outfalls from power stations of the same configuration. Right now the station's output potential is up to fifty per cent of maximum . . . Correction – fifty-five per cent. Christ – they're winding it up fast!'

Lesa revved up hard, jammed the car into bottom gear and let in the clutch. She wedged the Klipfone between her neck and shoulder so that she could talk to Darryl and drive at the same time. 'Okay, Darryl. Don't clear the channel. Stay on line and stay logged in to SPOT, and keep me posted.'

The little car left rubber on the road as it took the turning towards the power station.

'You have fifty per cent power,' the power station superintendent reported.

'Initiate arming,' Koniev ordered.

'Arming initiated,' Pachmann responded.

Koniev turned to his guests. 'We've now reached the stage where we arm the nuclear artillery shell that's housed in the ignition chamber, gentlemen.'

First Deputy Yuri Salvanis shifted uncomfortably in his seat. 'Just how powerful is the shell?'

'It has a yield equivalent to one hundred tonnes of TNT,' Koniev replied reassuringly. 'Please don't worry, comrade – the torus coil will be fully energized when the power station reaches one hundred per cent power output. That's when we detonate the shell. All its unleashed energies will then be focussed through the torus coil and fired into space as a beam of pure energy. Keep your eyes on your target monitor. In fifteen minutes the Soyuz will be vaporized.' Koniev caught Hegel's eye towards the end of his little speech. The physicist's grin irritated him.

'You have sixty per cent power,' intoned the superintendent's voice.

Lesa took the bend too wide and too fast and nearly collided with a thirty-tonne quarry truck coming in the opposite direction. Her reactions were fast, which was just as well, because in a dispute between a Skoda and a quarry truck, the diminutive Czech saloon was likely to come off worst. The truck blared its anger and disappeared into the night. She wrenched the wheel over and managed to correct the hard swerve. The Klipfone fell onto the passenger seat. She could hear Darryl's voice, sounding thin and reedy and alarmed. He had heard the truck's horns. She snatched up the instrument. 'It's okay, Darryl,' she reported breathlessly. 'Nearly hit a truck.'

'Christ – you should see these false colours! The outfall's turning the Pacific red. Come on, you stupid computer! Where's my figures? For God's sake, Lesa – the output's up to sixty per cent! What the hell are you going to do?'

At that precise second Lesa suddenly knew exactly what she was going to do. She spun the wheel, wrenched the handbrake on, and succeeded in spinning the Skoda through a hundred and eighty degrees in the narrow road.

'You have sixty per cent power,' the superintendent's voice declared over the speaker in the control room.

'Ignition in ten minutes,' said Pachmann. 'Ignition count down sequence initiated.'

Lesa overtook the quarry truck whilst frantically sounding her horn and flashing her headlights. The huge vehicle stubbornly swung towards the centre of the road, forcing her to jam on the brakes and drop back. She slammed into a low gear and managed to squeeze past the truck on the nearside. Her sudden cutting in was rewarded with an explosive hiss of pneumatic brakes and the truck blaring its horn in retaliation. She accelerated to a safe distance in front of the vehicle and braked the Skoda to a standstill in the middle of the road. Certain that the truck was going to flatten the saloon, she leapt from the driver's seat. Another angry hiss of compressed air mixed with the squeal of protesting brake shoes and the truck ground to a shuddering halt a few metres from the Skoda. The driver was a big Slav who was used to getting his way in arguments. He jumped from his cab and advanced on Lesa, swearing profusely in Russian.

He never saw or even felt the kick. Having no wish to add to his injuries, Lesa caught his unconscious body as he crumpled and dragged him into the undergrowth, well clear of the road. She grabbed her Klipfone, vaulted into the driver's cab and left the door open so that the interior light enabled her to study the complex arrangement of gear levers. For the moment she ignored Darryl's querulous pleas to be told what was going on.

388

The quarry truck had ten gears with additional levers to engage crawler gears, the six-wheel drive and the tipper. Luckily the Soviets had adopted international symbols to mark the various controls. Doubly lucky that the driver had left the engine running. She found reverse and a low forward gear and spent a few anxious moments shunting the mighty vehicle forwards and backwards to turn it around. Despite its intimidating size, the truck's power steering made manoeuvring relatively easy although the slightest pressure on the throttle resulted in the diesel engine revving furiously and creating a shattering uproar.

'What the hell's going on?' Darryl's voice was demanding from the seat beside Lesa. She snatched up the handset and yelled, 'Just keep me posted on that power station! And please shout!'

Lesa crashed the gear-box into a low gear and gunned the engine. The truck lurched back the way it had come. She twisted the driver's spotlight mounted on the door so that its moquito-filled beam was trained on the jungle.

'It's running at at least seventy per cent power!' Darryl's voice yelled. 'Lesa – will you *please* tell me what's happening!'

'Just keep me informed!' she screamed, not picking up the handset and not taking her eyes off the encroaching jungle along the side of the road. The truck buckled and jolted as its tyres mounted the verge. She was not accustomed to driving such a wide vehicle.

Victor Koniev was explaining to his guests that the roaring they could hear outside was due to ionized air being sucked through the torus when the superintendent announced that the power station's output had reached eighty per cent.

'Three minutes to ignition,' said Pachmann.

Hegel worked a tracker ball with his palm to centre the target graticule more precisely on *Colorado*'s flight deck. He gave Pachmann a broad grin that was a mixture of anticipation and triumph.

'Eighty-five per cent,' stated the superintendent.

Lesa spotted the trail that led into the jungle and wrenched the wheel over. The quarry truck smashed into the jungle like a demented tank. Foliage slashed at the windscreen and ripped the wipers away. She wrestled the wheel left and right to avoid the larger trees. Saplings she flattened and bushes she ground to pulp beneath the massive tyres. She was following the trail that Harry had taken during his unfortunate escapade with the wild boar that had led to them being expelled from the island.

'It's got to be well over eighty per cent now!' she heard Darryl yell.

By now the noise of air blasting through the torus coil was painfully loud in the control room. First Deputy Yuri Salvanis eyed the monitor that showed the Beta mirror from a distance. The air being sucked into the torus and ejected could be seen as a faintly glowing beam of light lancing into the night sky.

'Imagine a circle of torus beams around all our cities,' said Koniev proudly. 'Never again will our people know fear. Never again will our motherland be invaded.' He looked in anticipation at General Zworkin, hoping for a nod of approval, but the Soviet officer remained passive and silent.

'What happens if the torus coil fails after the shell has been detonated?' Yuri Salvanis inquired, sensing that he knew the answer.

'I can assure you that it won't fail, comrade,' said Koniev suavely. 'The few minor tests we have already carried out have been a great success.'

'But supposing?' the first deputy persisted.

'Then you get to find out what it's like to sit on top of a nuclear explosion,' General Zworkin growled. 'Now cut the cackle.'

'Two minutes to ignition,' said Pachmann quietly.

'Abort level C passed,' said Hegel.

'At abort level A we are committed to detonation,' Koniev explained to his visitors.

'One minute to detonation.'

'You have ninety per cent power.'

Lesa gave up her blind groping for the lever that worked the tipper. She brought the quarry truck to a standstill, hunted for the lever, found it, and yanked it up. The idling diesel dropped a few revs as the hydraulic motor that powered the tipper rams absorbed some of its energy. Branches snapped and showered onto the cab as the tipper elevated. She twisted in her seat and peered through the cab's rear window. The sight of the gleaming nakedness of the hydraulic rams was all she needed. She grated the gearbox and revved the engine and the giant truck surged forward through the jungle. It felt wildly unstable and tended to veer alarmingly at the slightest provocation. It frightened her at first, especially when she came close to hitting a tree that looked capable of stopping the charging vehicle. She fought the steering wheel and realized that the instability was due to the truck's raised centre of gravity now that the tipper was at maximum elevation.

The crazy charge along the boar trail seemed to go on forever. There were repeated dull metallic booms from overhanging branches smashing into the raised tipper. 'Where's the clearing!' she wept aloud. 'Where's the fucking clearing!'

'Lesa! Lesa! Can you hear me? It's now at maximum output!'

Suddenly the trees thinned out. The headlights picked out the gleam of ceramic insulators and the two monster power lines suspended from their row of concrete cross-arm supports.

'Thirty seconds and counting . . .'

'Ninety-five per cent power.'

'Abort level B passed.'

'Twenty . . .'

Pachmann glanced at Hegel and saw that the big man was clenching and unclenching his fists as he stared at the picture of the shuttle on his target screen.

'Fifteen . . .'

'One hundred per cent power. You have one hundred power. Good luck, everyone.'

The scream of the artificial hurricane was now almost deafening.

'Ten . . .'

'Gentlemen – this is a proud day for our country.'

'Abort level A passed.'

Hegel rested a finger on the firing key.

The *Colorado* was perfectly centred.

'Five . . . four . . . three . . . two . . .'

At the exact moment that Pachmann counted 'five' Lesa drove her foot to the floor. The quarry truck leapt forward. The power line was racing towards her. She opened the door and steadied the bucking wheel as best she could. Fifty metres . . . forty metres . . . left a little . . . No . . . right! That's better! Hit the lines between the concrete columns.

'Lesa! For chrissake talk to me!'

Thirty metres . . . twenty . . . ten! Jump!

She hurled herself from the cab. Her body possessed the momentum of the truck's crazy charge causing her to roll over several times when she hit the soft ground. Badly winded, she looked up in time to see the careering, unbalanced vehicle, with its tipper fully elevated, smash into the power lines like a huge, gaping steel maw. The impact ripped them from their insulators and short-circuited them together.

The searing flash was blinding. It left vivid patterns dancing on her retinas. There was a thunderclap of an explosion that slammed a hammerblow shockwave through the ground with enough force to toss her backwards even though she had been lying down. She heard and felt trees crashing all about her. Her first thought when she had sorted out her reeling senses was to get away from the clearing as fast as possible. She climbed groggily to her feet and staggered back along the deep ruts made by the quarry truck's tyres.

Meanwhile, a few kilometres away, an even more awesome event was taking place on top of Mount Kuromia.

## 51

*Sparkle* was two miles off Kuro when all three men saw the bright light appear on the peak of Mount Kuromia. First there was a flash that left a residual brilliance that burned like a beacon in the night, lighting up the jungle on the mountain's lower slopes.

'Holy shit!' Krantz breathed.

It was like watching an incandescent gas lamp being gradually turned up to full brilliance. Quite suddenly the seemingly peaceful but brilliant light became an expanding ball of energy. Ten seconds after the first flash, the sound of the cataclysmic explosion reached the trimaran, followed closely by the shockwave. Had *Sparkle* been carrying sails they would have been ripped away. The three men recovered their balance and stared aghast at the hideous spectacle of a mountain top being vaporized by a small thermo-nuclear explosion.

## 52

When Diem heard the tremendous explosion his first thought was that Mount Kuromia had erupted. His second thought when he saw the terrible sight from his window was for the safety of his beloved *Rasputin*. The telescope had vanished. In its place was a glowing inferno lighting up the underside of an expanding mushroom cloud. He dragged on a pair of shorts, stuffed his feet into a pair of sandals, grabbed the boat's keys, and raced out into the night. Windows were being thrown open all around him. People were shouting. He ignored them all. His scooter refused to start so he abandoned it and set off for the harbour at a run.

## 53

Lesa reached the abandoned Skoda and leaned against it to get her breath back. The devastation on Mount Kuromia was total. In place of the telescope was a crater, glowing blood-red and vomiting arching streamers of liquid fire into the sky. There were secondary fires burning in the jungle on the mountain's lower slopes. She heard vehicles approaching, but before she could move there was a screech of brakes. The light van had to mount the verge to get past the car. The driver yelled a curse at Lesa and accelerated towards the town. She heard several other engines but they took the turning leading to Mount Kuromia.

As soon as she had recovered sufficiently to think straight, she climbed behind the wheel and headed towards Kurograd. The cooling effect of the slipstream on her face helped clear her head. She stopped just before entering the town and stared across at the glowing aftermath of the mighty explosion on Mount Kuromia. She was in no doubt that her intervention was responsible for what had happened. Hegel and Pachmann, and the fourth man – the fat, bald man whose name she had never learned, were undoubtedly dead, but she saw her failure to kill them face to face as yet another betrayal of her vow to avenge the massacre of her family.

*Could you have killed them if you had come face to face with them, Lesa?*

Always that questioning, treacherous voice inside her – challenging her motives; querying her courage and undermining her self-esteem. More vehicles hurtled past. She could hear shouts. People were running about in the township and pointing.

*There's still Diem! I'll prove it to you, Neti! I'll kill him! I swear!*

She started the Skoda's engine and angrily rammed the gear lever into first. She rounded the bend; the first thing she saw was that *Rasputin*'s navigation lights had been switched on and there were clouds of exhaust smoke billowing around the transom. A figure in white shorts was untying the mooring springs.

Diem!

She skidded the car onto the quay and accelerated.

Diem saw the approaching headlights and thought that the harbour captain was coming to stop him taking *Rasputin*; a reasonable assumption because the car Lesa had stolen belonged to the harbour captain. He cast off the last line, jumped aboard, and raced into the wheelhouse, praying that the engines had warmed up sufficiently to deliver full power without stalling. He thumped the engines into gear and opened the throttles. The engines faltered and then climbed to peak revs. He glanced over his shoulder but was too late to see Lesa dive into the water.

Two strokes took her to the transom. She grabbed hold of the swimmers' boarding ladder and nearly had her shoulders dislocated by the sudden acceleration as *Rasputin* swept in a wide circle towards the harbour entrance. For a terrible moment she lost the ability to think coherently as a flood of ugly memories trampled over her reason. It was this very rung that she had clung to all those years ago . . . But this time everything was different. She had learned to hate; she had learned to kill; and, perhaps most terrible of all, what little she had learned from Lin of the love and trust that men and women could have for each other had been brutally extinguished. The savagery that burned within Lesa gave her the strength to overcome the terrible drag on her arms from the backwash of *Rasputin*'s propellers. She managed to transfer her grip to the next rung. And then the next. Her legs were flailing wildly in the wash, making it difficult to hook them onto the boarding ladder, but somehow she succeeded.

*Rasputin* cleared the harbour entrance and Diem began to feel better. He throttled back to eight knots. No point in wasting fuel – there was no other boat on Kuro that could catch him in a chase. He glanced at the fuel gauges and thanked his foresight in always keeping the tanks full. He had more than enough fuel to reach Hong Kong or Macau, or just about anywhere that took his fancy.

And then a voice from the past spoke softly to him.

'Diem.'

He spun around on the helmsman's chair and goggled at the apparition framed in the doorway, silhouetted by the first light of the dawn. It was a girl – no a woman – a beautiful woman swathed in a skintight suit. Her lovely face and round eyes possessed a Eurasian quality that was timeless in its beauty. But in those eyes was a tiredness – the tiredness of a long journey nearly over. And then a sensation of icy horror stole into his guts with the realization that he knew those eyes.

When he spoke his voice was a croak barely audible above the diesels. 'Lesa!'

'Hallo, Diem.'

His mind raced – reaching blindly for the most plausible explanation from a kaleidoscope of improbables that hoarded in upon him. 'Lesa! It's not you!'

She answered him in Vietnamese. 'I'm not the Lesa that you knew, Diem. I'm no longer the Lesa that you raped all those years ago.'

'You're dead! You were shot!'

She shook her head slowly and lifted her arms. 'No, Diem. I'm not dead. But very soon you will be.'

Diem saw that she was holding a catapult just like the one she had had when she was a kid. She slowly extended the elastics so that the missile pouch was aimed unerringly at his head. He saw that she was compensating for the movement of the boat so that the pouch never strayed from its target. He remembered her skills with the weapon which she used to love showing off in the village and how the boys would never compete with her because they hated losing face. He remembered how she had killed a soldier with the deadly slingshot. In the space of a few seconds Diem remembered a number of things that he had tried to blot out over the years: the time he had stared at her nakedness when she was covered in leeches. And then the memories that were hard to forget: the killings . . . the silky feel of her when he had raped her . . .

He sank to his knees, his hands pressed together in supplication. 'Please forgive me, Lesa. *Please. Please* – I beg of you to spare me.' He searched her eyes for a flicker of compassion and saw nothing. Not even hatred. But the catapult was still aimed at his head, its elastics fully stretched, her grip on the pouch was all that stood between him and death.

Lesa shook her head. 'That I can't do.'

'*Please!*'

'What happened to the fat one?'

The question gave him hope. 'Leo? He died some years ago. An accident.'

'And the redheaded woman?'

'I don't know. She was a prostitute from Macau.'

The elastics tightened. 'So that leaves only you and her, Diem.'

Diem started to cry. 'Lesa – you don't know what it's been like all these years – living with the memories. I've been punished a thousand times over every night! You must believe me.'

'In that case, Diem, your suffering is over. You were involved in the killing of five of your own people. Your life is a poor trade for their lives.'

'No – not five people.'

Lesa frowned. 'Neti, Thi, Hinny, Lin and little Suzi. That makes five.'

'Suzi wasn't killed. The redhead took her back to Macau.'

Lesa stared at Diem. The catapult elastics suddenly relaxed. 'You mean Suzi is *alive*!' Such was her shock at the news that Ko's training in Sham Shui Po was forgotten. Diem saw his chance and charged past her. She lashed out with her foot but was too late. Diem was about to round on her but seeing her aim the catapult, chose instead to dive into the sea. Lesa was about to fire at his head when he broke the surface but then she realized that she needed Diem alive. She *had* to find out what had happened to Suzi. By now Diem was swimming with long, powerful strokes towards the lights of Kurograd about two miles distant. The gap between *Rasputin* and Diem widened rapidly because the motor-yacht was still making about eight knots.

Lesa spun the wheel causing *Rasputin* to heel violently. She tried to bring the bows on course for the lone swimmer but over-corrected the turn. With a sick feeling of despair, she realized that the accurate control of a boat the size of *Rasputin* required a good deal of experience. She closed the throttles slightly and managed to bring the bows around. Diem was now two hundred metres from the boat and still swimming strongly. This time she avoided over-correcting but failed to realize that she was moving too fast.

*Rasputin* bore swiftly down on Diem. Lesa saw that she was going to run him down so she closed the throttles to a fast idle. Diem's head disappeared down the side of the boat and reappeared in its wake. Lesa pulled the gear levers into neutral and leaned over the side. 'Diem!' She yelled. 'I won't kill you! I must know about Suzi!' To emphasize her point she threw the catapult into the sea. Diem stopped swimming and trod water. By now he was about twenty metres astern of the yacht.

'*Please*, Diem! I swear that I won't harm you.'

The Vietnamese seemed undecided for a moment and then he struck out for the boat. Lesa pushed the gear levers into reverse and nudged the engines open with the intention of helping him by reducing the distance he had to swim. *Rasputin* surged astern straight at Diem.

'No, Lesa!' He suddenly struck out sideways to avoid the hull that was bearing down on him.

In panic Lesa snatched at the controls. Instead of knocking both engines into neutral, she inadvertently left the starboard engine in gear with the result that the boat suddenly crabbed. Diem's head disappeared beneath the transom. His terrible scream of agony chilled her blood. She hurriedly put both engines into neutral and raced to the transom. Diem surfaced in the centre of a spreading pool of red.

'Lesa!' he gasped and appeared to faint. Lesa jumped into the sea and grabbed his hair before he went under. She jerked his head up and got him to the boarding ladder. The red was spreading everywhere. It couldn't be blood – there was so much of it.

Diem's head was lolling and his eyes were glassy as Lesa struggled to lift him out of the water with one hand while holding onto the boarding ladder with the other. She braced herself and heaved, expecting Diem's body to be heavy as it came out of the water. Instead it was surprisingly light. A groan and a trickle of blood escaped from his lips. It was when she got him to the top rung that she saw the extent of his terrible injuries; the propeller had virtually carved his torso away at the waist.

'Lesa . . .' He was staring at her with the expression of a man who knew he was dying.

'Diem!' Lesa wept. 'I'm sorry. I'm so sorry – it was an accident! You must believe me! *Please*, Diem!' She allowed him to slip back into the water so that she could no longer see the full horror of his horrible injuries.

He gave a nod. 'Believe . . .' The word came out with a mixture of red froth that dripped from his lips.

'Diem . . . please tell me about Suzi. What happened to her?'

'Redhead . . . took . . . took . . .'

She felt his life ebbing away even as she clung to him. 'What was her name?' In desperation she shook Diem's head.

'Marie . . .'

'Marie who!' As much as she hated herself for doing it, she had to shake him again quite hard to get him to speak. It was as if she were keeping him alive by the overpowering force of her iron will.

When the words came they were mixed with more of the crimson froth. 'Jimmy Pria would know. She was one of his Macau girls.'

It was Diem's last sentence and his most lucid. Lesa held onto him for a few more seconds, uncertain what to do. She let him go and watched the hideously truncated corpse drift away on the swell for a few moments before climbing back onto the broad after deck.

She stared around her, unable to fully comprehend that she was standing on exactly the spot where those terrible events of 1985 had taken place. She aroused herself: there was much to do. First there was the motorboat to be lowered on its davits into the water. Once it was afloat and she had made it secure, she went forward into the saloon. Unlike the bungalow, there was evidence of Hegel and Pachmann all around. The hated faces were staring at her from several photographs. She found a small desk with its drawers crammed full of papers and notes. The professional in her took over – she had come to Kuro to do a job. All these papers were evidence of Hegel's and Pachmann's activities on the island. She found a large plastic sack in the galley and crammed it full of all the papers she could find including an electronic memo pad with a substantial memory. She screwed newspapers into loose balls and built them into a heap in the middle of the saloon's floor. Next she opened all the windows before setting the paper on fire. She stood back and watched with detached interest as the fire took hold. Once the furniture was burning, she swung the sack over her shoulder and dropped it into the motorboat. The eastern sky was brighter now; the sun would be up in an hour. She climbed into the motorboat and cast off.

She paddled a safe distance from the *Rasputin* and watched it burn. The smoke billowing from the saloon windows swirled in the wind and thickened steadily. After five minutes the intense heat made it necessary for her to paddle even further away. She was so intent on the spectacle of flames engulfing the bridge that she didn't hear *Sparkle*'s engine until it was within two hundred metres of her. She gave it a cursory glance and went back to watching the *Rasputin* burn. Two seabirds, attracted to the scene by so many boats, wheeled and cried. They circled for a few minutes, decided that there were no pickings to be had, and returned in the direction of Kuro.

'A tidy insurance claim for someone,' Harry observed using a loudhailer.

Lesa continued to ignore *Sparkle*. Des went about and stopped the engine. Sea surged past the trimaran's graceful hulls.

'Do you want a lift or are you going to stay there all day?'

Lesa gave Harry a withering stare. He was standing on the outer hull, steadying himself by hanging onto a mast shroud. 'You shot at me with a rifle,' she accused.

Harry looked blank. 'I did? When?'

'When I took the Zodiac.'

Harry's expression cleared. 'Oh, that.'

'Yes! That!'

'Lesa – I swear no one shot at you. I fired a couple of rounds into the air to attract your darn-fool attention. God help me, Lesa – you're the last person I'd want to shoot at.'

Lesa looked up at him and saw the genuine concern and dismay in his eyes. Quite suddenly she weakened. She cradled her head in her hands and wept. She wept for her family; she wept for dear Neti; she wept for Lin; she wept for the misery and wretchedness of a life dictated by childhood events that prevented her accepting that there were men in the world who could be trusted, and who cared for her, for her own sake.

General Gus Whittaker tossed a bound report across his desk to Harry who picked it up and leafed through its pages.

'What am I supposed to do with it, general? Read it and eat it?'

'It's interim. Read it and let me know if there's anything left out.'

'Is there anything on the papers Lesa Wessex recovered?'

'Oh, yes. They'd built a working torus beam sure enough.'

'So now we're going to build one?'

'Yes and no.'

There were times when Harry hated Gus Whittaker. This was one of them.

'We're going to build a joint one with the Soviets. The exact details will be announced by the president next month.'

'General, what good will a joint US/Soviet torus beam be? That'll leave both sides without any enemies to use it on.'

'It's not going to be a weapon, Harry. It's going to be the basis power unit for a manned mission to Proxima Centauri around the end of the next decade.'

Harry opened his mouth to say something and promptly closed it. A slow grin spread across his face.

'What's so funny, Harry?'

'That was Alexi Hegel's original dream, general.'

'A pity he didn't stick to it. Has the Wessex girl been in touch with you?'

Harry shook his head. 'I've no idea where she is. I know she's in America because her fingerprints have been processed through immigration. The trouble is, the EPA have fixed her up with so many fake IDs, it's hard to keep tabs on her.'

General Whittaker grunted. 'Let me know when you find her. We might be able to fix up some sort of award for her, even though she's not a US citizen. She deserves something. And her partner – Darryl Grade.'

Harry wished he could point out that Lesa Wessex's father had been a GI. Lesa had told him her full story after their return to

Hong Kong having first sworn him to secrecy. Harry's feelings for Lesa were such that it was a promise he would always keep even though she had run out on him in Hong Kong.

'If I find her, I'll tell her,' Harry promised.

'You do that, Harry. Okay – let me have your comments on that report tomorrow.'

'It's good of you to give me time to read it, general.' Harry stood and moved to the door.

'And, Harry.'

'General?'

'All round one helluva mess, but you did well.'

Harry grinned. 'Thank you, general.'

'But don't do it again.'

# JACKSONVILLE, FLORIDA June 1

A smart house on a smart estate marked the end of a trail that had extended half way around the world.

Lesa parked her rented car where she could keep the house under observation. She put on a pair of dark glasses and pretended to be studying a street map. The newspaper on the seat beside her concealed a PebbleZing catapult that she had purchased from a sports shop at a nearby mall. The store owner had insisted on calling it a slingshot. Her small supply of round, slightly flattened pebbles were the products of a walk along the beach.

Despite the length of the trail, it had not been too difficult to follow. The hardest part had been tracking down Jimmy Pria to his luxury home in Portugal where he was spending his retirement. He had become quite helpful once he was satisfied that Lesa wasn't an official from the People's Republic of China trying to track down profits that he had smuggled out of Macau. He had studied Lesa's pencil drawing of the redhead with interest.

'This is a good likeness,' he had said. 'But she will have aged now . . . like all of us. That's right – her name is Marie. She was one of my best girls. One of the cleverest too. She saved all her money and she made a lot more than she told me about. Stupid kids – they all thought they could fool Jimmy Pria. The kid? Yes – I remember her getting stuck with this baby. Her story was that the guys on the cruiser who had rented her services found the kid as the only survivor on a drifting sampan full of dead boat people. The authorities in Macau accepted her story. After she was stuck with the kid she became respectable: got a job with Pan Am and married a flight engineer. He died a couple of years back. She still writes to me. Do you want her address?'

The throaty sound of an air-cooled engine broke in on Lesa's thoughts. She looked up and saw Thi jump from a beach buggy and turn to wave at the freckle-faced boy who was driving it.

She couldn't be Thi and yet she was: Thi's face; Thi's carriage; Thi's hair; Thi's everything. But no – it wasn't Thi. This lovely young girl was smiling happily as she watched the beach buggy drive off – Thi had never smiled. Thi had seen too much suffering to smile whereas this girl had known the life that Lesa remembered dreaming about in her village when she had poured over the glossy American magazines that her mother used to bring home from Danang.

A woman aged about fifty emerged from the house and waited in the doorway for the girl, smiling patiently as though eager to hear how the date had gone. It was the redhead. She hadn't changed that much. Hatred suddenly blazed in Lesa's heart like a furnace door being thrown open. Her hand slid under the newspaper but was stilled when the woman went forward to meet the girl. They hugged and kissed and laughed, and walked towards the house with their arms about each other's waist.

In that fateful moment Lesa realized that killing the redhead would destroy more than one life. Tears pricked her eyes. Her helplessness was yet another betrayal in a lifetime of treachery. She pressed her forehead against the steering wheel.

*Neti – dear, beloved Neti. I can't do it. I just can't! Please understand. Please forgive me, Neti, I beg of you.*

She started the car angrily, banged the shift into drive, and accelerated away. She stopped at a trash bin on the outskirts of the town and dumped the PebbleZing and the pebbles.

Two miles further down the road she stopped the car suddenly when she realized that the digital watch Lin had given her was no longer on her wrist. She stared at the white band of skin. She had worn the dud watch for nearly twenty years; it was a part of her. A part of her past. And now it was gone. It must have come off when she dumped the catapult. She was about to turn the car around when she had second thoughts. Suddenly the black cloud had lifted. She felt cleansed; renewed. The watch was her past which she sensed had suddenly lost its domination over her. She needed a friendly voice. Someone with whom she could share this wonderful experience; this new awakening. She seized her Klipfone and called Harry's number. She stretched luxuriously when she heard his voice.

'Hallo, Harry. Guess who?'

'Lesa! My God, Lesa – is it really you?'

'It's me all right. How are you keeping, Harry?'

'I'm absolutely goddam miserable with all these calls of mine to you that keep getting re-directed. Where are you?'

'Jacksonville, FA.'

'Jacksonville! Lesa – that's fantastic! You're right on my doorstep! You must come and see me and put me out of my misery.'

'Harry, I'd love to but I have to get back to New York. And then home. I've left Darryl alone for too long. This is just a friendly call to let you know I haven't forgotten you.'

'*Please*, Lesa! All you've got to do is take Ninety-Five south and you'll help cut the year's suicide figures by one.'

Lesa laughed and started the car. 'I'll be taking Ninety-Five, Harry, but I'll be heading north. I've finished here now. I really must get home.' The car picked up speed.

They chatted animatedly for a few more minutes. 'I really must concentrate on my driving now, Harry. US Ninety-Five is coming up. I'll call you from a motel. God bless and keep you. Goodbye.' She finished the conversation by blowing him a kiss.

Within five minutes of ending the call she was yearning to hear his voice again. It was a lovely day. Shadows flitted across the windscreen. She looked up into the flawless blue sky and saw a flock of pelicans flying south. She wanted to stop and watch the graceful birds but the traffic on the approaches to US Ninety-Five was getting heavy.

Five minutes later she swung the rented car onto the ten-lane highway. She pressed her foot to the floor and wound up to the legal limit.

Heading south.

*Also available from Mandarin Paperbacks*

JAMES FOLLETT

# A Cage of Eagles

The locals call it Hush Hush Hall. The British Army calls it No. 1 POW Camp (Officers), Grizedale Hall. British intelligence calls it the Cage of Eagles.

It is the biggest concentration of German prisoner-of-war talent in wartime Britain. Gathered together are airmen, navigators, radio experts and U-boatmen. One hundred skilled and determined men with one thought uppermost in their minds – escape. But all that changes when U-boat ace Otto Kruger takes over as the senior German officer. With ice-cool, deadly efficiency he turns the camp into a clearing house for sending vital intelligence back to the Fatherland.

The battle of wits between Kruger and his captors draws together such diverse characters as Ian Fleming and Beatrix Potter in an explosive story that has the British in the unfamiliar roles of guards and hunters. It is a battle that the Germans fight with fortitude, grim determination . . . and humour.

# JAMES FOLLETT

## Swift

### A small explosion:
### the greatest crime of all time

There is a satellite through which, daily, pass all the interbank transactions between London and New York, currencies to the value of billions of pounds – moving not as bank notes, but as vulnerable streams of electrons. This, the most vital computer system in existence, is operated by SWIFT, guardians of the system on which depends the delicate stability of the world's currencies. And one man has a plan to destroy it.

That man is Charlie Rose, disaffected mobster boss with millions at his disposal. Assisted by a Soviet Tass correspondent with his own motives to pursue, and a brilliant but psychotic computer programmer, Rose has the audacity, the power and the driving will to dare the biggest, most sophisticated act of theft ever conceived...

JAMES FOLLETT

# Ice

Beneath the desolate wastes
of the South Atlantic
lurks a malign force
of unimaginable power

The top brass of Western Intelligence are badly rattled when transatlantic cables are inexplicably and provocatively cut, and Russian and American relations reach freezing-point when a luxury ocean liner and a Soviet supersub go down in a sea like honey.

Only Glyn Sherwood and Julia Hammond, two scientists working on the Antarctic can dare to guess the identity of an enemy well outside the diplomatic compass. It is a gargantuan slice of the glacial continent bearing millions of tons of rock in its grasp.

Swathed in its own fog, the frozen colossus triggers a series of disasters as it drifts inexorably north. On collision course with New York and impervious even to nuclear blast, it has the seismic force to cause Manhattan to shake like a dog.

With *Ice*, James Follett has conceived the teeth-chattering possibility of how Nature can punish those who foolishly believe they have mastered her.

'The most sensational thriller – and chiller – of the year.' *Edinburgh Evening News*

JAMES FOLLETT

# Dominator

**Hijacked – the world's
most sophisticated weapon
in space**

High above the earth's surface orbits one of NASA's
latest space shuttles, Dominator. But the crew and cargo
on board are beyond the control of the US space agency.
Dominator has been hijacked and a nightmare is about to
be unleashed.

How could it happen – and how will it end? James
Follett's heart-stopping novel spans three continents as it
follows the fearfully possible outcome of a new deadlock
between the warring Middle East factions and the
United States. Standing innocently at the centre is Neil
O'Hara, ex-astronaut, ex-drunk, whose rare skills and
debatable loyalties may ultimately be the only barrier
between us and the holocaust . . .

# A Selected List of Fiction Available from Mandarin

While every effort is made to keep prices low, it is sometimes necessary to increase prices at short notice. Mandarin Paperbacks reserves the right to show new retail prices on covers which may differ from those previously advertised in the text or elsewhere.

The prices shown below were correct at the time of going to press.

| | | | |
|---|---|---|---|
| ☐ 7493 0003 5 | **Mirage** | James Follett | £3.99 |
| ☐ 7493 0134 1 | **To Kill a Mockingbird** | Harper Lee | £2.99 |
| ☐ 7493 0076 0 | **The Crystal Contract** | Julian Rathbone | £3.99 |
| ☐ 7493 0145 7 | **Talking Oscars** | Simon Williams | £3.50 |
| ☐ 7493 0118 X | **The Wire** | Nik Gowing | £3.99 |
| ☐ 7493 0121 X | **Under Cover of Daylight** | James Hall | £3.50 |
| ☐ 7493 0020 5 | **Pratt of the Argus** | David Nobbs | £3.99 |
| ☐ 7493 0097 3 | **Second from Last in the Sack Race** | David Nobbs | £3.50 |

All these books are available at your bookshop or newsagent, or can be ordered direct from the publisher. Just tick the titles you want and fill in the form below.

**Mandarin Paperbacks**, Cash Sales Department, PO Box 11, Falmouth, Cornwall TR10 9EN.

Please send cheque or postal order, no currency, for purchase price quoted and allow the following for postage and packing:

| | |
|---|---|
| UK | 80p for the first book, 20p for each additional book ordered to a maximum charge of £2.00. |
| BFPO | 80p for the first book, 20p for each additional book. |
| Overseas including Eire | £1.50 for the first book, £1.00 for the second and 30p for each additional book thereafter. |

NAME (Block letters) ............................................................................................................................

ADDRESS ............................................................................................................................................

............................................................................................................................................................

............................................................................................................................................................